A
Convergence
of Evils

A Novel
By

Thomas Hofstedt

Many evil things there are that your strong walls and bright swords do not stay.

(J.R.R. Tolkien)

Table of Contents

Incident on the Bay (Three Months Ago)

She watched his eyes change and knew then that he had decided to kill her.

Standing nude in the moonlight, she felt the improbable hope slip away with his rejection of her forlorn proposal. It was just the slightest shift in his expression; the sliver of curiosity that she had stirred in him turning to regret, like a shopper momentarily seduced by a product almost within his reach, only to decide the cost was too great. She even thought that she detected the whisper of a sigh but distrusted her perceptions, confused as they were by the sound of the wind and her whipsawing emotions.

The realization did not surprise her. The possibility of this ending had always lurked just below her consciousness, a fatalistic brew of her own fear and the menace that accompanied the man like his personal cloud. So her first reaction to the certainty of her death was a tangle of questions, verbalized entirely within her own head.

Where did I screw it up? So careful … never a wrong move … I've done everything he asked. No complaining, not even to the others. So careful … How could he --

The man interrupted her internal monologue, as surely as if she'd been speaking aloud. "You called home. Talked to the wrong people. Said the wrong things."

It was a measure of his dominance over her that she simply accepted his clairvoyance and did not even wonder how he could possibly know what she had done or what she was thinking. Nor did it occur to her to protest his lethal intention.

I'm going to die! Here! Now! With the thought came a sudden rage, a surprising heat wave of pure sensation, a silent scream, blurring her vision, making her lightheaded and causing her to stumble forward. She caught herself by bracing against the deck chair next to her, the one where she had carelessly dropped each article of her clothing as she stripped naked before him, knowing even as she went through the motions that this last desperate gambit would not work, that any appeal to lust, mercy or any of the other human instincts was doomed by his utter lack of any emotion except indifference.

She neither knew nor wondered whether her surging anger was at her, at the man or at some uncaring god, and it quickly passed, replaced by apathy, a form of mercy in its own way.

So stupid … to think that this could work … to think that changing your life was as easy as putting on a new dress and moving to a different address … So fucking fucking stupid …

He spoke again, softer and with what might have been regret, reaching out and gently touching her bare shoulder. "You were very good. I wish …".

He stopped, looking startled, as though surprised by his own words. Much later, he would wonder about, and be bothered by, this first-ever need to explain. His hand moved from her shoulder down to her elbow, a gentle pressure turning her to face outward, directly facing the lights from the tall buildings that seemed to extend fractured pathways of light along the rippled surface toward them.

"It's hard to be the first … the one who exposes our mistakes … the one who makes us look bad."

He went on, but the words did not reach her, as though the wind caught them and carried them away toward the bright lights that mocked her audacity in thinking that she deserved to be among them.

She was naked, cold and afraid, but it was his talking that did it, that caused the emotional switch to flip one more time, this time to the mode that had carried her throughout her brief life, a way of behaving that had brought her so heartachingly close to those lights and all that they signified. It was a curious blend of defiance and selfishness contending with a learned helplessness. *To hell with this little man and his regrets! I'm going to get what I want! Let him do whatever he has to do!*

She was ten feet from the edge, a lifetime of distance. She shook his hand loose from her arm and took three quick accelerating steps. She heard the man say something. The words did not register, but when she heard the lack of surprise in his voice, with its tacit acceptance, even approval, of her gesture, it confirmed for her the futility of her effort. Only then did she feel the despair that she had fought so hard against for so very long. *To come so far! So unfair!*

She didn't think she was very far above the water and, on her fourth step, she leaned forward, extended her arms behind her and launched herself upward and outward in a shallow dive. It was unwitnessed but – if there had been an observer – he would have admired the graceful way that she coiled and then pushed off, the way that the reflected lights striped her classically nude form in such contrast to the darkness awaiting her.

The sound, a faint 'pop' swallowed up by the wind and vastness around them, seemed unrelated, a mere coincidence, surely not the cause of the sudden and dramatic change in her flight. The lean and arrow-like form accelerating outward with such purpose and linearity suddenly became a tumbling lifeless bundle with trailing limbs, falling solely according to the dictates of gravity, without volition or grace.

The man watched the whiteness that was the woman slowly dissolve as she receded into the dark waters, still admiring his retained image of her body and the spirit that drove her to the very end. He stood motionless for a long ten seconds staring at the black surface. Before turning away, he said something that only he could hear, in a language that was not English.

Vladivostock, 1991

*E*vil empire, hell! More like a fourth-world banana republic! How in the living hell could we have feared these screwed-up people?

The question was rhetorical and silent, voiced only to himself as Ellerby stood looking at the line of forlorn Soviet warships rusting in place, great grey hulks as devoid of sailors as they were of the menace that was their right. In that respect, the naval forces seemed about as capable as the air force, with its fleet of MIG-21's and Backfire bombers sitting heavy-winged and pathetic alongside the potholed runways of the Vladivostock Airport, grounded by the lack of parts, fuel and sober pilots.

As if to confirm his vision of squandered power, a pair of gaunt sailors veered in his direction, holding their hats out to him, an obvious Westerner, therefore a person with more wealth than was fair in such a place as this. He shook his head, noting how his gesture elicited the now-familiar expression of disgust; the "it's your fault I'm so badly off and you could fix it if you weren't so damn selfish" reaction that seemed to be the prevailing Russian view of visiting Americans. The sailors sheered away on a new course, crossing the street and zeroing in on a cluster of Japanese tourists crowding around a pushcart vendor selling nesting dolls, brightly painted caricatures of American presidents. *Grass roots capitalism at its best!*

He watched Aleksei returning from the kiosk, a drab dumpy man wearing a badly fitting and stained suit. *The human equivalent of the damn sad ships!* He was carrying two steaming paper cups of what the Russians called "coffee", really just hot water with clumps of instant something stirred in. His English was heavily accented, just barely intelligible. Not so surprising, given that he had learned the language by reading the personal mail of the American residents of the Russian Federation. It provided him with a workable vocabulary that, unfortunately, came out as something not quite English, as though a deaf mute had just acquired the power of speech and was determined to use it.

"Did you see war monuments?"   Aleksei pointed vaguely toward a cluster of statues across the boulevard.

After five days in Russia, Edgar Ellerby's cynicism was at maximum levels. *War monuments? There are no other kind! Heroes of this, heroines of that … Huge gray blocks of stone commemorating heroic striving for the great Soviet cause… silent about the quantities of suffering and millions of deaths for the sake of a doomed vision. The truly monumental features of the society that I have seen are stupidity and shortsightedness. They savaged their environment and their people and called themselves a "great power"!*

The festering anger surprised him. It was as if he had bought into all that 'Evil Empire' bullshit and suddenly learned it was a scam perpetrated against him personally.

He looked beyond the ships, out to Amur Bay. From here, it looked pristine, although he knew that it was hopelessly polluted, dangerous to the surviving fish and to humans along its shores. As if to confirm his point, a sailor walked to the rail of the nearest ship – a tender of some sort – and emptied a pair of buckets into the harbor.

Everything is gray – gray ships on a gray sea, with a gray city looking on. It was the same monochromatic and depressing vista wherever you looked. The buildings behind him, across the broad avenue, were covered with layers of grime and soot from decades of neglect, a cancerous film that at least was visible, unlike the nominally breathable yet toxic air. Ironically, the street itself was clean. Even as he watched, a quartet of sweepers was moving along the curb, women using brooms made from twigs – *besoms?* – a technology that dated from the Middle Ages. Through gaps in the buildings, he could see the gigantic above-ground pipes carrying hot water from the central water utility throughout the sprawling city, reminding him that *centralization* had been carried to ridiculous extremes in the Soviet new order. He wondered if anyone in the suburbs ever experienced a hot shower.

And we feared them! Thought of them as a rival!

He realized that Aleksei was still standing there, holding the watery coffee. *They do have the edge when it comes to patience... something they learned while they were always waiting for the future they were promised, I suppose.* An entire nation of individuals who had learned to live without expectations. Even Aleksi, an ex-KGB official, was now quite under-unemployed in the new "market economy", but seemed incapable of either surprise or irritation.

The vodka helped. Every male Russian he interacted with after midday seemed at least moderately drunk. And he knew that Aleksei's coffee was laced with the stuff. In the few short days he had been here, he had come to believe that the vodka and the surge of false optimism that came with the sudden absence of rules were the mainstays of existence in the "new Russia". Alcoholism was an adaptive mechanism in such a world.

He took the coffee that was held out to him. "Where are the others? I seem to have lost them."

"At the station. It's what they wanted to see first. They always do."

The station was steeped in history and rightly famous. The Vladivostock train station was the terminus of the Trans-Siberian railway, 5,616 miles and five time zones from Moscow. Theoretically, and according to the official schedule, the trip from Moscow to Vlad and the Russian Far East would take five days. In reality, the deteriorating Soviet infrastructure and the rigors of trans-Siberian travel made actual transit time quite variable. Western travel agencies were billing it as "adventure travel".

Martin came up behind them and said, "Of course they're at the god damned station. It's all there is in this godforsaken hellhole, for Christ's sake! Except for the women, of course. Tourism was never much of an emphasis in Stalin's Five Year Plans."

Aleksei said haltingly in his agonized English, "It was closed city, Martin. Even Russians couldn't travel here. No point in tourism." Then he added a rapid ten-second burst of Russian, incomprehensible to Edgar.

"Right!" said Martin, with undisguised sarcasm. "Your mighty Pacific Fleet had to be shielded from prying eyes!" And he gestured grandly at the line of rusting warships behind him. "Christ, Aleksei! Our satellites knew more about your non-readiness than your own admirals!"

So much for undercover tradecraft. Martin has to be the most obvious "secret agent" ever sent into the field. Might as well wear a nametag that said "CIA" in big black letters. I wonder what he expects to learn?

Maybe he's trying to look like a Russian, one of those middle-aged males without work, relevant skills, or prospects who were so prevalent in the new order. A casualty of the collapse of the Soviet social contract… particularly that part about 'to each according to his needs'.

As usual, Martin looked like he'd slept in his suit and shaved in cold water with a dull razor. Everything about him projected an air of indifference, of not paying attention to appearances, of being just this side of a grand rebellious gesture. There were two exceptions. First, his eyes: they were alive, attentive and calculating. The other was Svetlana, his companion. She was young -- perhaps twenty – with long blond hair and the body of a Playboy centerfold.

She surprised Edgar twice. The first time was when she walked into the room clinging to Martin. *How did he get a woman like that?* was Edgar's immediate and involuntary reaction, so spontaneous that at first he thought he had said it aloud. Since then – it seemed weeks ago but in reality was only a few days – he was no longer surprised by the sight of strikingly beautiful young women on the arms of older thuggish men. He came to see it as the first confirmation that the market economy was starting to work at its most primitive level, needing only legal and moral infrastructure to flourish.

The second time she surprised him was when he learned that Svetlana was fluent in English, smart & quite aware of the impression she made on him. They were standing in line waiting for the van. Without any preamble, she looked at Edgar and said, "I think I seem like a bimbo to you."

He fumbled for a response, finally settling on a lame "I'm not sure I would know a bimbo if I saw one."

"Dumb blonde? Courtesan? Prostitute? Escort?"

Observing his embarrassment, she went on "What the Victorians referred to as a fallen woman, maybe?   How about 'gold digger', a more American term?"

He recovered and noted that she was smiling slightly. He realized that she was more interested in teasing him than in expressing any insecurity or lack of self-esteem on her part. He said, "I don't know about your morals, but you certainly have a better vocabulary than I do." And then he added, quite genuinely, "And I think Martin is lucky to have you around, no matter what label you use."

Her smile broadened, apparently pleased by his response. As she turned to get in the van, she said, "Martin is an interesting man … for an American."

Edgar detested Martin.   He was either drunk or absent most of the time and as transparently disdainful of the Americans he was escorting as the Russians who were their nominal hosts. In the five days they had been in close proximity to one another, he had been obscene, sarcastic, insulting or angry in about equal doses. He shared nothing about himself, with one notable exception.

After a particularly vicious obscenity-laced harangue by Martin, Edgar said, "It's hard to tell who you dislike the most – us or the Russians." He made it a question by looking directly at Martin, challenging him to choose.

Surprisingly, Martin seemed to take the issue seriously, as though it was important to him to declare his allegiance to one or the other. "Tweedle Dee and Tweedle Dum …You're all seriously fucked up. If we put on an intergalactic police lineup, you wouldn't be able to tell the difference."

Then he paused and smiled, an expression utterly without humor. "I've killed more Russians than Americans.

So I guess I must like the Americans more." The comment ended the conversation.

His name wasn't really Martin, but that's what he went by at the moment. He'd been assigned as "commercial liaison" to their group of visiting politicians and businessmen from San Francisco, supposedly to orchestrate their schedule and provide daily briefings on the local politics and economy. Edgar suspected that the reality was that Martin was being punished for some infraction of the intelligence code and that his assignment to Vladivostock was the CIA's equivalent of the outermost circle of purgatory. And based on what Edgar had seen of his behavior, it didn't seem likely that he was intending to work his way back into good standing.

For whatever reason, Martin seemed to attach himself to Ellerby. It was after midnight of Edgar's fifth day in Vladivostock. He had come to accept the continuous sense of unreality, no longer trying to sort out whether it was jet lag, cultural whiplash or simply the massive displacement he was experiencing, like Dorothy's arrival in Oz. *And don't forget the booze.* They had just finished their third "state dinner" in three nights. The speeches were clichés strung together, with vodka toasts proposed at regular intervals. The Americans had fallen in line, proposing ever more maudlin oratory. The venue this time was the ex-Headquarters of the Communist Party; in a cavernous room with twenty-foot-tall photos of Lenin and his successors, flanked by red banners with Russian phrases. When he asked Martin what the Cyrillic lettering said, he smirked. "Bumper stickers for the proletariat. Fortune cookies for the believers."

"Are there any believers left?"

"Oh my, yes. They've relabeled themselves. But they're still out there."

"So the cold war isn't over? The good guys didn't triumph after all?"

Martin laughed. "And who are the good guys? Us?" The last word was expressed with so much contempt that

Edgar wanted to ask him what he had done to earn his apparent exile. But just at that moment, Svetlana leaned into Martin, whispered to him and pointed to her watch.

Martin got up. "Round up Gillis and Feldstein. It's time to meet some real Russians."

"Why those two? Or me, for that matter?"

Martin looked at him in a calculating way, like a Tiffany's saleslady at a shabby vagrant who had wandered into her store. Edgar knew that he was trying to decide whether or not to lie.

"Because you're still reasonably sober." And then, after a long pause, "And because you're the only ones in this gaggle of capitalists that has enough curiosity to enable me to teach you something important about this seriously fucked-up place."

People to People

Thirty minutes later, the five of them stood at the front entrance of one of the architectural monstrosities that lined the hillsides around the cities, the "people's housing" that represented the bleak reality of the Stalin era far better than the heroic monuments dotted around the city. It was tasteless and shoddy construction, an ugly huge concrete rabbit warren that blotted out a mile of hillside. They climbed three levels in semi-dark stairwells, moving through distinct sound layers of crying children and angry spouses, finally arriving at a nondescript door like all the others facing onto the apparently endless hallway. The aroma of cabbage and cigarette smoke seemed to emanate from the walls around them.

Svetlana opened the door, not bothering to knock, and stood aside for them to enter. The room was small, lighted only by a single bare light bulb dangling from an electrical cord that was hanging from a hook in the ceiling. There were a few chairs, a day bed covered with large pillows, and a pair of card tables with a half-dozen bottles. Each of the walls other than the one where they entered was partially demolished, apparently to create a doorway into an adjacent apartment.

Six people were in the room. In one corner, three men – all of them smoking – looked at them. In the middle of the room, three women stood closely together, holding wine glasses. All of them, both men and women, were young – thirty at the most. Something about them, their resemblance to one another, the casual way they were dressed, but mostly the way they stood and looked at them as if appraising a threat, gave Edgar the sense of walking in on a group of employees banded together to complain.

Svetlana said something in Russian to the six, and then – in English – introduced them to the Americans as "good friends" and recited their names in a rapid-fire fashion that – ten seconds later -- left Edgar unable to recall who was named what. One of the men spoke. His English was excellent. He said simply, "Welcome. Please have a drink." And he gestured to the table filled with bottles.

Edgar found himself standing next to Svetlana, so he asked, "Who lives here?"

"I do, thanks to Martin."

"And who are these people?"

She looked around at the two clusters and smiled a very sad smile. "Just friends. We … Martin … thought you might like to meet some of the locals, not just the Governor's stooges that he trots out for the visiting Westerners."

He gestured at the gaping holes in the thin walls, partially framed but without any doors. His raised eyebrows turned the gesture into a question.

"Martin calls it 'remodeling'. For me it is one-hundred square meters of breathing room. An incredible luxury."

"And the previous tenants? From those other rooms?"

An emotion that he could not identify flashed across her face. She shrugged. "I think I shall call them early victims of the new market economy."

He asked, "But isn't this building owned by the state?"

One of the three other women had broken off from her group and was listening to them. She put her hand on Svetlana's forearm to forestall her response and asked Edgar, "'What does 'state ownership' mean if there is no state?"

She went on without waiting for a reply, her voice sarcastic, "Who owns the land, the buildings, the oil, the factories, the forests … the nuclear weapons?"

He said, "In America, we have a saying, 'Possession is nine-tenths of the law.'"

"And if there is no law?"

He smiled, "I am a lawyer and a politician. I cannot conceive of the absence of law."

"I envy you for that." And after a long pause, she added thoughtfully, "And I think you shall have a difficult time understanding either Russia or Russians."

Edgar looked closely at the woman. She really was quite beautiful. Tall, blonde, long-legged, with green eyes that looked directly at him, leaving him feeling inadequate in ways he could not define; guilty of *something*. It somehow reminded him of his earlier encounter with the two sailors. She was dressed casually – slacks and a loose sweater, no visible jewelry. *Elegant* was the adjective that came to mind first, then *exotic,* mainly because of a very faint and jagged scar from her hairline down to her left eyebrow. He judged her to be about his age, perhaps thirty, plus or minus a couple of years. The only flaw was the faint aura of uncertainty that clung to her – and to almost every other Russian that he had met in the last four days, as though the catastrophic collapse of the Soviet system might be due to some personal failure on their part.

He said, "I'm sorry. Svetlana's introduction was quite fast and I missed your name."

"Irina."

The one-word response intrigued him. The informality and the hint of mystery caused him to wonder again why they were here, moderately drunk, at two in the morning in this drab concrete warren. What did Martin and Svetlana have in mind? That thought immediately reminded him of the so-called "orientation" the group had sat through in the airport lounge just before boarding their flight from San Francisco to Vladivostock via Seoul. He remembered the slightly embarrassed Russian consulate official who cautioned them.

"Two things you need to be aware of. First, a Russian may ask you to bring something back with you … a letter, package, currency. Don't do it, no matter how innocent the request seems. Second, many Russians see Westerners as their way out of a difficult situation. This is particularly true for young Russian women. They can be quite … *creative* in finding ways to achieve that."

Irina broke into his thoughts. "Svetlana tells me that you are a 'city councilman' in San Francisco. You must be very important." It was a statement, not a question.

"Not very. I go to meetings and listen to unpleasant people complain. What about you? What do you do?"

She smiled impishly. "I go to meetings and complain ... unpleasantly."

She went on quickly, "I manage an orphanage. And I'm good at it, but since Mr. Gorbychev's perestroika ...." She waved her hand vaguely in the air.

"There are scarcities," he finished for her. "I imagine orphans are not doing well in the new economic order."

She said flatly, "They have no roof."

When he looked puzzled, she said, "An English term, but a Russian concept. 'Roof' ... 'krysha' ... is slang for 'protection' ... which is typically provided by our famous mafia or a party member with connections."

"I think I understand. Perhaps Martin is Svetlana's 'roof'?"

Her head snapped up and the green eyes flashed. Her face reddened, making the scar more vivid. She took a quick half-step toward him and the wine in her glass splashed onto his shoes. For half-a-second, Edgar thought she would strike him. When he instinctively stepped back, she froze in place and Edgar watched a progression of emotions move across her face. Fury gave way to indecision, in turn to be displaced by an expression of utter resignation. Watching, he was saddened, somehow reminded of a client long ago having to choose between a plea bargain and a trial that could lead to life imprisonment.

Nice conversational touch, stupid! And you're supposed to be a diplomat!

Her eyes down, she said, "You don't know anything about us, do you? What it's like when the world and everything in it changes?"

"No, I don't," he admitted. For some reason, he thought again about the two gaunt sailors holding their hats out to him. His vague feeling of guilt intensified.

He was trying to compose an apology when the sound of the door closing diverted him. The conversational hum in the room was gone and, when he looked around,

Edgar saw that the three Russian men had left, leaving four distinct pairs – the four Americans, each with a Russian woman in close conversation. Martin and Svetlana had withdrawn to the day bed, sitting close together among the pillows and watching the others, reminding him of parent chaperones at a high school dance.

The bastard has set us up with hookers! Arranged it like we're a bunch of out-of-town hick conventioneers come to the big city for fun and games!

The confirmation followed immediately. He watched Feldstein and one of the women – another blonde, shorter than Irina, in a noticeably over-tight dress – step carefully through the makeshift doorway in the opposite wall, the woman carrying her shoes in one hand and pulling Feldstein with the other. He glanced at Gillis. He was standing face-to-face with the woman, about three inches separating them with their hands interlocked. *Are they in on this? Am I the last one to catch on?*

He realized that Irina was watching him closely and probably knew what he was thinking before he did. Her look of resignation had shifted to amusement.

Edgar grimaced. "I must look like a real babe-in-the-woods, huh?"

"Babe-in-the woods? I do not know the expression."

"A person who is slow to catch on … naïve … unsophisticated."

"Those are not bad things. I think perhaps they have something to do with why I picked you."

"What do you expect of me? What do you want?" *Christ! Those have to be the dumbest questions ever asked!*

Irina shook her head. "Those are two very different questions. What I *want,* you cannot or will not give me – an exit visa to your country and for all my orphans to be adopted by rich Americans. As for what I *expect* …."

When she paused, Edgar suddenly realized that he cared intensely about how she would end the sentence. He felt as if he was being judged in some important way and that her expectations would tell him something about both his past and his future. Then, with a suddenness that startled him, he was aware of Irina's body, of what her loose sweater was concealing and of the shadows in the hollow of her neck.

As if sensing his shift in awareness, she smiled in a new and more personal way. Her voice became tentative, less edged. "… You are here for five more days … and nights. I would like to be your … shall we say, companion … I can help you to understand us better. I can please you in many ways."

"And in return?" His voice was unintentionally gruff.

"I read your press release. You are here to help the Russian Far East with – how do you put it – 'the transition to a market economy'. So we shall model that transition … I suggest two-thousand dollars as a fair market price for my companionship." As she spoke, she put her hand on his shoulder, her thumb resting under his open collar and one finger tracing faint arcs on his neck.

"Irina, I … I … Are you … professional? Why are you doing this?" He winced when he heard himself.

She laughed. "I'm divorced. Svetlana is my cousin. I manage an orphanage. I have no other sources of income. No 'roof'. I assure you that I am not *professional*." She picked up her handbag from under the wine table and took his arm, pressing closely against him. "And I'm Russian, so I adapt."

He asked, "Where shall we go?"

She laughed again, even more loudly. "Let me see? I live with two other women in a single room in a building like *this* – ". Somehow, the sweeping gesture she made with her free arm exposed the room's squalor more dramatically than if she had turned on a floodlight. "You are staying in a suite in the best hotel in Vladivostock. Why don't we go to your place?"

Edgar held the door for her. He glanced at Martin, who was looking directly at him with an unreadable expression. At the last second, just before the door closed, he winked and gave Edgar a 'thumbs-up'. The gesture sent a surge of anger through Edgar and he stopped suddenly, the door banging painfully against his heel. *The son-of-a-bitch thinks he knows what I want!*

Irina tugged at his hand, ending his need to distinguish himself from the others. But that wink and thumbs-up would become one of his most durable memories from his first-ever trip to a disintegrating world.

New Opportunities

The oldest game on the planet! Martin watched with satisfaction as each of the women did whatever they had to do to entice their targeted American into a liaison, intrigued as always by the triumph of biology over common sense. He had used two of the women before for similar entrapments, in the not-so-long-ago days when his job description called for a 'softer' approach to a disaffected bureaucrat or an intelligence officer with exotic tastes. But Irina was new to him, a concession to the *who the hell cares* attitude that went with the new East-West détente and made the old tradecraft seem like so much superstition, practiced only by ancient and irrelevant castes from both sides of the line.

Svetlana recruited her and vouched for her reliability. These days, that was good enough, but something about her bothered him. *She's different. Smarter. Harder, more calculating somehow, but at the same time ambitious in ways the others aren't. Realistic about the tradeoffs required to get what she wants. The kind that will extract the highest price for her information or services. No illusions about patriotism, the greater good. A recruit that would be hard to manipulate and therefore not to be trusted.*

Good thing she doesn't know about the secondary arrangements I've made for the two of them.

He would not recognize the important reality about Irina until much later; that she was not afraid of him, nor did she care about his agenda. Years later, he would come to believe that Irina was the sole person that foresaw the Soviet collapse with all of its collateral damage. And she had planned her exit strategy, using him – the cynical operator supposedly immune to manipulation – as the jumping-off point.

God! The world has changed! Whoever said that when Gorbychev opened up the wall, 'it was the end of history' had it nailed. A few hundred million ex-Soviet slobs whose only skill is fiddling the state systems are out-in-the-cold trying to adapt, believing that the capitalists have a magic formula that – once they drink the koolaid – will make them rich. And the Americans! Naïve fools like Ellerby and his delegation, who think they can parachute in and transplant their values into the Russian psyche, stir in a little technology and make the cold war disappear in a year or so! What a gathering of idiots!

The only realists – and the ones who will survive and prosper in the next decade – are the secret police and the mafia, the ones whose illusions were gone a long time ago. For them … us … it's like a gigantic cookie jar.

The Soviet implosion left the secret services on both sides scrambling. Martin had long ago made his own calculations, as coldblooded as any KGB agent looking to find new ways to apply skills no longer sanctioned by the 'official' policies of the state. His employer, the CIA, was caught unaware by the overnight collapse of the Soviet Union -- their archenemy and single most important reason for being. Field agents, such as Martin, found themselves with nothing to do, turned into 'commercial attaches' to facilitate new avenues of trade or commerce. Some, like him, became 'entrepreneurial'; rogues who used their unique knowledge to prosper in a world where all the old constraints were removed. Martin, for example, was good at killing people, an activity that – until recently – was done rarely and with layered approvals. These days, he had new clients who asked few questions and were willing to pay well.

The Agency is a dead end. They want satellites, computers, analysts … Clean and neat, data, algorithms …. not people like me … on the ground, messy, hard to control. They sure as hell would not approve of Svetlana, a completely unknown influence. In the old days, they would send someone like me to arrange an unfortunate accident for her – or perhaps even for me. Now they talk of early retirement and severance payments. Want you to study Arabic or Chinese and move to a different sector…. It's all bullshit! Always has been!

He did not dwell on and perhaps would not acknowledge the reality that he *enjoyed* setting the traps, finding and exploiting all of the human weaknesses to corrupt individuals, using either fear or greed as motivators to extract what was available and then terminating the arrangement – and often the individual. He knew that his official personnel file at Langley included the phrase, 'a highly intelligent psychopath with strong tendencies to violence'. He did not care. He was about to launch a new life, one where dossiers and personnel files no longer mattered.

There are millions of Ellerby's out there ... natural prey for the realists. And millions of Irina's looking for a better life. All they need is someone to bring them together in profitable ways.

The Deal (A few months ago)

There would be many deals – a series of off-the-grid transactions that enabled a certain life style -- but in his mind there was always *the deal*, the spectacular closing of a career, the criminal's equivalent of the corporate executive cashing in his stock options and 401K's to buy a boat and sail around the world. He did not yet know the specifics – who the victims would be, how the hooks would be set, how escape routes would be secured, or even the particular frailty that he would exploit – arms, drugs, or some other scourge so important to some upward-bound segment of the ever-shifting power structure.

In the early stages of this second career, he was like a young second cousin to a Mafia don, aspiring to be a made man but needing to establish an early rep by breaking legs and running errands. He brokered information exchanges, made some introductions, managed the diversion of arms, arranged cleverly forged documents, always getting paid a few thousand dollars. The high-value transactions were the infrequent assassinations. But the real payoffs for him were the connections, A-list names that could be cashed in or traded. His real currency was *leverage.*

It would take twenty-plus years. By then, his reputation was firmly established. If there was a Who's Who of 'facilitators of large scale criminal enterprises', he would be among the top few independent operators. But *the deal* was always just around the corner, a vague possibility that resisted taking on a definite form. It became clear that he needed to make the transition from a middleman to a principal, from a facilitator to *the man.*

He didn't press it. In his shadowy world, serendipity was a highly valued commodity, a fickle determinant of whether someone lived or died, whether a contract fizzled or turned into a lifetime relationship. Later, when he looked back on the complex set of arrangements that made up *the deal*, he recognized the nearly random convergence of three coincidences that made it happen, a coming together in time and space of small-time scams that – with some imaginative tweaking – could become something much greater.

The first of these three factors was his current sideline – exporting hopeful young Russian women and selling them into the US prostitution market. He did not know it then, but it would become the launching point for what would become *the deal*. By itself, it was small potatoes; a handful of women who required a lot of handling for not much money. He would much rather sell arms. The RPGs, Kalishnikovs and Uzi's at least were predictable, emotionless commodities.

Another apparently disconnected element was the emerging relationship with the American shipping executive. He was rich with inherited wealth, trailing all of the arrogance and sense of entitlement typical of the class. He reminded him of the Soviet apparatchiks – the ex-Communist bosses and their kin – who envisioned themselves as the new captains of industry or, for the more ambitious, as a regional governor of one of the resource-rich provinces. The decade after the wall came down was a feeding frenzy in Eastern Europe, fueled by the idea of trillions of dollars of state-owned assets that were up for grabs. They all wanted the biggest share and most of them wound up dead or in a Siberian gulag.

Like the ambitious Soviets, the American's self image was a serious personal weakness. He needed to see himself as something much more than a passive conduit for a few prostitutes that could be exploited for profit. *That need makes him vulnerable to people like me.*

The phone call was the final piece, the "click" of things falling into place, the intersecting of coincidences that would become serendipity.

"Necesito un submarino".

At the time, the simple message was unique both for its content – how many people need a submarine, after all? – and its source, a first-tier drug lord in Mexico. The call intrigued him. Up to this point, the largest piece of military hardware that he had brokered was an ancient turboprop Tupolev Tu-95 strategic bomber that went 'missing' when the Soviet empire imploded. To the best of his knowledge, the aircraft was still dropping bombs or even nastier things on African villagers from the wrong tribe.

Despite the call's uniqueness, it was a feasible transaction and the potential brokerage fee was substantial. He did some research on submarines, mostly by talking with ex-Russian naval officers in various Baltic ports. When he was ready, he boned up on the thriving US/South America drug trade and flew to Cabo San Lucas at the tip of the Baja peninsula with a young and very attractive woman named Tamara. Their passports said their name was Schneider and that they were from Hamburg. He refined his sales pitch during the long flight and the architecture of *the deal* began to emerge.

Interesting. The cartels need an ocean-based transport system for smuggling drugs and they're desperate enough to be thinking about submarines! I happen to know someone who runs a corruptible shipping line and wants to be a major crime boss. And I have some leverage on another party that controls a major port on the California coastline.

He spent three days in Cabo. The first two days were spent sitting in his hotel room waiting and wondering about the wisdom of his opening play. He rarely second-guessed himself, but he began to wish he had used other tactics. *All this Latin machismo shit! You should have paid more attention.*

The son-in-law of the cartel's boss met them at the airport two days ago. "Call me Estavan", was all he said. He instructed the limo driver to pull off the road as soon as they were off the airport grounds and turned in his seat to look at them. He looked like what Martin knew him to be -- a peasant, a man who should be in the fields with a machete harvesting the crop rather than in the upper levels of management in a multi-billion dollar criminal enterprise. His English was rudimentary and most of his attention was focused on Tamara's impressive breasts.

He probably practices that look in front of the mirror every morning. Scowl, dead eyes, pinched lips, unblinking ... Ends up looking like a TV ad for a laxative.

The conversation was brief and edged with hostility.

Might as well get right to the ground rules. "I need to meet with your boss ... the Jefe."

The look did not change, and his voice matched it. "For you gringo, I am the boss. Can you find us submarino?"

How to play this? He went with his instincts.

He spoke slowly and distinctly, making it seem a concession to stupidity rather than language differences.

"Yes, I can sell you a submarine. But you are too many levels down in the organization for me to deal with. And you're thinking too small ... Pero estás pensando demasiado pequeño."

The man's eyes changed, focusing on him rather than Tamara's breasts, apparently seeing him for the first time as perhaps something more than a broker, but still far from important. The eyes transmitted a total contempt for him, a reaction that he was not used to seeing. It amused rather than offended him, causing him to wonder if this son-in-law of a drug lord had ever in his brief life experienced fear or uncertainty of any sort. He reminded him of Dietrich, once one of the most feared members of the brutal East German Stasi. The man shot himself exactly one year after the wall fell, the day after a man in the street refused to show him his papers. Dietrich could not comprehend such a world, where ordinary people could defy him.

He took a deep breath and said again, slowly and with more emphasis. "I want to see your boss ... the Jefe." He made sure that the impatience came through quite clearly, despite the careful diction.

The man blinked twice and looked at the driver as if to seek advice. The driver stared straight ahead, his hands locked tightly on the wheel.

The eyes changed, signaling a decision. "We will drive you to hotel. Enjoy your time in Baja. It is a beautiful place." The tone was dismissive.

Nothing more was said until they parked beneath the hotel portico. The porter opened his door. Estavan stared straight ahead, clearly done. He leaned forward and put his hand on Estavan's shoulder. He could feel the strap for a shoulder holster become more prominent as the man's muscles tensed.

Can I even trust him to carry the message?

He said, in carefully spaced words, "Tell Jefe – his name is Jose Torres, as we both know – to take his expected profit from the submarino scheme and multiply it by ten. I'll be here until Friday if he wants to learn how."

"Do you understand? ¿Me entiende? Comprendo? Ten? Diez?"

That was two long and uneventful days ago.

The knock on the door came in the early afternoon of the third day. He was teaching Tamara basic street Spanish … nouns, phrases and adjectives, leaving the verbs and their conjugations for some unknown future instructor with a greater interest in improving Tamara's vocabulary.

The man at the door was tall and well-dressed. They looked at each other for a long ten seconds and apparently were mutually satisfied. "My name is Torres. I'm curious about the number ten."

He invited Torres in and started talking. He talked for an hour, extemporaneously and without interruption. His talk included statistics about DEA interdiction efforts, cocaine demand and prices in California, the surging market for methamphetamines, maritime regulation, the hazards of submarines, the economics of prostitution and his own extensive experience as a middleman between individuals and organizations who traded in corruption and violence.

His two listeners were a stark contrast. Tamara listened intently, although she knew virtually no English. Torres, on the other hand, appeared to pay only intermittent attention, leaning back in his chair and looking mostly at the ceiling or Tamara. However, when he stopped talking and allowed a loud silence to form around them, Torres leaned forward and said, "I have five questions."

The questions were brief and to the point.

"One. This shipping person? I understand that we need him, but can he be trusted?"

"Trusted? Of course not. He won't betray us. But he's an amateur and may do something stupid. My job is to make sure he doesn't."

"Two. Getting the stuff ashore? The gringo's DEA is getting better. Lots of risk there …"

"It comes in on our ship with our crew, is unloaded onto a pier that we have sole access to. And we have the means to divert the police at the right time."

Torres nodded. Then he leaned forward and looked directly at him. *So, this is the important question.* But Torres' tone didn't change. "Three. We already sell the product to the dealers in your city, the retail channel. Why should we help to put a wholesaler between us? And if we do, how will you convince them to buy from you?"

He kept his expression in place, but this was the question that most worried him. His answer was based on two critical assumptions. *He doesn't care who buys the stuff. And we need to impress him that we're serious.*

"I thought we'd kill several of the street corner dealers … send a message … and—once we've got their attention – emphasize that we can offer them a reliable supply of high quality stuff. Same day delivery … that kind of thing."

"Question number four. The price?"

"To be negotiated, but at least as much as you're getting from your small-time buyers now.   Depends on quantity, quality and the product mix.   But there's one condition going in – a non-negotiable."

Torres raised an eyebrow.

"The first one has to be a big shipment. At least a billion dollars – street prices - of product."

Torres' other eyebrow went up.   He sat back, obviously running numbers in his head. "We're the major provider for crystal meth and coke… probably some combination of the two to make it a billion dollar deal … and the crystal would have to be 85% purity or better to justify the price …   I might have to bring in some competitors … colleagues."

"That's your problem. We'll deal with you and you can work out the supply side any way you like."

For the first time, Torres really looked at him, a long intent stare locked on his eyes. When he spoke, his voice was different; both more serious and more confidential.

"If" – he stressed the word – "if we do this ... a shipment of this size ... you understand that you and everyone you represent is ... will be committed. And accountable. There's no going back."

"We are fully aware of your organization's reputation for enforcing contracts." *Like beheading family members of those who skim product off the top*

Torres sat back and stared at him with an expression that signaled he was satisfied with what he had heard.

He prompted him. "You said you had five questions?"

Torres inclined his head to indicate Tamara. "Who's she and what's she got to do with any of this?"

He smiled and began the second and much easier part of his sales pitch, made easier by Tamara who clearly had picked up on where the conversation was headed. She sat up straighter and smiled.

"This is Tamara. Think of her as a prototype for a different kind of product line." He talked about the "pipeline" and the strong motivation of Russian women seeking fresh perspectives. Torres had no questions when he finished.

They shook hands and set a meeting date in San Francisco two weeks in the future. As Torres turned to leave, he stopped him. "Tamara has some free time. I thought that she might hang around Cabo San Lucas for awhile ... improve her Spanish and pick up some local culture."

Torres smiled again and held out his hand to Tamara.

Deferred Consequences (Three Months Ago)

Ellerby's mayoral appointment calendar said "Grodin - Exchange Program" with thirty minutes allotted. But the person coming toward him was definitely Martin, his CIA escort from Vladivostock more than twenty years ago. He was older, thicker in the middle and even more cynical looking, but it was Martin. He wondered how Martin would describe the changes that he saw in him.

"Congratulations, Mayor. You've come a long way."

Ellerby stood up behind his desk and held out his hand, knowing that nothing good could come from this encounter, but finding himself curious about the shape it would take. "Actually, only a few hundred feet since we last met. From the offices of the Board of Supervisors to the Mayor's office. Better furniture, though. And a driver goes with the job." He said nothing about Vlad or the change of names.

Martin – or Grodin – ignored the extended hand and walked over and sat down in one of the four leather chairs surrounding the conference table in the corner of the office. He set his briefcase down on the table and simply looked at Ellerby, still standing by his desk. *So, some things have not changed in two-plus decades. He's still running his little operations, moving hypothetical pawns around on invisible boards.*

Ellerby shrugged and took the chair on the other side of the table. "As I recall, the last time we met, you were thinking about changing jobs. What have you been doing?"

"This and that. Facilitating, brokering, problem solving ... that sort of thing."

"So what brings you here? To San Francisco?" *To my office, you goddamned arrogant son-of-a-bitch!*

"I have a major client here in the Bay Area. A very high-minded do-gooder type of fellow. He wants to set up a cultural exchange program for graduate students from ex-Soviet states, mostly Russians."

"Sounds like something that one of our local universities would be interested in. Have you tried –"

"No. He wants the City of San Francisco to be the sponsor." His tone was dismissive, clearly making the point that this was already settled, not a matter for negotiation. "He feels strongly that *branding* is important." The slight emphasis on the word highlighted his amusement at its usage.

"And we want to locate it on Pier 37. It's sitting idle and rotting away. We'll rehab it and make annual rent payments to the city. We'd like you to sell that idea to your Board of Supervisors and the Port authorities. They'll like the idea of idle City property being used by a not-for-profit arts enterprise. And it's a nice little pop for the city budget."

Ellerby felt himself getting angry. He knew that part of that anger was at himself, stemming from his memories from a quarter-century in the past. It was not how he liked to think of himself, definitely not his fondest memory. The other part was Grodin's arrogance and his apparent presumption that he could dictate the terms of their relationship simply because he was aware of Ellerby's immature behavior more than two decades in the past.

I wonder if he knows of my present arrangements? That would seriously complicate things.

His mayoral instincts kicked in. *Time for a civics lesson.* He started to say, "The city budget does not allow for –"

Grodin cut him off, clearly anticipating this. "My sponsor will put up the funds. We'll hire and pay for a staff member, upgrade the space, recruit the students, manage their transportation and activities here, and be responsible for all the paperwork. All you have to do is endorse the concept and attend a few rubber-chicken dinners."

"It's not just the local authorities. You'll need State Department approval. There's visas and –"

"It's all taken care of. On both ends, Washington and Moscow." Grodin sat patiently and Ellerby realized that he would have a prearranged answer to every objection that he would make.

That's enough of this charade. Goodbye, Mr. Grodin ... or Martin ... whatever the hell your name is!

He stood up and held out his hand. "Tell your sponsor thank you for his public-spirited proposal. But the City of San Francisco must decline to participate at this time."

Grodin did not stand up or take the extended hand. He merely smiled in a way that reminded Ellerby of that depressing room in Vladivostock with the holes in the walls. Ellerby thought, *He's enjoying this. He expected me to go all righteous on him. And he's got something up his sleeve.*

"Please, Your Honor. Be patient for a moment. I want to show you an example of the benefits that will follow from the kind of cultural exchange that we have in mind."

He opened his briefcase and removed an iPad. He turned it on and faced it toward Ellerby. The video was clearly visible even from his standing position. It had been edited into three scenes, each one fairly short with accompanying sound. Each of the scenes had a time and date stamp. The first was a clip of Ellerby – almost twenty-five years younger -- giving a toast at the arrival ceremony for the San Francisco trade delegation in Vladivostock. He listened to himself, talking about looking forward to meeting Russians and sharing common values and stories. *God, I was pompous. And naïve. All at the same time!* The second and shortest scene showed Irina and him entering his ornate hotel suite in the center of Vladivostock. The video clearly showed how beautiful she was and how nervous he was. The third and longest clip was of them naked, making love on the carpeted floor of the hotel room. Irina still had her red heels on. *Funny. I never noticed that at the time.*

Both the visual quality and the audio clarity were impressive. There must have been two cameras and a skilled remote operator, because the zoom capability was being used extensively and effectively. *The son-of-a-bitch probably hijacked all of the CIA's equipment and assets in the Russian Far East.*

He watched without speaking. Grodin simply stared out the window, seemingly uninterested in whatever Ellerby was seeing or thinking.

An enormous sadness settled over him. The scenes reminded him of what he had once been and how much had been lost in that time. *I was so young and there were so many possibilities.* Then, for some reason, he remembered the way Grodin – Martin – had winked at him when he walked out of that squalid little bare room with the woman named Irina.

He spoke very quietly, knowing that whatever he said next would be irrelevant to whatever Grodin had in mind. The evenness of his voice surprised him and emphasized his sadness.

"That was almost twenty-five years ago. In another world entirely."

Grodin picked up the iPad and replaced it in his briefcase. "Yes, it was. For both of us. But your constituents – and your political enemies, maybe even your wife at the time – wouldn't care about time or place. Some of the most popular YouTube clips are actually quite old."

He stood up to leave, saying, "We thought a good name for the new program would be "The San Francisco Cultural Exchange Program". With that, Grodin simply nodded and headed for the door.

A few weeks after Grodin's office call, the Mayor found himself standing at a podium at the entrance to one of San Francisco's shabbier piers, announcing a new cultural exchange program. His opening phrase was, "A fine example of the power of people-to-people interaction."

He winced at the pompous expression, thinking *I need to get a better speechwriter.* He promptly revised his opinion. *Maybe you should read the speeches before you give them!*

There were less than a dozen people listening to him. The launch of one more cultural exchange program was not front-page news, particularly when the sponsoring donor chose to remain anonymous. *That's just fine with me. The less coverage the better.* Neither Grodin nor his supposed 'sponsor' were in attendance.

He thought back to the meeting with Grodin in his office, the part after watching the videos. Many times since then, Ellerby had tortured himself by scripting an alternative ending. *What if I had refused to endorse his scheme ... if I had just said 'no' and let him do whatever he wanted to do with his goddam video clips.*

Instead, detesting himself, he asked, "What exactly will this so-called cultural exchange program actually do?"

Grodin was headed for the door. Before he opened it, he turned back to Ellerby and said, "You don't want promising young Russian women – like Irina, with all those specialized skills – to be denied opportunities for growth in the United States, do you?"

The bastard knows!

The Tenderloin District (Present Time)

"I will not commit suicide today." McAdams said it aloud, listening carefully to the sound of it for any telltale insincerity, any hint of self-pity or histrionics. Anything that would make it less ominous. The word 'today' was emphasized, thereby allowing for the possibilities that made the commitment both possible and binding. The incentive for today's forbearance was the permission granted for tomorrow. That slight stress on the word 'today' also subtly changed his approach to the day. His focus shifted from the meaninglessness of his daily routine to honoring his single-minded commitment, the way an alcoholic uses 'one day at a time' as a protective mantra. Therapy was transformed into mere timekeeping.

At first, he was bemused by this newfound apathy. *How strange, this numbness, the not-caring. Will it ever end?* But McAdams had neither sufficient energy nor curiosity to chase after answers to such ambiguous questions.

A therapist could have helped. But McAdams shunned such types or even the idea that one should seek help for problems of the spirit. In any case, the certain cause for his depression was easily identified -- his belief that he had killed Gonzo and Freddie, his last two partners in the Homicide Division. Not literally, but as surely as if he was their appointed executioner. The fact that he was the only police officer in San Francisco who held that view did not lessen his guilt. To him, their very intense sympathy was proof of his culpability.

The other factor was the job itself. McAdams was COPPS – a member of what the SFPD called 'Community Oriented Policing and Problem Solving'. He was assigned to the San Francisco Tenderloin, meaning that he was responsible for balancing sociology & criminal justice in one of the infamous hot spots in the urban United States. The syndrome was well known -- "burnout", "compassion fatigue", "vicarious post traumatic stress disorder" – the semantic markers for an excess of caring; for beating one's

33

empathic head against a wall assembled from all of the woes of human possibility. If one were seeking a source of unending futility, COPPS in the Tenderloin would be a ranked contender.

The Tenderloin was the habitat of choice for drug dealers, addicts, prostitutes, panhandlers, gangbangers, and the entire whacked-out spectrum of mentally unstable street people. These days, it was also the current frontier for the gentrification movement, fueled by the influx of the mostly-young and geekish 'software engineers' and 'entrepreneurs' who could not quite afford the South of Market condos and deluded themselves into believing that today's Tenderloin was the re-creation of New York's Greenwich Village of the sixties, or today's Harlem. The mixture of the underclass and the nerds was a volatile one, and McAdams – if he were not mired in depression – would have enjoyed the interplay.

Murphy, the Captain of Detectives and his boss for the last six years, did his best to sell the transfer to COPPS. It was an awkward interview, each of them careful to not say certain things, an elliptical form of conversation common among men who care about each other but live within a macho culture that does not condone displays of certain emotions.

"We need someone like you there. Just walking around talking to the civilians." Somehow, Murphy's tones and inflection conveyed exactly the opposite message.

"I'm a homicide cop, not a social worker."

Murphy snorted. "First, this is only a temporary assignment. All you need to do is get it going. And, guess what? What part of the city do you think is the biggest contributor to our homicide rate? That's one of the reasons you're the right person for this assignment. You already spend half your time there now."

"I want to keep working on –". He stopped, not knowing how to finish the sentence. He didn't know how to admit to his boss that he was doing precisely what that same boss had emphatically prohibited him from doing.

Murphy looked at him with the same expression he would have used on a middle-class teenager picked up for truancy. He walked around his desk and closed his office door.

McAdams sat back in his chair, knowing what was coming. *Not a good sign. Murphy closes his door only when he's about to scream obscenities or to – what's worse – start one of his personal counseling sessions, of the "I'm telling you this for your own good" variety.*

Murphy sat back down, leaning as far back in his chair as it would recline. "Go ahead, say it. 'I want to keep working the Gonzo and Freddie cases.' Everybody in the goddam department knows what you're doing and half of them are running in circles trying to keep you from screwing it up without hurting your feelings!"

McAdams opened his mouth, but Murphy didn't even pause. "First of all, the cases are at dead ends. We're still working them, but we're stalled. It happens. We'll get the bastards, but it's going to take awhile. Second, you're a loose cannon. Nobody trusts you to follow the rules once we finally get a handle on somebody."

He leaned forward over his desk, as if getting closer to McAdams would give his words greater impact. "C'mon Mac. You'll still be in the loop. And it's probable that your Jane Doe – the dame washed up on the mud flats -- was hanging out there. In the Tenderloin. That's where people usually go when they're trying to stay off the grid."

McAdams had the flashback again, a sudden vision of a stark white nude corpse sprawled against a deep black background, as if a photographer trained in Fine Arts was apprenticed to the Coroner's office. He had trouble refocusing on what Murphy was saying.

"… not a cushy assignment. I know the mayor gave all those soft and fuzzy statements at the press conference where they launched COPPS –"

McAdams was derisive. "He made it sound like an offshoot of the Salvation Army!"

Murphy went on doggedly, "... But what he didn't say – and what you know better than most of us -- is that we've got some new and really bad players. There's a big push by somebody with South American connections to take over the really nasty stuff – drugs, prostitution, strong-arm stuff. They hurt people. And they view the Tenderloin as their personal playground. Those three street dealers that got shot in the back of the head were part of the succession planning."

"And Jane Doe," McAdams said softly.

"Yes, her too...". Murphy's voice trailed off.

There's more and he doesn't want to tell me. Who the hell cares!?

In the end, McAdams gave in. Mostly because he just didn't care enough or have enough energy to resist. The only option was to take the extended leave he was entitled to. He knew – and those around him knew – that the odds were that he would never come back, that he would be obsessed with the gun on his belt or on the bedside table, and that – sooner or later – he would pick it up and use it.

So, like today, he began each morning with a vow to try one more day. And once he was out on the street, it was as if the elements were aligned and determined to reinforce his resolution to stay around for one more day, that it was a good time to be alive. It was a warm spring day, in the seventies. The sun was out and keeping the fog at bay. A slight but steady breeze was blowing. It was one of those San Francisco days that could have been scripted by the Chamber of Commerce and compressed into a video for distribution to Midwestern cities during their long and dreary winters.

But if you're depressed, all incoming stimuli are tainted. For McAdams, all that the warmth did was to attract specimens into the open air that were best left in the dark; the shirtless over-tattooed dealers on Golden Gate Avenue or the winos and addicts propped up against the outer wall of Glide Memorial Church. The sunlight – so welcome to those who lived on the street – did nothing for

McAdams other than highlight unpleasant details and sharpen one's awareness of the urban squalor on all sides. And the freshening breeze brought odors to one's attention that triggered visions of decay and rot, reminders of what was behind the walls and beneath the streets.

"Nice day, isn't it? Reminds one of all the good things that are possible."

McAdams smiled. Garfield's timing was perfect, as if he was wired into McAdams' brain and could detect the precise low point. No surprise. He had learned long ago that the man leaning against the wall looking at him with a thoughtful expression had extremely strong empathic connections, what McAdams simply called a "bullshit detection capability". Some of it was surely genetic, some of it the kind of stuff you picked up from years of AA meetings, but most of it from just walking the streets and dealing with the cons, delusions and scams that were so prevalent in this place where "getting by" was a full time job. Most of the denizens of this place were looking for a way out, whereas Garfield gave the impression of a man just paroled from a personal hell, for whom life on the street was a gift.

"Give it time, Mac. The good guys always win in the end."

McAdams no longer tried to keep up appearances when Garfield was around. He found it simpler – and somehow comforting – to accept that his inner self was so visible. *Could be a basis for a marriage. I wonder if Garfield has a lover?*

"Hello Garfield. Good guys? I don't know who they are any more. I feel like the marine that was accused of killing civilians instead of insurgents. He said, 'I just kill 'em all and let God sort 'em out'."

Garfield was as much a part of the Tenderloin as the historic buildings with their colorful graffiti ever since he'd wandered into the scene ten years ago. No one was quite sure of his history, motives or even how he sustained himself. Rumors were all over the map. Some had him as an eccentric billionaire, a dropout from the high tech culture of Silicon Valley. Others figured him as an ex-con trying to atone for some extreme wrong. Garfield would neither confirm nor deny the various stories.

McAdams didn't care; he just wished the earth could be strewn with people like Garfield.

Garfield was somewhere between fifty and sixty. He looked well-worn, like someone who spent too much time in the sun and worried a lot. He had a perpetual semi-smile and blue eyes that seemed always to be looking directly at you. He dressed like one of the street people, but in a way that told you he still cared how he looked. The jeans were faded but clean; the shirt old with frayed cuffs, but it was a Pendleton and it fit. On cold days, he wore an old Army field jacket with darker patches where insignia and nametags had once been.

They heard Harry Howden coming before they saw him, a high-pitched voice behind them and getting closer. Together, they watched him approach. Harry stood out, even in a setting filled with the zonked-out, depraved, misbegotten castaways that littered the sidewalk around him. He was tall, perhaps six feet six inches or so, but bent forward from the waist and with his head down, so that he had to look upward at most people. Even then, he would not stand erect or lift his head but simply rotated his head from side to side as if tracking some internal metronome. *Making eye contact is not his strong point,* McAdams thought.

Howden was wearing his usual tan trench coat, belted at his waist, buttoned to the neck and with the collar turned up. McAdams had never seen what he wore beneath the coat, although the pants were clearly from a tuxedo, with a satiny stripe running down the outside of the leg, terminating at a pair of black shoes with the stitching torn, so that the soles flapped as he walked. The rest of his wardrobe and whatever possessions he owned were loaded in the red wagon – a classic Radio Flyer -- that he pulled behind him, attached to him by a short rope from the wagon handle to the belt of his trench coat. He was a caricature of a refugee from some third world conflict, although the scourges he was escaping from were entirely in his own mind.

He always carried a bible in one hand. McAdams had never seen him refer to it. Instead, he waved it aloft, an accompaniment to his perpetual oratory, a crude baton directing an imaginary orchestra of prophets.

Howden stopped when he saw McAdams and Garfield at the corner, his wagon bumping against his calf. His voice was loud, rising over the background noise of traffic, oratorical as always, in keeping with its cataclysmic content.

"Do not prostitute thy daughter, to cause her to be a whore; lest the land fall to whoredom, and the land become full of wickedness! For whosoever shall commit any of these abominations shall be cut off from among their people!"

"Good morning, Harry." McAdams spoke when Howden's head rotated on its forty-five degree axis to bring him within sight.

"The land is full of foulness and abominations," recited Howden, but at a lesser volume. "Can't you see it all around you, McAdams? Garfield?"

"Leviticus, isn't it? Makes your god sound like an angry old man with sexual hangups."

Howden scowled at McAdams' blasphemy and his voice regained its volume. "Thou shall not expose thy sister's nakedness! The whiteness of flesh is displeasing to God!"

"I don't have any sisters, Howden. But tell me, what's new around here? I hear rumors of new … foulness and abominations. A new breed of sinners inflicting woe on the Tenderloin. What's your take?"

McAdams no longer felt awkward in these elliptical conversations with Howden. In his pre-depression days, he would have worried about this compatibility with seriously unstable people. Now, he felt like their conversations held some real but elusive truths, if only he had the energy to sort them out.

Howden almost stood up straight, as though

McAdams' questions warranted better posture to reinforce his response. "They rise up from the waters, dripping evil! They are among us, with chemicals and swords, seducing us!"

"Who are they? These seducers? Where do you see them?"

But Howden's eyes had turned inward, attending to voices that only he could hear. His voice became shrill and he turned to leave. "God is displeased. The whores are multiplying among us, arising from the bed of the sea. And they are zombies, undead!"

I don't think there were any zombies in Leviticus. Or chemicals, for that matter. McAdams put a hand on Howden's arm. "It's a sunny day, Howden. We're safe for the moment. Can I buy you a cup of coffee? How about a cinnamon roll?"

Howden made a vague gesture at the street scene around them. "Can't stop. They're doomed. They need to hear." And he stepped off the curb, his wagon nearly overturning. Whatever he was saying was lost among the horns and engine noises as he crossed the busy street against the red light, forcing traffic around him and his red wagon.

McAdams checked his watch. Two hours gone since his oral commitment to stay alive for another day. A long way to go. He turned back to Garfield. "Gotta go. But Howden's right about the foulness and abominations, so I'm going to do my best to stem the tide. Maybe go arrest a prostitute for soliciting during daylight hours."

"You just missed your best bust for the day. You stood there and watched Howden commit a serious jaywalking offense." Garfield smiled, but his eyes stayed fixed on McAdams with an expression heavy on curiosity.

"That's what community-oriented policing is all about … ignoring the little stuff. Prioritizing. See ya."

Garfield watched him walk away and shook his head in a way that conveyed an immense sadness. *A good cop with very bad karma … I know all about those.*

Moonlighting Agents

Charles Desmond knew that he was a mediocrity and was content with the fact, thereby demonstrating an unusual degree of self-esteem among his middle-class peers. He was average looking, of average intelligence and made an average living working as an on-call claims agent for several different insurance firms. He had the average number and types of flaws typical of his class and generation. The exception – the flaw that would kill him within the next ninety minutes -- was his addiction to gambling.

He was an average gambling addict -- a net loser. Paradoxically, he worked in an industry – insurance – based entirely on a realistic assessment of probabilities. Yet he wasted his money in an industry – gambling – that was based on the assumption that its customers could not (or would not) abide by the self-evident probabilities. The irony never occurred to him. Like most gamblers, other forces propelled him. The first was the naïve belief that "next time will be different". Then there was the power of what the psychologists called "partial reinforcement", so that the positive feedback of the occasional "win" more than offset the negatives associated with losing. And, of course, there was the biochemistry of addiction, the release of dopamine that goes with risk-taking behavior.

Bad habits usually require extraordinary financing efforts. Accordingly, Desmond had developed a profitable but illegal little sideline: he accepted bribes to facilitate fraudulent insurance claims. Today's customer, Pacific Cargos, was an infrequent but reliable contributor to this sideline. Half-a-dozen times over the last couple of years, the company paid him several hundred bucks in cash to "expedite" a highly-overstated claim for damaged goods, workplace injuries or physical loss from weather or other causes.

Under "cause of loss", the company's form read, "External damage to crating allowed seawater to penetrate

41

container and damage the shipment of 1,000 personal computers." Under "extent of loss", the entry was "total". The insurer was a medium-sized Korean financial firm based in Seoul that Desmond represented in Northern California ports, which is why he was boarding a small freighter anchored south of the Bay Bridge on a gray and cold morning.

The container in question was sitting on the deck awaiting his inspection. Other cargo had been offloaded yesterday, so the ship was quiet. The deckhand who met him just pointed at the very large wooden box and said in a language that was just barely English, "That's computers. Cover we moved so can check inside."

"I'll need a flashlight. And to see the lading documents ..."

The man barked some kind of emphatic curse in whatever language he spoke and added "Said nothing about that." And he walked off toward the bridge.

Desmond shrugged. It was hard to get excited about dotting i's and crossing t's when the game was rigged in the first place. He walked over to the crate, picking up a six-foot stepladder leaning against one of the deck cranes as he went. The crate seemed to be a custom-made wooden container, about twelve feet by twelve feet and six feet high. A splash of paint highlighted a series of vertical gaps in the planking along one side, presumably the "cause of loss" mentioned on the form. *Fraud #1 – I'll bet those gaps were caused by a crowbar sometime in the last few hours.*

The cover was pushed back a couple of feet on one end. He placed the ladder and climbed up to peer inside. *Fraud #2 – there's probably about 100 computers left. The others are already on the gray market.* The light streaming through the open top highlighted obvious water damage to the packaging of the individual computer packages still in the container. *Fraud #3 – A definite loss, but almost certainly caused by the water hose that still lay uncoiled at the foot of his ladder. And the damage is confined to maybe the top twenty packages.*

He ran the numbers in his head. *Nine-hundred and eighty computers … maybe a thousand bucks each on the gray market, plus about the same amount or more from the swindled insurance suckers in Korea. Somewhere around a couple of million to be split up by the shipping company and whoever "owned" the computers.*

He spent about three minutes using the camera on his iPhone to document the damage to the exterior of the crate and the water damage to the contents, careful to compose his shots so that the reduced size of the shipment and the trivial amount of real damage was not evident to some paper-shuffling clerk in Seoul. He also appropriated three undamaged computers in their brightly colored boxes, as many as he could conveniently carry.

He smiled. *A skim on top of a scam! That deckhand looked pretty dumb. And, if asked, I'll just say I need a sample to verify that they were a total loss.*

He headed for the bridge. He did need those lading documents for his report, and – more importantly – he needed to pick up the thousand bucks in cash. His resentment grew with every step he took toward the bridge. *They pay me a thousand and take in a couple of million for themselves!*

Then the world turned weird. Ten feet ahead of him, a cabin door slammed back against the bulkhead and a figure lunged out, tripping on the bottom flange of the door and sprawling against the outer rail. The suddenness stopped Desmond in place. Then it got even stranger. The figure gathered itself as if to run, then stopped, realizing that Desmond was standing there gawking. She – it was most definitely a woman – looked back and forth between him and whoever was standing in the cabin she had just exited so violently. Desmond simply stared back at her. She was beautiful, quite young, with long raven-black hair, and wearing only a very flimsy, almost transparent black cocktail dress and red heels that called attention to startlingly white breasts and long legs. Her appearance – not even that, her very presence -- was so out-of-context that Desmond could not move for several seconds.

Then he registered that she was looking directly at him with a wild, terrified expression and was speaking, something incomprehensible but repeated in a rising tone. It sounded like gibberish. "Mama geet semye", was what he heard. *What the hell is going on?* The weirdness only increased when Desmond thought, *"I've seen this woman before!"* The thought was so implausible that he reached out to touch the cold steel of the bulkhead, as if to reassure himself that he wasn't dreaming.

Then the man came out of the cabin, turning to face him.

"Desmond, isn't it? The insurance guy?"

"Yes, I –"

But the man held up a hand to stop him and turned toward the woman, still looking as if she wanted to run. He said only "Anya", but she seemed to respond to something in his eyes. Whatever she saw, it diminished her. The tension that was keeping her poised for flight seeped away. The wild look faded into a dullness that could have been acceptance, and she edged past the man – careful not to touch him – and went back into the cabin. He closed the door behind her and then turned once more to Desmond.

The man looked at the three boxes under Desmond's right arm and then raised his eyes to look directly at Desmond. His expression was simultaneously questioning and disappointed. He took a roll of bills out of his pocket, peeled off ten one-hundred dollar bills and held them out.

Desmond took the money. "These?" he said, pushing the bright packages forward while he tucked the cash away. "I need them in case they want physical evidence of loss. They ask sometimes –". His embarrassment was obvious to both of them.

"Sure," the man said. "The damage is obvious. Those are really water soaked." Somehow, the absence of sarcasm made Desmond feel like a child caught lying about his homework being done.

"Uh, I need the bills of lading –"

"I'll email them. We're completely electronic these days. You should go now."

"Yeah." He turned away and took two steps toward the gangplank down to the waiting shore taxi. Then he stopped and faced the man, who was standing still, watching him. Desmond knew he was being stupid, but was still seeing that terrified look in the eyes of the half-clothed woman.

"Uh, that woman –"

The man looked directly at Desmond, and he understood why the woman's spirit and flight instinct had deserted her.

"What woman?"

When Desmond was descending the gangway to the boat, the man took a cellphone from his pocket and pushed a single digit.

"We have a couple of problems that need your attention. One is Anya. I think she knows what's coming and wants to change the outcome."

He listened for ten seconds. "Whatever. That's your area of expertise."

He went on. "Our other problem is Desmond, the insurance guy."

He listened briefly. "Yeah, I know. He's been reliable. But he's skimming product. And worse? He ran into Anya just now. At best, he's a loose cannon. Worst case? He blabs to someone."

He listened, this time for about thirty seconds.

"OK. And soon. Before he starts talking." And he ended the call.

Nude on the Beach

It was two months back. Before McAdams' life turned dark, a time when homicide was just a job, something that affected other people's lives, not his.

It looks like the opening scene for one of those depressing Scandinavian films, the sort with depressing music heavy on the bassoons, bleak wintry landscapes, where all the characters are monosyllabic and sad even when they're smiling.

It seemed an unlikely thought. McAdams did not frequent movie houses and, if he had, he would have avoided the crime shows, particularly the "police documentaries". He had far too much of that in his daily life.

The truth is that the overly melancholy Scandinavians could write a dozen scripts just by following me around for a few days. Lonely cop, forty-year-old workaholic, no real relationships, divorced for years. Eats takeout dinners standing at his kitchen counter while watching whatever sports are available on his ten-year-old TV. Thinks about women a lot, but doesn't do much about it.

 Not a drunk, however.

He looked more like a college professor or a genial small town GP – the kind that Norman Rockwell would paint -- than a big-city homicide cop. He wore the better brands of sport coats and they looked natural on him, not like just a garment thrown on to cover up a shoulder holster. Women would say he was intriguing, maybe attractive. Sandy unruly hair, brown eyes, a spontaneous smile. He was six feet tall and fit, due mostly to genetics rather than any discipline in diet or workout regimes. In spite of his current reverie about melancholy, he was a naturally cheerful and curious person. Other detectives ragged him about "how nice" he was, how the bad guys would laugh at him.

His ex-wife captured the image nicely. "He was an ideal first husband."

He was also highly introspective, probably not a good trait for a Detective Lieutenant in Homicide. But perhaps it explained why he was thinking such drab thoughts early in the pre-dawn morning.

The film analogy was apt because it did seem that the monochromatic scene was carefully designed to simulate a theatrical experience. The neon yellow crime scene tape was the only color in sight, marking out the rectangular borders of the hypothetical stage. The stark white body at center stage was a dramatic contrast to the ink-black mud and leaden waters of the tidal flats where it lay, half imbedded in the soft muck as the receding tide allowed gravity to take effect. Even the people – crime scene technicians and the assistant coroner -- were clad in white coveralls and seemed to move in a choreographed fashion. For added atmosphere, the dense gray fog served as a shroud for the entire scene.

She was the city's fiftieth homicide of the year, a milestone of sorts. *Not as bad as it used to be, but this is going to be one of those cases that is hard to forget.*

Once on a long and boring stakeout, sitting in a darkened car in an equally dark alley, he and Gonzo had gotten into one of their more atypical cop-to-cop conversations.

Gonzo had started it. "Does it bother you when somebody gets away with it? When somebody gets killed – your ordinary citizen type -- and we can't catch the sicko that did it?"

McAdams thought about it seriously. "Sometimes, but probably not as often as you think… and not for very long. But there are times …"

To his surprise, Gonzo persisted. "What's different about those? The times where it really gets under your skin?"

He answered without thinking. "Evil."

He could also feel Gonzo raise his eyebrows.

McAdams went on quickly, intrigued by his own statement. "Yeah, I know. Kinda overly melodramatic, isn't it?"

He went on, curious about his rising passion for his hypothesis. "Look. Most of the killing is easy to understand. Not excusable, but still something even the normies can relate to. Crimes of passion – the jilted lovers, paranoid schizophrenics, drunken arguments, meth heads. Even the gangbangers and their drive-by strafings are understandable. Pathetic, tragic and stupid, but understandable."

Gonzo nodded. "They're also easy to identify and put away. Passion and stupidity don't make for good alibis."

Then he added, "But that's not all of them …"

"Yeah, it's not. What's left are the ones that bother me. Still."

The conversation ended abruptly when the object of their stakeout appeared and they split up to keep him in sight. But McAdams had not forgotten and had gone on to flesh out his theory of evil during one of his sleepless periods.

It requires not just intent, but planning, what the courts call premeditation; a deliberate act to erase a person and everything that they are or could have become. It assumes knowledge, a full awareness of what you are doing and the acceptance – either explicit or tacit -- that their existence is unimportant…. An ultimate form of arrogance.

Later, he added to the depiction. *And they're smarter, the evil ones. No doubt about their 'ability to tell right from wrong'. And harder to catch.*

The woman hadn't been in the water very long, probably overnight. She was young, probably early twenties. Even with her face half buried in the muck, it was evident that she had been quite pretty, with long dark hair and regular features. She was naked, so it was easy to see that her body was well-kept and one that would attract men. The only obvious identifying mark was a tattoo of a butterfly on her left ankle.

Standing at the edge of the mud and looking at the crime scene, he somehow knew that this was going to be one of those cases that would stay with him, one of those that had evil at its core.

He wanted to find the person who had done this and to ask him "Why?"

At first, his compulsion to ask such a question puzzled him. He knew that the answer – if forthcoming -- would neither exonerate the killer nor explain his action. He wondered if perhaps, against all odds, his intention was to trigger some latent self-insight in the person. Not remorse, because that would complicate McAdams' feelings about evil, that it can only exist within an entirely self-absorbed individual. Perhaps fear was what he hoped to stimulate; the realization that a cop asking *"why"* could be his executioner.

He thought a lot about what he would do after he asked the question. Like most homicide and street cops, he supported capital punishment and it was easy for him to daydream about executing such a person. He was uninterested in the endless arguments about sociology, deterrence or morality. He simply wanted to exact vengeance, the ancient tribal form, with sharp blades and wailing women.

Gonzo approached him, ducking under the tape. McAdams noticed that his shoes were covered with black muck. *Knowing Gonzo, he'll throw them away rather than trying to get them clean again.*

"So, any early insights?"

"Three, actually. But pretty obvious ones. First, this is an assassination, not your usual hot-blooded affair. Single bullet in the back of the head. Second, she was tossed into the water last night, somewhere not too far away. The tides dumped her here. Third, I don't know why, but I'm thinking this may be connected to the same people that did the three corner dealers –head shots, dumped in the Bay, etc."

"That's it?" McAdams prompted him when he slipped into a brooding silence.

"No. There's one more thing." Gonzo paused and, when he spoke again, his voice was different, huskier. "I really want to get the bastard who did this. He's –"

When Gonzo paused, McAdams supplied the word. "Evil."

McAdams and Gonzo drew the case because they were first on the duty list that day. However, they probably would wind up with it in any case, given its sinister nature. They were the top pair of detectives in Homicide, closing more and tougher cases than the next two pairs combined. And this case was one of those that the politicians and ordinary voting citizens would get excited about. They would check their locks more carefully and think twice about late night outings in the city. It was bad for business. He knew that at least a couple of journalists would write it up in ways that would bring back memories of the so-called Zodiac murders that had the city terrified for months.

She was the fiftieth. But she was also the last of a quartet. Three other and far less-attractive individuals had been killed in the last three weeks. In each case, the male victims had their wrists bound with duct tape, were killed with a single gunshot in the back of the head and the bodies were dumped in the Bay. The three were low-level narcotics dealers, the bottom-feeders that stand on street corners and serve drive-by customers.

The woman at center stage on the tidal flats was linked to them by what the crime novelists called *modus operandi.* For now, she was known simply as Jane Doe.

The Journey

Every now and then – less frequently now – Sofia wondered what it would be like *not* to be afraid. *How can one conceive of an absence that you have never experienced? Fish without water. Eskimos with no snow. The blind deprived of darkness. Much easier to remember and relive those explosive increments to experience that made one aware of new worlds –sex for the first time, the incredible sadness of music, landing in America …*

The fear began in the orphanage, probably learned in the crib as an amalgam of hunger, loneliness and pain. Then it was perfected by adults in the series of foster homes; by adults that wanted things from her that she didn't know how to provide, at least at first. It was honed to a sharp edge by existing within a society devoid of trust, one that required cannibalization of its own members for survival. The fear remained, but at least was tempered by hope when she made her pitch to Andreiovich, who promised her things that she knew he didn't have. But he was the gateway.

"I want to go to America … to San Francisco."

He laughed. "So do I. We all do. But we're still in Vladivostock. What makes you different?"

"I want it more."

When he laughed again, she played her lone trump. "You did it for Sasha. You can do it for me."

He looked at her, this time seeming to appraise her seriously; not just her body, which she was consciously arranging for his approval, but also the intensity of her wishes, listening for raw hunger rather than the characteristic shallow materialism that had become so common in the new Russia. When he spoke, his voice was huskier.

"You say you want it more? Prove it."

She slowly began unbuttoning her blouse. *The first step. So easy. But will he do what I want him to do?*

A week later, while she was dressing, he said, "I have made some arrangements for you."

She did not ask about the details. She knew that he was being well paid for his services and that he would lie about what was in store for her. Instead, she practiced her English, working to eliminate the Russian accent. It was the most practical step she could take to further the plans that she had not shared with Andreiovich. And every night, she would recite her secret, like a small prayer -- the name and address in San Francisco that Sasha had told her about. And she worried that Sasha no longer called.

Her trip began on a Russian ship out of Vladivostock, a floating fish-processing factory that was the "mother ship" for a fleet of much smaller trawlers operating around the Aleutian Islands. Unlike the three other women, she was somehow exempted from providing sex-on-demand for the crew. She seemed to travel in some variation of protective custody, an investment to be nurtured for the moment. Apparently, Andreiovich had made "special" arrangements for her and she knew that this was not necessarily good news. The second leg of her journey was also by sea, on a fishing trawler owned by coastal Canadian Indians that picked them up at Dutch Harbor at the tip of the Aleutians and then transferred them at sea to the American freighter that was at last anchored in the middle of San Francisco Bay.

The trip was difficult for her and the other women. Natalia, Anya and Maria were younger, barely twenty, but the companionship helped, even through it was based on their shared fears. Anya was Sasha's younger cousin and looked uncannily like Sasha. The two of them did not discuss their fears about Sasha's silence and what it might mean, a tacit reluctance based on their fear that – if they talked about the options – there would be only one horrible surviving possibility. For a while, seasickness made her indifferent to whether she lived or not, driving the fear into remission. All four of them suffered from it, but Anya seemed to wither away and become old before their eyes, as if they were watching a time-lapse video of her lifetime.

Anya disappeared somewhere during the second night they were docked in San Francisco Bay. It was if she had never existed. Sofia and the other two women did not talk about her after that, as though their silence absolved them of any responsibility for her fate.

On the third night, the American came aboard with new dresses for them. He was the younger of the two men, even though he was the boss. He watched them strip and put on the new clothes, but seemed more interested in how the dresses looked than in their nakedness. She remembered the way he had looked at Maria when she had pulled off her T-shirt. She somehow made it an eloquent expression of contempt. Sofia envied Maria her breasts – large and quite natural – but the man's expression became even colder, if possible. Sofia watched him, thinking *this man will not be tempted by anything we can show him or do to him. He is missing some important part of himself.*

When they were dressed and standing before him, he said, "Tonight I shall introduce you to some very important men. I want you to please them."

Natalia asked, "Will we be paid?"

"I'm sure they will be quite generous … if you please them."

"Who are they?" Sofia shuddered when Maria asked the question. Somehow, she knew that both the question and the answer – if it was forthcoming – would be dangerous.

The man looked very hard at Maria. Sofia was very impressed that Maria did not drop her gaze, but stared defiantly back. *Very brave, Maria. And stupid!*

"They can tell you their names if they choose, but it is better for you if they do not. They do not speak your language, or even English very well."

"And one more thing … You may overhear some talk. Who knows? They may talk in their sleep." He paused and looked at each of them in turn, his eyes dead. "You should forget whatever you hear. Even better for your future: forget that you met these men."

They left two hours later, long after dark. They climbed a ladder onto a pier, awkward to do in spike heels, and walked the length of the darkened shed built onto the pier, exiting onto a wide walkway that reminded her of Vladivostock for a brief second. Sofia was the last to cross the sidewalk to the waiting vehicle. She looked up at the lighted skyline and the lights on the bridge spanning the Bay, so different than where she had come from. *So this is San Francisco. I've made it this far … so little distance to go now.* And that is when the fear returned, surging in from the dark recess where it had been waiting, gaining strength.

To come this far, to get so close …

Breakaway

Sofia did not think very much about herself other than an occasional assessment of what internal strengths might be required in a particular situation. She saw an American commercial once that was built around the theme *"Just Do It!"* and she recognized that she had been living according to that motto for as long as she could remember. And given the obstacles in her path, she had done very well indeed. One of her institutional minders once recited some statistics that she never forgot: Within two years of leaving a Russian orphanage, fifteen percent of the girls commit suicide. Another sixty percent are involved in prostitution or are drug addicts.

She was not curious about the other twenty-five percent even though – upon her emergence from the orphanage at age sixteen -- she became one of them. Presumably, each was an example of what social workers call the "resilient child syndrome", the exception that carves out her own private world amidst the chaos. She would have scoffed at the label. To Sofia, simply *existing* in Russia was ample testimony to one's resilience.

To say that she had a *plan* to escape would have been a vast overstatement. But in her mind, she had now completed two of the three legs of her journey to freedom. Her first goal was simply to *get out of Russia*. Once that was achieved, the second goal became to *get to San Francisco.* When she stepped onto the pier, after traveling more than six thousand miles, she mentally crossed out those two and focused on the third and most dangerous leg: *an address in Pacific Heights.* She did not think beyond that point, either out of superstition or – more likely – because she could not conceive of getting that far, like a teen ager boasting "I'm going to Mars" and then being asked "But what will you do once you get there?"

A month before leaving Russia, she downloaded and studied a street map of San Francisco, committing it to memory. She learned the name of every major street, neighborhood and tourist attraction in the city, as if she was competing for a "taxi driver of the year" award. So she knew that she was – at this moment -- about 2.4 miles away from her third goal. She also knew it would be the hardest to attain. The distance was trivial, but the obstacles were both large and dangerous.

The vehicle at the street entrance to the pier was a black Cadillac Escalade, huge and ominous, with black windows. Ironically, she was quite familiar with it because it was the car of choice for the Russian mafia chiefs that she was acquainted with in Vlad. The door was held open by the other American, the older one who spoke fluent Russian and called the younger man "Boss" with a barely detectable irony. Sofia feared him more. The younger man was frightening because he viewed the three women as freight, packages to be delivered. If Sofia ran, he would seek to minimize the economic loss. The older man – the one holding the car door -- smiled a lot, but Sofia knew that he would hurt her for no reason other than his own amusement, like a cat playing with a mouse.

She was intensely aware of the ten feet of sidewalk between her and the Escalade and even more aware of the way that the sidewalk stretched away into darkness to the left and to the right. *I will get only one chance. Now or later? Run at the first opportunity or wait for a better chance? How will I know when it's the right time?* In that instant, she knew it was not a real choice. She knew that the longer she waited, the more powerful the fear would become, until it served to imprison her as effectively as any iron cage. *But I will get only one chance.* And looking at the long stretch of empty sidewalk, she knew that this was not the time.

The three women sat in the last row of seats of the Escalade, so that making a quick exit while stopped at a traffic light was an impossibility. So Sofia studied the buildings and the people in the cars next to them or on the sidewalk. *Normal people, with normal fears. I wonder what they worry about.* Even the homeless beggars with their illegible cardboard signs at the traffic lights were intriguing to her. *So close, and still so far.* When she looked ahead, she realized that the older man was watching her, turned sideways in his seat. He smiled at her, in a way that told her that he knew she intended to run. And she also realized that he was looking forward to that.

Looking directly at her, he said, "You remind me of a woman I met a long time ago, in Russia."

"What happened to her?" She asked the question, knowing that she did not want to know the answer.

"She disappeared, like Sasha. And Anya." He turned away, but his smile was so at odds with the simple phrases that Sofia shivered and hugged herself tightly. *He knows. And he wants me to know that he knows. I've just been warned.*

The map in her head told her they were traveling along the Embarcadero. When the Cadillac stopped and the doors opened, she knew they were in North Beach, the "Italian neighborhood" according to the guidebooks. The SUV was parked on a steep hill outside of a house that Sofia recognized as one of the classic Victorian homes that San Francisco was famous for. It was tall, four stories, but very narrow, sandwiched between a two-story brick apartment building and another Victorian. Every light in the house seemed to be on. There were a dozen steps leading up from the sidewalk to an ornate front door. Two men stood on the sidewalk, one on either side of the stairway. They were dark in every way – dark skin, dark hair, wearing dark clothing and dark in subterranean ways that Sofia recognized and feared. *They are the same in Russia. Cruel little men who protect the bosses. The Americans say 'riding the coattails'.*

The two Americans went inside, leaving the women in the car. One of the dark men came and stood next to the car, an obvious minder.

Maria was the first to break the silence that had settled on them during the transit from the ship. "I wonder how much they'll pay us?"

Not enough, Sofia thought, but did not say.

"Less than they should," Natalia scoffed. "But more than Yuri paid you for what you did for him in his dacha, that's for sure!"   Her tone was scornful, but Sofia could hear the underlying nervousness. It was confirmed by her next question.

"Sofia? … The American … the quiet one who smiles all the time … he frightens me. I think he is not like most men, yes?"

I cannot help them without hurting myself. They are still girls, with girls' dreams.   So young in so many ways. They do not want what I want.

She said, "I think … I think we should be very careful around these Americans, especially the quiet one who smiles. Do you remember our proverb …   'It's the still waters that are inhabited by devils'? These men are not our friends."

They waited in a tense silence. Sofia used the time to study the Victorian and the surrounding area. *There are many windows and there must be fire escapes. A very narrow alley on either side, but with a watching man at the end of it. But there may be a way. If, just if ….*

After about twenty minutes, the sentry answered his cell phone and told them to get out of the car. They were met at the front door by another of the dark-skinned men. He directed them up the next flight of stairs, where they found themselves in a living room that took up the entire floor. The only apparent exit and entry points were the staircases at opposite ends of the room, leading either up or down. *It's like living in a series of luxurious railroad cars stacked on one another.* The furniture seemed ponderous, with lots of heavy velveteen fabrics. Three men were sitting at one end of the room, around a coffee table with a dozen or so sheets of paper scattered on its surface. *So, these are the important ones … the ones we need to please.*

The three men were alike in many ways. She guessed they were all Latin and from somewhere else. They all wore obviously expensive suits and – to Sofia – seemed to be posing, trying to project an air of authority, even while sitting down. *These men are competitors, not partners, trying hard to impress each other. And maybe us.* Sofia guessed them to be somewhere in their forties. Two of the men were lighting enormous cigars and the third was engaged in opening a bottle of red wine. The scene – and the satisfied expressions common to the three – indicated that the business of the evening was concluded.

No introductions were made. The two Americans conferred in one corner of the room in inaudible tones, leaving the three women standing uncertainly in the middle of the room, looking everywhere except at the men. The three men grouped around the table sat back in their chairs with their cigars and wine glasses, clearly appraising the women. *It is exactly like Russia. We are here for the men's temporary pleasure. They are like babushkas in the market, trying to decide which piece of meat is best.* She tried to keep her contempt from showing.

After about thirty seconds, the one who seemed the youngest of the three grinned broadly and said something to the man opposite him, indicating with a sweeping gesture that it was up to him to make the first move.

"Elige primero, Jose. No le diría esposa."

The man – Jose -- glanced at the third man, who simply inclined his head toward the women. Then Jose stood and walked slowly but directly to Sofia, taking her hand to separate her slightly from the other two. His English was heavily accented, but he spoke slowly and distinctly.

"My name is Jose. I am delighted to meet you, Miss -- ?"

"My name is Sofia. Your friend … the one who spoke to you just now in Spanish? What did he say?"

Jose, if that was his name, was startled by the question. Then he smiled quite genuinely. "He said that I should choose first. And that he would not tell my wife."

She watched him closely, but also observed the other two men introducing themselves to Maria and Natalia.

"And why are you entitled to be first? You must be more important? A boss? El Jefe?"

Sofia had no plan. She had not thought about how to play this game. But her instincts, and something about the way Jose had looked at her as he was deciding which of the three he would prefer, was dictating her recklessness. *I need to become something more than a quick fuck to this man. So little time and so few chances!* The way that both Sasha and Anya had simply ceased to exist was continually running through her mind. She also was aware that the Americans were watching her closely.

The unexpected Spanish phrase and her rapid-fire faintly hostile questions caused Jose's smile to fade, to be replaced by an expression that was an interesting mixture of exasperation and curiosity. He paused, clearly thinking about what to say. She wondered if she had pushed too hard.

Jose shrugged. "Forgive me. My English is muy malo … very bad. But your questions ….? It's funny. I do not know how women think. But the question I would ask … if I were you, in your position … is Por qué se eligió a mí?"

It is a beautiful language. So unlike Russian. No wonder they call it a Romance language.

She shook her head. "I know no more Spanish."

"It translates as 'Why did this man pick me as his first choice?'"

Sofia was intrigued despite herself. "So. And how would you answer the question?"

"What if I said, 'Because of your beautiful body?' "

"I would think you had bad eyesight or very strange taste. Maria's tits and legs are clearly better, and Natalia is exposing everything she has to offer, which is considerable. I'm skinny without much of an ass."

He frowned, as though the crudeness bothered him. Then he said, halfway between a question and a statement, "Perhaps I should change my mind … if you have so little to offer me?"

Sofia turned slightly, still facing Jose, but with her back toward the others in the room. She simply loosened the sash on the wraparound dress she was wearing and let it fall open. She wore nothing beneath the dress.

He did not move, but his breathing quickened slightly and his eyes changed. "I think perhaps you … understated … your appeal relative to Maria and Natalia." He reached out one hand to adjust the way the fabric fell across one breast. "Perhaps we can talk more about this in another room?"

She retied the sash and held out her hand. Her own breath quickened. Not for any erotic pretense but because she knew that her best chance for escape depended on what happened in the next few minutes. Once she had determined that she would run at the first opportunity, any *waiting* would be unbearable and dangerous. But the plan that she had formed while waiting in the car required three more outcomes that were beyond her control.

When Jose started to the staircase going up rather than down, she thought to herself, *that's one.* She put her arm around his waist, inside his suit coat and pressed herself close against him, as if to reward him for unknowingly making the right choice. The third floor seemed to consist of four bedrooms, two on either side of the staircase. When Jose turned to the right at the top of the staircase, she breathed to herself, *that's two.* When they entered the last room on the right, she saw the large windows and lights of the city beyond. *That's three. This is the time.*

She turned to face him. He reached out and gently loosened the sash one more time, this time using both hands to part the dress. She stood quietly for a few seconds, then held her arms to the side and spun slowly in place, allowing the silken material to form interesting shadows around her. He took off his suit coat, dropping it on the overstuffed chair. She said nothing, but raised her eyebrows and inclined her head to indicate the table near the four-poster bed. A bottle of Champagne in an ice bucket and two glasses were waiting.

She said, "I would prefer vodka – "

"And I tequila. But the gringos are conventional in so many ways."

"We shall make do." She hooked a finger into his shirtfront and moved with him to the table alongside the bed. "Let me," she said and picked up the bottle. She opened it and poured one glass. When she reached for the other, she fumbled it and it fell to the floor. He reached down to retrieve it so that his head and upper body were moving upward to meet the champagne bottle on its downward arc. She swung as hard as she could, using both hands.

The bottle did not break and Jose fell forward onto the bed, sliding slowly from there to the carpeted floor. Sofia stood over him, breathing rapidly. He did not move. A slow trickle of blood ran from his temple onto the bright white collar on his shirt. *I wonder if I have killed him?* She realized that she hoped not, and was surprised by the emotion.

She moved quickly and efficiently, as though her actions were carefully planned, following some hidden choreography rather than spur-of-the-moment desperation and an instinctive animal cunning. Much later, she would marvel at her coolness and the rightness of her choices. She retied her dress around her, and then took Jose's coat and slipped it on, rolling the sleeves to free her hands. She went to the window and found that her run of good luck was continuing. The window was large, with two vertical panes that opened sideways. There was no screen. Leaning out, she found herself overlooking the roof of the adjacent brick apartment building, about five feet below her and across a three-foot gap. She held her shoes in her hand and jumped, landing lightly. She found a metal staircase at the rear of the building and went down it three steps at a time into an alley that led to the side street, around the corner and out of sight of the dark sentries at the front of the building.

Glancing at the street signs and visualizing the grid that she carried in her head, she began the final leg of her journey, walking fast with her head down and the fear welling inside her. *Only a little more than a mile!*

Sanctuary

Sofia took off her shoes after the first half-block. The stiletto heels were simply not made for walking fast, especially when climbing hills in San Francisco. She knew that she was drawing attention, barefooted, wearing a man's suit coat with her long white legs and her shoes in her hand. Fortunately, it was dark and there were not many pedestrians on the streets that she chose. There was almost always a siren somewhere in the distance, as through to remind her that she was a fugitive in a strange city, without friends or resources.

Something in the coat kept bumping against her leg and for the first time she became aware of the sheer weight of Jose's coat. She stopped, considering possibilities. She saw a lighted Starbucks window across the street, recognizing the name from TV commercials. She went in, finding a leather stuffed chair in a corner, fairly hidden from the doorway. She kept the coat on, knowing that the neon red dress would draw attention. She went through each pocket. The thing bumping against her leg was a cell phone. *Sofia! So stupid!* She remembered reading about the tracking devices built into the latest phones. She opened the phone, pulled out the battery and sat looking at the pieces, wondering if it was already too late.

Another pocket held a thick wallet, the longer kind that travelers use for documents as well as currency. She riffled through the notes ... at least a couple thousand dollars, probably more. There was a Mexican passport with Jose's picture – his name was Jose Reboso --and in the other breast pocket a thin sheaf of papers. She scanned them quickly, noting a lot of tables and numbers. There were handwritten notes in Spanish, with arrows and exclamation marks in the margin. She put the coat back on and left, throwing the battery in a wastebasket near the door and the body of the phone into a storm drain outside the door.

Three blocks to go, all of them uphill.

Sasha said that she was sure that the woman would help. How could she be so sure? What if she slams the door in my face? Or worse, takes me in and then calls the police ... or someone much worse than the police?

Then the damnable thought that would not go away. *What happened to Sasha? Did she go to this woman? And if she did, ...*

It took her an hour. She headed *downhill* from the Starbucks, away from North Beach. If they traced the phone and found witnesses, she needed misdirection. Twice more, she diverted right or left for a block, but always away from the Victorian. After twenty minutes of zig-zagging, she headed uphill. Once in sight of the house, she stood in a darkened doorway across the street and watched for twenty minutes, studying the shadows and passing cars. She saw lights go on in the upper story. Someone was home.

Standing there, she thought of the orphanage six thousand miles away, remembering iron beds, cold food, thin blankets, lice and – most of all – the natural and unrelenting cruelty of abandoned children. She wondered whether she would be able to leave her daughter in such a place, if she had one. To her credit, she could not decide, because she also remembered much about life after the orphanage, things unsuitable for mothers with children – being hungry and cold, her dependency on men incapable of love, friends who disappeared. Most of all, she remembered the constant fear. It was not a world she wanted to bring a child into, perhaps because she recognized the possibility that she was capable of consigning her child to an orphanage. *Would that be an act of love? Or rationality? How would I know the difference?*

She found a comb in Jose's coat pocket and ran it through her hair. She put on her heels and made a final attempt to smooth the dress. She took off the coat and folded it across her arm as if she was just carrying it for her man. Finally, she took a deep breath and walked without hesitation to the enormous front door of the house across the street.

She reached out and pushed the bell, hearing it echo within the house. A few seconds later, she was sure that she heard faint footsteps approaching.

She almost prayed, but long ago had vowed never to ask anything from a god that could allow such a world to exist.

The door opened. Light spilled out from the brightly lit interior, silhouetting the woman but leaving her face in deep shadow, unreadable. Each of the women stood mute and unmoving, as though their encounter required a moment of silence to commemorate either an unchangeable past or something yet to come.

She took a step forward, breaking the spell.

"I am Sofia. Sasha said you would help me."

Visions on the Waterfront

It was a realtor's dream listing, except for the one flaw.

The location was perfect -- a waterfront location with an unobstructed view of the Bay Bridge, shielded from traffic noise, with easy access to public transportation and the bright lights of the Embarcadero and financial district. The rent was nominal, and there were no walls or common space to be shared with obtrusive neighbors. It was a rare find in the hotly-contested housing market in San Francisco.

The only problem – the flaw that kept it off the market -- was that it was only sixty square feet and lacked heat, running water or any utilities. But for Howden, it was his best home ever. Howden saw it as a natural extension of what the voices had promised; a divine sign confirming his status as God's spokesman to the benighted San Franciscans.

As a veteran of the city's homeless population, Howden was constantly looking for a better situation. In his wanderings around his territory, he scouted freeway overpasses, alleys, abandoned buildings, sheltered doorways to retail stores. Essentially, he was seeking an urban cave, something out of the elements and defensible against predators. The option of using the available public shelters had been ruled out long ago by some cognitive short-circuit that would not allow him to fall asleep in a room with other people. The clinicians called it "paranoid schizophrenia", but to him it was a sign directly from his personal God.

His God sent him the key. He found it on the pavement in front of one of San Francisco's lesser and little used covered piers south of China Basin. It opened a normal sized door at the side of the shed-like structure on the pier, providing access to a cavernous interior that opened to the Bay. At the very end, where it projected into the Bay, he found his space – a small doorless closet with a window facing the Bay. Its function was unclear but, for Howden, it affirmed God's promise to provide for his children.

His only problem with it was that it was haunted.

It had happened twice before, each time somewhere after midnight. First, there would be bumping against the pier, directly below Howden's den. Then the unclean women -- painted women, whores -- would rise up from the water. Their white faces would appear over the edge of the pier, bearing expressions that seemed thousands of years old. They were unashamed of their nakedness, barely concealed under gauzy garments that emphasized rather than hid what should remain unseen. They spoke angrily, and in strange tongues that God had cursed long ago. As Howden watched, their milky white skin seemed to float through the darkness of the pier until they disappeared at the far end as though passing into a liquid medium. He remained frozen in place long after they had passed.

Howden's inner voices were silent, as though they too were afraid to challenge the passage of the other-worldly procession.

Reminiscence

As the water taxi pulled away from the ship and its bogus insurance claim, Desmond was engaged in a serious internal debate. It didn't last long because it required him to choose between loyalty and greed, a choice that was both familiar and easy. He knew now why the woman was familiar. He'd seen a picture in the Chronicle not very long ago, a full-face photo of a murder victim that the cops were trying to identify. It was so much like the 'Anya' he had just seen that he shuddered. *There has to be a connection.* Most importantly – and the trigger for the greed -- he remembered that there was a reward for information as to who she was or how she came to be dead, along with a phone number.

So, I get a thousand bucks for filling out some fraudulent forms ... or maybe a few thousand bucks for making a legal phone call ... I don't owe the guy on the ship anything. Not a hard decision. And I can do both! All I need is that phone number.

He had an app for the Chronicle on his iPhone, but the reception in the middle of the Bay was not good at the moment. He settled back on the hard wooden bench and spent the remainder of the brief trip reconstructing the image of the half-naked woman sprawled on the deck.

His killer, on shore and headed for the pier where the water taxi would deposit Desmond, was also engaged in trying to recall images of past events. Like Desmond, the images were pleasurable ones, although completely at odds with the reality that generated them.

It was an anniversary of sorts. He had first killed a person exactly thirty years ago today. It puzzled him that that particular date was so firmly fixed in his mind, especially because it was by his standards such an ordinary event. It was a killing sanctioned by society because he was a soldier. The victim was five hundred yards away, featureless, without a personality, seen only through the scope of his specialized sniper rifle. So unlike the subsequent killings, the ones so up close and personal, so intimately involved with a specific victim in an end-of-life dance that brought out their uniqueness even as he extinguished it.

In the early days, he could – if he wanted to -- defend his actions as "moral", sanctioned strikes against particular individuals operating outside of what society – or some obscure government official -- deemed acceptable limits. Then the killings became merely "legal", defensible in a court-of-law because he was "following orders", but no longer for any discernible good other than protecting some politician's ass or diverting cash flows into an alternative pocket.   Finally, he simply stopped thinking about the rightness or wrongness of what he was doing. He no longer remembered how many people he had killed; nor could he recall particular names or faces of victims.

Perhaps it was the significance of a thirty-year anniversary, but today's assignment evoked a more reflective side.   "Reminiscence" or "nostalgia" would be incorrect in describing his thoughts. It was more analytical than that, a curiosity about patterns and trends. For instance, he could not recall a single instance where he had killed in self-defense. Even as a soldier, he was killing people at great distances that could not possibly be a direct threat to him. And always under orders or a well-defined contract, nothing spontaneous or impromptu. Even in these latter days – what he thought of as his 'entrepreneurial period' – the killing was purposeful … unemotional, furthering some larger plan.

He was still surprised at how easy it was to kill someone, helped along as it was by the surprising passiveness of the victims. No one *expects* to be killed; the idea is inconceivable, even as it is happening. Resistance is lessened by the implausibility of the threat. Perhaps the passiveness is enhanced because *hope* is such a powerful emotion, and he learned to foster it in his victims so as to keep them cooperative.

He remembered one ordinary citizen in particular. He'd tied his hands, put him in the trunk of his car and drove to an old mining site with deep shafts. When the man was standing in the moonlight with his back to him on the edge of a shaft penetrating deep into the earth's blackness, he was still uncomprehending.

"This can't be real! Who are you? Why are you doing this?"

He was amused by the questions at this point in the game. "Why are you asking? What good would it do you to know the answers?"

"I can fix it. Whatever it is. There has to be a mistake. I'm sure we can work something out."

"I don't think so." And he fired one shot, toppling the hopeless optimist into the darkness.

This one – Desmond, the one he thought of as 'the thirty year target' – was typically oblivious to what was about to happen to him. He watched him come ashore carrying the three brightly packaged boxes and pick up his car from the lot near the pier. He drove directly to his condo complex in South San Francisco, easy to follow in the light traffic at that time of day. When he parked, he stayed in his car and the stalker watched him punch buttons on his iPhone, apparently searching or texting.

When Desmond held the phone up, punched it seven times and held it to his ear, the killer made a mental note. *As the man said, we don't want him talking to people, do we? I wonder who he's calling?* He jimmied the locks at the back entrance at the door of Desmond's condo. When Desmond came in, he was sitting in the living room waiting.

The killer was working on a theory about how people behaved when confronted with an obviously lethal threat. He was motivated by reading a New York Times article about the "five stages of grieving", the so-called Kuebler-Ross model. He thought that – in the case of the individuals he was about to kill – there were four possible stages. First was *indignation*, the "You can't do this to me" stage. That was quickly followed by *fear*, the "Jeez, that's a gun he's pointing at me". Third was *calculation,* the "How can I get out of this?" stage characterized by a sly look and furtive glances looking for help. Finally, some – but not all – would

70

get to a fourth stage – *acceptance.* In those few cases, he would experience a fleeting sense of admiration for them. But never sympathy.

He did not test his theory with Desmond. It was the middle of the day in a populated area. Speed was essential. And there was that troublesome phone call to be dealt with. Then Anya.

When Desmond started "What the hell –", the killer fired one silenced shot from ten feet away. When Desmond fell, he stepped forward and held the muzzle about six inches from the back of Desmond's head. He stood for twenty seconds, thinking about police procedures and four other killings. *No reason to give them a link.* He knelt and felt for a carotid pulse that was not there. He replaced the gun in his briefcase along with the cell phone from the leather holder on Desmond's belt. He found and kept the bayside parking receipt from Desmond's pocket. Finally, he picked up the spent cartridge and the three boxes that Desmond had been carrying and left the building as he had entered.

When he had driven several blocks, he stopped and hit the "redial last call" button on Desmond's cell phone. It rang several times before a voice came on.

"SFPD. Homicide Division. Detective McAdams speaking."

Gonzo

Gonzo and McAdams put in double shifts for four straight days on the Jane Doe murder and had nothing. No leads to the killer. No ID on the victim. There was no apparent connection between the street dealers and Jane Doe other than the single headshot, the Bayside sites, and their hunches. They had given the press a photo of the woman, wheedled some reward money out of the departmental budget, and set up a hot line that rolled to the phone on McAdams' desk.

The case bothered each of them, but for different reasons. Which they could not talk about. For McAdams, it was the need to confront the killer, to ask him that "why" question that he would not answer. For Gonzo, it was the need to restore the victim in some way, to make her something more meaningful than a slab of dead meat found on the tidal flats and given a temporary name.

He did not articulate this, not even to McAdams, but Gonzo knew that his obsessions were entangled with his personal history. He identified with the underclasses and the anonymous victims, the kind that too often wound up on metallic tables in the morgue, unclaimed and there through no fault of their own. The kind that the press liked to describe as "caught in the crossfire".

Guillermo Gonzales was the only son of migrant farmworkers from Michoacán, Mexico, two of the millions of illegals looking for a better life in the US. His story would be commonplace, a tale of two generations. From Mexican to American, from uneducated to educated, Spanish-speaking to English-speaking, illegal to legal, poor to middle-income, from insular to assimilated, from street-smart hood and gang member to detective sergeant in the SFPD. McAdams once teased him by suggesting that he should convert from Catholic to Unitarian, just to complete the transformation.

He wore a suit and polished his shoes every day, standing out among the motley dress code of the modern plainclothes force with its emphasis on scruffy and utilitarian.

He claimed that he became "Gonzo" because he got tired of telling Anglos how to spell "Guillermo", let alone pronounce it correctly. In fact, McAdams had come up with the nickname after their first month together, and it stuck. The name seemed to capture his style as well, his enthusiasm and tendency to shift into a higher gear at the slightest opportunity, the playfulness that was always lurking just below the surface.

They had been partners for six years, long enough to form something quite unique, a friendship to be valued but never acknowledged, a uniquely male form of currency to be drawn on only as a last resort. In the last two months, McAdams had spent countless hours thinking about their relationship, trying to figure out what made it work, why he and Gonzo effortlessly worked through the same kind of disagreements that had caused each of their marriages to disintegrate in a flurry of epithets. He knew about the bonding that goes on in combat units and during crises, among sports teams, paramedics, figure skating duos, and identical twins. But this seemed something more than that.

They had saved each other's lives. Put themselves in harm's way for the sake of the other. Spent hundreds – thousands? – of hours sitting together drinking bad coffee in a darkened car waiting for someone or something to come along. Played "good cop – bad cop" games with sixteen-year-old gangbangers and mafia capos. Shared as much as any modern male is capable of sharing with another male, always listening with compassion, although they would not use that term.

In the end, he simply accepted their relationship for what it was – a rare gift, one that he did not appreciate until it was taken away.

McAdams still would think of Gonzo every time he saw a Hispanic male with a suit on. And, without fail, he would think, *It's my fault.* Then he would relive, in exquisite detail, the sequence of unthinking casual choices he had made that killed his partner.

The call came on McAdams' desk phone. When he picked up, a male voice said, "I have something from the woman that was murdered last week – the one you're calling Jane Doe." He recognized neither the voice nor the slight accent. The tone was peremptory and triggered an instinctive hostility.

"What do you have? And who are you?"

Typical cop! All questions, never any information.

"I'm a cabbie. She left something in my cab. I figure I should give it to the police." *The hook. Not your usual crackpot call. The promise of something tangible.*

This was the tenth call that McAdams had fielded in the last hour. About as many had rolled to his voice mail. The announcement of a five thousand dollar reward "for information leading to ..." had brought out a swarm of hopeful informants, a lot of them the kind that always call, whether it's a mass murderer or a lost dog. But each potential lead had to be treated seriously. He logged every one of them faithfully. This one sounded like the most promising of the lot.

"So bring it in. To me. I'm Detective McAdams, on the third floor –"

Ah! The slight change in tone! Still arrogant, but now with very faint overtones of real interest. Almost a request rather than an order...

"I know who you are. But I'm not coming in any police station. I'm out front, the only Yellow Cab you'll see. You come down and get this stuff." *The critical point ... I figure a fifty-fifty chance he'll see it as a challenge to his manhood.*

"I'll be there in thirty seconds. You stay put. But we need to talk." Then there was only the dial tone.

McAdams stood up and motioned to Gonzo who had just walked in. "I'll be right back. There's a cabbie out front that says our Jane Doe left something in his cab. Doesn't want to come inside."

"I'll check it out," Gonzo said. "I haven't had my Starbucks fix yet, so I'm going out anyway."

McAdams walked over to the window that faced out onto the street. He could see the Yellow Cab double parked alongside the long row of black-and-whites at curbside. Because of the angle, the driver was a barely visible dark shape.

How did he know to call me? Or that we had labeled her Jane Doe? And he said he knew who I was. And then he realized the far more important puzzle … *How does he know that his fare became a murder victim? I think this guy needs a closer look!*

He watched as Gonzo emerged from the front entrance and crossed the sidewalk. He leaned down to talk to the cabbie through the driver's side window. McAdams pulled his cell phone from his pocket and hit "two", the rapid-dial for Gonzo. He remembered thinking *I could just yell out the window, but the damn windows don't open.* Gonzo straightened up and turned around as he looked at his cell phone, as though he knew he would see McAdams watching from the third story window on the corner.

"Gonzo, this guy is more than he's letting on …"

The windows were double-paned and thick, so McAdams did not hear the shot. Gonzo's head snapped back amid a pinkish haze of blood and brain matter, his body sprawling like a straw dummy flung from a moving truck. The cab leaped forward, accelerating around the corner.

The images were not captured on any film or digital media, but they were hard-wired into McAdams' brain and he watched the same ten seconds repeat themselves over and over, always ending with Gonzo dead while he stood at the window watching. The video – that's how he thought of it -- ran on a 24/7 loop, always at the periphery of his consciousness. He tried to imagine and then impose alternative endings, but the details reasserted themselves – Gonzo's expression looking up at the window, the way his left foot was twisted so awkwardly, the "occupied" light on the roof of the cab, the running blue uniforms, the pinkish haze.

On-the-Job Therapy

Freddie came two weeks after Gonzo, assigned to McAdams because the Captain said that he was the least sexist of the senior detectives in the Division. McAdams agreed with him on that score, although he did not believe that was the main reason for the pairing. *He thinks I'm fragile; that I need the empathic touch rather than a locker room companion.*

"You'll match up well," was how the Captain put it.

"What you mean is that I'm an emotional wreck and she's really good at managing PTSD head cases."

The reference was to Freddie's last job. She had just completed a twenty-year hitch, retiring as a captain from the U.S. Army's Judge Advocate General's division. Her specialty was investigating violent crimes committed by returning Iraq and Afghanistan veterans. She was forty-two years old and had seen almost as much gore and mayhem as most big-city homicide detectives.

"No, McAdams," Murphy said with a sigh. "What I mean is that you'll match up well because she's smart and you're not. Because she knows nothing about the SFPD and you know what's under every rock in the goddam city. Because you need a partner and she needs a good teacher."

McAdams let it ride. Actually, he thought she would make a great partner. She had no history with Gonzo, making it less awkward.

"Freddie" was Frederica Felicia Fulbright. Some of the old-timers in the Division tried to stick her with the label "4F", for "Fucking Frederica Felicia Fulbright"; but the movement died out quickly thanks to her standard comment whenever the term came up -- "I'm Freddie, just Freddie." But the way she said it – her look and the tone of voice – made it stick. McAdams had never seen a walk-on detective – let alone a woman -- fit in so fast, so well. Within a few months, she earned the respect of all ranks.

About two weeks into their partnership, McAdams commented on it. "It's very impressive. You're imbedded in the most sexist organization in the world, but it's like you've cast some kind of gender-blindness spell on the whole crew. How do you do that?"

"First, you're wrong about your rankings. I just spent twenty years in an organization that makes the SFPD look like the National Organization for Women. Where I came from? A woman – a competent female officer – in the army is going uphill the whole way. And the higher you go, the steeper it gets."

"That's not the Pentagon line. They pull out these stats --"

"Stats!" She looked at him as if gauging his intelligence level and finding it wanting. Finally, she just shook her head and said, "It's all in how you keep score."

"You mean 'body count'? Like in a war? The best warriors are the ones that kill the most people?"

"Yeah, it's just a gentler kind of body count for the Pentagon PR types -- how many women are entering the service, being promoted, etc. Use those metrics and the U.S. military looks like affirmative action run amok. But look where those women are in the modern army – logistics, planning, recruitment, medical… They call them 'pussy jobs', regardless of whether it's a man or a woman in place!"

"And they keep the women out of combat …", he added.

"Precisely. How would you feel about, say, an Internal Affairs officer who had never served a day as a line cop?"

McAdams realized that part of Freddie's style was to answer a question with another question. *I think I'll try that too.*

"I get your point. So what makes police departments so much more enlightened than the military?"

"Let's stick to our own small world, shall we? How does the SFPD keep score? How does it judge the relative merit of its detectives?"

"It's easy. The number of cases closed."

"Yep. And that happens to be the point of what we do. As the policy wonks like to say, you manage what you measure. Oh, and another thing? They count cases closed by the *team* of detectives … promotes and rewards teamwork, discourages grandstanding."

He started to talk, but she cut in. "And you and Gonzo were tops in the Homicide Division for three straight years …". She stopped abruptly in mid-sentence.

"Oops!"

Am I that bad? Do they tell the rookies that they shouldn't mention Gonzo in my presence?

"It's OK, Freddie. Gonzales was my partner and now he's dead. You can say it." *You could even say it like it is: He's dead because he was my partner!*

The Department mandated at least one visit to a psychiatrist, a conversation that left him more rather than less depressed. Using Google, he tracked down and read from across the spectrum of psychotherapy – ranging from chat rooms to blogs to formal research papers by people with hyphenated degrees and strings of credentials. He had unwillingly become an expert about grieving and loss when a close friend is suddenly taken away.

But he was still a walking basket case.

Freddie helped. Not overtly and maybe not even intentionally, but her presence and the banter that went with it was restorative. The experts would give it a fancy label, but to him it was just proof of the clichés – 'time heals all wounds', 'this too shall pass' – all those awkward bromides that people mutter to the survivors while avoiding eye contact.

They spent most of their time on what the press had labeled 'the duct tape killer', the guy with – so far – three drug dealers and – maybe -- Jane Doe to his credit. They worked a few new cases, but the Captain made sure that they were the easy ones. McAdams was still considered to be fragile goods and Freddie was new, so it made sense. They kept him away from the day-to-day work on finding

Gonzo's killer. Murphy was right: His obsession with revenge would have ruined the case if it ever got to court.

The Gonzo story was national news for a few days, the kind of compelling drama that journalists feed off of – a popular cop shot in broad daylight, squarely in front of the police station. It was not just a cop killing; it was a bold assassination. It galvanized the entire community and became the priority case for the entire department.

Not so for the other two murders on the same day, an ordinary citizen named Desmond and a sixteen-year-old caught in a drive-by. They were worked, but driven into the background by the sensationalism of a cop killing.

The investigation into Gonzo's shooting went nowhere. One of the ironies was that most of the potential witnesses were cops going in and out of the station. But no one paid any attention to the double-parked cab or noticed the man who was driving. Three different people got the ID number of the cab, but it had been stolen twenty minutes earlier from a nearby taxi rank and was found abandoned near Fisherman's Wharf an hour later. Every detective and uniformed officer rousted their informants. Rewards and other inducements were offered. Everybody Gonzo or McAdams had ever arrested was interrogated and their private lives were looked at for possible enemies. The crazies were pulled in and sweated.

Nothing.

Ditto for the so-called duct tape killer. No one cared a whole lot about the three dealers. Cops thought 'good riddance', and the shooting of a street dealer didn't cause any of the law-abiding citizenry to worry about their own safety. All of the male victims had been bound with duct tape and shot once in the back of the head with the same gun, but that was about the only forensics evidence that they had to work with. McAdams had Freddie circulating pictures of Jane Doe among the local working girls while he spent most of his time trying to pin down the swirl of street rumors about a new supplier trying to muscle in on the narcotics distribution network.

The phrase 'crime wave' gained traction in headlines and TV newscasts for a few weeks, but the simultaneous occurrence of a public-transit strike and the sighting of a pod of three whales in San Francisco Bay diverted the public's attention in new directions. Stories about unsolved murders without suspects were no longer interesting.

Freddie

He's a lot like Britton. A nice guy ... a good man ... who never learned to get some distance between himself and other people's problems.

The comparison she made between McAdams and Britton worried her. Britton was her last case in her Army JAG career. More than that, he was the reason she left the army. He came back from his third tour in Iraq outwardly calm, a poster boy for the returning veterans, the kind the Army would send out to small towns to sell what used to be called 'War Bonds'. The truth came out later and in a bad way. He was stressed, a psychiatric hairline away from mass murder. Not surprising, given that he was a platoon leader engaged in almost daily combat. Half of his unit was killed or wounded, most of them by IED's placed by a faceless enemy.

Two weeks after his homecoming, he strangled his wife and shot his sixteen-year-old son. He called his commanding officer to come and get him and sat with the bodies until the MPs removed him. Freddie was on the scene within an hour, starting a murder investigation that promised to be both short and irrelevant to the outcome.

Her first interview with Britton depressed her enormously. He spent the entire time talking about his First Sergeant and what he looked like when he and his jeep were shredded by a 105mm artillery shell hidden in a trash heap on some crummy dirt road in Mosul. It was important to him that she understood how blunt force trauma and flying metal fragments acted on human flesh and bone.

"We couldn't find all the parts. It was dark and there were snipers. One foot ... his face... We threw everything we could find into a bag. I left it with the chaplain."

She had the impression that he was trying out in his head alternative images of rearranged body parts, seeking one that somehow could lessen the indignity of the appalling reality that haunted him.

The next day, Britton hung himself in his cell, using a noose fashioned from his own clothing.

She would not admit it, even to herself, but Britton was the reason she retired from Army JAG. His case – and her handling of it – got national attention and a very positive New York Times feature about the military justice system. She was a sure thing on the next promotion list. But all it did was depress her. *It doesn't work when there's no outrage, no villains, only victims. How do you prosecute a system!?*

She could have gone anywhere. She chose San Francisco because she liked the idea of being a homicide detective in a real city and the fact that the police chief was a woman. The decision was helped when she learned that all the big military bases around the area had been decommissioned and that murder in San Francisco was a mostly civilian enterprise.

How naïve I was! Thinking that a big city homicide cop would not have to face all the ambiguity involved when good people kill innocent people. That somehow, murder in the civilian world would be unequivocally wrong, not riddled with contradictions and 'mitigating factors'.

That was one of the reasons she fixated on finding Jane Doe's killer. It would help McAdams and at the same time lessen the injustice of the woman's death. *It's funny how I impute innocence to unidentified corpses, especially women. For all I know, she may have been an absolute bitch. Maybe that's why the Church doesn't make someone a saint until they're dead.*

They released a retouched head shot of her to the media and got the usual calls from the usual people. None of them checked out. Freddie was spending a lot of after-dark time talking to the street girls and their pimps on the theory that Jane was earning her keep through prostitution, although she didn't show the kind of wear-and-tear that goes with the profession. *Other than being dead, of course.* She wasn't a junkie, but she was killed in the same fashion as the three dealers, so Freddie was working on the assumption that there had be some connection to the world of narcotics.

   The break came from one of the girls who worked the Union Square area with its ever-changing crop of conventioneers and tourists, the kind of visitors that called the city "Frisco" and wanted something special. Her name was Emma. Freddie found her near the cable car stop and talked her into taking a break at Starbucks. She looked like an anorexic college student from somewhere in the Midwest, with needle marks instead of freckles. But she lit up when Freddie showed her the photo. Too late, she remembered Freddie was a cop and went cold.

   "Nope. Never seen her before." She got up to leave.

   "Would she look more familiar if I told you she was dead? Shot in the back of the head and tossed into the Bay like a piece of trash…."

   Emma stopped cold, seeming to shrivel in place as though Freddie's words had punctured something. She said "Jesus!" in a way that left it unclear whether it was a prayer or a curse. Then, "Shit!" She sat back down and took the picture back from Freddie.

   "I only saw her once. But she did stand out, even in this stinking lousy business. She looked like a model, like one of those young starry-eyed types trying to break into the movie business. She had an accent, something from central Europe, I think. And some made-up name for the johns – Natasha or something that's supposed to sound exotic."

   "Was she working the streets?"

   Emma laughed. "Her? No way! The whole deal was prearranged; not your usual curbside negotiation. It was for some trade union here for a convention that week -- Amalgamated something-or-other. Me and two other girls were in the bar at the Fairmont, like we were told. This big-shot – one of the higher ups in the union – brought these three guys to the table and paired us up, making a big deal about his 'matchmaking' abilities. A real asshole. Then another guy came in with your woman – Natasha or whatever – and handed her off to the big shot like she was the Queen of Sheba instead of an extra-good-looking hooker early in the game."

Freddie asked, "Could it have been a legitimate escort service?"

Emma snorted. "No way! The guy that brought her? He told her straight out that she should do whatever Mr. Bigshot wanted her to do. I remember he said, 'The dude is horny. Make him happy. He's paid a lot of money for the next few hours.' And she – Natasha or whoever – was afraid of him – the guy that delivered her. It showed."

"This guy – the one that brought Natasha – "

Emma interrupted, "He was a short fat little guy who looked like he was trying his best to look really mean."

Freddie spent another few minutes trying to zero in on the approximate date. They finally concluded that it was somewhere in the week before Natasha turned up dead on the tidal flats and became Jane Doe.

So, two definite and not-very-original suspects ... a pimp and a john. Natasha was being shopped around by this mean-looking little fat man. A personal service for relatively heavy hitters who don't want their whores right from the street. I need to find out who these guys are ...

Emma got up to go, clearly needing to top off whatever magic powder was driving her. Freddie could see the muscles twitching under her skin. She put her hand on her arm to keep her in place, saying, "Give me three more minutes for some basic police work ... what they used to call 'pounding the pavement'?"

Emma sat down, although she did not sit still, her hands fluttering in her lap and a slight tremor creating ripples down her bare right arm.

Freddie took an iPad out of her purse and began tapping. It took forty seconds to identify the convention that had brought the so-called asshole to town ... something to do with pipes and boilers. Another thirty seconds to identify the Amalgamated Engineer's Union and get on their website and find a page devoted to pictures of the key officers of the union. She showed the screen to Emma who took five seconds to scan the photos and point to one in particular.

"That's the asshole! The loudmouth that has to pay women to fuck him!"

Freddie noted the details on the site. His name was Jacob Leibman, the public relations guy for the union. She gave Emma twenty bucks in exchange for her cell number and promise to testify if called upon. *If she doesn't OD before we need her in court!*

Another sixty seconds with the iPad and she had Leibman's biographical data and address on screen. His office was fifteen minutes away. She shut down the iPad, shaking her head in a now familiar amazement about how technology was transforming police work. Turning cops into web crawlers.

But not this next part ... unless RoboCop is closer than I think!

New Dialects

She caught Leibman as he was leaving his office. He was a big man, angular, as though constructed from overlapping metal slabs of varying sizes. Even his crew cut hair was arranged to square off his head, each strand vertical and of uniform length. He seemed familiar somehow to Freddie. At first, she thought it was because he looked like so many of her ex-military colleagues of a certain generation, a genotype that she did not do well with. Beyond that, he also reminded Freddie of one of the villains from a Batman comic book.

"Mr. Leibman. I need to talk to you."

His first reaction was to stop and appraise Freddie, his eyes running an overt full-body scan and a smile starting to form, the kind that a self-important middle-aged man with an excessively macho self image uses when approached directly by a strange and younger woman. *He'll probably call me 'Missie'.*

Before he could open his mouth, she held two objects up to his face, her arms straight out. Her left hand held her SFPD badge and the right hand the 5x7 glossy photo of Jane Doe. "I'd like to ask you some questions about this woman."

That got rid of the smile. In its place came a look of uncertainty that lasted only a microsecond and was displaced by an expression that combined slyness and arrogance in about equal parts. He used it as a defensive force-field, staring out from it at Freddie with hostility.

"Never seen her. Don't know who she is. Now, I need to be …" He turned to leave.

Freddie shifted to stay in his path, still holding the photo six inches in front of his nose. "You met her at the Fairmont two weeks ago. In front of several witnesses." *'Several' is technically true, although only one of them has been identified.*

His eyes narrowed, as if to mask the calculations that he was clearly sorting through. "So? I meet lots of people. It's my job. And I still don't know her."

"According to the witnesses, your job that night seemed to be procuring prostitutes. That's the lesser charge, but it's worth maybe five years in jail and a boatload of really bad publicity for your union."

The effect was like a slow motion implosion. The force-field collapsed inward, leaving Leibman looking just plain bewildered. He waved his hands in front of him as if to block any more accusatory words. "They got it wrong! I didn't … I don't … Wait a minute! You said 'lesser charge'?"

Still holding up the picture, Freddie said, "She's dead. Murdered." And then, speaking slowly and distinctly to make the threat very clear, "And you were the last person to see her alive." *That's almost certainly not true, of course. Jane Doe was killed days after that meeting. But it's too good a line not to use!*

It had the desired effect. Leibman started spewing words, random phrases, sometimes blustering, other times pleading, but spilling out. "It was one night. Christ! A few hours. I never … She didn't … The guy said …"

Freddie held up her hand. "We'll get to the details. Right now, I need to know what you can tell me about her."

"What's there to tell? She was a whore."

Freddie almost hit him in the face. The instinct was so strong that she squeezed her fingernails into her palms, using the pain to refocus her. *He isn't worth it. And it wouldn't change anything. But I'd like – just once –to forget all the civil rights bullshit and make them hurt!*

"Leibman…"

Something in her tone or posture alerted him. He moved back half a step. "She was Russian. Said her name was Natasha. That's about all I got. She was --"

Freddie interrupted, "What about the guy who handed her off to you. Tell me about him."

"The first and only time I saw him was at the Fairmont when he delivered the dame. I don't know who he is or where he comes from. No name … nothing."

"Who set it up? The girls and all that?"

Leibman turned away, mumbling. "Nobody set it up. Like I said, she was a hooker. She came on to me and we made a deal. That's all it was – a one shot deal."

Freddie spoke slowly, spacing her words as though talking to a six-year-old. "Leibman, Leibman! First, we have witnesses who are quite clear about your part in the arrangements. Three of them are your colleagues. You're what the courts would call a procurer, not just your average horny john. Second, I couldn't care less about your pathetic sex life. I want to find the bastard that killed this woman and I'm perfectly willing to splash your picture on the front page if you don't help me. Now, tell me about the guy that turned up with Natasha."

He looked at her and she could see the familiar transition taking place: the shift from fright to calculation when a suspect realizes that he has something valuable; something a cop needs. Tradable goods. *We can help that along.*

"Y'know, Leibman. If I can find the guy that delivered Natasha to you, you'd be a lot less important to me. Maybe even forgettable." *That's a stretch. But his lawyer will get some mileage from it when they sit down with the DA.*

He looked away and started talking. "I don't know him. He called me. Said that he could provide a dozen whores, whenever and wherever I wanted them. And promised something extra special for me. That was Natasha."

"Was he local?"

Leibman thought for a bit. "Yeah. I think so. And I think he works or lives on the waterfront. A couple of times … on the phone … I could hear a foghorn, maybe one of those extra loud whistles that ships have."

Great! That narrows it down to maybe a hundred miles of shoreline! But it might have something to do with why she was dumped in the Bay.

"And he's some kind of boss. Once, when we were on the phone, he got interrupted by somebody. The guy said, 'Hey, boss, we got a problem'. My guy asked me to hold on, but he didn't mute the phone. It was kinda weird."

"Weird? Like kinky?"

"Nah. Just, it didn't make sense. I could hear most of what they said. The guy that interrupted … the one with the problem … said something like 'the war finger was poking around the boxes.'"

"The war finger was poking around the boxes!"

"Yeah, I know. But that's what I heard, " said Leibman. "And the guy I was talking to? The boss? What he said?" Leibman paused, as if for dramatic effect before delivering a punch line.

Freddie just scowled at him.

"He said, 'You know what to do. Tell the gang to start hard-timing the row row.'"

A Golf Game

Ellerby putted – a short, stabbing stroke -- and watched the ball stop short of the crest of the slope and then roll back, stopping within a foot of where it had started.

"Shit! I should quit this damn game.""

McAdams winked at Fallon. "Where you gonna go? To work? Home to your empty house? "

Ellerby grinned. "Actually, I was thinking of the bar. Somewhere I have a comparative advantage. A dark place where I do not have to prove my manhood by trying to outsmart a vicious little white ball."

"Mayor! Mayor! Remember your image! Politicians are supposed to play golf. It builds character – unless your constituents know that you routinely cheat." Fallon spoke around his cigar as he was putting, the ball tracking along a smooth arc that terminated six feet left of the hole. He was the best of the three of them and still a lousy golfer.

The repartee was part of a Wednesday afternoon ritual at the Harding Park golf course. The three of them had been meeting late on Wednesday afternoon for the last two years, playing nine holes or until dark, whichever came first. For each of them, it was the only fixed point in their chaotic calendars and they went to absurd lengths to show up, blowing off both social and professional obligations to do so. Not one of the three ever commented on the obvious quirkiness or what it implied about their needs.

It began when they met at the annual Policeman's Benefit Dinner. Semi-drunk, they pooled their money and won an extravagant bid for a golf game with a touring pro at Pebble Beach, outbidding a slightly less drunk covey of Vice cops. They organized a three-day boys' outing around the game and came away with a sense of mutual comfort and a camaraderie that defied analysis.

Given the crowded conditions at San Francisco's premier municipal golf course, they spent most of their time waiting between shots and the idle intervals became more important than the physical act of playing golf. Conversation could go anywhere at any time.

"You know. I tried to teach this game to Carlo," Fallon said. "Thought it would be one of those father-son bonding experiences that everybody talks about but nobody ever seems to achieve."

Ellerby shook his head. "Bad idea. All it does is bring out all that Freudian stuff about fathers and sons … the really dark stuff that Greeks wrote plays about."

McAdams rolled his eyes and said, "Gentlemen! We've got exactly one child between the three of us – and that's Carlo – so I think maybe we shouldn't be giving parenting advice."

He looked at Ellerby. "You and I don't have any experience and…" -- with a glance at Fallon -- "he obviously can't be objective about his own kid."

What he *didn't* say – because it was tacitly understood among them – was that they couldn't -- shouldn't -- talk about some of the realities of the Fallon family business, particularly the line of succession between father and son. Everybody knew that Fallon was involved in shady activities, lines of business that often strayed across the line that separated "legal" from "illegal". Not quite "victimless" crime, but as far as McAdams knew, Fallon stayed away from drugs and prostitution, the kind of stuff with violence at its core.

The exceptions involved Carlo. Both father and son were seemingly locked into their roles as spoiled child and the enabling/rescuing father. Carlo went through childhood with an immunity to consequences. Dominick was a classic enabler, providing Carlo the freedom to practice truancy, bullying, insubordination and all of the other transgressions that – if consequences were permitted -- could have provided opportunities for character development. But Dominick saw such consequences as threats to his only son.

It was a vicious cycle, each incident more serious than its predecessor, each rescue reinforcing both father and son in their pathologies. There were stories: increasingly lurid accounts as Carlo became of age. Stories of broken bones, even a late night execution, and Dominick's monumental rages directed at any threat to Carlo. The stories flourished in the waterfront subculture, embellished to the point where they became urban legends, usually with a moral thrown in about Italian fathers and their obsessions with their only sons.

As mayor and a member of the police force, both he and Ellerby were careful not to know too much. It helped that McAdams was a homicide cop with little interest in the more genteel criminality that Fallon flirted with. And Fallon had never sought to play on their friendship in his occasional formal brushes with state or federal inquiries. In any city other than San Francisco, their weekly golf game would be scandalous and unsustainable. Here, it was local color, simply another affirmation of the city's sophistication.

McAdams didn't worry much about his image. He liked Fallon and as a homicide cop didn't worry much about the kind of rough capitalism that Fallon was engaged in. *That's what we need more of … criminals with an aversion to violence and a strong commitment to their family.*

However, Carlo was another matter. McAdams was hearing stories – both on the street and from other officers in other divisions – that Carlo was thinking of branching out into some of the more violent variations. *I wonder if Fallon knows what his son is doing?*

He tried a change of subject. "So Mayor, how's your love life? I see the gossip columnists are picking on you again?"

"They are an excitable lot, aren't they?" Ellerby paused to hit a nine-iron about fifty yards dead left into a stand of eucalyptus. He was truly a remarkably bad golfer, redeemed only by his acceptance of his ineptitude. "They write about as well as I play golf."

Fallon picked up on their conversation. "They take good pictures though. The woman you were with on Saturday night at the Opera – Elaine somebody-or-other? She looked real good in that dress. I've heard of backless gowns, but that was almost frontless! And that's not the first time you've been sighted with her either."

"Her name is Eileen, not Elaine. And she's just a friend. A person that likes operas. She helps me with my image – the socially-active bon vivant politician. Like you said, image is important. Kind of like the way you drive your 1956 Thunderbird with the top down on Sunday afternoons."

The dialogue depressed McAdams. He had seen the pictures and promptly envied Ellerby. He thought he could see something in the way the woman was holding his arm and leaning ever-so-slightly against him that signaled something more than a chance to see the opera. *You're imagining things. Just because you're so goddam all alone.*

The suddenly darker mood made the golf game seem senseless. He said, "You two public figures carry on talking about your images. I've gotta go. And it's already half-dark anyway."

Ellerby grinned, "That's the problem with being a homicide detective. Most of the murders happen after dark. You're like a vampire, allergic to daylight."

McAdams had already turned back toward the clubhouse, but looked back over his shoulder. "Lots of interesting things happen after dark. Especially when you're hanging out with good-looking blondes in skimpy dresses. Good luck with Eileen what's-her-name that likes opera."

Fathers and Sons

"The kid's OK. He just needs to do his own thing … cut the apron strings… like any other kid. You should give him some slack."

Dominick Fallon almost laughed out loud. *A hit man giving parenting advice! Not your usual family therapist.* As far as he knew, Grodin had never been married or produced any offspring. To make it even more absurd, he had never demonstrated the slightest concern for the needs of others unless it gave him an edge with that person. He was a transparent and unrepentant sociopath that liked to disguise himself as an amiable cynic.

So he's running another agenda. One that is furthered if I do as he asks … give Carlo more freedom … to do his own thing… such a stupid expression! Let him kill women and children to make a few more dollars for his offshore accounts!

He said, "Let it go, Grodin," knowing that he wouldn't, that he would note the point of resistance and simply slide off to a new angle of attack, always probing for the soft spot, the hard-to-find but inevitable imperfection that could be exploited. As patient as water dripping on sandstone. Fallon often marveled at Grodin's supreme indifference to what others thought of him; how he could absorb criticism, even ridicule or gross insults without apparent effect. *What do you call a person who has no emotion? Inhuman? Insane?*

Ironically, it was that very absence that made Grodin useful to him. An advisor unswayed by anger, love or hatred, always there for a second opinion on matters where Fallon mistrusted his own judgment. But unlike other advisors, his lack of ego enabled him to reliably carry out orders that he disagreed with. Like having a robot or a computer that responds to voice commands. *But what if someone else gets at the programming? Like Carlo …*

The thought of Carlo depressed him and – as it always did these days – triggered an internal dialogue

Thomas Hofstedt

between two individuals that seemed to exist side-by-side within him.

Lighten up! He's exactly like you were at that age.

But that's the problem! I want him to be different ... to make different choices.

You know better. He's your son. He's watched you for thirty years. He wants to be like you, but bigger, richer, scarier.

He can do all that. But he doesn't need to be a gangster! He could be ...

Respectable? Admit it. Say the word. That's what you want... respectable!

What's wrong with that? It's a lot safer. He's already got the college education, the society wife, the two perfect kids. Why not hang around with the people that go to the symphony, have a private jet, play golf at the country club and get talked about for political office?

He doesn't want that. Thinks it's dull. Those people? He calls them schmucks!

He and his son did not even resemble one another. The elder Fallon was tall, slender and aristocratic-looking, with thick gray hair and piercing brown eyes. Carlo was short and pudgy, with thinning blond hair and pale eyes that were neither interesting nor interested. Side-by-side, he and Carlo would not appear to be even remotely related to one another.

The differences were more than just physical. They seemed to come from different centuries and cultures. Dominick was married to the same woman for forty years and still mourned her death three years after the actual event. Carlo was married to a woman he detested, who produced children that he seemed indifferent to. One of those scorched earth divorce trials was in process, delighting the local press as much as it saddened and puzzled Dominick.

He's my son. But what is it that we share?

Two days ago, Dominick had dropped in on Carlo at his office without notice and had surprised him in the act of caressing a young woman sitting on the corner of his desk. She was young and strikingly beautiful. Both she and Carlo

96

looked up sharply when the door clicked, but with very different expressions. The woman was startled and embarrassed all at the same time, moving to pull her dress back into place and slide off of the desk. Carlo was merely annoyed, as though a waiter had interrupted his conversation. Dominick simply turned and walked out of the office, but left with the impression that the woman was clearly more frightened of Carlo than she was curious about Dominick.

Fallon tried to recall what he wanted when he was Carlo's age, but all he remembered was the fear and greed that seemed to drive him as he progressed from neighborhood bookie and numbers runner to extortion schemes and – finally – to becoming a major crime factor on the Oakland and San Francisco waterfronts.

The truth was that Dominick Fallon was the dominant player in a well-defined market niche, approximately halfway between 'white collar' crime and the more violent mafia thuggery. Behind the scenes of the legitimate business, a host of genteel criminal enterprises flourished. Goods were diverted. Fake contracts facilitated money laundering. Counterfeit goods were brought in from Asia. Insurance scams, work stoppages, union "organizing" … It made for a nice living, and was sufficiently 'respectable' to keep Fallon below the radar of the organized crime task forces.

He didn't know how Grodin had found him. He just turned up one day with a briefcase filled with cash, looking for a ship to rent. Since then, Dominick and he had collaborated on a pair of ventures that made each of them a lot of money, leaving far-away corporations poorer and in the dark as to what had happened to them. It became apparent to him that Grodin's ambitions and capabilities far exceeded his. He made Dominick feel parochial, like a small-time hood confronted with a criminal mastermind.

Grodin, the ultimate cynic, told him, "Think of it this way. On the criminal spectrum, you rank just below the greedy snobs who sell penny stocks and practice insider trading and Medicare fraud. And *way* above the legbreakers and drug pushers, not to mention the politicians who sell their votes for cash."

The respectable front was the Fallon Transportation Company. The Chronicle called it a "diversified transportation services company". It owned and operated a small fleet of cargo carriers operating between Asia and ports on the West Coast of the U.S., ran stevedoring and brokering services in LA and San Francisco, and provided specialized marine engineering and consulting services on a global basis.

Dominick had made Carlo the CEO of the shipping subsidiary – Pacific Cargos, Inc. -- with the intention of insulating it from the shadier parts of the business and giving Carlo a springboard to respectability. However, to his consternation, Carlo had suggested a number of "innovations" that would take it in exactly the opposite direction. To make it worse, Grodin had clearly signed on with Carlo and Fallon feared that the combination would be a fatal one. When Fallon complained to him that Carlo was booking deals with major drug cartels, Grodin had recited the "kids will be kids" line.

Like most fathers, Fallon had unreasonable expectations for his son; and -- like most fathers -- he assumed that he could use some combination of reason and authority to make his son be what he wanted him to be.

It was an assumption that would prove fatal.

Family Monologues

Scientists and others have speculated about and studied the causes of criminal behavior for thousands of years. The 'classical' view is that crime is the result of economic forces, motivated or deterred by comparing self-interest against the likelihood of punishment. It springs from the belief in an inbred rationality and implies that crime is a free choice.

A strikingly different view – generally labeled as 'positivist' – is that crime is determined by specific non-economic forces. Some researchers and criminologists emphasize biological deficiencies; others focus on psychological and/or sociological factors.

Carlo would satisfy both camps.

Certainly, his decision to take over the flow of narcotics in the Bay Area, thereby expanding his opportunities in prostitution and other violent offshoots, was intrinsically rational, motivated by the belief that he could make a lot of money without running much risk. His authorization of the execution of the three street-level drug dealers was based on a straightforward cost-benefit analysis. If he subjected himself to study, it could be easily demonstrated that he was not very smart and had few attractive attributes, so that criminality may have been his 'best' career option.

On the other hand, he grew up in a loveless home, with a domineering father and a mother who was probably bipolar, although heavily self-medicated with alcohol and an assortment of prescription drugs provided by friendly shrinks. He exhibited a resistance to authority very early in his childhood and bounced from school to school and counselor to counselor, transitions triggered by increasingly violent incidents and smoothed over by family money and influence. Several court-mandated therapists along the way commented on his inability to connect with others, on the absence of "a moral compass".

He quickly realized that his father was a limiting factor. He refused his father's attempt at advice and counsel, even on straightforward business matters. Carlo had no confidantes until Grodin came along, but if he had, he would have described Dominick Fallon to them as 'weak', 'timid', 'conservative', or 'conventional', summarized in Carlo's vocabulary as a "pathetic old fucker". The fact that his father loved him unconditionally was simply irrelevant to the choices Carlo made. He was also unappreciative of the several times that Dominick committed felonies ranging from bribery to murder to bail him out of nasty situations. He thought of those rescues as 'premature', thinking – wrongly -- "I would have solved the problem myself if he'd stayed out of my way."

Their last conversation was typical. Dominick was fidgety, clearly wanting to talk about something that was bothering him. Carlo recognized the symptoms.

"Carlo, I –"

"No."

"But you haven't even heard –"

"I don't need to. It's the same goddam thing one more time."

"I've left you alone. I thought you'd do the right thing … Break away from all … this." Fallon waved his arm, a gesture intended to include the family history as well as their immediate surroundings.

"I am. Breaking away. Just not in the direction you wanted me to."

"Carlo. Look at me. I've never killed a woman. Never pushed dope to teenagers. I don't kidnap women who think I'm their ticket to a modeling career."

Carlo considered the list. *Not bad. He's nailed almost every one of the new lines of business. He's missing the one that he might approve of… the one that started me on this track. And he's the one who kick started the whole thing by sending Grodin my way.*

Carlo did not know where Grodin came from or any part of his colorful history. He simply showed up in his office, using Dominick's name to gain entry. His proposal was simple.

"Some friends of mine would like to rent a ship for a month."

"We got ships. Send your friends by."

"They're very shy. Asked me to handle it. And they are very big on privacy. Don't like a lot of paperwork."

Grodin watched Carlo, seeing the expression of slyness creep into his eyes, the giveaway that he was looking for. The deal was essentially done at that point, although Carlo didn't exactly know it yet.

Grodin's 'friends' required a small merchant ship to pursue a meandering route in international waters for a month, putting into port only once for fuel and provisions. No cargo was ever loaded on and only the Captain and Engineer remained on board. Ten men came aboard late at night. They did not declare that they were CIA, just "the crew and some special technicians". There was a single passenger, brought aboard by a helicopter near the Algerian coast in shackles and wearing a hood over his head, apparently semi-conscious. At the end of the month, the ship delivered the passenger to three black-clad soldiers who appeared in a Zodiac raft about ten miles off the coast of Yemen. Pacific Cargo, Inc. received a cash payment of two million dollars in cash from one of the special technicians as he left the ship.

Carlo did not watch the news nor read newspapers. He did not know the phrase "involuntary rendition", but would not have cared one way or the other if he had.

The term he did know was 'connected', and Grodin was seriously connected. He brokered some covert arms shipments and talked Carlo into setting up a human pipeline smuggling young Russian women into the U.S. prostitution business. In the course of their business dealings, Carlo learned an important fact about Grodin: he was highly skilled at killing people as well as arranging shady business deals for his clients.

Grodin let him believe that it was his – Carlo's -- idea to open up discussions with the major South American drug cartels. "You can do the biggest narcotics deal in the history of the US – a billion dollar deal – a deal so big that the Mexicans, Colombians and Venezuelans will all want a piece of it."

When he had him hooked, Grodin tutored him on how to run a narcotics wholesaling operation in a major American city. He kept it simple. "Bring the stuff in on one of your boats. Stash it in a waterfront location that you control. Hire some thick-necked goons for security and convince the local gangs that they've got to deal with you if they want good stuff at the right price."

He didn't talk about financing until later, until Carlo was obsessed with doing 'the biggest deal ever'. Then he introduced the Russian money guy, an ex-KGB agent transformed into a Moscow banker. Over a two day meeting, they developed the plan whereby the Russian would lend the money in return for a significant share of the profits and a lien against the assets of the Fallon companies.

Grodin also brokered the meetings with Vargas and Torres, although he let Carlos think that it was his own brilliant idea to use the Russian whores as a perk for their summit meeting in San Francisco, thereby making Sofia's escape a personal failure for him. It still enraged Carlo every time he thought of her. *That bitch Sofia nearly ruined the whole deal*! Once it was clear that she was gone, he and Torres had made an agreement: Whoever found her first would keep her intact and on ice until both of them could be in the same room with her. That prospect had taken root in his nighttime fantasies, to the point of obsession.

Grodin helped him hide the new lines of business from his father, although he knew that couldn't last much longer. Dominick was at Carlo's house for a rare Sunday dinner. The dinner was catered, given that Carlo's wife had moved out with the children. The evening did not go well and ended on a note that worried Carlo.

Dominick handed Carlo a copy of the San Francisco Chronicle, folded over to highlight a front-page article with the headline "Another Duct Tape Murder".

"Carlo. One more time. I want you to run a shipping company. Make money the old fashioned way. No more of this ... other stuff."

"Dad" – pronounced with a drawn-out inflection that mimicked an outright sneer – "Fuck off. I don't know how to say it any more clearly."

Dominick did not look offended, just enormously tired and sad.

"I can't."

After a pause, he added, "But I know some other ways to get my point across."

Cold Cases

McAdams took a week off after Gonzo's death. He didn't have much choice. The Captain was quite emphatic.

"You're not worth shit to us in your condition. Take some time and get your head together. We'll find the fuckers that did Gonzo!"

McAdams thought that it was an accurate assessment of his mental state, although he wasn't so sure about the last part; they were no closer to finding Gonzo's killer than the day he died.

The day he came back to work, he was partnered up with Freddie and they were handed the Charles Desmond and Jane Doe cases.

He knew that the assignments were carefully selected with several criteria in mind. First, they were still open cases after two weeks or more of investigation. And the victims – at least Desmond -- were apparently upstanding citizens, unworthy of dying in such a fashion. At least according to the newspapers. So it did require some attention. More importantly, the Desmond murder occurred on the same day as Gonzo was killed, so McAdams would have to focus on Desmond rather than on Gonzo's activities on that day. It was a not very well disguised diversionary tactic.

Finally, both cases showed signs of becoming classically 'cold' cases. So if a still distraught detective and his rookie partner weren't at their best, no harm would be done.

He had Freddie take the lead on Jane. Mainly because thinking about the still-unidentified woman reminded him of Gonzo with his muddy shoes on the tidal flats.

The Desmond file was depressingly thin. Charles Desmond lived alone, apparently had neither friends nor enemies, and was seen by no one on the day that he was shot. He made his living as a run-of-the-mill insurance adjuster. More than one of his acquaintances described him as 'Caspar

Milquetoast'. His records and recent employers did not point to any controversy in his career or personal life. The only lead was his apparent addiction to gambling. Due to that, his finances were chaotic and would drive a personal financial planner nuts, but they were not at the level that would get him killed.

There was no physical evidence. He'd been shot once in the chest just inside the entrance of his condo. No signs of a struggle. Robbery was not a motive as he had a thousand dollars in his pocket and his wallet was still there with all of its credit cards. The condo had several valuable electronic items lying around in the open. One neighbor said that he had been out that morning because his car had been gone when she left for work.

The only curiosity was that his cell phone was missing. Interestingly, according to the phone company, the last two calls had been to the SFPD.

Freddie said it. "Either he had a very valuable cell phone or we're missing something. People like this don't get shot. They declare bankruptcy and go back home to the Midwest."

McAdams had stopped worrying about it. He had already decided that this one wasn't going anywhere, destined to be one of the many unsolved homicides in the files. He was already reallocating his investigative time to Gonzo.

He decided to spend a couple of hours reviewing the listing of incoming calls for both of them for the last couple of weeks before Gonzo went downstairs to that taxi. All of the detectives maintained a call log, a simple list of incoming 'business calls'. Most of the logs were haphazardly kept, but both McAdams and Gonzo were pretty good about it, using the old-fashioned method of writing down each call in a bound notebook and sometimes adding a comment if there was something to follow up on.

He pulled the log from his desk drawer and set it squarely in the middle of the bare surface in front of him, staring at it the way a widow with two kids and no job might regard an eviction notice. The ringing of his cell phone was a welcome diversion.

It was Freddie.

"Got a break on Jane. Turns out she was a high-end working girl. Street name was Natasha or something like that. I've got a witness – a prostitute, kinda dubious, if you know what I mean – who saw her being handed off at the Fairmont about a week before we found her."

"So, do we know anything about her handler? Or any johns?"

"I'm working on that now. But I'd rule out any customers as her killer. She was assassinated and dumped in the Bay. Definitely not the hot-blooded modus operandi for a presumably satisfied conventioneer in his upscale hotel suite."

McAdams grinned despite himself. *Fast work, good thinking, and a working knowledge of Latin … I think I'm going to like this partner.*

"What's next? And is there anything I can do at the moment to keep this moving along?"

There was a long silence on the line and when she spoke again, it was if she was embarrassed.

"Uh, Mac? Bear with me for a sec, will you? I feel like I've walked into one of those old Sherlock Holmes stories – the kind where there are lots of clues, but none of them make sense?"

"So the game is afoot, is it? OK, I'll be Watson. What's bothering you, Holmes?"

"Somebody overheard something. I think it's relevant, but it's gibberish." Freddie recited carefully, enunciating in an exaggerated way. ""The war finger was poking around the boxes! Tell the gang to start hard-timing the row row.'"

McAdams laughed out loud.

"What the hell does it mean?" Freddie sounded offended by McAdams' laughter. "It sounds like either a terrorist plot or Gaelic, maybe both!"

He stopped laughing. *Not her fault. She probably grew up in Kansas.*

"Welcome to San Francisco, Detective Fulbright. The City by the Bay. The place where ships come and go and ancient dialects persist. What we have here is a classic exchange between stevedores – the workers that load and unload cargos from freighters."

"Thanks for the history lesson. What did the *stevedore* say, exactly?"

"OK, a step at a time. *Boxes* are containers, those big steel things you see stacked up on ships, sitting in piles on the waterfront and riding on flatcars around the country. *War finger* is one word – wharfinger –meaning the manager or owner of the pier where the boxes come ashore. *Gang* is a stevedoring work crew, the ones moving the boxes on or off of a ship at the wharf. *Hard timing* is stevedore slang, meaning a work slowdown. And your *row row* is an acronym, usually expressed as *RO/RO* -- " He spelled it out for her. "It stands for 'roll on, roll off" – a special purpose cargo ship where the cargo – usually vehicles of some kind – can be driven on or off the boat on special ramps."

Freddie spoke mostly to herself. "So – translated -- the head guy on the wharf is being nosy, so the workers will make their point by dogging it for awhile."

"By George, I think she's got it!" McAdams used his best English accent.

"That's from My Fair Lady, not Sherlock Holmes. And you're being sexist!"

"And you're dealing with someone on the waterfront. I gotta go. Stay in touch."

He hung up. The call log was still sitting in the middle of his desk.

When he opened the log to the last page that had any writing, he noted that the dozen or so calls for that day were mostly citizens responding to the reward offers on the Jane Doe case. His eyes went immediately to the last call on the page, the one from the shooter in the cab. The date, time and his written comment, "Jane Doe tipster, Yellow Cab". He remembered sending Gonzo downstairs to his death as he sat down to make the entry. He sat staring at the one line in the notebook, willing himself to look away, anything to stop his brain from going there again.

He sat back, staring at the page with an unfocused gaze, trying to see it as a mass of words rather than as some kind of epitaph for Gonzo. He turned back to the page, determined to work his way through the book, starting with the most recent call and working backwards in time.

Three lines up, the name was there in black and white. It was equally cryptic, but screamed for attention. It read, "AM: Charles Desmond, tip re: Jane Doe". A phone number followed, with an asterisk. The code "AM" meant "answering machine". The asterisk was his code for "Follow up!"

Charles Desmond called me half an hour before the killer showed up for my assassination. Both of them said they knew something about Jane Doe. Now Desmond is dead and I was supposed to be dead.

The Mayor

Grodin walked out of Ellerby's office, not even bothering to close the door behind him. His contempt was as transparent as if he had challenged him to a duel by slapping him across the face with a pair of riding gloves. Ellerby walked over to close the door and stood staring at its blank face.

What the hell happened? Where did it all go wrong? As though it could be traced to a single, discrete cause... Like agreeing to set up a cultural exchange program.

He looked at the photos on his office wall, the ones showing him shaking hands with power brokers at higher levels of government. *I remember how naïve I was. About politics and power, what was possible. How much good could be done without cutting corners. Compromise, of course. But always in the right direction, giving up something to get something, always with that slight gain. All those urban problems – crime, housing, homelessness, traffic – that seemed so tractable to new ideas. A life lived trying to do the greater good.*

So where did it go off the rails? Wrong question. Like asking an octogenarian 'When did you become old?' Whatever had happened to get him to this point, it sure as hell wasn't a sudden cataclysmic event, more like a long, slow slide down that famous slippery slope.

Some of it was disillusionment, the inevitable realization that the problems aren't going to be solved in your term of office, maybe not in your lifetime; that you're just one of a long line of idealists butting their heads against the same wall. That good intentions don't go very far against the vested interests with their money and power. That a four-year mayoral term is a short time and can be waited out, especially if one is playing against institutions rather than individuals. That the people you want to help don't trust you or are themselves apathetic about the possibility of change.

At first, the disillusion led to frustration that morphed into a willingness to bend the rules, but in a constructive way. A practical means for getting things done. Idealism tempered with a constructive amount of realism. The tools were time tested – patronage, giving and receiving of favors in exchange for the right kind of concessions, the skillful use of "spin" – the recasting of policies and decisions to make them seem more honorable than they were.

If it had stopped there, I would be a simple and representative case study of the modern big city mayor, worthy of a documentary with a title like 'the maturation of a politician'.

Clearly, the old adage about 'power corrupts' was also at work, although I tend to think of it as 'entitlement'. I've served the people for thirty years and gotten nothing back except abuse, indifference and free rent. I've helped tens of thousands of people get jobs, homes, city contracts, medical treatment, education. For what? The right to second-guess every thing I do on their behalf? Anybody would start to look for ways to get what you're owed.

And there are so many slippery slopes to choose from. It was easier to get away with it when I first started in politics. But then came 'investigative journalism' and every newspaper and TV station in town formed a task force to dig up dirt, even if it wasn't there. No wonder that so many politicians are serving time for everything from accepting bribes in exchange for lucrative city contracts to appointing their mothers-in-law to cushy jobs..

Would it have happened if Grodin hadn't shown up? Probably. But Grodin knew how to package it. Not just for me, but for the newspapers and my staff members that were still committed to my reform agenda. Beyond that, he knew how to cover it up, right on down to setting up bank accounts, dummy corporations and photo ops designed to create an impression exactly counter to the reality.

The conversation was crystal clear in his memory. Grodin was sitting in the same chair as his last visit.

"This crazy idea of the Governor's? Using the city as a testing ground for a war against crime? We want you to kill the idea."

Ellerby didn't bother to disguise his sarcasm. "I know what you want and why you want it. But remember, I'm a so-called reform mayor. I'm supposed to be serious about reducing crime. I make major speeches promising the citizenry that I'm on top of it. And you want me to decline to participate in a program that's directly focused on reducing violent crime in our city?"

Grodin was dismissive, clearly not listening. "Spin the statistics. Use the numbers to show violent crime is decreasing as a result of the policies you already have in place. Play the individual liberties card. Talk about the police state tactics that the Governor has in mind, the erosion of civil rights that would be inevitable if you have layers of state and federal cops swarming around with a so-called special mandate. Your Board of Supervisors will eat that up."

He knew Grodin was right. "I can't just say no. I need to give them an alternative."

Grodin smiled in a way that told Ellerby he already had the answer. "Use your COPPS idea. Move it off the drawing board and into the streets. And not just the Tenderloin. It has the same objectives as the Governor's plan, but the methods are exactly the opposite – soft instead of hard, organic instead of bolted on, internal rather than external. Get your new female Chief of Police to back you up. She's been yelling about the need for better community relations for the last three years. Sell that to your Board of Supervisors and you'll make the Governor look like Genghis Khan on steroids."

He's right, as always. I can make it look statesmanlike, strategic. All I'm doing is advocating for a sensible policy choice. Hard for an investigator to get excited about something that didn't happen. And no risk. No bagfuls of cash changing hands, no subordinates wearing wires, no editorials about 'soft on crime'. The Governor can yell about it, but he's almost a Republican … not much status in San Francisco.

But there is one more thing.

Grodin was ahead of him. "Fifty thou for your personal campaign fund as soon as you derail the Governor. Very carefully laundered. Wherever you want it."

That was a month and several murders ago – the ones he knew about, including a cop. This morning, he called Grodin, intending to change the deal. The language was veiled – they talked about "breach of contract". But twenty minutes later, Grodin showed up in his office. His language was more direct -- pungent phrases including words like 'corruption' and 'criminal malfeasance' -- and he didn't close the door when he left.

A Dreary Day in San Francisco

It was a dreary Wednesday afternoon in San Francisco, one of those winter days where the grayness not only infuses all the surroundings, but seeps into the attitudes and outlooks of the people, causing fatigue or a vague sadness for which there is no apparent cause. Officially, it was not raining, and it was true that if you held out your hand palm up you would not feel any drops. Yet if you go outside in a woolen garment, you begin to smell and moisture penetrates through to your skin. You are continuously cold.

He hadn't seen Freddie for two days. When he called her on his way to the golf course, she was vague about what she was doing. "Murphy's got me following up on some stuff for him. Pure grunt work. Way too ordinary for skilled veterans like you to waste time on."

"Freddie. It's not good to lie to your partner. You know the concept. We're supposed to be each other's alter ego. Remember?"

"Alter ego? I don't think so, Mac. Too many dark recesses where you hang out in your head."

She's hiding something. About the only possibility is that Murphy's got her working some piece of the Gonzo investigation. And I'm not to be trusted on that one!

"OK, but I'm picking you up at seven tomorrow morning. I need your help more than Murphy does. And by the way, it's beginning to look like there's a connection between Jane Doe and Charles Desmond."

"I'll be on the curb with two double lattes." Then her voice changed. "Uh, Mac … You are doing your Wednesday afternoon threesome today, aren't you?" It sounded more like a plea than a question.

"Of course. The rain keeps all the riff-raff away … No waiting."

When they disconnected, Freddie sat staring unhappily at the screen on her iPad. It displayed a street-level Google picture of a warehouse/office building on the

113

Oakland waterfront. It sat in front of the only pier on the Bay where stevedores worked the roll on–roll off type of cargo ship. A boatload of Japanese automobiles arrived twice a week. But the reason for her unhappy expression was not the building itself; it was the name of the owner.

She was headed for the entrance when she noticed a cluster of women – clearly prostitutes working an early shift – on the corner. She headed for them, but not without a grimace. *Freddie. You're just putting it off. Mac needs to know who he's dealing with, and sooner is better than later.* But she pulled Jane Doe's picture out from her coat pocket and approached the scantily clad women who were already tightening their formation against what was obviously a cop intent on hassling them.

As it turned out, Ellerby and McAdams did tee off right on time. Fallon met them at the driving range and hit a few balls, but decided not to play, saying, "I've got better things to do than get wet and not have any fun doing it."

The two of them tried for three holes, then gave up and headed for the bar.

With Fallon absent, it was probably inevitable that the conversation drifted toward their common interest in police matters. Ellerby long ago admitted that his favorite part of being the Mayor was that he could hang with cops.

Ellerby started it. "They say that felonies go up when there's a full moon. In my opinion, it's this damn weather! Makes me feel like running down a jaywalker or stabbing a city council member!"

"Maybe it's the opposite. Bad weather makes folks more depressed, passions cool, murder rate falls?"

"That's too many causal links for me," Ellerby said. He went on before McAdams could continue. "Speaking of murder rates, how are you Sherlocks doing with finding the guy with duct tape who shoots people in the back of the head?"

The transition was too quick, too pat. And Ellerby's gaze was just a little bit too intense. *This is a planned conversation, but why with me? He could get better answers from the Chief.*

Ellerby read his reaction correctly. "Yeah, I know. Sorry. Why am I pestering you rather than going through the chain of command?"

"It's not just that. I'm not even on that case any more. Since … since the Gonzales thing."

"Christ! That. Jeez, Mac, I'm sorry –"

"Forget it. Ancient history." He tried another tack. *Anything to avoid talking about Gonzo.* "But about those duct tape hits? I can tell you that we've got nothing. Well, almost nothing. There's an emerging theory that a new bunch is trying to move in… Take over the nasty end of the business … narcotics, prostitution. The killings are their version of advertising."

"Oh, and the coroner thinks that our Jane Doe – the fourth in that bloody little series – is from one of the ex-Soviet states. Apparently, their dental work is distinctive; i.e., so bad that it stands out."

Ellerby blinked twice and froze. McAdams could almost feel the sudden intensity from across the table. Ellerby's attempt to cover up his reaction was far too late. He said, "That's a start, I suppose."

That was an interesting reaction. Needs revisiting. But he kept his voice neutral. "Not much of one. The Bay Area has lots of citizens hailing from those parts. We're working that angle, but nobody is reporting any missing persons from that category."

Ellerby looked thoughtful, silent for the moment. McAdams was content with that, watching the grayness intensify over the eighteenth green. He realized that it had begun raining again, real rain this time. A foursome was coming up the fairway, their brightly colored umbrellas somehow making the gloom even denser.

Ellerby's voice was soft, tentative, as if asking for some kind of reassurance. "I'm under some pressure on this. The Governor wants to use San Francisco as the site for a new approach to the violent crimes problem. He wants me to get the players in line." He paused. "He thinks that the recent surge in our murder rate makes us a prime candidate for his experiment."

"Another 'fad-of-the-month' program from the pointy-headed crowd in Sacramento?"

"Probably. But it would be a pretty dramatic change. The idea is the old 'shock and awe' technique. A show of overwhelming force. Federal, State, County and City law enforcement combined. A dedicated task force. Zero tolerance. Expedited judicial procedures ... the whole works."

"I see why they need your support. It sounds more than a little militaristic." McAdams smiled, thinking of San Francisco's liberal reputation. Among other things, it was the only major US city that did not allow officers to carry or use Tasers. "This is going to be a hard sell, politically speaking. Especially in this particular left-coast city!"

"I think I can sell it. But what bothers me is whether it would actually work? The get-tough kind of stuff? I need a street-level perspective on this."

McAdams tried. He honestly tried to weigh the pros and cons, to render some halfway-informed opinion. But the rational and the analytical were crowded out by the cycling visions of the white body on the black mud and the pink haze that exploded from Gonzo's head. His response was driven more by his barely suppressed need for vengeance than by any rational calculus.

"Yeah. It would work. It's an idea whose time has come."

His cell phone rang. Much later, he would wonder why he answered. To do so was a violation of his Wednesday afternoon rules. Maybe because the conversation was at a natural breaking point. Or the falling barometric pressure was affecting his mood. Perhaps the ring tone somehow transmitted the excitement of the caller. Or maybe it was simply ordained by a callous and uncaring god with yet another cruelty to be practiced on him.

"McAdams"

"Mac, this is Freddie. You've got to get over here, right now!"

"Where the hell are you? And what's going on?"

She was almost whispering, her words coming fast and excited. "Jane Doe. Desmond. You're right. They're linked. And I've got the bastard. He's running the women, drugs –"

"Freddie, I'm at the golf course with Ellerby –"

"That's just it. I know all about your golf buddy. The killer? It's your golf part—"

There was a distinct sound, a *thunk,* and then the voice stopped, leaving only a blinking light on the face of his phone.

He was a primary witness and was asked to describe the sound that ended the call. He was pressed for adjectives. The best – and worst – that he could come up with was, "It sounded like hitting a melon with an axe."

Freddie's body turned up two days later, stuffed into the trunk of a stolen Audi abandoned in South San Jose. Her revolver was still in her bag. Parts of her cell phone were imbedded in her skull, driven there by the force of the blow that killed her. According to the autopsy, she was killed instantly by a single violent blow to the side of her head with 'a blunt metallic object'. The pathologist's judgment was that she was struck from behind by a right-handed person using a sidearm type of motion. Informally and off the record, she thought the weapon might be a crowbar or the blunt end of a hatchet.

McAdams didn't – couldn't – go to the funeral. For the first few days, he drank a lot. He could not sleep, hearing the "thunk" sound over and over. After a while, he began to think of it as the sound of a car door shutting.

Ellerby made a major anti-crime speech centered on Freddie's death. He promised revenge but called it justice. But all that McAdams could hear was Freddie's voice, her last words. "The killer? It's your golf part--"

117

An Unremarkable Murder

The pier was dark, the only light coming from the open end of the vast shed facing onto the Bay; not enough to do anything except somehow make the darkness more apparent. That light barely reached the killer sitting on an overturned wooden box waiting for his victim to appear. Perhaps it was the darkness and the sensory deprivation that it fostered that made him briefly depressed, more reflective than was his custom.

It started as a simple burst of irritation. *Thirty years of this bullshit! And I'm sitting in the goddamn cold waiting for a madman to come through that door so I can kill him. I'm as crazy as he is!* The unusual pang of self-doubt amused him and it was that sensation that triggered his attempt to reconstruct how he got to this particular point.

It was an uncommon journey; one that – if he were to write a book – would expose a world that would shock "ordinary" readers by unmasking players and transactions that exist in the shadows and crevices of the systems that govern their lives. It would be like throwing a voter into a septic tank before asking him to vote on a bond issue for a new sewer system.

The goddam CIA! With their 'cold war' and 'evil empire' bullshit! Bureaucrats huddled in their offices worried about the politicians who are worried about their constituents getting worried enough to vote them out! Running their 'operations' like they're playing a video game! Sending people like me – 'deniable', such a nice word! – to do things – nasty, vicious things – that they couldn't admit to doing and had no idea whether the viciousness even achieved anything at all.

Ah! But for me, it was the ideal career. I would have played the game forever. I met people ... I networked my ass off. Just not the usual class of people. Mafia, arms dealers, warlords, poppy farmers, pimps, corrupt politicians, revolutionaries ... Best of all, the people like me on the other side. The Stasi, KGB, the PKK in Turkey, ISI in Pakistan, more Arabs than I knew existed ... people who make up their own rules. Need money? Rob a bank. A policeman bothering you? Shoot him. A politician asking questions? Bribe him. Or, in the rare case where that doesn't work, send in a whore and take some pictures.

Then détente and technology happened and real spies became obsolete, underemployed. Some – the ones who needed more structure, less risk, or more respectability -- stayed mostly legit, becoming soldiers of fortune or provocateurs in obscure places, agents for shadow governments and greedy corporations with less-than-honorable agendas. The rest of us did what we were trained to do, but entirely for ourselves. Independent contractors.

Clients were easy to find. They needed us for their dirty little deals…. Our deniability. Most of all for our willingness to do what needed to be done. Especially once the 'war on terror' became the rallying cry. We became 'brokers'. The obscure faceless middleman that could funnel drug money into political campaigns; set up 'back-channel' meetings; get sophisticated weapons into the right hands of 'preferred' guerilla factions; kidnap suspected terrorists from foreign settings and arrange for their 'interrogation' by skilled professionals who were not constrained by treaties, conventions or even a natural compassion.

Good money to be made. All those deals with fees to the brokers. Paid in a variety of currencies. Heroin for stinger missiles. Assassinations for cash. Information for sex. Trade secrets for a drilling concession. Suitcases filled with cash. All that skim off the top. No receipts required.

Then this deal. A capstone to his career. Fifty million bucks and change for a thousand kilos of chemicals and a few women thrown into the package.

The killer waited patiently in the dark with his thoughts, as certain of his prey as a tiger circling a fawn with a broken leg. The lack of a challenge – what the naïve novelists termed 'the thrill of the hunt' – did not bother him. Even in the early days, it had never been about risk. Nor did lust for power, justice, conquest, vengeance or any of the other storybook emotions have much to do with his choice of a profession. Occasionally, an interesting puzzle would make a particular job more satisfying; the need to find a novel way to kill someone in a certain time, place or manner.

He knew, of course, that he was a psychopath. Even the CIA had finally rejected him for that reason. *Although they overlooked that little detail while he was efficiently killing the official enemies of the state.* The label did not bother him. He had read a quotation somewhere -- 'Insanity is the absence of every emotion except reason' – and it pleased him greatly.

His one professional quirk was his intense curiosity about his victims. It was not the disabling kind of curiosity; the kind that led to the question, 'Why has this person been chosen to die?' Answering that question required delving into philosophy, morality and the underbelly of human emotions. He had no tolerance for sophistry of this sort, although some curiosity was necessary in that it was prudent to study their habits and behaviors, their strengths and weaknesses, so that the job could be done safely and without incident. But once the routes were mapped, trajectories calculated and escapes plotted, curiosity was a luxury.

Not so for the killer. He wanted to know what they thought and how they felt when they knew they were about to die. He did not torture them in any physical sense. He simply made it clear to them that he was going to kill them, and then he watched. It was voyeurism of the most obscene form.

In any case, this night's work had little mystery to it. He had come across the man's possessions at the end of the pier and knew that he was a danger to their enterprise. Witnesses were not permitted. Particularly a witness that talked loudly and continuously all day long about the visions he had seen.

He heard the man long before he saw him, spewing a continuous sing-song stream of apocalyptic curses. The door opened, allowing the light from the halogen streetlights to penetrate into the interior of the shed; a single long shaft of light that split the darkness into two halves. The man's silhouette was backlit and cast a vastly enlarged and misshapen shadow of some fantastic creature on the opposite wall. The light also revealed the killer, seated on a wooden crate halfway across the shed. He held a powerful flashlight in one hand and a large revolver in the other. Both were visible to the man in the doorway.

"Come in. I've been waiting for you."

Howden stood in the doorway, peering closely at the killer. "I know you. You are godless, cast out, not of the people. You bring the white-skinned women, the whores out of the sea." Howden's voice boomed, amplified by the acoustics of the blank walls and empty space.

To his surprise and for the first time, the killer experienced a premonition, an emotion less than fear, a sense of ... something new to him. Insecurity? His own mortality? He did not like the sensation and pushed it back down.

This is a madman. Something about Howden's appearance in the doorway set off memories about primitive cultures that venerated their madmen, viewing them as emissaries of their gods.

"Come inside, and close the door."

Howden took one full step through the doorway, his eyes fixed on the killer, his backlit waving arms creating an eerie strobe effect to enhance his rising voice. "Thou sin. Thou shall not deliver up thy woman to another man. Thou shall not uncover the nakedness of thy sister. Thou dishonor God."

The killer stood and shouted at Howden. "Stop your stupid ranting! Stop and listen to me. I'm going to kill you! Do you hear me?"

The voice did not change. If anything, it became louder. "Thus says the Lord God, Put every man his sword by his side, slay every man his brother, his companion and neighbor. But the Lord God commands, thou shalt not kill."

He fired two quick shots into Howden's chest. The rounds drove him back into the open doorway, his outstretched arms preventing him from falling outside. He stood swaying, his hands braced against either side of the door. He looked directly at the killer. His voice was shrunken, but the words were still those of an angry Old Testament God, reverberating.

"I will require the life of he who murders! Whoso sheddeth man's blood by man shall his blood be shed! He that killeth shall surely be put to death!"

The killer's hand was shaking. He lifted the gun and fired a last shot into Howden's face from a foot away. The impact drove the man back across the narrow walkway and toppled him into the water at the foot of the pier.

The silence was profound.

A Cocktail Party

McAdams had never attended a political fund-raiser before. Like most cops, he didn't think very highly of politicians as a class. With the lone exception of Ellerby, they were empty suits. They made the policeman's job more difficult, either by their public bitching about "the lack of progress" or their tendency to take credit for whatever progress did come about. The idea of giving them money was laughable, even if he had any to give away, which he didn't. But Ellerby had invited him and Fallon in a way that made it clear it was important to him.

It was in the bar at Harding Park, after a rained out golf session. "It's for my reelection campaign. Eileen Moresby is hosting it at her home."

When McAdams began to protest, he interrupted. "I know it's not your thing. I hate them myself, and I'm the guest of honor. But I want you to come. You can meet a different class of people."

"That's precisely what I'm afraid of," said McAdams. He didn't add what he thought of that particular class.

Fallon was more serious. He was watching Ellerby closely and asked, "C'mon, Your Honor! There's something you're not telling us."

McAdams had a thought. "Isn't Eileen Moresby your companion at the opera? The one with the frontless dress?"

Ellerby held up his hands in a defensive manner. "OK! OK! First, let me say that I would actually like you to come. For my sake, so that I could have some real people to talk to. But the real pressure is coming from Eileen. She really wants to meet the two of you. When I told her about these golf games going on for years, she apparently thinks it's something she needs to know more about."

He paused. "Truthfully? She and I have –"

He broke off when both McAdams and Fallon began to grin. He was clearly embarrassed. " … have become … close. I think she wants to meet my friends. It's a woman kind of thing."

McAdams was startled by the sudden personal turn of the conversation. He badly wanted to ask, "Are we friends?" *There's a question for you! Funny how much I want to see how they would answer.* And then another thought occurred, one that literally jolted him. *I never asked Gonzo – or Freddie – that question.* A deep sadness settled over him, clearly picked up on by the other two men who were already hypersensitive to his moods. He cleared his throat and tried for a light tone.

"I'll be glad to come. Free drinks, I presume?"

"I'll be there," said Fallon.

Moresby's house occupied about one-third of a block of frontage near the top of Scott Street, guaranteeing spectacular views of the Bay and the city. He rang the bell and the door was answered by a young woman who for some reason looked very uncomfortable. She was wearing a traditional maid's kind of thing, a white apron of sorts. She said nothing, but just stood aside for him to enter. She had on a lot of makeup, but still was very pretty. Brown eyes, blond hair, tall and slender. But he had the distinct impression that she was afraid of him and he could not help wondering what particular crime she was covering up. It was a professional disability unique to cops dealing with nervous citizens. Among other things, it made it hard to get a date in a singles bar.

Sofia was terrified, but not for the reason that McAdams was attributing to her. *This was crazy! Every time I open the door, I expect to see one of them standing there... the quiet American, or Jose or one of those small dark men!*

McAdams walked into a living room about half-full of important looking men and women, all of them engaged in intent conversation with one another. Not your usual cocktail party conversations somehow. More intense, more like a negotiation than a friendly chat. *Maybe because they know they're about to be asked to give Ellerby some of their money.* Dress styles ranged from blue jeans to business suits for the men. The women were uniformly well dressed. *Strange. How all the women seem younger and better looking than the men with them.* Ellerby was on the far side of the room talking with the anchorwoman from one of the news channels.

A woman approached him and held out her hand. "I'm Eileen Moresby. Thank you for coming, Mr. ….?"

"McAdams. I'm part of the golf team."

Her expression instantly changed from professional hostess to something much more intimate, a visible curiosity. *Ellerby wasn't kidding. She really does want to meet us.* "Mac! I'm so glad you could come. Now I know what I'm competing against on Wednesday evenings!"

Before he could think of a reply, she turned to greet another couple just coming into the room. She gave his forearm a squeeze and promised, "I'll catch you after the speeches. Please don't leave before we can become better acquainted. And Fallon too!"

He watched her move around the room talking with people, never for more than two or three minutes and then moving on. She looked different than the gossip column pictures, just as beautiful but more human. He guessed her to be about Ellerby's age and he was pleased to see some wrinkles at the corners of her eyes. She moved in an assured way that reminded him of an athlete, maybe a dancer. She was completely at ease, talking, listening and laughing in about equal amounts.

"She's good, isn't she?"

The question startled him. He turned to his left to find the woman who had opened the door. Like him, she was watching Moresby work the room. She'd taken off the apron and was wearing a simple outfit with black slacks and a plain white shirt. No visible jewelry. She was holding a glass of white wine and switched her gaze from Moresby to him, studying him quite closely without any pretense. His first reaction was a very slight indignation, quickly displaced by discomfort for having been caught staring at Eileen Moresby.

He settled for a neutral tone. "She does seem very competent. I wonder where one learns that sort of thing?"

"How do you say? Necessity is the –"

"Mother of invention," he finished, turning to look much more closely at this woman who seemed not to fit into any convenient category. "My name is McAdams … Mac to most people."

When she was silent, he prodded her, "What's yours?"

She jumped. "I'm sorry. I was still thinking of your question … how one adapts to new situations. My name? It's … Anna."

The verbal hesitation was curious, reinforcing his first generalized suspicion that he tried to suppress. *Damn! I wish I could shut off this cop attitude. Just talk to an ordinary person without trying to match them up with a wanted poster. Well, maybe not so ordinary.* She was distinctly better looking than most, although she gave the distinct impression of a woman who was doing her best to look otherwise. She had wound her obviously dyed blond hair into a severe bun, offset on one side of her head and had on too much makeup, badly applied. Her clothes seemed over-large and mannish. Overall, the effect was to suggest a Hollywood starlet trying to act the role of a frumpy German housewife.

She surprised him again. "You're a cop, aren't you?"

"Am I that transparent?" The comeback was obvious. "And you're a maid? Right?"

She smiled as if pleased with his question. "Actually, Ellerby told me about you. As for me, today I'm a maid. Pressed into service for the fund-raiser."

"Maybe I've watched too much British TV, but you don't look much like a maid."

"Actually, I'm a volunteer. Trying to help Eileen out while I'm visiting."

He was picking up a faint accent, barely there. "You're living here?"

It was so quick that he thought he imagined it, but for the briefest second, she looked frightened. And she clearly was thinking hard about how to answer the innocuous question, maybe just to keep the witty repartee flowing.

"Eileen has been very gracious. Otherwise I'd be camped out with the other poor tourists."

He saw Fallon come into the room and wave at him. She asked, "Who's that?"

"His name is Fallon." After a pause, he added quite deliberately, "He's a friend." *Such a simple phrase. I wonder what it really means?*

But Anna hugged herself and seemed to shrink. As soon as Fallon started toward them, she left, simply turning away and walking quickly with her head down, toward the door on the far side of the room.

She's guilty of something. But interesting as hell.

He could not know that it was fear that propelled her, not guilt. The name *Fallon* was imprinted on her memory. First, because that was the name of the owner of the shipping company that owned the freighter that brought her on the last leg of her trip to San Francisco Bay. And she overheard one of the seamen refer to the younger American as *Mr. Fallon.* She had never seen the man who waved at McAdams before, but the name by itself was enough to drive her from the room, fear at her heels.

The fear and the haste it triggered narrowed her focus to her immediate objective -- the door on the far side of the room -- so she failed to notice the small dark man in the doorway to the kitchen as she went by, almost running.

Tonight the man was working as Dominick Fallon's driver. The parking valet took the car from him when he dropped Fallon at the front door, so he had ducked into the kitchen for coffee. If Anna had looked, she might have recognized him as the minder who stood by the SUV outside of the North Beach Victorian the night she ran.

That's the puta! She's done something to her hair, but that's her! He dumped the coffee and left by the back door, cell phone in hand. Once outside, he dialed a number and left a simple message: "The girl you're looking for. I know where she is." He went looking for the car, hoping Fallon would not stay long. His waiting time passed quickly. He spent some of that time speculating about what he might do with the ten-thousand dollar reward Jose had offered to the man that found the woman called Sofia, but those speculations inevitably merged with his lurid visualizations of various things that might be done to the woman when they took her.

She will not be so pretty when they finish.
The thought did not bother him.

Conversation with the Hostess

The speeches were short and predictable, testimonials for Ellerby followed by his polished response. McAdams was faintly surprised by the real sense of hope that seemed to pervade the gathering, apparently motivated by the belief that meaningful change could be brought about within the existing political system. *Providing, of course, that the right people are elected.*

The exodus was a long drawn-out affair, the room emptying gradually, leaving pairs and trios still in heavy conversation. Apparently, some of the movers and shakers viewed this as the time for an extended unofficial caucus, the time to sell a particular idea to a particular person. They moved in a few inches closer, smiled less and lowered their voices.

McAdams was standing talking with Fallon when Eileen Moresby came over.

"Gentlemen. I'm sorry to leave you stranded."

Fallon responded for them. "No problem. It was interesting for me to see our Mayor in this light. And some of your guests are quite charming." He emphasized the word "some" very slightly and McAdams was pleased that she smiled at the inflection. When she looked at him inquiringly, he said, "I enjoyed talking with Anna, the volunteer working the door."

She stared at him sharply, as though expecting his expression to be at odds with the words. Finally, she merely said, "Yes, Anna is interesting, isn't she?" Again, he thought he could hear the faintest hint of an accent but could not place it.

He thought about what he had heard of this woman. *Here for the last year or so. From somewhere outside the U.S. Mexico, according to some of the rumors. Lots of money stemming from a major divorce settlement from some prominent foreign individual with dubious sources of income. Patron of the arts. Often seen in public with prominent figures. No known long-term relationships or personal scandals. Slowly and steadily built a niche within San Francisco society. Connected.*

"Shouldn't you be saying goodnight to your guests?"

"Edgar is doing that. I've got him stationed at the door." She stared off in that direction, biting her lower lip as if trying to remember something important. "I told him that I'd send one of you to keep him company. Do you mind, Mr. Fallon ... Dominick?"

Fallon seemed amused. "Not at all. I'll hold the hat out while he shakes their hands." He strolled away, detouring to pick up a glass of wine from the bar.

They watched him walk away, being careful not to look at one another. The silence stretched long enough to be awkward. *She's leading up to something. And it's not cocktail party chatter.*

"Mac. What if ... "

She reminded him of his ex-wife in the latter and declining days of their marriage; the interlude between 'trying to work it out' and 'I give up'. Part of it was the sentence fragments that never went anywhere. The other part was the look of uncertainty; the fear that a comment or question would open up a new front in their long running war of attrition.

She took a deep breath and he could trace the impact of sudden resolution as it transmitted itself from the brain to her body. She stood straighter and the words came out without hesitation.

"If I suspected – just suspected, without any proof – that a crime, a serious crime, was about to happen, could I tell that to the police without getting myself involved?"

"Theoretically, yes. Practically, I'm less sure."

Not surprisingly, she seemed troubled by the equivocation. Her shoulders slumped and she frowned.

He went on. "We get lots of calls from citizens to warn us of something bad that's going to happen. Frankly, most of them are false alarms or crank calls. If you want to get real attention, you have to tell us how you happen to know about this bad thing.... Provide some plausible context.

Usually, to do that, you have to give up something about yourself. If a caller says 'I think my neighbor robs banks', we don't get very excited. But if the caller says, 'I overheard my husband talking to his ex-con brother-in-law about robbing the downtown branch', then we'll take a hard look."

She was still biting her lip, clearly troubled. He tried again.

"Look. There's a simpler way." He gestured toward the front door, where Ellerby was shaking hands with departing guests. "You know the mayor. Use that. Tell him what you're worried about. He can tell the Police Commissioner who will tell the Police Chief who will tell the Chief of Detectives … who will probably tell me to go check it out. And no one except the Mayor will know that it was you who started the snowball rolling downhill."

Her expression did not change. She said, "I can't."

He asked, "Can I ask what you're afraid of? Publicity? Some kind of blowback? What?"

But she had changed back to the textbook hostess, shedding the uncertainty and obvious concern. With professional briskness, she said, "It's just a hypothetical question. Somebody told me – I think it was your Police Chief at a party last week – that most crimes are solved by a tip. I'm just curious how it works."

She patted him on the arm. "Thanks for coming. I'm so glad to have met you." With that, she walked off toward the front door.

She's lying. And she's scared. McAdams had seen the combination many times. In his experience, the pressure could not be contained. *I think I will be seeing Ms. Moresby again, and before very long.*

Fallon offered to drop him off, seeming to want to pick up their conversation. As they stood out on Scott Street waiting for the driver, Fallon asked him, "Our hostess was quite eager to talk with you without me around. What did she want?"

Later, McAdams would wonder why he lied. "Not much. What the PD thinks of Ellerby, that kind of stuff."

Fallon looked skeptical, clearly unsatisfied with the answer. *Am I just a bad liar? Or does he really care that much about what Eileen Moresby said to me?*

His internal debate was cut off by his cell phone. He looked at the caller ID and shrugged at Fallon. "I have to take this."

The call was brief. "I have to go. They've fished a body out of the Bay."

Fallon grinned. "I have to admit that's a really good exit line. OK, see you on Wednesday. I've got some new clubs that I'm eager to try out."

McAdams was already headed down the street, but said over his shoulder, "Hope does spring eternal, doesn't it? At least in golf."

Stilled Prophets

McAdams got out of the cab when they ran into the pair of panda cars blockading the street and walked the thirty or forty yards to the knot of people clustered around something lying at the waterline.

A floodlight was being set up. But for the moment, the form was a shapeless bundle. It could have been a pile of wet rags thrown together, or a bag of somebody's yard trash fallen from an overloaded pickup. Then the light came on and McAdams saw the trouser leg with the satin stripe and the shoe with the sole coming off, exposing a bare foot.

"Shit!"

An enormous sadness descended on him, a gray weight that made him conscious of the enormous effort required for each step to bring him to the edge of the lighted circle. *That's good, isn't it? If depression is the inability to feel, to experience emotions, then maybe I'm not so depressed.* The irony was obvious, but he shunted the thoughts away for a later time.

"You know him?" One of the uniformed cops asked.

"Yeah, I do. His name is Harry Howden. One of our more colorful homeless types. Usually hangs out in the Tenderloin." He listened to himself and thought, *Harry deserves more than that.* So he added, "He was a prophet, just ahead of his time." *That's probably as close to a eulogy as Harry's gonna get.*

Finally, he added, "He was harmless." *Not what you would usually say about a prophet.*

"Not to somebody. He's been shot three times, the last one between the eyes from about a foot away."

"When? What do we know?" Even as he asked, he could feel the sadness becoming anger and knew that – for him – the killings were becoming personal, a threat to the detachment that homicide cops must cloak themselves in.

A plainclothes cop heard the questions and joined them. His name was Scanlon. McAdams knew him slightly. *A transfer from Vice a couple of years ago. OK, I think.* Scanlon was seriously overweight. Maybe that's why he was dressed like he was coming from the gym; jeans and a hooded sweatshirt with his badge stuck on the front. He waved the uniform away.

"When? Maybe two, three hours ago." He pointed up the street, apparently indicating a truck, one of those mobile food wagons that service construction sites. "The driver parks there at night. He says he saw this guy – Howden? – go by him about nine o'clock, headed this direction. He was alone, talking to himself. Crazy preacher kind of spooky stuff, the guy said."

"He tended to see things the rest of us couldn't and he wanted to warn us." *Why do I feel this need to defend Howden?*

"Yeah, whatever." Scanlon took a half step back and looked closely at McAdams, like someone having second thoughts about someone he'd just met. "You asked 'what do we know?'. Quite a bit, I think. You OK? You wanna walk through it?"

My reputation precedes me, I think. 'Be careful with Mac. He's still pretty shaky.' Pretty soon, they'll be confiscating my belt and shoelaces before they tell me the details of a crime scene.

He nodded. "Yeah, I would. I'm supposed to be a homicide detective in my spare time."

Scanlon became a tour guide.

"A couple of joggers – they're over there with the uniforms – saw the body in the water about an hour ago, called 911." He pointed at the pier that was about thirty feet away and about ten feet above the water level at that point. "He got shot up there, fell off the pier. Dead before he hit the water."

"And you know all that because …?"

Scanlon led him back up the bank to the sidewalk and then to the pier, really a covered shed with an open walkway around its perimeter, projecting maybe sixty or seventy yards into the Bay. A side door into the shed was standing open.

"We figure he walked in the door, met the killer, got shot and fell back into the water."

McAdams began, "That's a lot –", but Scanlon interrupted. "He – your homeless guy -- has a key to the door; it was in his pocket." He pointed to the planking just inside and outside the door, to a series of dark spots circled in some kind of neon chalk. "Blood, still slightly wet."

McAdams said, mostly to himself, "So the killer was waiting inside …"

"We think so." He indicated a single small crate, about twenty feet from the door. "A handy place to sit and wait. It looks like an ambush to me."

"So he had a key too?"

"Maybe. But the shed is open at the far end. It's possible to come in that way, up a ladder from the Bay. You'd need a boat."

"Any idea what Howden was doing here? It's pretty far from his daytime hangouts." But he thought he knew the answer.

He followed Scanlon toward the end of the pier. It was quite dark, the only light coming from the open door behind them and from the uncovered end of the pier. Scanlon switched on a small flashlight. When they reached the end, Scanlon used his flashlight for a pointer. The small enclosed space had three items in it – a little red wagon piled high with goods, a ratty sleeping bag, and a King James bible. Crime scene tape was across the entrance.

"That's Howden's stuff," McAdams said. "Looks like he found a home."

As they turned to leave, a pair of portable floodlights came on at the other end of the shed, revealing a mostly bare interior. A few boxes and what looked like small piles of debris dotted the plank floor along both sides. Both sides were lined with clusters of barrels against the walls.

Halfway to the end, near the centerline of the pier, a large red spike was sticking up from the flooring. McAdams knelt for a close look. It wasn't a spike, strictly speaking. It was a heel from a woman's high-heeled shoe, at least four inches long and covered with a neon red fabric that was torn where it had wedged itself in the crevice between two of the twelve-inch planks.

Scanlon took a piece of chalk from the pocket of his hoodie and drew a crude circle around the heel. "Could be something. Can't quite picture our killer in four-inch heels, though. More likely it's been here for years."

But McAdams was hearing Harry Howden's voice. Not the exact phrasing, but the booming tones and the language. "Zombies ... Whores coming up from the sea ... "

Harry's visions got him killed. He was struck by the thought that followed. *Just like the ancient martyrs, prophets who pointed out unpopular realities.* He tried to remember the bible stories from his long ago youth and a jumble of nouns ran through his mind – Sodom and Gommorah, Nineveh, Jonah, Lot. In the end, he gave up on the specifics, but it's how he wanted to remember Howden.

I hope Harry had a chance to see himself in that role before the lights went out.

He walked back to the bayside end of the shed, looking out at the lights on the Bay Bridge and, in the distance, the lights of Oakland. Closer in, there were the masthead lights of the half-dozen freighters waiting to either load or unload cargo at the Oakland terminals.

But he did not see them. For the first time in months, he was focusing on a smoldering anger that was slowly building within him, stoked by his long dormant awareness of the self-destructive cycle that he had come to accept. Later, he would recognize it as a turning point.

Gonzo. Freddie. Howden. He's killing people that I know, that I care about, that have depended on me in some way. That son of a bitch!

Later, he would recall and wonder at his use of the singular pronoun 'he"; at his assumption that the killings were linked. He did not know it, but it was as if he had designated himself as the avenging agent, a being evoked by Howden's dying curse: "He that killeth shall surely be put to death!"

Divided Loyalties

McAdams could not stop thinking about Ellerby. Freddie's last words in her too-short lifetime were, "The killer? It's your golf part--". McAdams was sitting three feet away from that very person at that moment, the same moment that Freddie was bludgeoned to death.

McAdams did not share that quote with the detectives who asked him about the call. It was a calculated omission and at the time he couldn't explain – even to himself – why he withheld essential information. When he started to think about it, his first excuse was that he wanted to understand it better. *What did she mean? Was it merely the start of some semi-sarcastic dig at him for golfing when he was supposed to be working? Or for hanging out with the Mayor?* He didn't think so. There was too much urgency, even a hint of breathlessness, in the phrase; like somebody about to make a major and unexpected announcement.

All the more reason to tell the rest of the team. What's wrong with you?

He invented other excuses for himself; nothing that would exonerate him in a departmental inquiry, but nevertheless real. He entertained himself by imagining the reaction within the Division if he announced. "Freddie said the mayor is a killer". The investigation would be hopelessly mired in politics before it got off the ground. And, in the end, Ellerby would skate by.

Half-a-dozen detectives were working the case. Murphy had assigned his number two – a twenty-year vet named Slater – to lead the investigation. McAdams knew him to be thorough and competent but rule-bound. He was moving up through the management hierarchy and couldn't afford to make the kind of morally ambiguous choices that street cops were confronted with every day. *If Ellerby's name pops up, Slater will instinctively look for ways to keep it quiet.*

Still, he felt disloyal. It took a while before his subconscious got through to him and even then he had trouble accepting the real reason for his silence. *I want to do this myself. For Gonzo and Freddie.*

Consciously, he knew this was stupid. Effective police work requires manpower, logistics, collaboration, networks -- all of the organizational fluff that can become deadweight bureaucracy but, when it works, puts the right people away. The lone wolf "rogue" cop is fodder for Hollywood, especially in high-profile cases like this one.

His other problem was his obsession, the one that made no sense and he could not share. *Jane Doe, Desmond, Gonzo and Freddie were all killed by the same person ... and Howden.*

It was crazy. There was nothing to link them except that Gonzo and Freddie were both working the Jane Doe case and Desmond had made a phone call to him just before he was killed. A call saying that he knew something about Jane Doe.

His first line of inquiry was obvious. He asked Murphy, "Freddie was off on her own for two days. She said that you had her working on some stuff for you. Dull stuff. What kind of stuff?"

Murphy raised his substantial eyebrows. "That's interesting. I didn't see or talk to Freddie for at least the last week before she ... before that day. Whatever she was doing, it wasn't for me."

McAdams said, "We can track cell phones. You must know where she was when she called me ... when she got hit."

"Yeah, we supposedly can do all that, but it – and you know this – it involves cell towers and something called triangulation. As of yet, all we can do is narrow it down to about two or three blocks on the Oakland waterfront. It's an area popular with street corner prostitutes, so we think she was meeting with an informant on the Jane Doe case."

She said she'd found one of the street girls who could ID Jane. Her name was Natasha. He pushed. "So who was she meeting? You must have –"

Murphy was clearly running out of patience. "The lab thinks they might be able to zero in on a specific location by using fragments of the phone that were imbedded … that were recovered when Freddie was found. They're working on it."

McAdams opened his mouth, but Murphy didn't let him even start the question. "Detective Lieutenant McAdams, how are you doing on Jane Doe? That's been open a long time, hasn't it?"

So I'm on my own and back to basics, the old fashioned stuff. For the next five days, he tracked Ellerby at odd intervals during the day. He couldn't manage a lot of time for surveillance, but Ellerby was pretty predictable. He left his home about eight in the morning, went to City Hall and from there to meetings with various city officials, the kind of stuff that mayors do in big cities. Interestingly, he went to Eileen Moresby's home on two of those five evenings, but left before ten to return home. As far as McAdams could tell, Ellerby did not meet any sinister or even questionable characters.

It was tough to stake out Moresby's place. PG&E was doing some underground cabling work on Scott, closing off one lane and leaving some space for him to park up against their equipment, but within sight of Moresby's entrance. The foreman came by to roust him, but he just showed the guy his badge and told him he'd bring a bag of doughnuts along on his next trip. The guy asked for half glazed and half plain.

Ellerby had just gone into Moresby's front door, ringing the bell just like any other friend or neighbor. She greeted him with a near kiss on the cheek, standard San Francisco protocol among the leisure classes. As usual, he arrived about eight in the evening and, if history was a predictor, he would stay for a couple of hours and then go home. McAdams was tempted to quit for the day, assume that Ellerby would stay with past patterns. *I need a team for 24/7 coverage, wiretaps, … What did Freddie find? Why is she dead? What's Ellerby got to do with this?*

139

Think about something else! He pushed the questions and the rising doubts that went with them into some less active part of his brain, trying instead to focus on basic surveillance principles. He knew the territory, one of the city's prized neighborhoods with its multi-million dollar homes, parks, private schools and chic restaurants. Not the kind of place where you see a lot of plainclothes types conducting stakeouts. At eight o'clock, there was still enough light to pick out the features of the dog-walkers and other pedestrians, but none of them went into the Moresby house.

He used his cell phone to start to scroll through his email messages, his eyes flicking back to the front door at frequent intervals. Most of the emails were departmental announcements, the kind of trivia that used to be pinned to overflowing bulletin boards that nobody paid attention to. Like the teenagers, he now relied on texting when he wanted to get somebody's attention.

Then, as if to emphasize that the new technologies were no substitute for primitive human instincts, something in the environment caused a distinct *Ping!* to sound in his brain.

Damsels in Distress

He scanned the street scene and picked it up immediately. Two large black SUV's were driving very slowly past Moresby's house, a two-vehicle caravan. The 'ping' was activated because it was their second pass within the last three minutes. They double-parked just around the corner on Jackson, a form of vehicular arrogance that suggested authority. *Somebody from the Mayor's office? Security? Airport limos? Maybe there's somebody important – either already here or about to arrive?*

He wished for a real camera with a long lens. Something more than his cell phone. The plates were not readable from where he was, nor could he see any details of whoever was inside. *Reconnaissance time, on foot.* He retrieved the hooded black sweatshirt with the huge orange Giants logo from his trunk and slipped it on. He might look a little sinister, especially in this neighborhood, but Ellerby couldn't identify him from five feet away if he should happen to come out of the house. He made sure his phone's camera was selected and headed for the corner.

At the same time, inside Moresby's home, Sofia was also dressing for an outing. She had tried what she thought of as a normal life – shopping, going to movies, being a tourist – living in the daytime in an open society. It didn't mitigate the fear. Even after all this time, the possibilities lurked at the margins of Sofia's day, shadows that pulsated with a non-specific menace. But the worst was the nighttime, when she was alone, awaiting sleep that would not come. Now she stayed inside. The only exception she permitted herself was a nightly walk. An hour in randomly chosen directions. Since Moresby's house was at the top of one of San Francisco's seven hills, she was assured of decent exercise; the last bit was guaranteed to be uphill.

Her outfit was the same each time. Sneakers, slacks, sweater and a mid-length black windbreaker with a big collar that she turned up. Combined with the scarf she tied around her hair and the sunglasses, she was as anonymous as possible. Eileen said, "You're either a Hollywood starlet trying to sneak past the press into a rehab program, or a Saudi princess trying to go Western without offending the sheik."

It was a bit earlier than usual, but she wanted to give Ellerby and Moresby some space. She waved at them as she passed by the arched entry to the living room. They were sitting as usual, on opposite sides of the unlit fireplace. They each had a glass of wine and looked … content, maybe? Like an old married couple?

McAdams was about a hundred feet from the doorway when the woman came out. His first reaction was "Oh shit!" but then he realized that it wasn't Moresby. In any case, she started walking the other way, so they wouldn't cross paths. Something about her was familiar and, when she turned at the corner and he glimpsed a profile, he remembered the maid/volunteer from Ellerby's fundraiser. Anna? The woman of mystery.

Then it got weird.

The two rear doors on each of the two black SUV's opened simultaneously and two men got out of each vehicle. They all looked alike, dark with dark suits and about the same size. The precision with which the doors opened and the uniform appearance of the men made McAdams think *it's the goddam Secret Service.* That thought disappeared when they began running, trailed closely by the SUVs.

Anna, or whoever she was, was clearly their target and she knew it. She was already in an all-out sprint. And running directly at him, about thirty yards ahead of the quartet that was obviously in pursuit. McAdams stood in the middle of the sidewalk directly in front of Moresby's house staring at the scene and trying to decide what to do.

Cop instincts helped. First, he took a picture of the oncoming runners. When he looked at it later, he was impressed – as always – with the quality of amateur photos taken – for god's sake – on an instrument that was supposed to be a phone. Everybody was in motion, but there was little blurring, thanks to it being a head-on shot of running figures.

The faces of the two men at the rear were obscured by those in front, but he got excellent shots of the woman and two of the men. Her sunglasses were gone and the fear clearly showed in her eyes. He doubted if she even saw him.

Then he dialed 911. Knowing he wouldn't have time for a long explanation, he put the phone on "speaker" and shoved it in the front pocket of his hoodie. The dispatcher would have to work it out. Or not.

He tried to gauge the relative speeds of the runners. He figured that she might have fifty or sixty yards before they caught up. But even as she flashed by him unseeing and he was making the calculation, she stumbled, catching a foot on a part of the sidewalk pushed up by one of the trees that made the neighborhood so inviting. She sprawled face first.

He heard the voice of the 911 operator. He said loudly, hoping it got through, "Scott and Pacific. 207 in process! Send units!" He reached for his badge but realized it was still in his sport coat, back in the car. Somehow, he didn't think these guys would be influenced much if he flashed it. They were running in a fairly tight bunch, focused on the fleeing woman. The two SUV's were maintaining position behind them. He stepped to the extreme edge of the sidewalk, trying to look like a scared civilian.

It reminded him of high school football. He wasn't that good, so the coach used him on "special teams". His assignment was to throw himself at the wedge of blockers that formed in front of the kickoff returner. So he did.

The impact was considerable. He hit the front two with what the coach used to call his half-assed cross-body block. The two in back slammed into the falling bodies, but one of them stayed on his feet. McAdams was on top of two of the men and another one was sitting up shaking his head. The guy still standing was pulling on the woman's arm, trying to drag her to her feet. She was having trouble standing up.

He scrambled to his feet, registering that his left knee was not working like it was supposed to.

Events moved incredibly fast. But, for McAdams, it unfolded in slow motion. The woman's scarf was pulled down -- she was clearly the one from the cocktail party – and she was being pulled wild-eyed to her feet by her captor. He wrapped her in a face-to-face embrace, her arms locked to her side, and backed toward the open rear door of the nearest black SUV, dragging her along. They looked like a couple in the last stages of a marathon dance contest. Then she went on offense. McAdams watched with admiration as she kneed him in the groin with considerable force and then stepped back to kick him in the face when he crumpled onto the sidewalk. It was not your usual amateurish kicking motion, the kind of poking effort a young girl would use in her first soccer lesson. This was applied kinetics. She pivoted on her left foot, bringing her right leg around, hips and shoulders turning to add force, striking with the side of her foot and following through, leaving a faint spray of blood in the air from his smashed nose.

He turned back to the other three. There was a lot of cursing in Spanish coming from the two of them scrambling into the second SUV. He ignored them, turning to the one still in play.

The last of the dark men was ten feet away, bent over with his hands on his knees, but looking first at the woman and then at McAdams with a disgusted expression, as though trying to decide what to do about them. When he stood up, McAdams knew he'd made up his mind.

He started to say, "I'm a police …", but stopped cold when the man reached behind him and drew a large black handgun from beneath his coat. McAdams was impressed that the suit coat was still buttoned, despite the running and fighting. He thought about his own weapon, still on his belt with the safety strap securing it. He watched the man smile and raise his pistol, holding it straight out with one hand and pointed directly at McAdams' forehead.

Time slowed and his vision narrowed to a tunnel with only the muzzle of the gun at one end. He was vaguely aware of sirens getting closer and the sound of a door opening and closing. He was unaware of his reflexive movements, reaching for his gun and holding out his other hand to deflect the certain bullet. The one crystal clear and overwhelmingly sad thought was, *Gonzo and Freddie would have backed me up.* He closed his eyes.

He heard the shot, then another. When he opened his eyes, time was running at normal speed. Eileen Moresby was standing in her doorway in a classic shooter's stance, holding a pistol in the recommended two handed grip, squeezing off carefully spaced and aimed shots. Ellerby was standing behind her, open-mouthed, holding his cell phone.

The two SUVs roared away, one of them with a shattered rear window, leaving the lone man lying on the sidewalk in a fetal position with blood streaming from his nose and McAdams standing with a puzzled expression, wondering why he was alive.

The woman was a hundred yards away, disappearing at a dead run around the corner of the next block.

Debrief

The uniforms moved them all inside Moresby's house. They put the guy with sore balls and a smashed-in nose in handcuffs in the back of a squad car. They put out high-priority APB's on the woman and the SUVs based on what McAdams told them. The street cops were clearly nervous about the mayor's presence, so they waited for the suits to arrive.

Murphy showed up along with what seemed to be half of the Commissioner's staff, not so surprising given that the mayor was involved. He pulled McAdams aside, saying, "Mac, please tell me that you being in the middle of this is all a big coincidence. Nothing to do with homicide … especially nothing to do with Freddie or Gonzo."

He lied shamelessly, noting that it was getting easier. "It's pure coincidence. I was in the neighborhood to call on a friend and got caught in the middle."

When Murphy asked, his skepticism apparent, "What friend?" he did the best he could on short notice.

"Actually, I wanted to talk with Moresby. Last time I saw her, she had asked me some questions that I promised her I'd get answers for. It seemed like a good time." *That's about as flimsy as it gets.* He looked at Moresby as he recited his lines for Murphy, hoping she would remember the context and back him up.

To his surprise, she stepped in immediately, as if they had rehearsed their alibis. "That's right, Captain Murphy. I met him here at a party for the Mayor last week and asked McAdams to come back." He relaxed, but then she went beyond the facts. "In fact, I asked him to come here this evening. He was a little early, which was lucky for us."

Luckily, Murphy was not looking at Ellerby, whose expression was registering serious doubt about what he was hearing.

What the hell? Why does she see a need to keep me out of trouble? He looked at Ellerby, but he just shrugged and turned away, paying no attention to any of them.

Murphy turned to her. "And the gun? Witnesses tell me you fired five or six shots."

"It's a Beretta 9 millimeter. And yes, it's legally registered to me. And I fired four shots."

"Why?"

She looked at him with the expression a kindergarten teacher might use on a slow learner at the end of a really long day. "I heard the shouting. Screaming really. I opened the door and saw him" – she pointed at McAdams – "standing there. The other man pulled out this big gun and pointed it at him. I keep the Beretta at the front door, so I grabbed it and started shooting." She paused, and then added, "There wasn't much thinking involved in it, actually."

One of the uniforms standing at the edge of the room cleared his throat. When Murphy looked at him, he said, "We think two rounds hit the sidewalk, one went into the rear window of the SUV. We can't find the other one."

She said, "If it went where I aimed, it's at the bottom of the Bay, about halfway to Angel Island."

Murphy asked mildly, "Are you experienced with handguns, Ms. Moresby?"

McAdams remembered the shooter's stance, the two-handed grip and the deliberate spacing of her shots. But she smiled sweetly and said, "Heavens, no! They make so much noise! I just hoped it would scare them!" She did everything but bat her eyes at the Captain.

Murphy looked decidedly unhappy. McAdams empathized. A near kidnapping and gun battle in Pacific Heights with the Mayor looking on were not the kind of news that the city fathers wanted in the headlines.

Murphy asked the question that McAdams was waiting for. "Who was the woman? The one they were chasing?"

Moresby looked at Ellerby as if to seek permission before she answered. "Her name is Anna Rubin. She's a friend of a friend."

"She's staying here?"

"Just until she finds her own place."

"Who's your friend? The one that sent her to you."

"We're not exactly close. She's a woman I met on an Alaskan cruise two years ago. We got along well, but we haven't stayed in touch. I didn't hear from her until a few weeks ago when she called and asked me if I could help Anna get settled. I said 'sure'."

Murphy had pulled out a notebook and was ready to write. He asked, "This woman who referred Anna, what's her name and how can we find her?"

Moresby's eyes looked upward to the right, the classic expression of someone trying hard to recall an obscure memory. "She called herself JJ, some kind of childhood nickname. The last name was something like Hawkins, or Hoskins, maybe Dawkins. She said she was living in Italy, but I'm pretty sure she was an American."

McAdams almost laughed out loud. *If I was a suspicious type, I would admire the way she just gave us a whole string of facts, not one of which would enable us to verify the supposed person named JJ. Then again, maybe she's telling the truth and I've just been a cop too long.*

Murphy seemed to have reached the same conclusion. He put away his pen and changed topics once more. "What do you know about Anna? Do you know of any reason that these men were trying to abduct her?"

Moresby looked quizzical. "Abduct? Are you sure it wasn't just a purse snatching?"

McAdams thought. *Four goons in suits, two black SUV's staked out on the street. Purse snatching?* And Murphy didn't even bother to respond; he just kept staring at Moresby with raised eyebrows, his question hanging in the air between them.

She shrugged. "I don't know much. She says she's looking for a job in interior design and wants to stay on the West Coast. She hasn't been real communicative, to tell the truth."

McAdams was watching Ellerby. He had closed his phone and was listening intently to the Q&A between

Murphy and Moresby. His body language was telegraphing a serious amount of internal tension.

She went on, "As far as someone having a reason to carry her off, all I can tell you is that she was afraid of something. She didn't like going out. She even got nervous when guests would come to the house."

"Is there somewhere she might go? Other friends here in town? Favorite restaurants? Anything at all?"

For just an instant, her face clouded. "I don't think she has any friends." But she went on in a neutral tone that managed to convey that she was tired of talking about Anna Rubin. "I'm sorry. I've told you everything I know about Ms. Rubin. I have no idea where she might go."

That's not even close to the truth. McAdams recognized the fleeting expression that came and went. *That was fear. She's terrified. But for whom?*

Police Procedural

McAdams spent most of the rest of the day in and out of Murphy's office, trying to make sense of the information that was trickling in.

The one they had in custody had no ID on him and claimed that he spoke only Spanish. Even that was hard to understand because his nose was thoroughly smashed up by the woman's textbook soccer kick. McAdams could still visualize the satisfied expression on her face before she turned to resume running. The guy with the broken nose was being interrogated but so far had told them nothing.

The iPhone photo that he had snapped had clear shots of two other men who looked like cousins of the one in custody and of a white-faced, terrified Anna in an all-out sprint. They circulated that and the booking photos in the morning rosters but none of the men had been identified by mid-morning. The uniforms on the street were checking transient hotels and shelters for recently-arrived single young women looking for a place to sleep. The usual databases were trolled, but no Anna Rubin popped out.

The room she was using at Moresby's was checked out. It was surprisingly bare. There were a few articles of clothing, all of them apparently new with Nordstrom's or Saks labels on them. Some tourist maps of the area, but nothing personal other than a cosmetics case and a toothbrush. The detective who made the search said, "Whoever lived here either was dropped on the planet from a spaceship or did not want to be found."

The SUVs didn't turn up. There were hundreds of black SUVs running around the city and they didn't have the plate numbers. The involved vehicles were probably stashed in a private garage somewhere in the city.

The media was having a field day with the story, speculating about gangland shootings in Pacific Heights, the Mayor's questionable relationships, and the identity of the "beautiful young woman" being chased through the streets. For once, McAdams thought that the media might actually be understating the drama. The city was experiencing a mini crime wave, and the police were getting nowhere.

Then a street cop from the Oakland waterfront called in. His name was Tedoski and he'd just been handed the booking photo of the Latino they had locked up.

"I don't know his name, but I've seen him on the streets lately. I've heard him called Pepe, but that's it. The word is he's Mexican, here in town to set up a new pipeline for all the good stuff – weed, meth, skag, the designer pills. He's got some local contact and he brought some friends with him. The word is that they don't mind killing people who get in their way."

McAdams asked, "Do we have any idea who he's working for?"

"Yes and no. 'Yes' our theory is that he's hired out to whoever the local warlord is who's trying to take over the delivery system. And 'No', we don't know who that is."

McAdams repeated Tedoski's story to Murphy. Murphy took some notes and said, "We've got some formal and informal contacts between the Mexican Federales and our LA and SF departments. We'll see what they know about this guy and his friends. It may take a while."

McAdams said, "Send Rubin's picture along. Maybe she's tied up in the drug business too."

It was an automatic and cop-like reaction, but the strange and new feeling was his sudden realization that he was hoping it wasn't true.

Something else had changed, but he was slow to pick up on it. Until he found himself pawing through his desk drawers looking for the name of his contact in the narcotics division. *I'm not depressed.*

He accepted it, only briefly wondering why the black cloud was gone. Whether it was the absolute certainty that he was going to die when he was looking into the muzzle of the pistol or the exhilaration that transfused him when he launched his body into the four running men.

A day later, Anna Rubin was still missing. She wasn't wanted for any crime, so the pressure to find her was pretty low key. Her picture was posted on the bulletin boards and a cursory check had been made of the low-end hotels and shelters, but that was about it. Moresby had promised to call if she returned.

McAdams gave up on watching Ellerby for a couple of days and caught up on his other jobs. Part of the reason was his feeling that Anna Rubin could tell him more about Ellerby than he would learn by following him around town. That feeling seemed more like a leap of intuition than any rational deduction. He couldn't trace the source of that feeling other than his sense that she was wrapped up in some kind of household intrigue; that Rubin, Ellerby and Moresby were linked in some way that he needed to understand.

He replayed what he could remember about their cocktail party conversation. One phrase in particular came back to him. When he'd asked her if she lived there, she responded, "Eileen has been very gracious. Otherwise I'd be camped out with the other poor tourists."

Where do poor tourists stay? Did she mean 'camped out' literally? He thought about it for a few seconds. Then he woke up his desktop computer and googled "hostels in San Francisco". The first site that he clicked on listed twenty-eight of them and displayed their locations on a map. *She's on foot and scared, needing to get off the streets. Let's start with the closest ones.* The majority of them were downtown, easily reachable, but two hostels were closer to Moresby's, one on Divisidero and the other at Fort Mason near Fisherman's Wharf.

He tried the Divisidero prospect first, on the grounds that she was running in that direction. As soon as he showed the receptionist his badge, the kid started a tirade about "the goddam Homeland Security" and the "erosion of civil liberties" and "overreaching Gestapo goons". McAdams finally got him to notice that he was just a San Francisco cop, but it was the "homicide" label on his business card that turned him into an active supporter. *The TV shows are good for something anyway.*

"Anna Rubin? Last couple of days?" He paged through an actual scruffy ledger, no computer screens for the poor tourists. "Nope, sorry." When McAdams described her as vividly as he could, the kid was even more emphatic. "We've only had three women in single rooms in that time. And I promise you they didn't look like that."

Fort Mason seemed more promising. It was a hodge-podge of old buildings with peeling paint, set off by itself. The hostel itself was a low-lying ex-barracks at the end of the main entrance road. He decided to try a less official approach, doing his best to impersonate a friendly uncle. "Hi. I'm looking for a guest of yours – Anna Rubin?" He was already turning away when the matronly looking woman behind the desk said, "Why, you just missed her. She said she was going to walk down to Fisherman's Wharf. She's only been gone five minutes."

Anna watched McAdams go into the reception area from about fifty yards away, at the edge of the green toward the community garden and the Bufano statue that she wanted to see. *It is the same man. The policeman from the cocktail party. And the one who saved me from Reboso's people. Who was about to be shot.* She pulled even further back into the trees that lined the green and watched. He came back out within a minute, looking at his car and obviously undecided. If he chose to walk to the Wharf, she'd have to find a better place to hide, and quickly. But he got back in his car to make the circuitous trip to the Wharf.

She was momentarily sad about leaving the hostel. She enjoyed the young tourists, so eager to see the sights, so transparently unworried. *Time to go, anyway. I'm much too visible, especially using the Rubin name. But where?*

She felt the weight of her shoulder bag. It contained everything she owned except for the few items she had left at Eileen's. Maybe that's why she had chosen the name Rubin, a Jewish name. Perhaps she felt some mystical sort of affinity for the generations of Russian Jews that were driven from their villages – shtetls – by the Cossacks, taking everything with them that they could carry. The irony was exquisite since she traced her ancestry back through the line of Cossacks, rather than the Jews they persecuted.

She thought of what she had in her bag. She did not know what it was, but she knew that it was important. It gave her ... what was the word that Grodin used ... "leverage". *But who do I approach? And where am I going to hide now?*

Then she smiled. *Of course! Remember where you are. This is America. Where do Americans go when they are in trouble and need help?*

Off Duty

McAdams canvassed Fisherman's Wharf for the next few hours; first by car, making two complete passes on every street that permitted cars, from Fort Mason to Van Ness, and three streets in from the Bay. Then he walked the rest of it, including the tourist madhouse that Pier 39 had transformed itself into. From a distance, he saw a half dozen possibilities, each of them a good-looking woman but not the one he was seeking. The last of them called him a pervert and threatened to call the cops.

He sat on a bench near the entrance to the ferry to Alcatraz and took a call from Murphy.

"Mac. I got a hit on Pepe. The Federal Police in Mexico know him. I talked to a Captain Ramon Alvarez in Mexico City. He says Pepe's a low-level all-purpose gofer for the Tijuana cartel. Works for one of the really bad guys there, name of Jose Torres."

"Does Alvarez know why Pepe's up here?"

"Nope. But he tells me that Pepe does whatever Torres tells him to do. In fact, they would very much like to talk to him about that very same question. They see him as a way to get at Torres. I promised we would share anything we get."

"What about Pepe? He said anything?"

"Nope. Same old story. He's more afraid of his colleagues than he is of us. And frankly, unless your Miss Anna Rubin turns up and files a complaint, there's not much we can do to him. American jurisprudence at its democratic best – No harm, no foul. We can probably deport him if we work at it."

Murphy asked, "Anything on your end?"

"Nothing yet." *Another lie. You'd think it would get easier.*

"OK, tell Slater if anything breaks. I've spent too much time on – "

McAdams didn't let him finish. He interrupted, his voice rising, "Slater. Why him? Does this have something to do with Freddie? Or Gonzo?"

"Damn it, Mac! Cease and desist! I'm sorry I mentioned Slater. And no, this does not – repeat, does not – have anything to do with either of them."

The line went dead. "Call ended" showed on his screen. Ten seconds later, the phone rang. It was Murphy again.

"One more thing. Ellerby called. He wanted to make sure you were OK. Very touching. And to let him know if we found Rubin. Says that Moresby is really concerned." He ended the call before McAdams could respond.

Ellerby's got my private number. If he wants to know how I am, he could call. So I think the real purpose of his call to Murphy is to find out about Rubin. I wonder what his interest is in her?

It was dark, well after nine. *Too many dead ends. Time to go home.*

McAdams' "home" was a strange place, even by San Francisco's Bohemian standards. His ex-wife couldn't stand it and he wondered if it wasn't a contributing factor to their divorce. Under the community property laws of California, she was entitled to half of it when they divorced. When he asked her if she wanted to keep it and buy out his half, she began laughing so uncontrollably that he thought it was hysteria, but gradually accepted that it was quite genuine unbridled amusement. He was glad, because – to him – it was truly the only home, in every sense of that misused word, that he had ever had or could ever want.

His home was the second floor of a two-story brick building occupying almost half of a short block on one of the little-used feeder streets into Mission Street. It dated from just after the 1906 fire and earthquake, so it was built to last with thick walls and vertical steel beams at regular intervals. Until ten years ago, the ground floor of the building was an automobile showroom. Today, it was carved up into four esoteric retail shops – an antiquarian bookstore, a costume shop, millinery store, and an establishment that sold used ball gowns and wedding dresses. Every time McAdams walked past them, he felt like he was in Victorian London. Between them, they had about ten customers a day.

His home was the entire second floor. It had been a garment factory for much of its existence and somehow had retained that feel through successive waves of gentrification. It was accessed from the street by a center stairway onto a small landing at the front of the building. His front door was thick oak, eight feet wide and ten feet tall, originally designed to enable large pieces of textile machinery to be brought in. Some past owner had installed a fairly elegant pulley system to make it easy to open the enormous door. Once inside, there were thick oak planks for flooring. They'd been sanded and finished several times after the place was converted to residential use, but they still showed irregularities and scars from their industrial legacy.

The interior was sheer empty space punctuated by the occasional vertical steel girder, a single room measuring fifty by one-hundred feet on the floor, with twenty-foot ceilings. There were no interior walls. It was like walking into an art gallery before it was stocked. When his ex-wife first saw it, she said, "Christ, Mac! It's like living in a airplane hangar!" The entire front wall – the one facing onto the street – was made up of translucent glass bricks, tending to make the space seem even larger, although one visitor felt as if she was underwater and having difficulty breathing. The back wall of ordinary brick had a long series of windows high up in the wall. Enormous skylights allowed even more light into the space.

Interior design was easy, tending toward whimsical. Everything except the bathroom and kitchen – furniture, art, closets, bookshelves, lighting – was freestanding and moveable. The living room was wherever the couch was, the bedroom where the bed sat, and so forth. By moving the furniture, he could remodel the house! The only real concession to normalcy was the bathroom. It was in the corner, concealed behind gigantic banners hanging from the ceiling.

It was dramatic. A couple of snobbish local magazines had featured it in their annual architectural reviews and one of the CEOs of a Silicon Valley IPO had offered him three times what it was worth on the open market. On the other hand, a psychiatrist and ex-friend of McAdams had used it in a Chronicle feature article dealing with agoraphobia – the fear of open spaces – in a way that made it sound sinister and unhealthy. In the couple of years since then, he hadn't had many visitors.

He had never analyzed why the space had such a calming effect on him. Perhaps it was a feeling akin to the perspective about one's place in the world that settles over a person when they see vast deserts or towering mountains or millions of stars on a clear night. Or something as simple as the security that comes with thick oak doors and plank floors.

He used it as a litmus test for possible relationships, believing that a woman's first reaction was as good a predictor of compatibility as any battery of psychosocial surveys or a computerized inventory of personality traits. *Pretty small sample size, however.* In the five years since his divorce, exactly three women had been through the door. Each of them said the same thing expressed in slightly different language: "Jeez, whyncha put some walls up?" One of them even bought him some folding screens with pastel Japanese designs to – as she put it – 'create some privacy'. None of the three women lasted. He gave the screens to the costume shop.

Quit fooling yourself. The problem isn't the psychic clash between the women and the physical space. It's you. It's the damn job.

At first, they blamed the long and irregular hours, with canceled dates and phone calls in the middle of the night. For a while, he was seeing a resident in neurosurgery who had the same scheduling problems. They saw each other about two hours a week and spent most of that time complaining about their respective schedules.

But the real problem, the one that eventually ended even the most promising relationships, the elephant in the living room, was the job. It consumed the relationship as well as him. He would look at a woman sleeping in his bed and imagine her as a corpse, another murder for him to solve. He could not feel affection for a woman without conjuring up vivid memories of sobbing husbands or wives who had killed their spouse – whom they genuinely loved – for some incredibly trivial reason. The morbidness eventually contaminated whatever good there was.

The neurosurgeon summed it up nicely on her way out the thick oaken door for the last time. "You're a homicide junky. And you're not going into rehab. Who wants to be married to a junky?"

His homecoming ritual did not vary. He flipped the switch by the front door that turned on half a dozen floor lamps scattered around the vast space. He went from the front entrance to the refrigerator, took a bottle of beer and walked directly to a chair placed in the precise center of the floor facing the translucent wall of glass. He did not know why, but it was important to him that the chair was centered within the room. He actually had measured and marked the spot with a tiny dab of paint. The chair was his single most expensive piece of furniture, high-backed and covered with a soft black leather material. When he sat down, put his feet up on the matching ottoman and reclined to the halfway point, the chair seemed to absorb him. He had tried meditation for a time, but found "the chair" – he always thought of it with quotes – to be a more effective therapy. Not therapy, more of an antidote to the toxicity of his daily routine.

So. Anna Rubin is out there somewhere. Where? Who is she and why does a Tijuana warlord want to kidnap – or kill – her? For that matter, who is Moresby? Sure as hell not your average Pacific Heights aging debutante! And what's Ellerby got to do with either of them?

He laughed at himself. *Sounds like I'm scripting a pilot for a new TV series ... or creating the ad program!*

He was halfway to the refrigerator to get his second beer when the door chimes rang. It had been so long since the last time that for a few seconds he thought that the ringtone on his cell phone had somehow been switched.

The center stairway had no gate, so whoever was pushing the bell was standing outside of his door on the landing. He picked up his Glock out of habit and looked through the peephole that he had installed through the door. Whoever it was stood well back from the door, so the fisheye lens gave him a very distorted view. He looked about the size of a six-year-old, but that was due to the lens. He was wearing an extra-large hoodie that kept his face in deep shadow and obscured his shape. McAdams couldn't tell if he was black or white, man or boy. His posture was curious, standing erect but with his head down and his arms held out from at his side as if signalling 'I am harmless'. He resembled a cowled medieval penitent seeking entry to the monastery. The sweatshirt said "San Francisco" in large letters and had a neon imprint of the Golden Gate bridge across the front.

Then he lifted his head, looking directly at McAdams, and raised his arms, allowing the baggy sleeves to slide down his arms so that his hands were visible. He held nothing, his palms forward, white against the shadows.

"Christ!"

McAdams opened the door and stared. Anna Rubin, whoever she was, smiled back at him.

"How symmetric. Last time, I opened the door for you." She looked at the gun dangling from his fingers. "Are you going to shoot me?"

And she walked past him, into the vast inner space.

An Improbable Sanctuary

Like everyone else, she stopped one step past the doorway, struck by the room. She tugged the hood of the sweatshirt down and looked left and then right, rotating just her head and neck as if she was trying to economize on motion.

"It's very odd, isn't it? When you go into a house, you expect space to contract, to get smaller, not bigger. Outside is big, without walls. Inside is small, with limits. You've done it exactly backwards."

He had been about to protest, to ask what she thought she was doing here, but her remark stopped him cold. Before he could think of a response, she went on. "Some people must find it disorienting."

He said, halfway to himself, "They usually say 'It seems so empty.'"

This is not the kind of conversation I should be having with a material witness to an attempted kidnapping.

She shook her head. "They're wrong. It's not that it's empty. It just doesn't provide the kind of boundaries or physical cues that some people need."

She keeps referring to 'some' people. I wonder how she views herself relative to 'them'?

"Ms. Rubin. I've been looking for you –"

"Yes, I know. I saw you going into the hostel at Fort Mason."

"But you shouldn't be here … at my house. This is not the proper –"

"But you said you were looking for me. And please call me Anna. I cannot think of myself as Ms. Rubin."

"I was – I am – looking for you. Lots of people seem to be looking for you. Including some that seem to want to hurt you. But we need to be talking about this at police headquarters, not here."

Wait a minute. I'm not that easy to find. Supposedly.

"How did you find me? They keep the addresses and phone numbers of cops out of public view."

"I asked Ellerby."

Ellerby?

His voice sounded harsher than he intended. "Why? What did he tell you?"

She ignored his first question. "That you would help me."

This conversation was being conducted while she wandered around and through the clusters of furniture that were scattered around the space, in the manner of a real estate agent sizing up a potential client's listing. He followed her, mostly talking to her back, his Glock still in his hand.

"Help you? Me? How? What is it that you want?"

The last question seemed to freeze her in place. She stopped, turned slowly, and looked at him as if she had been accosted by a panhandler and was considering whether or not to give him a dollar.

"What do I want? Such a complicated question."

It was the first predictable thing she had said since he opened the door. A transparent stall. He waited.

"To thank you, maybe? And apologize …?"

"For…?"

She picked out one of the two chairs at his kitchen table and sat down, putting her shoulder bag on the table in front of her. "Saving my life…. That's the 'thank you' part, not the 'apology' part."

"And the apology part?"

"For almost getting you killed."

The gun was a Smith & Wesson, 40 caliber. Very reliable weapon. The guy was holding it all wrong. Hot dog style, one hand, sideways. But he was six feet away, close enough to see the tattoos on his knuckles. He knew that he had me cold. And he was smiling.

He moved to take the other chair, hoping to disguise the slight shudder that went through him. The movement also reminded him of the twinge in his left knee, a residual from the collision with the four men. He became conscious of the pistol and placed it on the table in front of him, feeling like a poker player in a B-grade western movie.

"Ms. Rubin ... Anna ... Who are you? Where do you come from? Why were those men after you? Why did you come here, to me?

Really good interrogation technique, McAdams! Bombard them with a thousand questions and hope they'll confess due to sheer confusion!

She ignored all of them. "I've been reading your newspaper. The one you call 'the Chronicle'. It has many – how do you say – 'typos'. Not long ago, there was a story about a killing. A woman shot and thrown in your Bay. I was wondering... Did she have a tattoo of a butterfly on her ankle?"

The tattoo definitely was not in the public record! "Yes, she did. On her left ankle." After a pause, "Who was she? We'd like to know." After a pause, he added, "She deserves to have a name."

It was if a cloud passed over her face. She closed her eyes for one second and when she opened them, they shone with a wetness that wasn't there before. Then she asked an odd question, the anger barely perceptible: "Why do you care who she was?"

He sighed. *There are so many possible answers to that question.* In the end, he picked the most personal one. "Because I want to find the man who would do that and ask him *why*. Then I want to shoot him in the face."

Anna leaned forward over the table and stared into his eyes as if she would find something there that would tell her what to do next. Her eyes were a deep liquid brown and very large.

"Her name was Sasha." Then, in a very soft and toneless voice, she said, "She was a friend of mine."

He stood up, partly to get away from those eyes, but also because of his growing discomfort with his lack of professionalism. "Ms. Rubin – Anna -- We need to go – right now – to police headquarters. You need to make a statement – "

"No."

"You're a material witness in a murder –"

"No."

"You're being chased by –"

"No."

Each time, the 'no' was a flat, uninflected denial, somehow making it sound completely non-negotiable.

He sat back down. She smiled at her small victory. He asked, "Why not?"

She shrugged. "I am … illegal. I have no papers."

"I don't work for immigration. I'm interested only in who killed your Sasha…. And some other people that I knew."

"I think I believe you. But you are a policeman. You fill out forms and those forms are seen by others – reporters, other policemen, judges, politicians, immigration officials. Sooner or later, one of them will say 'This woman, Anna Rubin, why is she getting special treatment?' And I will be 'repatriated' – such a pretty-sounding word!"

He knew she was right. The chances that she could stay below the radar in a case like this were non-existent. He hated himself for saying it, but …

"I can arrest you now. Take you into custody."

"But that would not do you any good."

"Why not?"

"Two reasons. First, if I am arrested, I will tell you nothing. I will deny everything I have said up to this point. I have nothing to gain by cooperating with the police."

"I disagree. But what's your second reason?"

"I'll be dead. Those men will find me again. And the next time, there will be no American hero to rescue me from them. And they will not kill me in the same quick way that they killed Sasha."

Her voice softened and her eyes turned inward. "It will take a long time and be very messy."

I should tell her that we will protect her. But that would be a lie. How many times have eyewitnesses told me that they were afraid to testify … that the state was powerless to protect them against the human predators that lived among them? Worse, how many times has a public-spirited witness turned up dead after some well-meaning cop said, 'Don't worry. We'll protect you. Trust me.'?

His indecision was easy for Anna to see. She felt a small burst of sympathy for him when he said, "Anna. I can't just let you walk out of here."

"You don't have to."

He threw up his hands in frustration. "What am I missing? You say you won't go downtown! You won't cooperate! You say I can't arrest you! Is there an alternative that escaped me?"

"I want to stay here ... in this wonderful big room. I need a place to hide." She giggled. "In a house that has no walls ... no place to hide."

He stood up, but before he could even begin to protest, she said, "And I *will* cooperate, but only with you. And only here."

He sat back down, finally recognizing that this strange woman had come here with a detailed plan of action and that she was about to share it with him. *I'm not sure I want to hear this.*

"What makes you think that I will go along with this ... this ... scheme? I can't even begin to tell you how many laws and regulations I would be breaking if I did?"

"Again, I have two reasons to be hopeful."

He waited, trying to look as skeptical as he could.

"I think I know a great deal. About many crimes. About some important people. And I have ... documents... documents that will be of interest to your police."

"Give me a sample."

"I know who Sasha is and who killed her."

"I assume that. What else?"

"Narcotics. Prostitution. You're seeing more traffic, different players. I know why."

"How – "

"Enough. That's your sample."

"You said you had two reasons for thinking I would go along with your scheme to hide you and be your private confessor."

"Ellerby said that you would be … approachable. His words were, 'You can help him get what he wants.'"

Ellerby again.

"Did he say what that was? What I want?"

"He said something that I don't understand. He said 'Just say to him, 'Gonzo and Freddie.'"

Pulling on Strings

Just say to him, 'Gonzo and Freddie'.

He couldn't help it. His first thought was of the famous Marlon Brando line in the first Godfather movie. "I'm gonna make him an offer he can't refuse." That was followed immediately by, *What the hell kind of game is Ellerby playing?*

However, with those seven words from Ellerby, his decision to violate the law, departmental rules and his own professional standards was an easy one. He did not try to justify it with any high-minded inner rhetoric about being true to oneself; nor did he invoke the classic 'ends vs. means' arguments. He did not weigh the possible consequences or think very far ahead about the implications of becoming a vigilante with a badge.

They talked for the next hour, sitting at the kitchen table with his gun and her shoulder bag between them on the table. It was mostly her talking, with him asking questions and taking notes. At times, he lost track of whether he was listening to her or to his own thoughts.

How many hundreds of times have I done this? Wheedling facts and semi-confessions out of people who fall somewhere between being victims or their predators. People who aren't quite innocent, but don't deserve what's happened to them. Scared people.

This one is different. She doesn't have an ounce of trust in her. Smarter. And she's tough. Is she scared? I think so, but she hides it well.

And she's got an agenda that only she knows.

At the end of the hour, they had negotiated a working arrangement. He would provide her with a temporary sanctuary – his home – and she would share the information she had about criminal activities. The other major condition was unstated, but clearly understood: The information would be rationed. He would have to prove himself.

Good enough for now.

"OK, let's go back to square one. Who's Sasha?"

"Her name is Aleksandra Vorokov. Sasha is what you would call her nickname. She's from Vladivostock and she is ... was ... twenty-two years old." Her voice became softer, more frail, as she went on. McAdams barely heard her say, "She taught me to play the piano."

"How did she get here? To San Francisco?"

She continued talking as though she had not heard the question. "I was with her when she got the butterfly tattoo. She'd been drinking. Just a little. A sailor teased her. Said he'd pay for the tattoo."

"Anna. How did Sasha get to San Francisco?"

Her eyes flashed and she leaned forward across the table, her fists clenched. "You ask *how*. First, you must understand *why!*"

Her monologue about *why* ran for half an hour. It covered the history of the Soviet Union, the pent up desires of one-hundred and forty million Russians suddenly exposed to capitalism in its rawest form, the savage culture of an orphanage in a broken society, and the fantasies of two young girls who saw a way to change the trajectory of their lives.

They both knew that the unfolding story was as much about Anna as it was about Sasha. He did not ask questions nor interrupt. He listened, alternating between anger at a system that trashed its people and grudging admiration for the two women who defied it. When she sat silent, slumped in her chair, he said nothing, waiting.

She stirred, seeming to become aware of where she was. She looked around the room and said, "It's easier to say these things in such a place. The bad parts disappear into all the space. There are no walls to contain them, to bounce them back to you. Not like one's memories, confined to one's head."

"Anna. *How* did Sasha get to San Francisco?"

"On her back." It was said without the slightest note of disapproval or anger. "She was pretty. And there were always men ready to help."

"An American came to Vlad and met with the bosses. He proposed a 'pipeline' – his word. A way to export pretty young Russian women to Western buyers. Sasha was one of five women in what he called their trial run."

"It was voluntary?"

"Voluntary?" She made the word sound like an epithet. "She had a choice. She could have stayed in Vladivostock, become old, and fat, and a drunk. Or she could believe that perhaps a small fraction of their promises could come true, and go with them. Meet important men, perhaps marry one of them. You need to understand – for us, America was ... to get to America ... that would be a new world. A new life."

"How did you know Sasha was dead?"

"The picture in your newspaper. It was a bad picture of her, but good enough for me to almost identify her. The 'almost' is why I asked you about the butterfly tattoo. But I knew she was dead when she stopped calling. Her last call ... I could hear that she was afraid. That she knew it wasn't working."

"Her last call? When was that?"

"A week before I knew I was coming. We talked mostly about me and what I needed to do. She had found ..."

She stopped and looked closely at McAdams. When she resumed, her voice and speech rhythms were different, more cautious, like a politician seeing microphones being turned on. *She's going to lie to me.*

"She said that she had found a place where – if I could get away from *him* – I could hide for awhile."

"With Moresby and Ellerby?"

"She didn't know anything about Ellerby. But she said Moresby was sympathetic to refugees, that she had been one herself. It was a crazy risk ... all I could think about was that Sasha had gone to her and now she was dead ... but I had no other choices. If she hadn't let me stay ...."

"You said *him* – the one Sasha had to get away from – who's *him*?

"I don't know his name or anything about him. But he killed Sasha. And you're going to get him for me."

Ah! The agenda emerges! He let it pass for now, but could not help feeling disappointment. *So naïve about how things work. About me and what I do.*

"How did it work? The pipeline?"

"Russian men – what you call the Mafia – would identify likely candidates. It was easy to qualify. Just be pretty and dissatisfied. There are many such women in the Russian Far East. You pay a few thousand dollars or Euros 'to cover transportation costs' and you're on your way."

She described the three-part sea journey, but claimed that she did not know the registries of the vessels involved. "We were kept in a cabin most of the time, or restricted to a small part of the open deck. The crew would not talk to us … even though we promised them … things. I did not know where I was until we went under the Golden Gate Bridge."

"Was it same for Sasha?"

"How she got here? Yes. But she told me that she was kept locked up, that the men just wanted to fuck her. That she was no better than a prostitute. She told me that she was going to try to run away. To Las Vegas."

"Is that why she was killed?"

"I think so."

"Do you know who killed her?"

"Yes, but I can't prove it."

"Who?"

"The American who came to Vlad to set up the pipeline. I think he has killed many people. And likes it."

"Do you know how I can find him?"

"I know two things that could help. The address of a Victorian house in North Beach where they took us when we left the ship. And the name of the ship. It was gone from the Bay by the next day, but I found a website that lists the names of the ships coming and going on any day. It was called 'Northern Lights'. I think that one other American – a younger man -- is his boss."

"Any names?"

"Two.   Here's one."   She reached into the shoulder bag and handed him a Mexican passport. He flipped it open to the photo and personal information.

"Where did you get this?"

"I stole it. From the man … I was with. When I ran away."

"Jose Rebozo?"

"He was one of three men – Latins -- at the Victorian in North Beach. I think that he is important. They were there for some kind of negotiations with the two Americans."

"And the other name?"

She hesitated, for the first time seeming unsure of herself. Then she looked at him intently, seeming to look for a sign that she could really trust him. Like a late night hitchhiker before getting in the car. Then he understood why.

"That last night, just before getting off the ship, I heard two of the crew talking outside the cabin. I heard the name 'Fallon'…. like your friend."

Easy Gains

The first part was easy. Using the internet on his laptop at home, he verified the existence of a ship called Northern Lights and quickly traced its ownership to a company called Pacific Cargos. But then he was in for a surprise. Pacific Cargos was part of "the Fallon Family of Companies". The CEO of Pacific Cargos was Dominick's son Carlo. He tried various sites to see if he could track the ship's movements, but quickly hit a dead end.

He googled "Jose Reboso", but quickly eliminated the three names that showed up as a possibility for Anna's "important man". He scanned the passport picture and emailed a copy to Tedoski, the Oakland cop who ID'd Pepe, hoping for a local sighting.

If Reboso was a major player, he figured the Mexican police would know him. Tedoski had mentioned the Tijuana Cartel, so started his Google search with that. He quickly learned that it was headed by a 'Jose Torres', one of the more vicious players in that world. He was able to download some fuzzy long-distance photographs of Torres, but they did not match up with the passport photo. Side by side, they might have looked like distant cousins at most.

Murphy said that he had gotten his info from a 'Captain Ramon Alvarez' of the Mexican Federal Police. Calling him would be tricky if he wanted to stay out of sight. He used a phone on an unassigned desk in the Division. He called Mexico, saying he was a "Lieutenant Mulloy" who worked with Murphy and was following up on Alvarez's earlier call. He got two police Captains named Alvarez before the right one.

"Murphy said to tell you that we're still working on Pepe, but nothing yet."

Alvarez's English was impeccable. He said wryly, "You should send him to me. Our methods are less ... shall we say, regulated."

"Can't do that just yet. But another name has come up – a Jose Reboso. Does that match up with any of Pepe's contacts?"

"None that I recognize. Do you have a picture?"

"I'll send one. Give me a fax number. I'll send the photo and call you right back."

He sent the fax and waited three minutes before redialing Alvarez. The phone was answered on the first ring. "Mulloy?" The tone somehow conveyed an image of Alvarez sitting on the edge of his chair, gripping the phone tightly. *Oh oh! I think my Officer Mulloy routine is about to be tested!*

"Yeah. Did the Reboso picture –"

"Tell Murphy that I'm sending three officers by charter jet. They'll leave Mexico City within the next hour. The officer-in-charge is a Captain Jorge Maldanado."

"Uh, Captain Alvarez –"

"Your Senor Reboso? We think it's Jose Torres. There were rumors of plastic surgery and he hasn't been seen for some time. Maldanado knows Torres very well and he is quite sure Reboso is Torres, with a new face."

"Mulloy?"

McAdams replaced the phone gently on its cradle, feeling like a needy parishioner taking money out of the offering plate as it passed by.

He left the building, trying not to look furtive, but knowing that he did not want to be anywhere in the vicinity of Murphy when his phone rang and Alvarez inquired about an eager subordinate named Mulloy. *I think I'm OK for a while. They'll have the phone number that the fax came from, but I don't think anybody noticed me.*

OK, she's right about Jose being important.

She's a piece of work. Knocks one of the world's arch criminals upside the head while he's trying to get her pants off and takes off with his newly-minted identity!

And that matches up with the streetside info we've been getting about new players and stepped up narcotics traffic. Still don't know who the other Latin types might be, or who the two

173

Americans are. But we know the women came off a ship owned by Fallon.

It was still before noon when he stopped back at his home. Anna was sitting at his desk using his laptop. She had on one of his flannel shirts – a blue checked flannel -- that extended to mid-thigh, leaving his imagination to work out if there was anything beneath it. A shaft of sunlight from one of the high windows on the back wall highlighted her bare feet extending from beneath the desktop. It was easy to imagine her as a studious graduate student working on her thesis.

Damn it! This has the potential to get complicated!

"Uh, Anna –"

She tapped a few more keys on the laptop and then looked up at him. "Your internet is fascinating. Did you know that you can order a Russian wife by email? Or that your Federal government seized five million pounds of narcotics last year? Or that a homicide detective in San Francisco has an average salary of sixty-one-thousand dollars?"

He walked over to the desk and closed the cover on his laptop. He sat down on the corner of the desk, folded his arms and tried to look stern. "Never mind the wonders of the Internet. If this asylum arrangement is going to work, we need to work out a few basic rules."

She pushed the chair back, bringing her long legs into full view. She crossed her arms and did her best to mimic his disapproving look. She said, "Oh good! I like rules." The word *impish* came readily to mind.

This is going well, isn't it?

She had moved directly into the beam of sunlight and he noticed that she had a sprinkling of freckles across the bridge of her nose and that one of her eyes had an arc of green across the deep brown. Her nails were painted a bright red, but he didn't think she was using any makeup. Her obviously dyed blond hair was short and tousled in a way that he suspected was deliberate, with definite tinges of brown showing at the roots.

The shirt was much too large and she had rolled the sleeves to her elbows. He could not help himself and looked casually at the buttons on the flannel shirt. She had fastened the middle three. In crossing her arms, she emphasized her breasts beneath the shirt and created tantalizing shadowy gaps in its folds.

She knows exactly what she's doing. But what about me? What the hell am I doing?

"Rules?" she prompted.

He cleared his throat, but realized he did not know what to say. Rather, he could not decide which of two options to go with.

What you're thinking is stupid! She's a completely unknown quantity in the middle of an investigation into multiple murders. She's got an agenda that you know nothing about. And you're supposed to be a professional.

But what he said was, "Yeah, rules. Like you need to get your own clothes. That's one of my favorite shirts."

She smiled and stood up. "OK. I'm sorry. I'll take it off." He watched while she unbuttoned – very slowly, without taking her eyes from his – the three buttons. He was intensely aware of his own silence, a fully aware accomplice to his own seduction. Then she wriggled her shoulders very slightly. The shirt slid to the floor. She was wearing nothing beneath it. She took a half-step toward him, bringing her within an arm's length.

God, she's beautiful. And she's really good at this. And I'm way past the point of no return.

He was breathing faster, but did not move. He said, "You don't have to do this, you know? You really don't."

"I know. But I have this thing about paying my bills. And I do owe you."

He began, "You don't owe –", but she reached out and held two fingers to his lips.

She took the final half step to close the gap between them. "And besides, I want to. Do this."

Much later, just as the natural light from the glass wall and skylights had faded to the point where he could barely see Anna's naked form as she crossed the room, he allowed himself to start thinking once again.

Funny. I'd forgotten how much fun that can be. With the right person... the kind that laughs and can be selfish some of the time.

The problem, however, is that his thinking – the rational kind – always circled back to the same question, the question that he had refused to allow to the surface during the last few hours. *Who is she and what does she want? Am I just a stepping stone on her way to wherever she's going – one that can be bought cheaply with some friction, skin and heavy breathing?*

He thought briefly about the other problem – that she was a material witness to multiple felonies and he was – supposedly – a professional police officer. He was surprised at how little that seemed to matter at this particular moment.

She slipped back into bed, lying against him with her head tucked under his chin. She said in a small voice, "That was very, very nice. Thank you." He thought, but was not sure, that she was crying.

Who are you, Anna Rubin? What do you want?

Anna and Others

In other parts of the city, other people were also thinking about Anna.

One of them was puzzled for the same reasons as McAdams and was asking the same questions. *Who are you, Anna Rubin? What do you want from me? Why are you here? Why do you look at me in that calculating way, as though you expect me to do or say something that I am supposed to figure out without any coaching? As if I have some obligation to help you do whatever it is that you're trying to do. You show up here, without my asking, become part of my life. But you offer nothing of yourself, at least nothing that seems of consequence to you.*

Another – a man -- although thinking of Anna, was asking questions of a much less benign sort. *Who are you? And where are you, you fucking bitch? How much do you really know? How can I get my hands on you? What are you telling people about me? What is it that you want?*

There was another man who thought about Anna, but was not curious about her. He simply wanted to kill her. She was one of his failures, and he did not like reminders of those.

The strange reality was that Anna was asking herself some of the same questions, particularly of the *what do I want* variety. She realized that it was a question she had stopped asking herself after the first few years in the orphanage, where what she wanted – achingly, continuously, above all else – was a mother and a father to take her away and love her. When it didn't happen, she no longer allowed herself to ask *what do I want*, or if she did, only for time horizons measured in hours or days. A lack of curiosity about the future was a defense mechanism. To care was to become vulnerable to people and events that she could not control.

Now for the first time, she could begin to think in terms of years, or even a lifetime. *I'm here, in San Francisco. So incredible, so unlikely that I never thought about what comes next. So different from Russia that I don't know the rules. There are so many more possibilities here, both good and bad ones. What*

should I want?   And what do men want from me?   Expect of me?
And am I able to provide that, whatever it is?
    Who are you, Anna Rubin?

Assimilation

For Natalia and Maria, it was like their life in Vladivostock in many ways. They were still mostly dependent on men for their existence; men who valued them for their bodies and did not care very much about whatever else made them unique. They were idle most of the time and had little to do, few places to go or people to talk with.

They had more money and time than they were accustomed to and they were in one of the most popular tourist destinations in the world, so the few available diversions were easily done. Movies, shopping, some sightseeing. And the men did not mistreat them other than by being indifferent to whether they were happy. They spent most of their time on a decrepit pier at the offices of something called "the San Francisco Cultural Exchange Program", sleeping on a pair of mattresses in a connected room. They practiced their English mainly by watching downloaded movies under the watchful gaze of a black woman named Madge who listened to music on her iPod throughout the day and seemed to have no other duties.

There were few demands on their time. The American – he told them his name was Robert – would arrange two or three nights a week where they would meet some men and do what they asked. By the standards of their previous life, it was a luxurious existence, free from fear and always lightened by the promise of things to come. "Las Vegas" was the mantra that calmed them and kept them compliant.

The important men they had been given to on their first night off the ship – the night that Sofia took off – became regulars. The Colombian paired up with Natalia and the Venezuelan with Maria. Once both women had worked just with the Columbian – he said his name was Emilio – who had instructed them quite carefully as to his exact needs over the course of several hours, needs that demanded more stamina from them than from him. On the other hand, the Venezuelan – Reynaldo – was crude and unimaginative, easily serviced. He also talked a great deal about how important he was and how much he was worth. Other than his accent, he was interchangeable with most of the men they had known.

They did not ask about or ever mention Sofia, sensing that the very topic was dangerous. They saw Jose, the man she had gone upstairs with, once more at the North Beach Victorian house. He was with a Latina woman and paid no attention to them.

They *felt* free, probably because they were in America, a place where people took freedom for granted and the TV promised them – in so many ways – that everything was possible. No one that they met seemed *afraid*, a condition that was new to them. They did not know that their cherished cell phones enabled them to be tracked at all times, although it is likely that they would not have cared very much if they had known. The older American told them that they would be leaving for Las Vegas within a few days, where they would have their own apartment and much more freedom to choose their own men.

Life was good.

Conversation in a Coffee Shop

The four men met in mid-morning at a cafe in North Beach, sitting at an outdoor table in an isolated corner of the patio. Even a casual observer would note the tension, the two-against-two group composition that made the quartet stand out. Carlo and Grodin arrived first, then Jose and Emilio. The other man, Reynaldo, was back in Colombia to oversee the packaging of the shipment. Each of the four ordered coffee.

Jose started. "We have three more days. Is everything ready?"

"Yes, on our end." Emilio answered after everybody looked to him. "Reynaldo watched the Sigilo leave Cartagena yesterday with the goods. They're as good as it gets … the crystal's at 85% purity."

Carlo added, "And I talked to Voyager's captain this morning. He picked up the ten packages yesterday. All they have to do is find each other."

Jose reached across the table and put his hand on Carlo's forearm. His grip was more than casual. "So that's the supply side of the deal. But the financing? Fifty million dollars is more than you have, I think?"

Grodin watched Carlo closely. *That's a very good question.* He was pleased to see that Carlo's expression did not change. Which might have meant– despite Grodin's low opinion of him – that Carlo was perhaps a very good poker player. But what Grodin suspected was that Carlo simply did not understand the seriousness of the deal he had struck with the Russian money, that he thought this was all some kind of game that he could control. Carlo had pledged his company – really his father's company – as collateral for a fifty million dollar loan, to be repaid from the sale of the drugs on the street. The first one-hundred million of revenue went to the Russian, making it a very expensive loan.

Carlo was dismissive. "Never mind where *we* get the money. It all spends the same regardless of where it comes from. You'll have it wired into your accounts as soon as the goods change hand on the dock."

Jose shrugged, but his grip on Carlo's arm did not change and he kept his eyes locked on Carlo. "And the drugs? All those kilos? You'll need a distribution network. But you are a respectable businessman. My associates … they wonder how their product will get to the street … to the addicts that we all depend on for future sales. Some of them have questioned why we are dealing with an amateur." His voice rose on the last phrase, turning it into a question.

Grodin looked hard at Jose, who merely smiled blandly back at him, an expression that somehow conveyed both sarcasm and contempt. *I wonder if he knows how thoroughly I've conned Carlo into thinking he's a future Al Capone?*

Carlo glanced at Grodin and then recited the lines that Grodin had been feeding him for the last month. *The same story I told Torres in Cali when this all started.* "We're the wholesale side of the business and our deal with you gives us more and better product than the competition." He paused, and then added with a distinct smirk, "And we've convinced the local retailers that it would be safer to deal with us … much healthier. "

Time to change the subject. Grodin broke in before Jose could go on. "This Reynaldo? He talks a lot. To the whores. I wonder who else he talks to. And what he talks about."

Emilio nodded, looking at Torres. "And then there's our Sofia. I wonder who she is talking to."

Carlo shook his head. "She won't talk to anyone. She's in the country illegally and doesn't want any kind of contact with police. And, even if she did, she doesn't know anything that could hurt us."

Too quick … and too pat. "Are you sure of that?" Grodin asked Carlo, but he was looking intently at Torres as he asked the question.

"We've got everybody watching for her," Torres said, knowing that his answer was non-responsive.

He thought about the passport and the slip of paper that was in the pocket of his coat that Sofia had taken with her. He agreed with Carlo that Sofia – he inwardly winced whenever he thought of her – could not afford to go to the police, but he had already arranged an alternative route back to Mexico, just in case. He had other passports with other names, and as soon as this deal was done, he'd be gone. The real worry was that damned scribble in one corner of the notes that Sofia had. If she figured that out and talked to the right people …

He thought about the men sitting at the table with him. *The gringos have a saying … What you don't know can't hurt you. But they're wrong. If these two knew what was in that coat pocket, they wouldn't be sitting here with me.*

Added Staff

*T*hat's it. No more of this.
McAdams woke to the sound of blaring horns behind him. He had fallen asleep waiting for the light to change on Geary Boulevard. If one appreciated irony, it was good news. He had been having trouble sleeping, partly because his mind wouldn't stop running what he had come to think of as "the Freddie & Gonzo show". The other deterrent to sleep was his fear of the nightmares. They varied, but always reached the same point – him running in place, hopelessly lost in the city he knew so well, trying to reach one of them kneeling before a faceless executioner. He never made it.

He was trying to juggle three full-time jobs. The official ones were as a lead investigator on the Jane Doe and Desmond murder cases and as the primary on-site face of the COPPS program in the Tenderloin. The third one, the one that obsessed him, was trying to find out why Freddie had said "I know all about your golf buddy". He'd been shadowing Ellerby for a week, learning absolutely nothing.

I need help.

The next morning, a breezy clear Sunday, he systematically canvassed the streets that defined the Tenderloin. He felt like a Coast Guard crew searching the grid for a missing sailboat. He found his target on his second go-round and stopped in his lane of traffic.

He yelled, "Garfield! Got a minute?"

Garfield held up a finger, signaling "one minute". He apparently was one of the crew that parked cars for the drive-up parishioners at Glide Memorial Church. Most of the valet parkers were street people, sober but decidedly ragged. Garfield was definitely the most trustworthy looking one of the lot. McAdams watched as an elderly Mercedes driver waved off a black man in army fatigues and tried to give his keys to Garfield instead. Garfield took the driver by his arm, walked him down the line of cars and introduced him to the black guy, who was standing patiently with an expression that indicated he'd been through this routine before. McAdams couldn't hear what was said, but at the end of the exchange, the black guy drove the Mercedes away and the elderly couple standing on the curb seemed OK watching their expensive car disappearing around the corner.

"Bridging class differences?" said McAdams as Garfield slid into the passenger side seat.

Garfield laughed. "Not me. It's Glide. Best melting pot in the world. I cried the first time I went to one of their services. It's a metaphor for human possibility."

How does he know I know what a metaphor is? McAdams drove half a block and pulled to the curb next to a hydrant. "I need some help, so I've got a proposition for you."

The perpetual semi-smile wasn't so perpetual after all. It went away, replaced by a quite genuine frown.

"Mac. You're a cop. I'm a ...". He stopped and from his expression, he was thinking hard about what to say, or how to say it.

I wonder how he would have finished the sentence. Would it change what I think of Garfield? I think not. Whatever he was or is, I trust him.

"Garfield, I don't care what you are or have been. I don't need a hit man. I'm not asking you to snitch on anybody on the street. It's not official, just a deal between you and I. I don't want you to do anything illegal. I can pay you a little bit for helping me, but basically I'm asking a favor."

"Mac, I can't! I'd like to help you, but I can't."

His body language was at least as convincing as the words. He was gripping the dash hard enough to leave a slight indentation in the plastic molding. His other hand was clenched. He was looking down at the floor of the car.

What the hell have I triggered? He remembered something that Garfield had said during one of their casual conversations on the street.

"It's a cliché, Mac. But it's true." He waved his arm at the chaotic street scene and all of its characters. *"Everybody*

here – every one of us freaks -- has a story. And it's an interesting one if someone knows how to get them to tell it."

McAdams asked, "Do you remember telling me how everybody has an interesting story?"

Garfield nodded, looking puzzled.

"Did Harry Howden ever get a chance to tell you his story?"

Garfield's eyes gleamed with something that may have been anger. After a long pause, he said, "No. He didn't." Then, after another gap, "And he's lost his chance, hasn't he?"

"Suppose I told you that this project – what I need your help with – could help find the bastard that killed Harry?"

Garfield leaned back in his seat. The fingers that had been squeezing the dash were now lightly drumming on the leather seat. McAdams guessed that a significant internal debate was taking place. *I wish I knew this guy's story. It sure as hell would be an interesting one.*

"Tell me more." And McAdams knew that he had an assistant. He started to talk.

Ten minutes later, Garfield was grinning outright. "You want me to spy on the Mayor?!"

"That's not the official language I would use, but yes, I want you to spy on the Mayor."

"There's one more spot where you can help." McAdams gave him a carefully edited version of what he had learned from Anna and asked him to spend some time watching the North Beach Victorian. He cautioned him, "Don't get spotted, and whatever you do, don't approach anyone coming in or going out."

"Don't worry. I've done this before."

Done this before? Garfield, who are you?

They talked for another five minutes. Garfield was headed back to the parking queue when he suddenly reversed course and stuck his head in the open car window. "I need a fifty dollar advance."

McAdams was surprised, but handed him two twenties and a ten. "We'll set up something more systematic after we get going."

"No need for that. I don't want to be paid. This is for Gus."

"Gus?"

"The black guy parking cars? He needs some special pills for his arthritis."

Why am I not surprised? A one-man Medicare sub-system. McAdams nodded and started to pull away. Then a sudden thought made him brake quickly enough that Garfield stopped and looked quizzically at him. He made a motion with his hands – 'something else?' -- but McAdams waved him off and eased into the passing traffic.

My last two partners are both dead because they worked with me. And there's a superstition – 'Bad things come in groups of three'.

Cryptography

Anna was wearing his flannel shirt again, this time with a pair of jeans. He tried to decide if he was relieved or disappointed to observe that all but the top button was fastened. She seemed as nervous as he felt, each of them avoiding eye contact, like two strangers who had witnessed an embarrassing incident rather than a pair of recent and intense lovers. Each of them avoided looking at the king sized bed that was in the far corner of the vast space.

They did not know it, but they were thinking the same thoughts. *What is this strange hesitancy? Yesterday, we were naked together. We made love. Why this uncertainty? I feel like a teenager with acne on a first date with someone smarter and better looking than me!*

She took something from the shirt pocket and handed it to him, holding it at arm's length pinched between two fingers. It was if she was being careful not to touch him.

"This was in Jose's jacket with the passport. I saw him writing on it and then he put it in his pocket when we walked into the room."

McAdams took the bit of paper with equal care. *So I've passed some entry-level test and can be trusted with the next bit of information.*

It was a single sheet of yellow lined paper, torn from a spiral notebook and folded into thirds. There were a half-a-dozen lines of writing near the top of the page. At first glance, it could have been a shopping list.

> **Us**
> Coke –1,000 kg
> Meth – 1,000 kg
> **Them**
> $50 mm + 10 (5/$3 mm) PK

It's a shopping list … For the major illegal substances. Two thousand kilos, all in one shipment. At street prices …

probably a billion dollars plus. This would set someone up in the distribution business in a major way.

Near the bottom of the page was a string of numbers and symbols, printed in blue ink. The writing was faint and the pen had punctured the paper in two spots, as if the note taker was writing on his lap.

The string read, "NV&S@30&-132-1730/!!m13.4".

She asked, "A code?"

"I don't think so. At least not one that he's going to use to send the information to someone else. I think it's a bunch of abbreviations strung together. It looks like he scribbled it down in a hurry, like someone who wanted to be sure to remember something. Like someone making a shopping list before dashing out the door."

They stared at it. She said, "Looks like an algebraic equation. Not my strong point in school."

"I was pretty good at it. And that's what I thought too. But the '&" and the '@' sign don't fit with that theory."

"Could the '@' symbol be part of a web address?"

"I don't think so. Not with that kind of trailing gibberish."

He copied the writing from the page onto a yellow post-it note and handed it to her. He put it the original sheet in his coat pocket. "Keep looking at it. Maybe something will occur to you. We've got a couple of detectives downtown that like word games and puzzles. I'll see if they have any ideas."

They stood silently, each of them looking at the scrap of paper as though hoping to find their next lines written there. The silence stretched, became awkward.

Anna did not understand her sudden ineptness. *What's going on? It's the oldest game in the world … and I'm good at it. Why this shy schoolgirl act?*

He got halfway to the door when she said very hesitantly, "Mac …".

He stopped but did not turn around, not even knowing what he was hoping for. Ten seconds went by, then she said in a very small voice, "Never mind."

He was on his way to the Tenderloin substation when he got a call from Garfield.

"We should meet. I wouldn't call it a progress report; that's a little too hopeful a label, I think. But I've got some info that might be helpful."

"Can you meet me at the park?"

"Ten minutes. See you there."

"The park" was emblematic of the changing Tenderloin. Not long ago, the space at the corner of O'Farrell and Larkin was a fenced-in trash heap and hangout for junkies and dealers. Now it's a family place, where parents -- mostly mothers – watch their kids devise elaborate games on brightly colored slides, chutes and things that spin. Garfield was leaning against the wall watching the kids. He in turn was being closely watched by several of the parents.

When McAdams walked up, Garfield grinned and said, "Welcome to the suspected pedophile club", and gestured at the cluster of glowering parents about twenty feet away.

"Hey, it's our version of Neighborhood Watch. But let's go get some coffee. I'll buy."

He was parked immediately opposite a Starbucks, so they sat in his car to drink their coffee.

McAdams said, "Let's see. You called me. So, I guess you're required to go first. Anything from the front line in the war against crime?"

"First, the non-news. Ellerby is as predictable as the tides. He goes to the same places, sees the same people, and makes the same speeches. And all of those – the places, people and speeches – are as dull and ordinary as tap water in a bar. His most deviant act is playing golf with you on Wednesday afternoons. And by the way, you could use some short-game lessons."

"I've tried. It's hopeless. What about the Moresby visits?"

"This is San Francisco. The only scandal would be if she was ugly. And she certainly isn't that! But …"

McAdams waited.

"I'm not sure about this, but I think her house is being watched. There's a Mexican-looking guy in a beat-up Toyota pickup that has been sitting just down the block both times that I've been there. He doesn't seem interested in anything except her house."

Jose's people. Waiting for her to return.

"I think I know who he is. And stay far away from him or any of his friends. You said 'non-news'. That implies there's something else ... Something that may be more interesting."

"That Victorian in North Beach. It's either got an interesting cast of characters or I've seen too many gangster movies."

McAdams said, "I think both may be true."

"I think there are five residents. They all wear dark suits –"

McAdams broke in, "Suits, huh? That automatically makes them suspicious in this city."

Garfield smiled politely and went on. "Two of them – Hispanics again -- look like gofers... grocery shopping, buying a paper, everyday stuff ... in and out several times a day. I think they're living on the first level."

He pulled his cell phone from his pocket and continued. "I've only seen the other three one time each, either getting in or out of a limo. I think they're living on the upper levels."

"What do they look like?"

"Judge for yourself." Garfield held the phone up where McAdams could see the screen. "Here's one of them. He left two days ago and came back yesterday."

The picture seemed to be taken from across the street. It clearly showed a Hispanic male in a dark suit ducking down to enter a black limo. McAdams guessed that he was middle aged and in good shape, but that's about all that he could tell.

Garfield scrolled to the next picture. "Here's another one." He was standing on the lowest step, looking into the street. The picture was slightly blurred, but it clearly was Jose Reboso/Torres. From the angle, McAdams figured the picture was taken from the sidewalk on the same side of the street.

"There's one more Hispanic guy, about the same age as that one. But I wasn't able to get a photo. He left yesterday with a small suitcase, looking like someone headed for the airport. I heard the driver call him Mr. Espinoza."

He's getting way too close to these people. And taking pictures!

"Garfield. You're going way beyond the job description! This is great stuff, but –"

"Relax Mac! I'm way below their radar." He held the cell phone up again. "I've got one more picture. It was getting dark and I was across the street, so I'm not sure it'll help."

The picture was of a man and two women going up the front stairs of the Victorian, taken from behind. The women were in very short dresses with high heels. Even in the poor light, their legs looked very good. The man was of medium size and build, wearing what looked like a leather jacket. McAdams judged him to be middle-aged or older.

"They were in there a couple of hours. The girls looked like pros, but young ones, the kind you get from the high-end 'escort services'. I haven't seen them on the street, for what it's worth. And I know most of the regulars, at least in the Tenderloin."

"How about the guy with them?"

"In the fifty to sixty range, maybe. Average looking white guy. I'm about eighty-percent sure he's an American. The impression I got was that he was delivering the women. He was holding on to them, not the other way around."

"Can you send me the pictures? I'll have our computer types see if they can enhance them to the point where we can get an ID."

"Sure." Garfield hesitated, and McAdams knew what he was going to ask. "Mac, what's going on? I'm picking up vibrations from you that worry me."

What do I tell a civilian when I'm withholding the information from the official people that I'm supposed to working with? The world is getting screwy! Then he had a thought that made him sit up straighter. *I've asked him to do something that could get him killed... and I'm worried about the ethics of sharing information?*

Even then, McAdams tried to hedge. "I don't know a whole lot, but I do know that these people – the ones that you're snapping photos of – are very, very nasty." He paused, not for effect, but because he was genuinely conflicted. "They kill people."

"Like Howden?"

"Yeah, and anyone else that bothers them." He paused and raised his voice, looking directly at Garfield. "And they're easily bothered."

Garfield's expression didn't change. *No fear, not even curiosity. Either he's a complete innocent or he grew up in a very tough neighborhood!*

McAdams took the Post-It note with the curious string of numbers and symbols and showed it to Garfield. "I got this from a source. I think it's got something to do with our narcotics trade, but it could be something else. Any ideas?"

Garfield read the string out loud, "NV&S@30&-132-1730/!!m13.4."

He laughed. "Looks like someone testing the 'infinite number of monkeys theory. Absolute nonsense to me. But if it's a code of some sort, Hooker can decipher it."

"Hooker?" *The paranoid schizoid at the Alcazar?*

A significant fraction of San Francisco's homeless population suffers from some sort of mental illness. Like a lot of them, Hooker was delusional. He heard voices. His particular oracles warned him that an ultra-conservative Tibetan sect was plotting to take over the world and was determined to kill him. The voices also assured him that he would be safe as long as he stayed within a one-block range of the old Alcazar Theatre in the Tenderloin.

"Hooker's an expert codebreaker? Our Hooker, the one who hears voices from the Himalayas?"

Garfield said, "I told you that everyone on the street has a story. Hooker's is more interesting than most. He was a full professor of mathematics at Berkeley when he was twenty-three years old, specializing in number theory. He consulted for NSA and the like before ... before the voices started."

OK. Sure. Another team member, this one a paranoid schizophrenic codebreaker. To go with my illegal Russian prostitute/lover, and my benefactor of the homeless who takes closeups of the world's most wanted criminals. What the hell! Why not? You're already operating way off the reservation.

"Garfield, would you track Hooker down and see if he can make any sense of this gobbledegook?"

"Easy. I take him a burrito every Monday afternoon."

Of course.

"Oh, and here's another fifty bucks." McAdams handed over a brand new fifty-dollar bill.

"For what?"

"Let's see ... for surveillance, portrait photography, and talent scouting among other services you've provided. But something tells me it's going to wind up as a grass-roots addition to our social safety net."

Fishing for Information

"Where's McAdams?" Fallon asked as they waited on the second tee, a four-hundred-thirty-yard par four. "And please don't tell me that he's suddenly developed a conscience about working."

Ellerby was also bothered by McAdams being a no-show and had already given the question some serious thought. *It's all getting tangled up – Grodin, Eileen, Sofia, Carlo. Now McAdams. And I'm smack in the middle, not a good place to be. Like juggling balloons in a high wind. Might as well add one more unknown to the equation …*

"It's complicated." Ellerby said as he turned away to tee up his ball.

Fallon put his hand on Ellerby's forearm to hold him in place. "Complicated? As in 'interpersonally complicated'?"

"Let's just say that Mac and I have some professional and personal issues that require us to maintain some distance for the moment." *Christ! What drivel! I'm starting to talk like my press releases.*

They each hit mediocre drives down the right side of the fairway. Fallon picked up the conversation again as they started walking. "Look, Edgar. I don't want to get all mushy about this, but if there's anything I can do …"

There is, actually. Would you please, please get Carlo under some kind of control? But I can't ask it. What the hell! Give it a try!

Ellerby asked, "Do you know a guy named Grodin? He works for Carlo, sort of an all-purpose right-hand-man is my impression."

Fallon didn't break stride and tried to keep his expression as neutral as possible. "Yeah, I know a little bit about him." *A little bit. Like he kills people that he finds to be inconvenient. And he's got Carlo by the nose ring!*

He was trying to figure out how to deal with the inevitable awkward followup questions about Grodin, but

Ellerby's next question came out of the blue. "How's Carlo doing with his cultural exchange program?"

Before answering, Fallon took some time to set up and hit his next shot, a topped three wood that left him still a hundred yards from the green. He used the interval to script a carefully worded answer.

"Actually, I don't know anything about it. As far as I know, Carlo has zero interest in any such thing. What's he doing? Some kind of community involvement thing?"

"More than that. He's taken over one of our piers on an annual lease and is bringing in Eastern European students – all women as far as I can tell – for short stays. Apparently, they study American culture and institutions. I … rather, the City … endorsed it. It's supposedly an anonymous donor, but I know that Carlo's firm put up all the money and they run the day-to-day operations."

Ellerby watched Fallon intently for any telltales, but so far his expression remained as bland as their surface conversation. They carried on an intermittent dialogue for the rest of the game, as they paused to hit their shots, often on opposite sides of the fairway. Ellerby fretted about what he had said. *Does he really not know what Carlo is doing? Am I doing myself any good with this calculated leaking?*

They played another five holes before darkness ended their game. Fallon declined to stay for the ritualistic beer, pleading a social engagement. In fact, he needed to follow up on what he had learned … and the suspicions that had been created.

Carlo's importing women from Eastern Europe. 'For cultural exchange.' And has unrestricted access to a pier. I wonder what else he's importing? I think I need to take a look at this civic-minded venture!

Elementary, My Dear Watson

"You've insulted Hooker."
            Garfield slipped into McAdams' car as soon as it pulled to the curb. "He said to bring him something more interesting. He solved your so-called code in ten seconds."

McAdams just looked at him.

"First of all, it's not a code. It's a pretty obvious form of shorthand once you know what you're looking at."

McAdams said, "Garfield. I'll concede that Hooker is smarter than I am. Almost everybody is. Please just tell me what that goddam string of hieroglyphics says!"

"It's a *meeting*. Somebody will meet somebody else at a particular place and time."

Garfield took the Post-It note from his shirt pocket, considerably more crumpled, and produced a pen. He underlined the last third of the cryptic string -- 1730/!!m13.4 – and held it up to McAdams. "Here's the time – the '1730' is military code for 530 PM. The '!!' marks are to stress the importance of the time or date. And the 'm13.4' is the date, using the European method of putting the month last. It means Monday, the 13th of April."

"The next piece is *where* the meeting will be held." He underlined @30&-132.

"The '@' sign means literally 'at' – the place to be on the 13th of April at 5:30 in the evening. What follows the @ sign is '30&-132'. Hooker says that the 30 refers to latitude and the minus 132 to the longitude, in degrees."

McAdams summarized. "So we have a meeting to take place at 5:30 PM on April 13 at 30 degrees of latitude and minus 132 degrees of longitude?"

Garfield nodded.

"So, and please forgive the obvious question, where is that exactly?"

"According to Google Earth, about one hundred miles due west of the Golden Gate Bridge."

"Not many street signs out there. So we know 'where' and 'when'. The only unknown is 'who' …"

"And Hooker says that's going to be two people – or companies, or probably ships, since we're meeting at sea -- with the initials 'NV' and 'S'."

McAdams thought a bit. "It does look obvious once you see it like that, doesn't it? But there's still one more missing piece. We've got most of who, what, where and when. The missing piece is 'why'?"

"Hooker thinks it's the Tibetan Navy coming to extradite him. Me? I think it's something much more ordinary. Like drug smuggling, maybe?"

Unraveling Motives

Ellerby had become a central character in the story that McAdams was constructing in his head. Anna said that Ellerby sent her to him for help *because of Gonzo and Freddie*. The last thing Freddie did in her life was to almost declare his golf partner -- who was Ellerby – to be Gonzo's killer. Eileen Moresby – the woman who provided sanctuary for Anna and saved his life with her marksmanship – was being courted by Ellerby.

I think it's time that I talked to Ellerby.

McAdams sat in his car working out a script, one with many branching points since it had to allow for the highly unpredictable lines of the other person in the dialogue. One serious complication was that Ellerby was mayor of the city, his boss three or four levels up the organization chart. The possibility that he might be engaged in criminal activity seemed very real, but McAdams pushed that thought aside. The final factor was that he liked Ellerby.

The hell with a script. I'll ask the obvious questions and we'll see where that takes us.

He dialed the Mayor's private number, the one that – so far – he had used only to make arrangements for their Wednesday afternoon golf games.

"Mac. What can I do?"

"I need a few minutes. Some puzzles I think you can help me with…"

"Such as?"

"A woman named Anna."

There was several seconds of silence, then Ellerby said, "That make take a little time. I have a parks commission meeting in ten minutes. Can we meet later? Say six o'clock, at Max's on Van Ness?"

When Ellerby ended the call, he swiveled in his chair, staring out the window at the Plaza. The view was slightly hazy, probably because of the extra-thick glass that they assured him was bulletproof. *But bullets aren't what I need protection from. At least not right at this moment.*

It's your own fault. You sent her to him. One of your more self-destructive decisions ... among the many. And you knew he'd come back at you. So, is this where the unraveling begins?

McAdams got to Max's first and staked out a booth in the most remote corner. Ellerby showed up ten minutes later, looking uncharacteristically nervous. He spent the first three or four minutes bantering with the waiter, discussing the varieties of beer that were available. McAdams just waited.

Finally, Ellerby leaned back and looked directly at him. He looked unhappy, like someone expecting to hear bad news. "OK, Mac. It's your meeting."

"Who is she? Anna Rubin?"

"A friend of Eileen's. That's all I can tell you."

"That's an interesting choice of words. Does it mean 'that's all I know'? Or does it mean 'that's all I'm willing to tell you'?"

Ellerby did not respond immediately, but seemed to become even more depressed by the question. "Look. I'm in a difficult spot. Eileen has sworn me to secrecy on some of this stuff. And I can't – I won't – violate that."

Maybe I know more than he does. Let's try that angle.

"Did she tell you that Anna Rubin is a runaway from a human trafficking scheme? That she's Russian and recently knocked flat a Mexican drug lord?"

A flash of anger – but not surprise -- came and went in Ellerby's face. "So, if you know all that, why are you asking me who she is?" Beneath the surface bluster, however, Ellerby was running rapid calculations. *So. Anna trusts him. That was fast. And he hasn't handed her over to the immigration Gestapo, so he's hung out there just like I am. Either of us can be fired for what we're not doing about Anna Rubin.*

Ellerby went on, "So you know as well as I do why those men were chasing her. That she's being hunted."

"Yes." McAdams wondered if Anna was telling the same stories to her different protectors. He decided to run a small test. "But she doesn't seem to be much of a threat to them. She knows almost nothing about the sleazebags who are running the trafficking op. Frankly, I don't think she's in much danger."

He watched Ellerby struggle to frame his response. But his next question surprised him. "Mac. You will keep an eye on her, won't you? She's had a rough time and deserves better."

"She seems to be doing quite well on her own. She's gotten from Vladivostock to San Francisco by outsmarting serious gangsters on both ends and getting help from everybody around her – including the two of us. I think Ms. Rubin is an extremely capable young woman." *She certainly managed me quite well.*

Ellerby looked worried, but McAdams couldn't know that the worries were as much about his own welfare as that of Anna's. *I endorsed Carlo's 'cultural exchange program'. I took bribes to influence civic decisions. It's one big daisy chain of consequences. If she blows the whistle on Carlo, I'm toast.*

Before he could respond, McAdams asked "Did she tell you about Sasha?"

Ellerby did not react except with a slightly puzzled look. "Sasha? No."

"How about Jose Torres aka Reboso? Did she talk about him?"

"Not that I recall. I don't think I've ever heard that name, anyway."

McAdams thought he was telling the truth. *If he is, then Anna hasn't told him a lot of what she knows. Maybe she doesn't trust him? Or sees him mostly as a bystander ... someone that doesn't need to be involved. But he seems quite concerned about her ... something more than you'd feel for a temporary house guest of a friend. And then there's that reference to Gonzo and Freddie!*

So let's ask. "Why did you point her at me? I'm a cop. Not the kind of friend you want if you're trying to hide, especially if you're in the country illegally."

"She called me. The same night that you played hero in front of Eileen's. Wanted to know who you were. Then I didn't hear from her until yesterday. She called and said she needed to talk to a cop, but one that she could trust. Your name came up again. I wanted to call you ... give you a heads up, but she vetoed that ... said she wanted to surprise you."

"Edgar," McAdams said very distinctly. When Ellerby looked at him, he said, "You did more than give her my name and address. You said 'Mention Gonzo and Freddie to him'. You knew that that phrase would get her in the door."

Ellerby looked highly uncomfortable, like someone caught in an outright lie.

"It's not exactly a state secret that you're extra-sensitive about the topic. I figured it would get your attention... that you'd give her a hearing."

There's more.

McAdams pushed the subject. "Y'know, there's something I never told anyone about Freddie. The day she died, you and I were sitting at the golf course, and she called me and said 'I know all about your golf partner.' *A slight restatement.* That's you. I wonder what she meant?"

Ellerby remembered the phone call vividly, particularly the chaotic way it ended, with McAdams dashing off to check on his partner, knowing that he already was far too late. And it was clear from McAdams' face that he was re-visioning the same scene. He was looking at Ellerby with an expression showing coexisting symptoms of pain and anger. *Be very careful what you say in the next ten seconds.*

"There's a man named Grodin...."

There. It was done. Five simple words that – one way or another – were likely to change the course of several lives, including his. Maybe to shorten it.

It took about five seconds for the words to penetrate. McAdams blinked twice, as if recovering from a consuming daydream, and then focused on Ellerby. "Grodin?" he asked.

They continued for another half hour, with Ellerby doing most of the talking. An outside observer might have remarked on the seeming transfer of energy between the two men. As the minutes passed, McAdams seemed to become more animated, more alive, even as Ellerby seemed to shrink within himself and lose interest, as if they were enacting a form of emotional symbiosis or transfusion. When McAdams finally stood up and looked down at Ellerby slumped in his chair, the tableau could have been the closing scene in a morality play, a drama where vast wrongs were confessed and forgiveness was withheld.

Interagency Cooperation

I think my lone wolf routine is about to end. I wonder how many of my infractions are up for discussion?

Murphy's message was short and to the point. However, it was the tone that made it quite clear to McAdams that time had run out. Murphy sounded like a father talking to a teen just kicked out of school. "McAdams. In my office. Now!"

He stopped long enough to download and print the photos that Garfield had emailed to him. He put them in a manila folder and put that in his desk drawer. He called Anna. "Stay inside. Don't answer the door – for anyone -- unless you hear from me." He was about to hang up when another thought occurred to him. "See if the internet will tell you who NV and S might be. And Torres had "PK" included in his shopping list. What does that mean? I'd start by trying to find out the names of the cargo ships that Pacific Cargo is running." He hung up without waiting for a reply.

Murphy's office had glass walls on the upper half, so McAdams could see Murphy leaning back against his desk, his arms folded. Three Latino men in dark suits stood in the corner of his office, talking among themselves. *I'll bet one of them is named Maldanado.*

"McAdams. About time."

McAdams said nothing, knowing what was coming. The three men were watching the two of them intently, as if readying themselves to break up a tense situation. They were very much alike – dark suits, dark skin, dark eyes, somewhere in their thirties, and very intense. For some reason that he could not identify, they impressed him as being soldiers rather than policemen. *It's probably the intensity. Cops pride themselves on their indifference.*

"You don't happen to know a Sergeant Mulloy in our Division, do you?" Murphy asked. The sarcasm was sufficiently obvious that McAdams knew that Murphy had made up his mind already about Mulloy's identity.

"The only Mulloy I know was a patrolman in the Sunset Division. He retired three or four years ago, I think. A seriously overweight fellow with a drinking problem."

Murphy glared. McAdams gazed back at him, trying to look merely curious rather than defensive.

Murphy sighed audibly and gestured to the trio of onlookers. "This is Captain Jorge Maldanado of the Mexican Federal Police Force. He just arrived from Mexico City and I've received very clear orders from the Chief that I'm to provide him every form of assistance I can." He did not sound happy about the situation.

The tallest of the three men stepped forward with his hand out to McAdams. They shook hands, neither of them saying anything. Once more, McAdams got a very strong feeling that Maldanado was military.

Let's try some empathy. He said to Murphy, "That's … unusual, isn't it? That kind of open-ended cooperation with people we don't know very well?" He smiled apologetically at Maldanado, whose expression did not change.

"I damn well do not like it! And neither did the Chief. She more than hinted that she was doing this under protest. Said something quite profane about DC meddlers…"

"Sounds like a rock band to me. But I'll be glad to cooperate. What can I do?"

Maldanado reached into his coat pocket and brought out the photo of the Reboso passport, the one that "Mulloy" had faxed to his boss very recently. He held it for McAdams to see. All four of the men in the room seemed to be watching him very closely.

Maldanado's English was impeccable. "Do you know who this is? And have you seen him recently?"

I wish I'd taken those acting lessons I once thought about. How did I ever get myself into this charade?

McAdams pretended to study the picture carefully. *OK, face. First we display nonchalance, then we shift the expression to quizzical, followed quickly by an 'Aha' look, and then segue into a mix of certainty and satisfaction.* In the end, however, he simply handed the picture back and said, "I

Thomas Hofstedt

think I've got a match for this. Murphy, I need to run to my office for something. I think Captain Maldanado will be very pleased."

Murphy looked like he was trying hard not to laugh. *Was my acting that bad?*

"A round trip to your office takes about 30 seconds. We'll wait. And it had better be good!"

He retrieved the manila folder from his desk drawer and took out Garfield's cellphone snapshot of Torres on the front steps of the Victorian. He was back in Murphy's office in about sixty seconds. He put the photo alongside the other on the corner of Murphy's desk.

"Is this the same guy?"

Murphy and the three Mexican cops leaned over and studied the two photos for about ten seconds. They straightened, looked at each other, and then at McAdams. Murphy looked intrigued; the Mexicans just looked intense, although Maldanado was showing a calculating gleam.

"He's about twenty minutes from here."

An Unofficial Reprimand

"He's about twenty minutes from here." The phrase seemed to change the quality of the air in Murphy's office. Each of the other four men seemed to stand straighter and become more aware of the others around them. One of the Mexicans said something very softly in Spanish. Murphy went around his desk and sat down in his chair. Both he and Maldanado started speaking at the same instant.

Murphy held up his hand. "Captain Maldanado. I need about two minutes with McAdams here. Then we can work out the jurisdictional details about what happens next."

This should be an interesting conversation.

The Mexicans filed out. Maldanado was dialing his cell phone before he was out the door.

Murphy motioned McAdams to the chair in front of the desk, then leaned back and folded his hands over his stomach, looking like a favorite uncle about to give advice to a nephew about where to go to college.

He held up the passport photo of Jose Reboso. "Mac, just for my personal entertainment, what's your official for-the-record *theory* about where this photo came from? His name is Torres, by the way."

He knows who 'Mulloy' is, but didn't mention him. Should I worry about that?

"I'd say it's a passport photo. It has that look about it. And we know he's here in town, probably using that name -- Reboso -- as an alias."

Murphy sounded as if he was reciting lines in a play. "So Mulloy must have gotten his passport picture from some source that he didn't want to disclose." His emphasis on the word 'Mulloy' was particularly heavy.

"I guess."

"And where did *this* photo come from?" Murphy held up the picture of Torres on the steps of the San Francisco Victorian.

Ah well, if you have to lie, stay as close to the truth as possible.

"One of those random things. The house where the photo was taken came up way out on the fringes of the Jane Doe investigation. It was a pretty remote possibility, so I asked one of my Tenderloin street people to watch it from time-to-time. He went beyond that to take cellphone pictures of people going in and out. That guy --" he pointed at the photo of Torres – "was one of them."

"One of them? You have other pictures?"

"Two." McAdams placed the photos of the women entering the house and the other Hispanic side by side on Murphy's desk. "Taken within a day or so. At the same location. And there's a third guy, another Hispanic, but I don't have any photos of him. His name might be Espinoza, but that's pretty slim."

Murphy looked closely at the photos. "Don't know 'em. But I'll bet our intense Captain Maldanado just might."

He leaned forward, his elbows on the desk. "Why don't you save us both a lot of time and stress and just tell me everything else you are withholding for whatever screwball reason?"

"The rest of what I've got is all conjecture, nothing hard."

"Conjecture, huh?" Murphy said. "I like conjecture. It's a sign of thinking. But it damn well better turn itself into the kind of evidence that the DA can actually use to prosecute someone. Please share your *conjectures* with us."

"OK." He pointed at the photos on the desk. "I think these people are here for some kind of narcotics summit meeting. Or to arrange a really big shipment. There's a lot of street buzz about new players coming in. And I've heard some talk about a transfer of some kind of illicit goods on April 13, at sea."

Murphy's one word question was eloquent. "Talk?"

"Actually, I've got some GPS coordinates."

"And there's this." He placed the post-it note with the 'shopping list' of chemicals that Anna had taken along

208

with Torres' coat. "It's also from Mulloy's anonymous source. He must have got it at the same time he got the passport picture."

Murphy glanced at the list and then sat straight up in his chair. "McAdams! For chrissakes! This is enough shit to keep every addict in the city topped off for six months!"

"I told you it's still just a hypothesis –"

"Hypothesis? Is that like a conjecture? Or something even fuzzier?"

McAdams ignored the sarcasm. *One more point to get out on the table. Then Murphy can get the right people going on the whole mess.*

"It's not just narcotics. I think they're involved in human trafficking as well."

"And that's based on …?"

"Remember our Jane Doe? The nude dumped in the Bay last month? Her name is Alexandra Vorokov, aka 'Sasha'. I'm guessing that she was a high-end Russian prostitute, one of several imported from the Russian Far East to be shopped around to people like Torres."

Murphy rolled his eyes to the ceiling, then smothered a mock yawn and asked, "Anything else Mulloy knows that I might like to know about? Any smuggling of nukes? Presidential assassination teams? Counterfeiting rings? Stock frauds? Intent to double-park?"

"I know it sounds –"

"It sounds goddamed paranoid is what it sounds like. Either that or you and Mulloy are writing a screenplay."

Murphy sat up straight and added, in a mockingly casual way, "By the way, a Patrolman Tedosky called from Oakland. He said to tell you that he's circulating the photo you sent him…. This one, I think." Murphy held up the other Torres photo, the one from the Reboso passport.

Oops!

"You forgot to use the Mulloy alias for Tedosky, like you did with Captain Alvarez."

"Murphy, I didn't … I needed to … Damn it!'

209

Murphy waved dismissively. "We'll revisit the rule book later. The one you seem to have such a hard time with. For now, I'm ignoring all your penny ante vigilante stuff because Torres is a genuine bad guy and I want him gone. In any case, you're not under my command at the moment."

"Not under –"

"I've been asked to lend you to the Feds, the DEA in particular. It seems that they're working closely with their Mexican counterparts to dismantle the drug cartels. They've got a team on the way to *co-advise on his detention* – such a nice phrase, don't you think."

"Why me?"

Murphy smirked. "Let's see. Let me count the ways."

He held up his right fist, raising a finger for each point. "First, it's a covert form of punishment for your 'I'll do it myself' form of policing. Second, you seem to know more about Torres than anybody else. Third, they asked for you, poor souls. Fourth, maybe it'll distract you from whatever you're obsessed about. Fifth, …. I can't remember."

"Murphy, I don't –"

"Oh, yeah. I remember." The thumb went up.

"Fifth, you're a damn good cop and I need somebody I can trust to make sure this goddam global law enforcement coalition that's been shoved down our goddam throats doesn't turn North Beach into a goddam war zone!"

McAdams asked, "SFPD is shut out of the op?"

"In Washington-speak, we can *observe and provide logistical support, if needed.* That's you, by the way. If they exceed the goddam speed limit attempting to escape, you can write them a goddam traffic ticket."

What isn't he telling me?

As if he'd heard McAdams' thought, Murphy said, "A couple of things …"

"First, Maldanado is not your usual cop. He's military, part of El Presidente's very bloody war on drugs … and drug lords. So he comes with some baggage you need to watch out for."

"Baggage?"

"Two things. One obvious, the other not so obvious. The obvious one is that he may not care very much whether Torres comes out of that North Beach Victorian in a body bag or in handcuffs. He gives me the impression of being on a vendetta. That is a Spanish word, isn't it?"

"Italian, I think. But they're both romance languages."

Murphy looked pained. "Whatever." Then he lowered his voice and looked around, like a politician about to tell a racist joke at the local country club.

"The other piece of baggage? The Mexicans have a wee problem with corruption. Scum like Torres scatter money around and it's hard to know who to trust."

"Maldanado?"

"Seems OK, but watch your ass."

It was a catch phrase, as common in cop-to-cop talk as "Have a good day" would be in the civilian world. But something in Murphy's voice or eyes gave the words an extra edge. It startled McAdams. *It's not just me that's grieving, is it? Gonzo and Freddie were a part of Murphy's world too. Two officers – part of a closely-knit family – are gone. And he was the father equivalent.*

He looked at Murphy, but he had turned to the window, his back to McAdams. He waved a hand in dismissal. "Now get the hell out of here and don't screw up the Torres op!"

Swat Team Time

I feel like a home plate umpire.
        McAdams was uncomfortable with the bulky body armor draped around him. *Makes my standard issue Kevlar vest look like beach wear.* On the other hand, Maldanado looked not only at ease with the outfit, but as though it was his natural style.

Twenty minutes to go.

They were watching the Victorian from across the street, using a third-floor vacant apartment that the SFPD had commandeered for the evening. They kept the lights out and stayed back from the windows. A dozen heavily armed DEA agents were waiting at either end of the street and in the alley behind the house. SFPD was ready to stop traffic and set up a cordon for two blocks on all sides when the "Go" signal came. It took some serious pleading, but Murphy had finally gotten the head DEA agent to agree to give the SFPD a chance to clear the buildings on either side before the Victorian was raided.

The feds had set up some fancy infra-red gear and were using McAdams' space for a monitoring station. The technician had already told them the essentials: "There are four people in there, two on the first level, two more on the second level. They're moving around some, so we know they aren't sleeping."

The deal was that this was to be a DEA operation, headed by a Washington DC agent named Ritter. With twelve agents involved, the main concern was to avoid getting hit by friendly fire if shooting broke out. The plan was for one six-man team to go in the back with the other team blocking the front from the outside and watching the narrow alleys on either side of the house. The SFPD and the Mexican trio of policemen were there to watch, told in no uncertain terms that they were to stay out of the action.

McAdams and Maldanado stood side by side watching the infra-red display. "Murphy said that you were military. On loan to the federal police?"

Maldanado smiled. "I am a colonel in our army … what you might call 'special forces'." My unit is presently responsible for drug enforcement for the state of Baja California."

McAdams flashed on what he knew about what that entailed, recalling horrific stories of atrocities and corruption. *Makes my job look about like a nanny at a day care center.*

"You've been chasing Torres for quite a while." It was a statement, not a question.

"Yes."

"Have you ever gotten this close before?"

"No."

"You must be looking forward to the end of this? To his capture?" He couldn't help putting a slight emphasis on the last word.

Maldanado looked at him and sighed.

"Yes."

"What will you –"

Maldanado stopped him with a raised hand. "Your Captain Murphy said that you were … independent … but I think he did not mean it as a compliment?"

"We have a complicated relationship."

When Maldanado just looked at him, he went on. "Two of my partners … friends of mine … were murdered recently. Murphy thinks I'm taking it personally … that I'm too impatient … vengeful … to stay within the boundaries."

The disclosure changed Maldanado visibly. For the first time, he looked directly at McAdams; a direct penetrating stare that somehow conveyed shared pain.

"Are you? Vengeful? Impatient?"

We got to the main question right away, didn't we? But I'm not going to answer it for a part-time Mexican quasi-cop with dubious motives.

"I just want to catch the bastard and look him in the eye."

Maldanado smiled in a way that told McAdams he knew two things, that he was evading the question and that he – Maldanado – already knew the answer.

McAdams went on the offensive. "What about you? What will you do when he's standing in front of you in cuffs?"

Maldanado looked out the window at the Victorian across the street for a long ten seconds, apparently studying its blank face. When he spoke, it was if he was talking to himself.

"You lost two partners, yes? That's hard. Did you know that there have been *fifty-thousand* drug-related murders in Mexico in the last five years? Did you know that the Torres cartel has executed *hundreds* of politicians, soldiers and policemen in Baja just within the last year? Did you know that three of those hundreds were my younger brothers? Their names were Tomas, Francisco and Pedro. They were beheaded and left in front of the Tijuana city hall."

Christ!

"Jesus, Jorge! I'm sorry. I feel like –"

Maldanado interrupted in a rough voice. "Your *feelings*" – he made the word into an epithet – "are irrelevant. What matters is that this butcher is stopped. Tonight!"

I have to ask him. I need to know. Is it just me?

"Jorge?" he asked tentatively. "I need to know. What will you do when he's standing in front of you?"

Maldanado's eyes blazed and his lips were a thin slash across his face. He started, "I shall –", but he stopped himself and forced a semblance of indifference into his features.

"That – what I might do or say – is as irrelevant as your *feelings*. Your DEA will take possession of him. We can try to extradite him, but that will be up to the politicians, not the policemen."

The door opened. One of Maldanado's men came in. "Es el momento de."

From their window, they watched the patrol cars deploy at either end of the block, stopping traffic but not displaying any flashing lights. The house opposite them seemed unchanged. A black box truck drove to the front of the house and six men piled out carrying assault rifles and other gear, positioning themselves to cover both the front entrance and the side alleys. McAdams knew that the other team was going in at the rear of the building. He glanced at the infrared screen and saw a confused mingling of hazy shapes in the small space.

The tactical radio on the small table near the window came to life. The voice of the lead agent was crystal clear. "We're inside. There's some noise –" The sound of semiautomatic weapons was strangely muted. *They must be using some kind of muzzle suppression devices.* When the voice came back, it was different, more staccato. "OK. We've got two hostiles down. Everybody OK here. We're going upstairs."

From the window, they could see muzzle flashes and dark shapes. The upstairs remained dark except for two windows facing the front, apparently rooms lit from within.

Ninety seconds later, the team leader's voice came on. "One more in custody, a Hispanic male. No sign of anybody else. House is clear. Team conducting in-depth sweep. Torres isn't here."

House is clear? But there were four heat signatures! One of these shitheads is on the loose! How?

Then he remembered Anna's story. *She was there. And she escaped. How?* She told him about the window that faced the alley and overlooked the roof of the adjacent building. *I found a metal staircase at the rear of the building … into an alley that led to the street. And that was from the Torres bedroom.*

From his third-story window across the street, he looked down on the next-door roof at a slight angle. It was in darkness, with several solid cubes dotting its surface – commercial air-conditioning units probably. A shape on the roof was moving slowly, crouching on the inside of the far parapet. The DEA agents on the ground watching the side alleys between the buildings were in no position to be aware of the person twenty feet above them.

Later, in the post-action debrief, McAdams was asked why he didn't use the tactical radio to alert the DEA team.

His lame "I forgot about the radio" didn't fool Murphy or Maldanado.

"Jorge! He's on the roof! Headed for the street! Come on!"

They careened down the narrow stairs and out the front door. A quick glance confirmed that both alleys onto the street were covered. So Torres could go only one direction once down the metal stairway – toward the Bay. He grabbed Maldanado's arm and pulled him that direction. They turned the corner at a dead run, Maldanado now in the lead by several yards.

The SFPD blockade had stopped traffic at both ends of the street. Pedestrians and cars were queued up in clusters on the corners. Most of the pedestrians were moving down the hill, trying to find out what all the excitement was about. A lone man was walking rapidly away from them, headed uphill about fifty yards away. He was barefoot, carrying a small backpack by one strap.

Maldanado screamed "Torres!" and ran at him, carrying his handgun like it was the Olympic Torch. The people streaming down the hill saw a madman running and waving a gun. They took off in all directions and McAdams found himself dodging wild-eyed civilians headed for safety.

Three hours later, McAdams was sitting in Murphy's office.

Murphy spoke through clenched teeth. "Let's see if I've got all my facts straight. We've got one in custody and three bodies, right? All dead by gunshot wounds?"

McAdams didn't even bother to nod.

"And the shooters are all gone, and I'm not to bother them with a lot of pesky questions. Is that correct?"

The Feds had slammed the lid on them, citing 'federal case', 'national security' and 'international relations' as the rationale. The DEA team was on their way back to Washington with a Colombian citizen named 'Emilio' and boxes of confiscated materials from the Victorian. Their public relations department was already issuing press releases saying that a major drug bust had taken place and that they were *evaluating a considerable quantity of documents that were confiscated*. Maldanado and his two aides were on their chartered jet and halfway home to Mexico City by now. Officially, in fact, they were never here.

Murphy went on. "Oh, yeah. I'm forgetting the dead guys. The ones that were so inconsiderate and stayed around so that we'd have to think up some plausible story to explain how they got dead? Let's see ... they are suspected members of an international crime syndicate, killed while resisting arrest. We're having trouble identifying them, but will let the press know as soon as can we discover who they are."

Murphy looked at McAdams with a considerable degree of belligerence. McAdams couldn't blame him.

"How am I doing? Do I have my lines down?"

McAdams said softly, "You missed the bit about 'a fine example of federal, state and local law enforcement agencies working together in the War on Drugs'."

"It's all bullshit, isn't it?"

"Yes, but it's newsworthy bullshit. TV networks will use it to sell a lot of ads. It will play well on the evening news."

Then Murphy looked straight at McAdams and asked the question that he could not ... would not ... answer. "What happened to Torres? Barefoot. Nowhere near the house."

His first and least serious lie was to Murphy. "I couldn't tell. I was too far away and dodging panic-stricken civilians."

Actually, he was only about twenty feet away when Torres turned around to face Maldanado. Torres put his right hand into the backpack he was carrying and waited. Maldanado stopped a few feet short of him, still with his weapon held vertically. Just for a second, if one ignored the pistol, they looked like two friends who had stopped to chat after a chance encounter on a city sidewalk. McAdams could not hear the words, but he clearly saw that Maldanado said something to Torres, who responded briefly, with a smile.

The second and far more serious lie was to himself. *Torres was reaching for a gun in the backpack. Jorge shot in self-defense. That's how I interpret what happened.*

What he *saw* ... the *facts*, free from bias or subjective interpretations ... what he *saw* was that Maldanado brought his gun down and fired a single shot into Torre's forehead from no more than a foot away.

What he still did not know, what he desperately wanted to ask Maldanodo but never had the chance, was *what did you say to Torres before you shot him? Did you ask 'Why?'"*

Call Me Sofia

An hour later, McAdams rang the bell to his own home, not wanting to alarm Anna by walking in on her unexpectedly. He stood so that he was easily identifiable through the peephole in the thick oak door, feeling as though he was posing for a picture. *They must teach this kind of reassuring behavior to the Mormon kids that they send on missions.*

She opened the door and stood looking at him, one hand behind her back. "It's your house, McAdams. You don't need to ring the bell." She was barefooted, wearing a plain black T-shirt and blue jeans. *Either she'd been shopping or her shoulder bag doubled as a suitcase.*

"I didn't want to frighten you by suddenly walking in on you."

She smiled a very sad smile. "I don't frighten very easily any more. I've been practicing not being scared."

"This helps." She brought her hand out from behind her back. It was holding the nine mm Beretta that he kept in his desk drawer. She showed it to him, lying flat on her palm and pointed away from him. He noted that the safety was off.

He experienced about a three-second surge of indignation, the kind of *you've been going through my things* reaction one might expect if you found a house guest rummaging through your personal papers. The sensation didn't last, pushed out by an image of her in his shirt – and then not in his shirt -- beneath him, moving in ways that were at first calculated and then uncontrolled rippling responses to waves of pleasure that engulfed them both. The whipsawing emotions left him feeling suddenly exhausted.

He cleared his throat. "Do you know how to use that thing?" he asked, pointing at the Beretta.

The simple question made her strangely still, as if she needed to be careful about how she answered. After a long pause, she said, "I had a boy friend once. His name was Dmitri. He was a soldier when he was young."

Her voice trailed off and her eyes lost their focus, visualizing a past life that was so remote and irretrievable that it might have been an existence from another planet or century. It was only for a few seconds, but it reminded McAdams that she had a past that he knew nothing about. *Who is this woman and what does she want from me?*

She literally shook herself and then looked at the handgun. "He was different when he came back from Chechnya. He was mean, and he drank a lot ... more than before. Dmitri loved guns. All kinds, but especially pistols. Every Sunday, we would go into the forest and shoot. He would teach me about his guns. And tell me stories about them. He even had names for them."

"What happened to Dmitri?"

The faraway look came back and she spoke in tones utterly devoid of feeling. "He chose the wrong side. One day, he just wasn't there anymore."

She held the Beretta up, looking at it like she was at Walmart looking at a power tool she was thinking of buying. "So you ask me if I know how to use this thing? Yes, I do."

McAdams was recalling Eileen Moresby in her front doorway. *She was in a shooter's stance, with the recommended two-handed grip, squeezing off carefully aimed rounds. Who are these women!*

She walked to the cluster of upholstered furniture near the glass wall that made up what McAdams thought of as 'the living room'. It was defined by a very large rectangular rug with a modern design, very Mondrian with lots of bright colors. An L-shaped sofa and two armchairs clustered around a two-level glass coffee table. A metal sculpture on the table was the centerpiece of the area; a contemporary stainless steel head of what might have been an Aztec princess. Two floor lamps at opposite corners of the rug provided light.

Anna sat in the corner of the sofa, pulling her feet under her and folding her hands in her lap. She put the

Beretta down on the cushion next to her. He noted that the safety was now on. McAdams sat down at the other end of the sofa. Except for the Beretta, it was all very domestic, looking like the prelude to an ordinary end-of-day scene that begins with the line, *And how was your day, dear?*

Anna was nervous for reasons she could not identify. *It's this damned domestic bit … the little woman waiting for her man to come home … for once not being afraid … this vague feeling that I'm missing something. No –losing something that I don't even know that I want … That I'm about to make a horrible mistake.*

The real cause of her nervousness was much simpler: For the first time in her life, she was unsure of herself. The "just do it" mantra was not suited to her current state of mind, where she neither knew what she wanted nor how to get whatever it was even if she could name it.

McAdams mistook her hesitancy. "About being afraid? Or not? There's some good news on that front."

She said nothing and did not change her expression, as though any acknowledgment of what he had said would somehow jeopardize the truth of whatever it was.

"Torres is dead, along with two of his bodyguards. Emilio Espinoza – or whatever his name is – is on his way to Washington and – I think -- a long time in a U.S. prison. Thanks to your information."

Again, she said nothing. She closed her eyes for about three seconds and, when she opened them, there was a perceptible change in her posture. It was as if the rigidity seeped out of her, like someone who'd given up on holding her breath. The transition somehow increased the fullness of her lips and changed what had been sharp angles into curves and rounded surfaces.

McAdams saw the question in her eyes. He said, "The others? They weren't there. No Americans. No other Latin types."

His cell phone rang. The caller ID flashed 'Murphy'.

He answered 'McAdams', listened for thirty seconds, said 'OK', and hung up.

"That was my boss. He circulated the descriptions of the men you called Reynaldo and this Emilio and got some quick hits. Reynaldo is Reynaldo Vargas. He's the Venezuelan equivalent to Jose Torres, very high up on the U.S. and Venezuelan 'Most Wanted' lists of narcotics types. Emilio – his real name is Esposito -- is a little harder to pin down. Apparently, he's the number two in a Colombian cartel heavily involved in human trafficking as well as drugs. Nothing whatsoever about the two Americans you've seen."

"What about the house? Who owns it?"

Interesting. That's the kind of question a cop would ask.

"Dead end. A Chinese landlord who lives in Shanghai and uses a local realtor to manage the property. The forms all lead to a non-existent address and the rent is paid in cash each month."

"But aren't there tax forms … disclosure rules …?"

"Yes, but there's a lot of cash slopping around. The agent is probably skimming off the top to compensate him for ignoring all the usual rules."

He asked, "How did you do at decoding 'NV' and 'S'?"

She shrugged. "'NV' was easy. All of the Fallon ships are named 'Northern something or other'. I'm betting that 'NV' equals 'Northern Voyager' … currently en-route from Anchorage to San Francisco with an intermediate stop in Seattle. 'S' could be anybody or anything... probably another ship from somewhere."

"Not many poppy fields in Anchorage."

"That makes this NV an unlikely candidate for drug smuggling, doesn't it? But if you're transporting ambitious and misguided women from Vladivostock …. "

"What about 'PK'?"

"That's even easier. Primorski Krai is the official name for the Russian Far East. It's a huge land area that includes Vladivostock. It would be very easy for a freighter on a far northern Alaskan run to make a call in any of several ports in PK. Or even easier to arrange a meeting with a Russian ship headed south. I'm sure Torres' notes mean that the NV shipment includes ten more Russian women."

She paused and the sadness came through very strongly. "Like me."

He stood up and went to the refrigerator, returning with a bottle of Chardonnay and two glasses. He poured two glasses and handed one to her. She smothered a laugh as she took the glass from him. When he looked quizzically at her, she said, "The last time I was in this situation, I hit the man – very hard – with the bottle."

"I remember. You told me." He glanced at the gun on the cushion between them and used the stem of his wineglass to nudge it toward her. "It's probably simpler if you just shoot me."

"But you promised me you would find the man who killed Sasha. If I shoot you, you cannot do that." She turned sideways on the sofa, her long legs spanning the gap between them, putting her bare feet into his lap. "Nor could you do certain other things that I like very much."

I think she's just changed the subject. It's funny – I never thought of feet as being erotic, or even interesting. Hers are so white. Maybe it's the contrast with the neon red nail polish. And the toes are so angular and bony, but the smooth curve along the ankle and top of the foot – a double inflection point, if I remember my geometry. Without thinking about it, he started stroking her ankle.

She sipped her wine, watching him intently, as if she was aware of the monologue he was conducting in his own mind and was trying to listen to it.

His jumbled thoughts kept changing course in his head. *Who is this woman? Can I trust you? Why are you doing this? What am I to you -- somebody to get you what you want in exchange for some world-class fucking? How many serious relationships have I had? Three? Maybe four if I count my ex-wife? And what have I learned? That cops – what they do and what it makes them – do not go well with certain kinds of women ... the kind I want. I know absolutely nothing about you except that you are a survivor and incredibly good in bed. That's not enough. Especially when you're screwing up my professional life.*

As if he had convinced himself of something, he lifted her feet off his lap, stood up and moved to the chair facing her. His voice even changed, taking on the weary tones of a person who believes he is about to be lied to.

"Do you have anything else to sell me? In lieu of rent?"

She reacted like she'd been slapped. Shock, then anger. She slowly condensed herself into the smallest possible space, pulling her knees up and wrapping her arms around them, with her chin resting on top of her knees. Somehow, it made her eyes look enormous. And sad. She just looked at him, saying nothing. She resembled a hurt child who had just been scolded for reasons she did not understand.

He did not relent, as though her silence justified the profound insecurity that was driving his inquisition. "You told me who Sasha was. You gave me Torres. And the Victorian. And the ship stuff. What's left that's of value to me? What else do you have to bargain with?" The unspoken phrase "except for …" hung in the still air when he stopped.

Indeed. Anna thought. *What else do I have to offer except good sex? He asked 'How did Sasha get to the U.S.' and I said 'On her back'. And yet …*

A series of vignettes flashed by in her mind. There was Ellerby, accepting her at face value when Moresby introduced her as a friend of a friend. The encounters at his fund-raising event where both men and women talked to her as though she was something more than a commodity. Even Torres briefly looked at her as a person. And then McAdams, especially McAdams. He offered her asylum without any real expectations on his part. And when she used the line to get his clothes off -- "And besides, I want to" -- she was startled when she realized that she meant it. And the sex was different, less calculated, more … mutual. With tantalizing hints of new and risky possibilities. *And now this*

… this distance, this … cop stuff. He's feeling guilty because he used me. Or angry because I used him.

She caught herself calculating odds, running through alternative scenarios in her head. *How can I get what I want? What will work right now?* But she had no answer to the first question, because she didn't know what she wanted. It frightened her and caused her to respond in a way that surprised her.

"No. I have nothing left to bargain with. I've told you everything that a policeman would be interested in." Her almost imperceptible emphasis on the word *policeman* was her only concession to her old self, the one that believed that men could and should be manipulated to get what one wanted.

McAdams knew that she had offered him a choice. What he did not know was which option to take. He tried for an equivocal middle ground.

"Where will you go?'

"Back to Moresby's house, if she'll have me. And Ellerby."

He remembered Garfield's description of the watcher sitting outside Eileen Moresby's Pacific Heights home. Even more disturbing, he thought of Ellerby's still-vague connections to the killings of Freddie and Gonzo.

He asked lamely, "Do you think that's safe?"

"You told me Torres is dead, with two of his guards. That Emilio is put away."

"That still leaves Reynaldo and at least two local Americans with an interest in keeping you quiet."

She shrugged. "By now, they know I've talked to you. They have no more reason to come after me." *Unless Torres told them what was on that slip of paper in his pocket.* Even to herself, the words sounded hollow, unconvincing. She stood up.

It was McAdams turn to be surprised by his own reaction. "Look. Stay here another couple of days. Just until we get a little more clarity about who's who and this drug deal that may or may not happen."

Now it's my turn to choose. Stay or leave? And on whose terms? She observed that her right hand was toying with the hem of her T-shirt, ready to implement one of her scenarios and pull the shirt off over her head. *But his offer to stay is because he's really afraid for me, not because I look good naked.* In the end, she also chose the middle ground.

"I'll stay for a day or so. On the sofa."

He tried not to let his relief show. Nor did he attempt to analyze the basis for it. "OK. And put the Beretta away, will you? I don't want to get shot if I get up in the middle of the night."

Somewhere around four in the morning, Anna crept into his bed, still wearing the T-shirt and jeans. He remained absolutely still while she wriggled her way under the covers and pressed her entire length against his back, breathing on the back of his neck, her right arm snaking around him so that her hand rested in the crease where his neck and shoulder met.

"Anna, I –"

"Sshh. Go back to sleep. I just wanted to hold someone."

Several minutes passed, long enough that their breathing became almost synchronized and all of the tension seeped out of him, leaving only a sense of bone-deep comfort from her warmth pressed against him. He was almost asleep when she whispered, "Mac. One more favor, the last one?"

"Um?"

"Call me Sofia. Please."

Renegotiated Contracts

*C*hrist, I might as well be back in the CIA! Grodin had caught the redeye to Miami for the eight AM meeting with Vargas in the Holiday Inn at the airport. The meeting was arranged by a phone call that lasted twenty seconds. Grodin had anticipated the call, so the barked series of commands did not surprise him. *They've heard about the raid and they know that Jose and Emilio are off the table, of course. They're wondering if the entire deal is blown. But they want to meet, so they haven't decided to pull the plug yet.*

"This is Vargas. You will meet me. Tomorrow. In Florida."

He said, "OK. Where and when?" Vargas told him and hung up.

The morning news headlined the raid on the Victorian, with dramatic pictures of bodies being loaded into the coroner's vehicles. Even with the minimal details that were made public, it was clear to him that Torres and his crew were dead and that Esposito was in the hands of the DEA. He also noted that the San Francisco cop on the scene was McAdams, the same guy Desmond had been dialing just before dying so unexpectedly.

I wonder if that's a coincidence? If they put Desmond and Sasha together … I think it's time for Plan B…

He called Carlo on his way to the San Francisco Airport. Carlo was barely suppressing his panic, firing rapid-fire phrases, each one closer to the hysteria threshold. "What happened? Have you heard from Vargas? We gotta shut down! Will Emilio keep his mouth shut? What the hell happened –"

It's like dealing with a ten-year-old. Grodin cut him off in a sharp voice. "Calm down. If we were blown, you'd be neck deep in cops by now. All that's happened is we've got two less players. Makes life simpler. And more profitable. I'm off to hold Vargas' hand. I'll see you as soon as I get back." He pushed the 'off' button before Carlo could respond.

Vargas's flight to Miami from Bogota was thirty minutes late. He showed up alone, clearly in a foul mood. He wasted no time.

"What the fuck happened?"

"Take your pick. Somebody blabbed. Or Torres or Esposito got spotted. Or one of your people is playing both sides. Or the DEA got lucky." The recitation was uninflected. He looked at Vargas with an expression that conveyed how little he cared about explaining past events.

When he started talking again, the tone was somewhere between sarcastic and angry, ratcheted up to match Vargas' hostility level. "Who cares! Shit happens. The real question is what happens to our deal?"

Vargas leaned back, folding his arms. "That's easy. We call it off. My people don't want to hand two thousand kilos of product over to some cop who's got a copy of the game plan." This time, his tone was softer, hinting that his words might be construed as a question, that negotiation was possible.

Christ! I might as well be back in Central Africa, negotiating arms deals with idiots with machetes; the kind that thinks the best negotiator is the scariest looking guy at the table. Any second now, he'll put on his most sinister look and tell me a gory story about what happened to the last person that tried to change a deal midstream.

"Not to quibble, Reynaldo, but your bunch – the Venezuelan side -- has only got five-hundred kilos at stake. In any case, the Colombians and the Mexicans might feel differently... especially with Jose and Emilio out of the game. More risk, sure. But also more money, fewer hands out."

Vargas' contempt came through quite clearly. "Your choice of words is interesting. *Only* five-hundred kilos is the biggest single shipment we've ever made of product of this quality. And I can speak for the Torres and Esposito people as well."

Now that's interesting. The Mexicans, Colombians and Venezuelans trust each other. Maybe there is something to this 'globalization' shit. And they still want the deal to happen. It's funny how quickly people get used to the idea of fifty million dollars in their pocket. And now he's going to tell me they need even more than that to cover the added risk. Time for a preemptive wrinkle.

"It can still happen. First, we don't think the narcs are aware of it. Nobody's been nosing around the ships and all the hotshot DEA bigwigs have gone back to Washington. And anyway, we're changing the procedures just in case."

Vargas sat without speaking, merely raising his eyebrows. Grodin went on. "We'll offload the stuff from the ships – both the drugs and the women – long before we go into the Bay. If they do raid the boats, they'll find nothing except consumer electronics products from the Far East."

Vargas agreed, much too quickly. "OK. That should help." He smiled at Grodin as though he had just passed some test.

The bastards were never going to call off the deal, just jack up the price.

But he was wrong.

"And the price is still fifty," Vargas said. "But we want it up front -- when the stuff goes on board the Voyager from the Sigilo. Same as before -- ten mill of it in cash, the rest transferred into our accounts. You own it … It's your problem how to get it onshore."

Cute! They get paid a premium price and take zero risk. Grodin did not hesitate in responding. "No deal. That puts all of the risk on us. That price was based on the stuff on a pier in San Francisco Bay, not a hundred miles at sea."

Vargas scowled. He started, "That was before …"

Grodin didn't even begin to listen. He interrupted, "First law of drug deals, Reynaldo. Both sides have to have skin in the game. How about this? Forty up-front, when the goods come on board the Voyager, direct wire transfer to your people. The other ten in cash, when the goods are onshore and ready to move."

Carlo's already on the hook for the fifty mill. The Russians won't take the money back now. No risk for me …

As if it was an afterthought, he went on. "And the women? No change. You still get five of the ten for three million in cash. You can pick which ones. On the dock."

Vargas sat back, looking at Grodin but clearly running various calculations in his mind. Finally, he leaned forward and smiled in a way that worried Grodin, telling him clearly that his counter-proposals had been anticipated. *We're following his script. We're exactly where he wanted to be. That's OK. Let him think he's in charge.*

But the next move was a game changer. Vargas shrugged and said, "Okay … with one more condition: We want you – you personally, not some low-level expendable – to be with the stuff from the time it's transferred from the Sigilo until it's on wheels and off the pier."

Grodin's expression didn't change as he thought of all the reasons he didn't like the proposed arrangement. *That puts me in the crosshairs if the cops are waiting.*

Grodin knew that his reaction would be critical. If he flinched, Vargas would be instantly nervous. *One of the oldest tricks around. The guide says, 'trust me, this way is safe, no risk of ambush'. So you tell the guide he's going to be at the head of the column, first in line if shooting starts. If he starts to whine and back out, you know he's setting you up.*

But that makes me the bearer of ten million in cash, the final payment on the pier. Plus the three million for the women. And nobody but me and Carlo know how or where the stuff is coming ashore.

He shrugged, an eloquent expression of indifference. "I'll have to run it by Carlo. It's his money."

Vargas smiled in a way that told Grodin he knew quite well who was making the decisions.

"You do that. I've got forty-five minutes before I have to be back at the boarding gate."

Grodin stood up. But when he turned to leave, Vargas stopped him.

"One more thing. It's not negotiable."

"The runner – Sofia – you still haven't found her?"

Grodin shook his head.

"The other two … her friends that were there when she ran … they're still around?"

Grodin nodded. *I know where this is going.*

He was right. Vargas stood up, saying, "They need to be gone."

Lethal Arithmetic

The two men sitting in the office on the top floor of the Pacific Cargos offices near the Oakland docks were alone in the building. The room was lit by a single hanging lamp that created a well-defined cone of light centered on the conference table, but each of the men had pushed his chair back so that they were in semi-darkness. It was as if a low-budget Hollywood film director was trying to suggest a conspiratorial setting. Such an impression was aided considerably by the silence, punctuated only by the sound of a foghorn at twenty-second intervals.

"This pipeline idea? It's all fucked up!" As usual, Carlo spoke in sharp, staccato sentences, in tones of absolute certitude. Grodin had come to think of the style as though Hemingway had become a conservative radio talk show host.

He responded mildly. "Twenty-six percent personnel losses is a bit high, I admit. But it's still a nice little business. It's made us a lot of money and friends."

There was a long silence. Grodin made a small bet with himself. *He's doing the math and wondering where the twenty-six percent number came from. That'll be his next question.*

"Twenty-six percent?"

Grodin smiled. "I'm rounding."

"You count funny. I only get –"

Grodin interrupted, "We've got ten on the way, if your rust bucket Northern Voyager doesn't sink before it gets here. And we've already placed four others with your new friends in Vegas – quarter-of-a-million each, as I recall."

"Yeah, so?"

"That's fourteen … the good ones … solid revenue producers placed with happy customers. The proof that the product concept is sound." *It's hard to keep from laughing, but the mutt likes the buzzwords. Needs to establish that he went to business school maybe. So we'll talk about 'pipeline economics' rather than 'importing whores'.*

As if to prove Grodin's point, Carlo went on, "So, how'd you get that twenty-six percent personnel losses? There's Sasha … Sasha-in-the-Bay." He giggled. "Sounds like a song title. And Anya. I liked her."

"And Sofia."

Grodin had the now-familiar reaction to the name. It always caused him to experience a strange combination of anger and admiration, a blend of emotions that had been long dormant until Sofia. *I could see it coming. She was going to run. But the bitch was way ahead of me. She's good. And she's a threat that has to be dealt with.*

Carlo's voice went up an octave. "Thanks to that fucking Torres! If he'd –"

"Carlo! You're lucky that Torres didn't have his quartet of dark-skinned personal goons carve you into little pieces. You handed him this gorgeous woman and guaranteed him a good time. You told him, 'A Russian … a woman that knows how to keep a man warm in the winter.' And then she clouts him with a bottle of champagne, steals his coat and passport with his brand-new identity which he'd just paid a million bucks for! If we weren't dangling a fifty million dollar deal in front of him, he'd be strangling you with your own intestines."

I wonder what else our Sofia got out of Torres? He's not telling us everything about that episode. It shows in his new face every time her name comes up.

Carlo was still doing arithmetic. He said sullenly, "OK. So. We lost Sasha, Anya and Sofia. That's three out of seventeen … nowhere near your twenty-six percent."

"You're forgetting about our current inventory – Natalia and Maria."

Even in the semi-darkness, it was easy to see Carlo's expression. He started with a frown that quickly migrated into the kind of smugness that a student displays when he catches the teacher in an error.

"So? That makes it even better -- three out of nineteen. Sixteen percent, not twenty-six."

He paused and then added, "I'm rounding." He leaned back with his arms crossed, like a debater who had just delivered a crushing argument, leaving his opponent wordless.

He reminds me of the desk jockeys at Langley. They loved to count things, to arrange them in little piles, to move tokens around on maps, to assume that the names or tokens had no volition or randomness that would screw up their 'scenarios' and 'initiatives'.

Grodin was pleased with the way the conversation had progressed, bringing them precisely to the point where his next words would have maximum effect.

"You've put Natalia and Maria in the 'success' column. I think they should be counted among our losses. That makes it five out of nineteen: twenty-six percent."

"But they're … they're working … they're …" He struggled for the word. "They're *happy*, for god's sake!"

Now there's a helluva characterization of prostitution. Wonder what he would say about slavery?

"The word I would use is *dangerous.* We've kept them around too long. They know a great deal about us – you and me – and about the pipeline. And about the deal that we're working out with the cartels. Reynaldo's been bragging about it to them. *And*, he thought to himself, *they've seen Sofia's example*.

"Christ, Grodin! Are you proposing … We've already whacked three street runners, Anya and Sasha … and a cop for Christ's sake! The insurance guy, Desmond. And the homeless guy running around saying the world is coming to an end. And you want to add two more?"

"It's not just me. Vargas and Torres suggested it as soon as Sofia ran." He emphasized the word 'suggested'. "They made it sound like a demand… a condition for going ahead with the deal. And I'm certain that Emilio would agree – if he still had a vote."

Then he used the buzzwords, always the clincher in a close call.

"Look, Carlo. They're expendable. Excess and obsolete inventory with all kinds of product liability if we try to put them in play in Vegas. Think of it this way: the potential cost to you if we keep them far exceeds the few hundred-thousand bucks you'll get if we move them to the end of the pipeline. It's a straightforward cost-benefit analysis."

"And a twenty-six percent loss rate? That's acceptable if your profit margins are big enough."

Carlo pouted, his usual reaction when he had to be talked into something. "OK, but I don't like it!"

Grodin figured that the stage was set for the real purpose of the conversation. "And there's one more thing … two, actually."

"On the drug buy, Torres and Esposito are out of the picture, and we've got a bunch of very nervous Colombians, Venezuelans and Mexicans. They're going to want to redistribute the risk – to us. I'm thinking we need to script a slightly different outcome – something that gives us more weight at the table."

Carlo's first reaction was alarm, but it quickly morphed into a calculating look, then became puzzled. "Why? Don't we need them?" And before Grodin could answer, Carlo asked the relevant question. "Isn't that dangerous? The cartels will rip us to pieces if we try to run a scam on them."

"No scams. Just some adjustment of the payment arrangements. Torres and Esposito are already gone. They won't blame us for them … that was the DEA, not us. And they still need us on this end. We pay well and we can get the stuff here … reliably."

"How would you do it?"

"That's the second thing I want to run by you. I think we need to change the arrangements for bringing the stuff in …."

235

A Form of Repatriation

Natalia and Maria were bored.
They had been cooped up in the offices of the Cultural Exchange Program on the waterfront for the last twenty-four hours. Madge, the stolid black woman at the desk, had gotten a call at eight that morning. When she hung up, she told them, "You two are to stay put. They're moving you to Vegas sometime today and they want you where they can find you on short notice."

She took their cell phones, saying they'd get new and better models in Vegas. They asked if they could use the internet, but Madge told them 'No'. And no TV. She said it was broken and had been taken away for repairs. They were reduced to reading the few magazines that were lying around.

Two hours later, Grodin showed up with a suitcase for each of them and some tourist literature about Las Vegas. He left again, saying only, "Sit tight. There are still some arrangements to be made."

Everything they owned had been thrown helter-skelter into the suitcases. They used some of their time to discuss what they should wear for their arrival in Vegas, finally changing into tank tops and mini skirts. Then they repacked everything neatly back into the suitcases.

They tried to go outside but Madge stopped them. They were beginning to view her like the matron on a prison ward.

"Not permitted."

"Madge! We're in a run-down warehouse on a deserted pier! All we want to do is change the view for ten minutes."

"Not permitted. You'll be gone in a couple of hours. Change your view then."

The only break in the long day was provided by a visitor, the first ever at the Center. Natalia and Maria had never seen anyone in the Center other than Madge and Grodin. He was a tall distinguished-looking man, about sixty years old, wearing a suit. Madge immediately tried to shoo him out, starting an intense confrontation featuring a low-voiced exchange that the women could not hear, although they heard him use the names "Fallon" and "Grodin" and "Ellerby".

Madge gave way, but immediately went to her desk and picked up the telephone. The man ignored her and walked directly over to them.

"Good afternoon, ladies. My name is Dominick". And he held out his hand.

Natalia was a year older than Maria and her English was better, so she had become the spokesperson for the two of them if there was any ambiguity in their inevitable encounters with ordinary citizens. But this posed a new situation.

Is this a client? So far, Grodin always did the introductions. He looks rich. And he got by Madge, so he's got some kind of clearance. But he doesn't have the look of someone about to get laid. And there's something else ... anger, maybe?

Neither of the women rose but Natalia took his hand and said, "My name is Natalia. And this is Maria." She spoke English, but deliberately used the thickest possible accent that she could muster.

"How's your stay in San Francisco?"

She played it safe. She smiled apologetically and said slowly and distinctly, "Sorry, no English. Frisco very nice."

Fallon tried for a few more minutes, but gave up when his questions elicited nothing but a fixed smile from both women and Russian phrases. It didn't help that Madge had stopped talking on the phone and was standing behind him glaring at the two women.

Fallon gave up. *OK. At least they're smart enough to stay in character. I wonder if they know yet what they've signed up for? Or if Carlo knows? Or if he even cares?*

He gave Natalia his business card, saying, "Let me know if there's anything I can do to help you during your stay." Natalia just looked at him, but when he added, each word stressed, "I mean it", she folded the card and tucked it into the pocket of her very tight skirt. Fallon left, thinking about the gap between him and his son, a gap defined by both age and value systems. He was also worried about why Ellerby had pointed him at the Cultural Center. *What's his agenda?*

Time passed very slowly for Natalia and Maria. Grodin finally showed up at midnight. He was carrying two jackets.

"We're taking a boat across the Bay. There's a small plane there that will take you the rest of the way. You'll be in Vegas in three hours."

Natalia asked, "I thought we had a date with Jorge and Emilio tonight."

Grodin looked closely at her, wondering if her question was an innocent one or if they had seen the news about the North Beach raid despite Madge's strict orders to keep them isolated. *No matter. The DEA raid on the Victorian is the clincher.* He could not help thinking of them as the *'twenty-six percent factor'*. Not a bad book title ... or epitaph.

He handed them the jackets. They were bright yellow and much too large, with several big pockets with flaps, the kind of garment a construction worker or a hunter might wear, someone who needs to carry lots of small objects around with him. "It's cold out on the Bay. You'll need these or you'll freeze to death."

"Let's go."

He led them to the end of the pier. Madge followed with the two suitcases. A boat with an open cabin and two very large motors on the rear transom sat at the foot of the ladder leading down from the surface of the pier. There was nothing to indicate that it had been stolen from a nearby marina thirty minutes earlier. By now, the women were accustomed to climbing or descending ladders with high heels, so it was an easy transit. Grodin made two trips up and down with the suitcases.

As soon as the boat moved away from the pier, its own speed and the onshore winds made it quite cold and the two women were grateful for the warmth of the lined coats. They stood with their forearms resting on the cabin roof and let the wind blow their long hair straight back. It was exhilarating, made more so by the change from their long confinement of the day.

After a few minutes, Grodin throttled back to about quarter speed and locked the wheel to maintain a straight course toward the bright lights of the gantry cranes lining the East Bay shore. He joined the two women, standing looking back at the even brighter lights of Fisherman's Wharf and the Embarcadero.

He said, "Say goodbye to San Francisco."

Maria started to say, "It's a wonderful –" but died before she could finish the sentence. Natalia lived approximately four more seconds, long enough to experience a surge of pure fear and then an all-consuming rage. To her credit, she was lunging forward toward the bullet that ended her short life.

Grodin checked his position, using the lights on either side of the Bay and trying to guess the midpoint. When he calculated that he was approximately in the middle of the shipping channel, he cut the engines to idle and propped the corpses against the sidewall of the boat. He lifted the plastic cushion that covered the bench along the one side of the boat and lifted out the lead weights that he had stowed there. There were twelve of them, each weighing ten pounds. He put one in each of the four large pockets on the jackets the women were wearing and fastened the snaps on the pockets. He wrestled Natalia's body upright, staggering with the motion of the boat and briefly looking like a macabre dancing master in a marathon dance contest, and let it fall back into the water. Then the same with Maria. Finally, he divided his last four weights between the two suitcases and dropped them over the side, watching them disappear quickly into the murk.

He was back at the pier within ten minutes. He used the hose at the end of the pier to wash down the deck of the stolen boat. It seemed strange to be pouring water into a boat. Finally, he started the motors, pointed the bow toward the southern end of the Bay, and locked the wheel. He stood on the ladder and engaged the throttle, watching the empty boat disappear into the darkness, its lengthening wake slowly becoming indistinguishable from the wind-rippled dark waters of the San Francisco Bay.

Collateral Damage

Murphy called McAdams at ten in the morning. "I think we've got some fallout from the Torres situation."

"Fallout?"

"Bodies, actually."

"Where?"

"The Coast Guard station on Alameda Island. There's a barge parked at the Spencer Avenue Pier. Oh, and don't wear your good shoes."

The barge was a very long strip of floating rust snugged up to the pier. About half of its length was taken up with a very large pile of black muck. A dozen individuals were clustered at one end of the sloping mound. Standing on the pier and looking down into the barge, he found the bottom was covered in the same gooey material, between an inch to three inches deep and still oozing salt water. A hodge-podge of boots was lying near the ladder going down and he found a pair that fit over his shoes. It made walking difficult, but he fit in with the other civilians in sight.

Murphy and Slater were the only ones he recognized. There were at least two cops with Oakland insignia and several in Coast Guard uniforms.

"Jurisdiction an issue?" He asked Murphy.

Murphy gestured with his thumb at the knot of people standing in a circle looking at the foot of the pile. "The evidence suggests they were killed on the Bay and dumped in the middle. Nobody really wants responsibility, so we're all being polite to one another."

"They?"

Murphy led him to the edge of the pile. Up close, it was the same muck they were slogging through, just piled higher. Two very dead women lay side by side at the start of the upslope, their weight pressing them down into the black goo. From twenty feet away, they looked like twins taking a break from a strenuous hike. They were wearing identical bright yellow workman's jackets and both of them had long white legs. One of the faces had been wiped clean, the whiteness a stark contrast against the blackness. The other woman's face was covered with a blue rag.

"Half her face is gone. And one arm is hanging by a thread. She got torn up pretty bad by the dredge. For now, they are officially known as Jane Doe I and Jane Doe II, but I'll bet they turn out to be Russian names – like your Alexandra Vorokov."

Natalia and Maria, last names unknown. Not much of an epitaph.

His vision blurred and he felt almost faint as a solid wave of sheer rage welled up within him without any warning. He wanted to scream, to cry, to hit something as hard as he could. All at the same time. It lasted only a few seconds, but left him weakened, leaning against the sidewall of the barge for support. He had never experienced any emotion or physical feeling quite like it.

I want the bastard that did this. I want to ask him 'why?' And then I want to shoot him in the face. Then he asked himself a question he had never before posed: *I wonder if I'm fit to be a homicide detective any longer?*

He managed to ask, in a squeaky voice, "What do we know?"

Murphy looked at him curiously. "Know? You mean, like a fact? A certainty?"

McAdams just waited, not trusting himself to speak.

"We are *fairly sure* – that's almost like a fact – that both of them were shot while on the Bay. There are bullet holes in their jackets, which they would not have been wearing except out on the water. We are also *fairly sure* that they were killed last night because of the condition of the bodies. And a stolen boat was found stuck up against the San Mateo Bridge at first light this morning. It had some blood spatter on the cabin windows."

McAdams looked at the two women. "We're lucky, aren't we?"

"You might say that. They weren't meant to be found. Whoever put them in the water missed the deepest part of the channel and apparently wasn't aware of the ongoing dredging. They came up in the first scoop this morning. Pure dumb luck." He glanced at the bodies and added, "For us, not them."

Murphy asked, "Mac, can you add anything to this? Any *conjectures* or information you might be *fairly sure* of, given your superior sources?"

"Yeah. Their names will turn out to be Natalia and Maria, last names unknown, most recently of the Vladivostock region. Last known employment was as consort for visiting drug lords you recently became acquainted with. Reason for their present condition? To coin a gangland phrase: they knew too much."

Murphy listened without a change of expression during his recital. "Someday soon, you're going to tell me how you know all these things, right?"

He said, "Absolutely!" even as he wondered if it was a lie. It would expose Anna – Sofia – to new hazards, both legal and lethal ones. *It's funny. My automatic response is to worry about her ... to think of ways to keep her under the radar. I need to think about that.*

He told Murphy what he had pieced together about the rendezvous at sea between Fallon's Northern Voyager and 'S', whatever that was, now two days off. "It's almost certainly a major narcotics deal and may involve more Russian women on the way in."

Murphy thought for a moment. "They'll probably call it off now that Torres is dead and Esposito is in custody."

"I don't think so. The deal is ninety-eight percent done. The two ships are already on the way, so they're partially committed. My guess is that a big chunk of cash is involved. And they don't need Torres or Esposito any more. In fact, with them out of the picture, that's more money to go around. You've still got active players with big stakes on both ends – the Venezuelan -- Vargas -- and our unknown Americans on this end."

"Put yourself in their shoes. A little game theory. They have two choices – either finish the deal or call if off. Turn the boats around. But they don't know if we're onto them or not. Two choices, two possible outcomes."

"Game theory, huh?"

McAdams ignored the sarcasm. "So assume they decide to finish the deal. If we -- the cops – in fact know about it, they're screwed. We'll confiscate, shoot or arrest anything in sight. On the other hand, if they *don't* go through with it, they're also screwed, because we'll still do the same thing. It will just take a little longer and we'll have to involve the naval forces of a couple of friendly countries."

Murphy nodded. "I gotcha. On the other hand if they go ahead and we *don't* know -- your other possibility -- they make a very large potful of money. So they might as well stay with the plan."

He smiled, "That's game theory, huh? I always knew that college education would pay off."

"Let's hope they're as smart as we are. This is the rare case where we don't want *dumb* crooks on the other side."

Murphy nodded thoughtfully. "And this" – looking at the two bodies in the muck – "wouldn't have been necessary unless they were going ahead with the exchange. Whoever shot them was making sure of --"

He stopped, his attention caught by something on the pier. McAdams turned and saw two figures climbing down the ladder into the barge. One was a uniformed cop, the other a familiar lean figure in a gray suit. He turned to Murphy and asked sharply, "What's Dominick doing here?"

Murphy pointed at the body whose face was covered with the blue cloth. "We found his business card on her. I thought his reaction to this" – gesturing at the bodies – "would be interesting. And we need an ID." He looked at McAdams closely. "You OK with that. Being his golfing buddy, and all that?"

McAdams didn't bother to answer. He stood back and watched Murphy greet Fallon, explain what he wanted, and then step back. Fallon walked the three or four steps to where the muck pile began, moving as if into a strong headwind, every step slower and more reluctant. He stood slumped, looking at the women, as if waiting for them to say something. Then he leaned down and lifted the blue cloth off of the ruined face. He stood staring for ten seconds and then replaced the cloth with exaggerated care. His expression did not change during the entire procedure, as though he was immune to surprise.

Without turning back to face them, he said, "I met them yesterday afternoon. Her name – the one with half a face – is Natalia. The other one is Maria. I don't know their last names or anything else about them." After a pause, he added, "They are ... were ... exchange students ...from Russia, I think. Part of an exchange program."

He spoke very softly, seeming to listen to his own words in a way that suggested he did not believe them. When he turned, he seemed to have aged by decades. "And I know your next two questions. First, they were fine when I left them, clearly looking forward to something. And second, I have no idea who killed them or what happened to them after I saw them."

That's a lie. I do know who killed them. My son. Either directly or indirectly. And then he said it outright. "No more. This has to stop."

When Murphy opened his mouth to speak, McAdams assumed it was to read Dominick his Miranda rights. But Murphy merely said, "Mr. Fallon, we'll need your full statement on this. I want you to go with Slater here to our office. He'll make sure you get home again. And thanks for your help."

They watched the two of them move off. Fallon moved like someone subjected to extraordinary gravitational force – slumped, his feet dragging through the muck.

McAdams pulled Murphy aside, not noticing Murphy's pained expression stemming from the force of his grip on his forearm. "Murphy, I want three things. And they're not negotiable."

Murphy didn't say anything, knowing that it would make no difference.

"First, we need to *see* this rendezvous at sea. You need to get the boys with the fancy toys – I don't care if it's NSA, CIA, SFPD, DEA or any other acronym – to turn on one of their fancy satellites at the designated time."

"Second, we need to plan an intercept at this end. And not the second they cross into U.S. waters, but after they're in the Bay and have offloaded. We need to know where this stuff is going and who's on the receiving end."

"Third, I want to be part of the team that goes in at the end. And not as an *observer!*"

Murphy just nodded, and McAdams knew that the slight movement of his head was as good as a notarized legal document.

"Fourth, I –"

"You said *three* things."

"Fourth, I'm going to pay a call on Carlo Fallon. His ship is part of the deal and I don't think he's an innocent bystander. And I'll bet that he's the anonymous sponsor behind the so-called foundation that provided the cover for these women. "

"OK, but you'll take Slater with you."

"This has to be my –"

"You'll take Slater with you. Or no deal. I mean it." Murphy's voice had taken on a new quality. The momentary therapist had become the boss again.

"OK. We'll do it this afternoon."

He turned to leave, but Murphy stopped him. "Mac. This is going to be a DEA operation. It's too big a deal to cut them out. And they've got the toys we need."

McAdams nodded. He climbed off the barge, took off his muck-covered boots and walked to the far end of the pier, away from the knot of people arguing who was responsible for the bodies and subsequent investigation. He dialed his home number.

Sofia picked up the receiver, saying nothing.

"Sofia. This is McAdams. I have bad news."

He heard the catch in her breathing and a rustling as she changed position. He pictured her sitting on the sofa with the cordless phone. *I wonder what she's wearing. God! I hate doing this!*

"It's Natalia and Maria. I think they're …". He hesitated, every professional instinct shouting at him that he didn't really know that it was them. But she solved the problem for him.

"Dead," She said tonelessly. "That's the word you can't say. Dead. Like Sasha."

"Yes."

There was a long silence. McAdams waited, knowing that there was nothing that he could say that would change anything.

"That leaves me …", she said. And then added in a thoughtful voice, "… and him."

"Sofia. We're close to finishing this. We can –"

His phone beeped and the 'Call Ended' banner flashed at him. He redialed, but heard only his own voice asking him to leave a message.

As soon as he entered the door to his home, he knew she was gone. The space seemed even larger and for the first time it *felt* empty.

She had taken the Beretta and his shirt with her.

Assisting the Police With Inquiries

Slater stood at the entrance to the Pacific Cargos offices and pier in Oakland, staring at the red brick building as though expecting it to have some message for him. Every few seconds, he turned his head to look at the cluster of prostitutes a hundred feet away at the intersection. *Christ! We've walked by this place twenty times without knowing what it was. Talking to the whores because the phone company says this was the street where Freddie's last call came from and we assumed she was working the prostitution angle.*

He was clearly startled when McAdams approached him. *What the hell do I tell him without Murphy taking off my head?*

That can wait. He merely nodded at McAdams and said, "Murphy said to let you take the lead. I'm just along for the ride."

McAdams acknowledged the comment with a grunt. *I'll bet Murphy added a few more details. Like making sure that I don't blow the case or kill anybody when I lose complete control of my emotions.*

Slater added, "And he said to tell you that we can't tie Carlo to the cultural exchange program. He's got about twenty cutouts between him and that pier. And – no surprise – the whole operation is gone. Cleaned out down to the studs."

"No surprise there. He's got a really good business advisor to help him with that sort of stuff." *The guy who doubles as his personal assassin.*

'There is one part I'd like you to take the lead on." He gave Slater the picture of Sofia, saying, "Put this in front of him when I cue you. I want to see how he reacts."

Carlo was talking on his desk phone and they waited prominently at his office door. McAdams had met Carlo a couple of times when he was with Dominick, but never paid much real attention. This time, he looked closely. He looked nothing like his father – short rather than tall, more fat, less hair.   Hollywood would cast Dominick as a ship owner, Carlo as a dockworker.

Carlo hung up and stood when they came into his office. Closer in, McAdams noted something in his washed-out eyes and the thinness of his lips that managed to convey both meanness and a simmering anger. It was immediately confirmed by the voice, an impatient reedy sound that was just short of whininess. He waved off their ID's and badges, saying, "I know who you are. What I don't know is why you're here. Tell me that, and we can be done with this bullshit real fast."

Definitely not the usual business executive behavior when confronted with homicide detectives in one's office. No nervousness, not even any real curiosity. Not even a token effort to disguise obvious hostility. That makes him either totally innocent of any criminal activity or else he's not very smart. Or very arrogant, which is the same thing in our world.

He glanced at Slater and could see his interest level jump in response to Carlo's greeting. *Red flags waved at bulls.*

He'd decided on a low-key approach, the 'soft' kind that is intended to come across as, 'We need the help of all you law-abiding civilians to catch the really bad people.' It really did create a useful support system for overworked cops and – if the subject was in fact one of the bad people – it sometimes lulled them into a false sense of confidence. The only problem was that it required the cop to keep his own ego in check, not an easy thing when your whole image is founded on projecting power or when the person you're being nice to has been killing people you know.

"Thanks for seeing us, Mr. Fallon. Why we're here? We've had several homicides either on the Bay or dockside in the last few weeks, including two women just last night. We are trying to find witnesses – someone who may have seen someone or something unusual going on. You run ships and stevedoring operations on both sides of the Bay. We'd like to talk with your crews – both the onshore and shipping hands."

249

Carlo waved his hand dismissively. "My ships are scattered all over the North Pacific. I might have a single ship, two at the most, in the Bay during any given week. There are only skeleton crews while they're in port and they usually don't speak English. There's zero chance they'd be able to help you."

"Would you give us a list of the ships that have been here in the past month and the dates? And access to the crews the next time in port?"

"No, I won't. The Port Authority will tell you what ships have been here and when, so you don't need me for that. And I don't want my crews bothered by cops asking them a lot of questions in a language they don't even speak."

"Other than stevedoring, do you have any offices or operations that front on the Bay?"

The slight hesitation was interesting. As was the hedged reply. "Pacific Cargos operates solely out of this building. And you're sitting on a pier. You can see the Bay if you lean out that window."

No mention of cultural exchange programs located smack on the waterfront. No surprise there.

So far, the questions were softballs. McAdams didn't pay any attention to the answers. His real curiosity was centered on Carlo's reaction to the next two items on his agenda. He nodded to Slater.

Slater slid the 8x10 photo of Sofia across the desk and asked, "Have you ever seen this woman?" It was a head-and-shoulders shot that McAdams had taken with his cell phone. The photo was taken in natural light against a blank wall. He told her, "I'm going to show this to one of the Americans – the younger one – to see what kind of reaction I get. I'd like you to think about what message you want him to take away when I show him the picture."

It took six tries. She reviewed each one, rejecting each of the first five and recomposing her face in ways so slight that he could see no difference. However, the final shot was compelling, even if one was unaware of the underlying context. She was unsmiling, leaning slightly forward, so that she was looking up at the camera, as if she'd been interrupted while reading a book. It could have been titled 'Woman Viewing Daughter's Rapist'. The utter calmness, the coldness in her eyes, the planes of her face, the set of her mouth … all of them combined to convey an all-consuming contempt.

Both of them watched as Carlo's eyes turned down to the photo. He started to say "I've never seen – " but stopped when the picture registered in his brain. He made no attempt to disguise his interest, but stared at the picture for almost ten seconds. His left hand, resting on his desk, formed a fist and the tendons in his neck stood out. His face reddened. Finally, he looked up at them, leaned back in his chair, and said, "I've never seen her before", each word enunciated distinctly through clenched teeth. His rage was so apparent that McAdams leaned back slightly and his hand moved involuntarily a few inches toward the butt of his pistol. He noted that Slater shifted his stance, ready to move quickly.

Time for the other question.

"Does a man named Grodin work for you?"

The transformation was remarkable. The rage dissipated as fast as it had appeared, replaced by a look that was a caricature of slyness. It was as if his facial expressions were being scripted by a cartoonist. *The DA will love this guy. Put him on the stand and watch him make a fool of himself.*

He had a hard time not laughing when Carlo said, "Grodin? Never heard of him. Now leave me alone. I've got some real work to do."

Out on the sidewalk, Slater said, "Mac, I don't know what you're doing and Murphy told me to leave you alone. But that guy" – he pointed back to the Fallon building – "is dirty as hell. He's –"

"Evil," McAdams said, "I know."

Slater nodded, but was clearly thinking about something else. Whatever it was, it clearly was making him nervous. McAdams didn't help him, just stood quietly watching.

Finally and very tentatively, Slater asked "Did Murphy tell you about the lab guy trying to piece together Freddie's cell phone?"

McAdams nodded. "Did he find something?"

Slater shook his head. "Nothing new. But there is something you should know. Freddie was here when she ... that day."

"Here?"

"You know how that triangulation technology works ... how iffy it is. We thought she was talking to the working girls." He gestured at the pair of hookers on the corner. "But maybe she was ..." He gestured at the building they had just left.

McAdams stood rigid, remembering his vocabulary drill with Freddie; about wharfingers and RO/RO's. His words came back to him. *You're dealing with someone on the waterfront.*

Christ, I killed her. Just like I killed Gonzo!

Garfield's Story

McAdams found Garfield in the cavernous St. Anthony's dining room. He was serving baked beans to a long line of men and women that exuded the kind of learned patience that came from a lifetime of dealing with institutions. The line stretched out through the door and along Golden Gate Avenue. When McAdams tapped him on the shoulder, he said, "I can't get away for another half-hour. Can it wait?"

Before McAdams could answer, Garfield said, "Better yet, Maggie here could use a break." He gently elbowed the woman standing next to him, an extremely tall and elderly lady in a print dress from another century. She was wearing a baseball cap with an LA Dodgers logo and white gloves that went almost to her shoulders. She was using an over-long pair of metal tongs to place a large white bun precisely in the middle of each plate that was held out to her.

"Maggie, why don't you go sit with some of our clients for a bit. Tell them about your cats. Mac here will take over for you."

Maggie handed him the tongs and smiled sweetly down at him. He unconsciously stood up straighter and smiled back, taking Maggie's place in the food line alongside Garfield.

"She's here every day, 365 days a year," Garfield said. "Lives in a big house somewhere near the beach and has a dozen or so cats. She says that they talk to her."

"Everybody has a story, huh? "

When Garfield only smiled at him, McAdams asked, "What's your story?"

Garfield's smile changed only slightly. "With Maggie on a break, it's OK if the buns are slightly off-center," he said.

They were silent for the next five minutes or so. McAdams watched the characters stream by with their plates in hand and downcast eyes. It was the "early" lunch, reserved for seniors. The majority were men, of every race and color. Most but not all were obviously street people and many of those were exhibiting classic signs of mental illness or drug abuse. But a significant minority reminded McAdams of ordinary people from his childhood, worn down by the circumstances of hard times. Garfield spoke to most of them by name, eliciting brief flashes of personality.

McAdams took advantage of a lull. "I wanted to let you know that those pictures you took – at the Victorian? – paid off. Some seriously bad characters have been taken off the table."

"I read the papers. Sounded more like an assassination squad than a professional police op." Garfield's voice was decidedly chilly.

Torres was standing there waiting. Maldanado raised his pistol and shot him in the face from a foot away. It was an assassination. How does he know that?

"It was a DEA operation. The SFPD was reduced to directing traffic at the time."

"Sure," Garfield said in a tone that implied the opposite. "The only thing? They never identified the officer doing the shooting. And no interviews permitted with the SWAT guys. That's handy, isn't it? No troublesome inquiries about whether procedures were followed."

McAdams said with some heat, "The newspapers also didn't mention that the guys inside the house – the two guys you called gofers? – they had a couple of Uzis handy. And they left out their rap sheets too, the ones that listed several suspected murders."

Why do I feel the need to defend the DEA? And why is he so upset?

"The Uzis – were they even fired?" Garfield's question jarred him.

They hadn't been fired, in fact.

"Can I have my biscuit, please?" The man held his plate out, his eyes still downcast. McAdams realized that he was holding up the line, standing there staring into space.

"Garfield, if you were a cop going into a dark building with known hard guys, you'd –"

"I have been. That's why I'm here."

It stopped McAdams cold.

So that's Garfield's story.

They dished food for another fifteen minutes in silence. Finally, Garfield waved over two nuns who took over for them. He led McAdams to an empty table in a far corner of the dining room. "I don't know what you want to talk about, but my history is off-limits."

"OK. Anyway, I have in mind sort of a humanitarian venture. Less of the cops and robbers stuff." *I wonder if I really believe that?"*

He slid the picture of Sofia across the table, the same one that he'd shown to Carlo. Garfield's reaction was one of intense curiosity. "She looks like someone who's just seen a venomous snake crawling across her kitchen floor. Am I supposed to know her? I don't."

"Remember the two women going into the Victorian – the ones you took a picture of?" He slid the photo across the table, of the two women going up the stairs of the house one on each side of the shadowy man holding their arms. "She was a friend of theirs."

"Was? That's the past tense."

"They're dead, fished out of the Bay yesterday." He put his finger on the photo lying between them. "And she's on the same list they were. Her name is Sofia."

Something changed in Garfield, but he merely said, "You want me to look for her?"

"Yeah, in a low key way. She's trying to hide, so the Tenderloin becomes a likely spot. Maybe you can enlist some help from the folks you know." McAdams pointed vaguely into the center of the dining room, about half-filled with the hard-core street people who didn't have a lot to do at this time of day. "And she might show up at Moresby's."

"And if I see her?"

"Keep an eye on her and let me know. I want to help her."

"To do what?" There was a very slight hint of disapproval, as though McAdams was asking to date his daughter.

255

To do what? I don't even know how to answer the question. To make her safe? Get my gun back? Get rid of the emptiness in my house? He finally picked the response that was closest to the surface, "I want to help her get rid of that snake crawling across her kitchen floor."

"Oh. And one more thing." He tapped the photo still lying on the table, the one of the two women and man. "You're the only person who's seen this guy. If you come across anybody that looks like him, let me know."

He went from St. Anthony's to his computer at his office. It took him only ten minutes to get the rest of what he thought of as *Garfield's Story*. He was a twenty-three year veteran of the Los Angeles Police Department, a detective sergeant working mostly in Hollywood. Twelve years ago, he and two other plainclothes types were knocking on doors trying to find a guy who liked to hold up people at ATMs, pistol whipping them for good measure. When they knocked on the front door of a house with foreclosure notices nailed to the frame, the only answer was three shots fired through the door. One of the cops went down. The two others – with Garfield in the lead – broke down the door and went in low and head first.

The newspaper account was predictably sterile, leaving out the terror and confusion that goes with the situation. It used phrases like *shots were exchanged* and *officers returned fire* and *normal procedure in officer-involved shootings*. At the end of the departmental investigation, all three officers were commended for their behavior and a lot of newspaper inches were used to demonize the dead gunman.

A pigtailed nine-year-old girl was struck by a police bullet and died in the crossfire. Her name was Amanda. Her parents received a significant cash settlement from the City of Los Angeles.

No mention was made of Garfield's retirement one month later.

Two Women at Starbucks

Garfield went from the Saint Anthony's dining room to his studio apartment in the Tenderloin. It was a short walk but filled with thoughts that would not stay suppressed. Once there, he went directly to the one closet. The gun was at the back of a dresser drawer, nestled amid stacks of boxer shorts, T-shirts and socks. Somehow, the articles of everyday clothing made the gun even more sinister. *Except for all of the memories and emotions that go with it, the ones I can't get rid of.* The clearest image -- the first to appear and the last to fade -- was always that of a nine-year-old blonde girl named Amanda.

Twelve years. I wonder if it still fires? But he knew it would. If he could pick it up.

Ten minutes later, he was back on the street. It took two hours of canvassing among the street people; the ones that would always notice a new and attractive young woman looking for a place to hide. He picked her up as she was leaving the Salvation Army shelter and followed her to a Starbucks. He stood on the curb looking in her and the other woman that joined her in the back corner.

The women did not fit in with the other customers. If one analyzed why they stood out, the first and most obvious difference was that they were not referring to cell phones or laptops. Then there were the scarves and sunglasses worn indoors. They looked like a pair of Hollywood starlets going incognito. Furthermore, they were holding hands in a way that made it apparent that it was important to them. Their heads were close together and, when they spoke, they whispered. And they were silent for long stretches, thinking.

The older woman thought mostly about past choices and the strange ways that they looped through her life, as though a playful Greek god was taunting her with reminders of her human failings, of all the wrong turns. The younger woman, on the other hand, thought mostly about the choices yet to be made, somehow knowing that the rightness or wrongness of her decisions would be withheld from her, that she did not have – could not have – enough self-insight to understand her own motives.

The complementarity of their misgivings would have amused them and perhaps comforted them if they had made them known to one another. The same motif ran through their disconnected thoughts, involving loss, renewability and the absence of absolutes between people that love one another. The many ways that forgiveness can be expressed … or withheld.

When they stood up to leave, there was a finality to the lingering way they leaned forward to kiss on both cheeks, in the European fashion. Perhaps it was nothing more than the pervasive sadness in each of them, a bone-deep regret that they had come so far and still could not be sure of the ending.

The older woman turned and walked away, hurrying in a way that suggested an attempt to escape rather than a desire to be somewhere. Her companion watched her go, wanting to cry but not knowing how. She turned to leave and saw the man staring intently at her.

The younger woman and the watching man could not know it, but they were thinking the same kind of thoughts. About loss and forgiveness, about going forward in spite of not knowing who exactly they were or what they wanted. Perhaps they sensed it in one another.

Sofia walked directly up to him.

"You're Garfield." It was not a question.

He nodded, saying simply, "Sofia."

"Why are you watching me?"

"Mac asked me to." And then without understanding why, he added, "He's worried about you."

The words jarred her. *Damn him! He doesn't have that right – to care like that. To obligate me to care!* Then the ambivalence surged back.

"Worried? I don't think so. He's a cop. Doing what he wants. And what he wants is revenge, the bloody kind."

He asked me, 'What else do you have to sell me? In lieu of rent?'

258

Garfield said nothing, just looked at her. *I wonder if she can hear what's underneath her words, the hopefulness? If she knows what's in her eyes?* He thought about McAdams and the muddling of duty and guilt and vengeance with the basic human need for trust and closeness.

What a trio! Me in a state of perpetual atonement. Her coming from a world where emotions are dangerous luxuries. And Mac? A case of terminal confusion.

She turned away. "Follow me if you like. But you won't like where I'm going. And stay out of my way."

She had gone two steps before he spoke to her back. "Give him a chance. You both deserve that." From his perspective, the words had no perceptible effect, but what he could not see was the instant tears that welled up. The tears were the first that she could remember.

That's important: that I can cry. I wonder what it means? But I can't think about that now.

She headed downhill, walking fast. Toward the Bay and the place where it all began.

A Confirmation

McAdams phoned, only to hear Moresby's voice saying, "Please leave a message." He had rung the bell at the ornate front door in Pacific Heights and listened to it echo faintly in the house. For the next ninety minutes, he sat in his parked car, watching the light fade as he waited for her to return.

The only distraction from his circling thoughts was a cell call from Slater.

"Mac. I've got a quick update on Freddie and where she might have been when she got hit."

He said only, "Uh huh".

"We still don't know if she was in Fallon's building or just talking to the pros on the street, but I can tell you that Carlo Fallon wasn't there when Freddie bought it. It wasn't him."

"Are you sure?" *That's too quick. No way he can check alibis that fast.*

"I cut some corners. Murphy wouldn't like it if he knew. Kind of violated both the letter and spirit of the due process laws. But I can tell you that Carlo Fallon was at 30,000 feet, on a Southwest Airlines flight between Las Vegas and San Francisco at the precise time Freddie was talking to you, just before …"

The silence lasted long enough to feel awkward for both of them. *So, Slater's a cop after all. Carlo got to him maybe. And Carlo didn't kill Freddie. But he knows who did. And he would have aimed Grodin at her.*

"Mac?"

"I'm here. Thinking. And Slater? Thanks. I mean that."

We're getting close. No, not 'we'. I'm getting close. Because I'm hoarding all of the information instead of sharing it with Slater, Murphy and others. Once again, he briefly wondered at his lack of concern with what was 'right'. *I'm supposed to be a cop. What am I going to do after this is over?*

The hell with all that! He began thinking about what he wanted to say to Moresby and how to deal with all that Ellerby had told him.

A hodgepodge of morality tales. A story about a failed empire and its inhabitants trying to adapt. About transactions between strangers that had consequences far beyond the satisfaction of their immediate needs. About refugees and their benefactors. About politics and reality. About women with secrets.

He saw her coming up the hill, watching in his passenger side mirror as she approached. When she neared, he got out and waited for her, leaning against the railing going up her front stairs.

She stopped ten feet short of him. Neither of them spoke. Finally, she took off the sunglasses that obscured half of her face and pulled down the scarf tied over her hair. He did not know if it was to signal her openness or her vulnerability to whatever he was about to say.

He asked, "Have you seen her?"

She looked at him for a long time with an expression that he could not classify. He did not know what she was hoping to see and did not know what signal he wanted to send. Nor did he care what she saw. In the end, he simply stood and let her look. Finally, she nodded and said, "Yes. Just thirty minutes ago."

"Where was she going?"

"I can't tell you."

"What is she trying to prove?"

"I can't tell you." And then, less harshly, almost a sob, "I don't know."

He said, "I talked with Ellerby."

She looked up sharply and some internal alarm was pinging at very high levels. "He told you?"

"About what's going on at the pier? The so-called cultural exchange? Yes, he told me."

Just as quickly as it arose, the alarm dissipated and she became quietly watchful once more. The only sign of concern was her slightly quickened breathing. *I wonder what frightened her? What it is that she was so afraid that Ellerby had told me?*

He tried again. "Can you tell me where she is? I want to help her."

She did not answer, but he felt the intensity in her gaze, the warring of curiosity, need and hostility. Finally, she said, "You're a cop; she's a criminal, in the country illegally. You're a man; she has a long history of being abused by men. You want her to be a witness; she wants to be an executioner. Exactly how is it that you intend to help her?"

It was the most damning indictment that he had experienced, made much worse because he knew he could not even begin to answer it. Perhaps that was why he said what he did, as his only means of retaliation.

"You're her mother, aren't you? The one who left her in the orphanage."

He turned away, back to his car, but not before seeing her face crumble and the green eyes mist over.

Rendezvous at Sea

About one hundred miles to the West, late in the afternoon of April 13, two bulk cargo carriers that were showing considerable wear approached each other at the spot designated as 30 degrees of latitude and minus 132 degrees of longitude. One of the ships – the one coming from the south -- was quite small and very rusty, about half the size of the other. Grodin and the ten women from the Russian Far East lined the railing of the bridge on the larger ship and watched the two ships approach within fifty yards of one another on the calm seas. Neither Vargas on the Sigilo from Cartagena nor Grodin on the Northern Voyager had any trust in navigation that lacked physical markers, so they were each relieved to see the other ship appear.

A launch brought Reynaldo Vargas and a horse-faced man unknown to Grodin from the Sigilo. Grodin met them as they came up the rickety gangway. "Hello Reynaldo. How was your trip?"

"Boring." He looked up at the cluster of women looking down at them from the bridge. "Unlike you, I had no female company. I don't know why I needed to go along with the shipment."

"That was the deal, remember … everybody's got to have some skin in the game. Once Torres got hit, all the rules changed. Don't feel bad. I had to fly to Seattle to pick up the ship."

Vargas said, "Poor Jose!" But the words were contradicted by the tone and the smile that creased his face. "All that money to be reallocated!"

The smile faded quickly, replaced by a worried frown. "But what if your DEA knows about our deal? That bitch Sofia probably tipped them to the Victorian. She may have given them this deal too." He looked over his shoulder at the empty sea, as though expecting the U.S. Navy to appear from the depths.

Grodin shook his head. "We've already covered this, Reynaldo. In Miami, remember? She didn't know about it.

She was only in the house for about four minutes, and it was after we'd talked about the details. She floored Torres before he could say anything. But that's why you get to return on the Sigilo. Even if they go after the shipment once we're in U.S. waters, you're still clear – with forty million dollars for company."

"The other ten million? You have it with you?"

The question sounded casual, but Grodin noted the intentness that infused Vargas and his companion as they waited for his response. *Fifty-fifty, I think. If I say 'yes', horse face will shoot me as soon as we transfer the forty mill. Take the ten million and the drugs and the women.*

"No, I don't. It will be on the pier … We'll give it to your guy when the goods are on wheels … with the women, assuming he's got three million on him."

Grodin didn't ask about the horse-faced man who had been standing quietly listening since coming aboard. He was older than either of them and looked both uninterested and downright mean. He wondered how Vargas would bring up the subject. Finally, Vargas nodded at the other man and said, "This is Pedro. He'll stay with you until the transfer on shore. A friend of his – call him 'Gomez' – will bring a van to the pier, along with the three million for the whores. Give him the ten million dollars and the women when the shipment is on the truck. Pedro and Gomez will find their own way home."

Grodin frowned. "Reynaldo. I'm hurt. You don't think we would try to cheat you?"

Vargas smiled. "Pedro has a satellite phone. I will check every now and then to make sure that you are on schedule. If Pedro doesn't answer …" The smile deepened but conveyed the threat quite clearly.

A clanking sound came across the water and they watched as two wooden crates were winched off the foredeck of the Sigilo and lowered into a ship's boat. The boat crossed the short gap to the Northern Voyager, riding very low in the water. The crates were lifted by a shipboard crane onto the deck. A pair of crewmen unsnapped a dozen clamps and slid the cover on one of the crates halfway back. They spent about ten minutes inspecting the contents. Vargas watched them with enough disinterest that Grodin was confident the Latins had not tried any amateur switches or shortages. One of the crewmen waved and gave a thumbs-up signal to Grodin. The crane then lowered both boxes into the forward hold of the ship.

Grodin watched, thinking about past transactions he had engineered. *Two stinking little wooden boxes. A billion dollars. Cocaine bricks and thin sheets of crystal meth. So much more civilized and profitable than moving bales of marijuana or tons of Kalishnikovs!*

Grodin waved at the ship's captain on the bridge. He smiled at Vargas and said, "That will start a forty-million dollar transfer of funds. It will take a few minutes to weave its way through all of the shell companies and cutouts. I'm sure your colleagues will let you know if it doesn't arrive within the next few minutes."

Grodin had practiced the art of evading financial regulators for the past twenty years. Assuming an interested financial regulator with sufficient electronic expertise – neither condition was likely in this instance -- it would appear as though a garment factory in Bangladesh, owned by a company in Curacao, was purchased by another company in Ghana, which was in turn owned by an individual in Mauritius. All of these individuals and companies were fictitious, existing only in file drawers. *The CIA would love it! The money conduit runs from Russia to Venezuela, probably two of the most corrupt banking systems in existence.*

Both of them watched as two apparently identical wooden crates were winched out of the Northern Voyager's hold, lowered onto the boat and taken back to the Sigilo.

Vargas looked puzzled. "What's the swap about?"

Grodin shrugged. "So the manifests match up. Each ship had a certain number of crates when they left port, and it's still the same number if anyone wants to check. Even the weights match up."

Vargas smirked. "I know what's in those I brought on the Sigilo. What did we get in exchange?"

"You should read your revised manifest. Big screen televisions. Made in Korea." *At least that's what the lettering on the boxes say. And that's what's on the top layer if you open the box.*

Reynaldo's worried look remained.

Grodin said, "We've got about an hour before heading for the Bay. What would you like to do?"

Reynaldo looked up at the women hovering above them, remembering Natalia. He said with a laugh, "What would I like to do, huh? I'd like to fuck my brains out! Which one would you recommend?"

Grodin smiled, but not for the reasons that Reynaldo would expect. *So predictable! I wonder how such people survive as long as they do? They confuse testosterone with brains.*

He said, "We've got a cabin set aside for you. Actually, I've asked all ten of them to be in your cabin in five minutes. Use your imagination. Personally, I'd stay away from the big blonde. Her name is Lena and she has a bad attitude. If you have time, you can even choose which five of the ten you want for your three million dollars. Your Pedro and Gomez team can take them along from the pier or, if you like, we'll hand deliver them in Mexico City in a month."

An hour later, Vargas waved from the bridge of the Sigilo as it began a sweeping turn to bring it onto its long southerly course back to South America. The Northern Voyager turned east at slow speed, aiming for the Golden Gate Bridge.

As the ships drew apart, the overhead satellite in geosynchronous orbit repositioned its cameras further south and closer in to the California coastline, no longer interested. It was a scarce resource and higher priorities were in play once the transfer was accomplished. Pictures of the two ships and the crates were already being studied by several law enforcement agencies on three continents.

Grodin had a pair of high-powered binoculars locked in a metal bracket on the bridge. Thirty minutes after the ships separated, he trained them on the horizon, aimed approximately at the point where the Sigilo had disappeared. With ten seconds to go, he put his eyes to the glasses and watched. At the precise instant he had planned for, he saw a bright flash over the horizon and – several seconds later – a crash of what sounded like distant thunder.

No satellite or anyone else except Grodin and a very shabby commercial fishing boat that was paralleling Sigilo's course saw or heard the massive explosion that ripped the entire bow off of the Sigilo. The ship's engines continued on and the forward motion drove the shattered hull downward, taking on massive amounts of seawater and sinking the ship within a minute. The only trace was some debris left floating on the surface. The trailing fishing boat traversed the debris field for the next fifteen minutes, three men with automatic rifles watching closely for survivors. A lone body floated to the surface and all three fired long bursts. When it was clear there were no more targets, the boat turned north at speed.

Sorry, Vargas. I lied. It wasn't really a shipment of TV sets in that crate. Now, just one more detail.

He found Pedro behind one of the launches on the main deck. He had one of the Russian women backed up against the railing with her skirt hiked up above her waist. Grodin shot him in the back of the head from a few feet away. Before he could fall, Grodin caught him and tipped him over the rail. The woman's screams were carried away by the wind.

An hour later, the Northern Voyager was met by the scruffy-looking commercial fishing boat. No watcher other than an indifferent gull or two observed Grodin, the crates, and the ten women make the short transit from the Voyager to the fisherman, which arced away to the southeast and – half an hour later -- joined a cluster of fishing boats making their way back to their berths in Half Moon Bay.

Plans for an Intercept

"What an asshole! They must find these guys in some secret government lab that clones idiots!"

McAdams noted that Slater leaned in close to him, to make sure that his remarks were not overheard. *What's sad is that he's right: the guy is an asshole. But Slater's got exactly the same problem –he's politically motivated, what my ex-wife used to call 'career-centered'.*

The object of their attention was a small man named Ritter, in a dark suit at the front of the room. He was using a laser pointer to highlight the bullet points on a Powerpoint slide presentation that – according to his introduction – "will clarify the chain of command, assigned operational zones, communication protocols, and seizure procedures for tonight's operation." Slater recapped it nicely: "What all that means? That no matter who fucks up, gets shot or does something brilliant, Ritter will get all the credit for the largest drug bust in U.S. history."

The briefing room was swarming with official personnel. The DEA, FBI, Coast Guard and Immigration were well represented. ATF was also there, for some reason McAdams did not understand. McAdams amused himself by betting with Slater that he could identify anybody from Washington DC or Sacramento. A dollar for every correct ID. They eliminated anyone wearing distinctive clothing, which got rid of half the room, the Coast Guard people in uniform and the DEA agents in black coveralls with "DEA" emblazoned on the sleeves. They called the bet off when he tallied four out of five by using just two criteria – Do they have short hair and do they look excessively serious and grim? The one he got wrong was a woman who turned out to be Port Authority.

The Torres 'shopping list' that Sofia had turned over was the attraction for the Feds. The street value of the items on the list would approximate over a billion dollars and – regardless of what metrics were used -- would be one of the

268

the largest single seizures of illegal drugs in the U.S. in its so-called 'war on drugs'. Everybody wanted to be involved in the operation and one of the higher-ranking Feds even lobbied to have the press on hand as it went down. He cited the use of 'imbedded' journalists in Iraq as precedent, but was overruled by the small guy in the suit. *Probably because he hadn't thought of it himself.*

There were three teams in place, each with a different sphere of responsibility. One cluster was on Yerba Buena Island at the Coast Guard Marina, mostly Coast Guard and DEA who would board the Northern Voyager as soon as the drug shipment had been sent ashore and seized. There were ten of them with a fast boat and access to a helicopter if needed. A second land-based group was staged on a pier on the Oakland side of the Bay and third group at a pier near the Bay Bridge on the San Francisco side. Each of these was a mix of DEA and either the San Francisco or Oakland police departments, mostly SWAT types. They would move to seize the drugs whenever and wherever they came ashore on their side of the Bay. The DEA agents all had night vision goggles sprouting out of their headgear. The few real cops just looked bored.

It all looks good in Powerpoint and on paper. Funny how everything goes to hell as soon as things get underway. I wonder where Sofia is and what's she trying to do?

Garfield had called him thirty minutes ago, leaving him a voice mail and sounding stressed. "I found your woman – the one looking at the snake. She was meeting Moresby in a Starbucks. Right now, she's on foot in the financial district, headed for the Embarcadero."

He hit 'redial', but was interrupted by Slater, who nudged him and said, "The ship is at the entrance to the Bay. Time to get ready."

Well over one hundred thousand vessels transit the San Francisco Bay in the course of a single year. Procedures for entering, anchoring and exiting are well established and overseen by half-a-dozen maritime or governmental agencies with very different agendas. The Coast Guard offshore radar system picked up the Northern Voyager about thirty-five miles from the Golden Gate and tracked it continuously from that point. As usual, a pilot boarded the ship prior to entry and swapped jokes with the captain during its relatively slow transit to its designated anchorage. In fact, the Pacific Cargos ship enjoyed an exceedingly normal passage through the various port and customs checks required of freighters entering the Bay. The harbor authorities had been instructed to behave normally, and not to look very hard for any unlisted passengers, illegal goods, safety issues or minor flaws in the documentation. The ship passed under the Golden Gate and the Bay Bridge and was directed to an anchorage about a half-mile south of the Bay Bridge, midway between Oakland and San Francisco. It dropped anchor shortly after midnight.

It was an exceptionally dark night. The Coast Guard had stationed an officer equipped with night vision binoculars on a freighter anchored about three-hundred yards from the Northern Voyager. Given the alignment of the two ships, he would be able to spot any boat launching activity on either side of the freighter.

At two-ten in the morning, the watcher keyed his radio. "Boats being launched." The message was transmitted to loudspeakers at each of the three posts.

The little man in the suit was the sole line of communication with the watcher. His alarm was apparent from his voice. "Boats? Is that plural, as in more than one?"

"They've put four boats in the water, two on each side. As far as I can tell, they're all the same -- standard launch sizes with two men in each. Could be carrying anything if it was loaded before they put them in the water. They just pushed off. All headed in different directions and they'll soon be out of my visual range."

The Coast Guard station picked up the boats easily, given the light traffic on the Bay at that hour. Each was headed on a straight line for a landing, two on the Western and two on the Eastern side of the Bay. The projected landings on each side were two to three miles apart. The

270

boats headed for San Francisco were aimed at points near Fisherman's Wharf and AT&T Park. The Coast Guard operator estimated the landfall points, but added unnecessarily, "That assumes they don't change course before landfall. And they're not moving real fast."

Ritter scurried off to consult with a cluster at the edge of the room. McAdams and Slater looked at one another and smiled as the loudspeaker remained silent. "He's probably revising his Powerpoint slides," Slater said.

The San Francisco-based team leaders caucused at the front of the room to adapt to the new circumstances. The group was split in half, each part assigned to one of the two boats headed their way. They would each go mobile, in a SWAT van that would constantly adjust its position to be at the spot where the boat finally came ashore. The Yerba Buena team would still wait to board the Northern Voyager until the landings were secured. The new tactics meant that each team had half its original complement and McAdams could almost feel the tension ratchet up as the men exited the pier with the new orders.

He told Slater, "You go with the Fisherman's Wharf team as the SFPD rep. I've got another idea."

Slater did not like it. "Do you know something I don't?"

"No. But I have a feeling that whoever's running the operation on their side is smarter than the little man in the suit who's supposedly on ours." He thought of voicing his other hunch, that all four boats were decoys, but didn't.

He sat on a stack of planks on the deserted pier listening to the crackling of the handheld radio as the shore teams – now operating as four separate units, each with a designated target heading for an unknown destination – changed their positions to adjust to the approaching boats. He thought about what Ellerby had told him about the man Grodin, and about Carlo and Garfield. Most of all, he thought about Sofia. *I don't know what any of them are doing at this moment, or where they are. But I think they are all going to come together in one place, soon. And it will be very messy.*

He took his cell from his pocket and dialed Garfield.

Dissolution of a Family Business

McAdams was wrong about Carlo. He was nowhere near the action, as far from the coming exchange as he could arrange to be, sitting in his library at home. If either a cynical observer or his own conscience pressed him about being so far removed from the danger zone that he had created, he would have talked about delegation and confidence in one's subordinates. And he probably believed his rationalizations. Grodin had pandered to that side of his self-image, feeding him lines that he could use to portray cowardice as leadership. And he made sure that his description of what could go wrong tonight was sufficiently vivid that Carlo was more than content to let Grodin manage the whole affair. Among Carlo's many disabilities, cowardice was high on the list.

Grodin told him what he wanted to hear. "It's all about the optimal division of labor. All this late night stuff on the Bay? That's what I do – the tactical stuff. You? You're the brains, the money guy. We need you to keep the big picture in focus." The fact that it would leave Grodin with acces to bags with thirteen million dollars in cash was not mentioned as part of his sales pitch.

Not that it would make any difference. He thinks we're a team. I wonder if he'll ever put it together – how truly stupid he's been!

The irony was that Carlo was afraid for the right reasons, but – as he was about to learn -- his fear was focused on the wrong actors.

"Carlo."

The voice from the pre-dawn darkness of the house seemed to come from several directions at once. And the single word had overtones and undertones that somehow transmitted sadness, anger and affection all within that one noun.

"What the hell! How did you –"

"You gave me a key, remember? So that I could visit the grandkids when I wanted to? The kids that now live with the mother who won't let either of us see them?"

"Dominick, it's three in the morning."

Dominick emerged from the darkness of the hallway into the library. He took the chair most distant from Carlo, so that he was still only a murky figure on the far edge of the lamplight.

"Yes. It's late. Or early, depending on your perspective. But I couldn't sleep. There's a lot of activity on the Bay tonight."

Carlo thought about all of the troublesome implications of that statement. *Does he have any idea of what's going on? How could he? Why the fuck is he here?*

Dominick didn't give him time to sort through alternative answers to the silent questions he was posing. "Do you remember our last conversation? About how I wanted you to spend your time on legitimate stuff? To stop your playacting as a mafia don? As I recall, you told me to fuck off."

Carlo enunciated each word very carefully. "It wasn't ... It isn't ... playacting!"

"No, it isn't. I realize that now." Dominick's sadness was quite pronounced. "It's very real."

The single desk lamp reflected its light upward from the glossy ebony surface of Carlo's desk, transforming him into something sinister, the kind of effect that kids seek on Halloween by shining flashlights up from below their chins, creating facial hollows and shadows that hint at demonic intention. From the semi-darkness where Dominick had seated himself, it made Carlo seem unreal.

A trick of lighting only. But I wonder if it isn't the real Carlo ... the one I could never see because of ... Because of what? Me? Him?

Carlo was talking, the words somehow falling unheard into the space between them as though the thick Tibetan carpet drew them downward while in transit. Dominick was in his own head, recalling Carlo at age thirteen. *He killed the neighbor's cat. Fastened it to a tree with duct tape and threw stones. Took an hour. And I bailed him out. A hundred bucks to the SPCA and a new cat for the neighbors.* Then he thought again about Natalia and Maria, how they were laid out so neatly on the pile of muck in their matching yellow coats. The only apparent difference between them was the blue cloth on Natalia's half-face.

Dominick's voice overrode whatever Carlo was saying, a reflective tone from the semi-darkness. "It's funny. When I gave you control of the company, I remember hoping that you would take some initiative, do things differently ... modernize it in some way. Maybe go into some new lines of business. Not just sit back and do business as usual."

"So? I guess you got what you wanted, didn't you?" Carlo did not even bother to attempt to conceal his contempt.

They sat in silence, as though allowing their clashing emotional states to contend in the space between them – Carlo's contempt and Dominick's sadness. It was not a comfortable silence, each of them knowing that they were locked together by family, but separated by an unbridgeable gulf without any way to reconcile their expectations of one another.

Dominick broke the silence. "I got a call from a lawyer in London today. Actually, a barrister or solicitor. They use different titles. He was representing a corporate client from somewhere in Russia. It sounded very global and glamorous, what with the English accent and all. But it was all a little vague."

Carlo waited, knowing what was coming and wondering how he would respond.

"He assumed I was still the controlling interest of the Fallon companies. I probably should have corrected him."

He went on, with a deep sigh. "It seems that this Russian firm has some kind of lien on the Fallon Group because they've extended a fifty million dollar loan to us. The barrister needed some quarterly financials to complete his documentation."

"Funny. I can't remember the Board approving a transaction of that size. And I checked with our banker. There hasn't been any cash inflow from any Russian lender."

Carlo asked, "So what did you tell the English asshole?"

"That I'd consider his request." His voice took on an amused tone, as though he was preparing to tell a joke. "That seemed to annoy him. He said that his client did not have a lot of patience, that it was really important to get all the documentation in order. Some nasty-sounding stuff about 'extraordinary consequences' ..."

Carlo spoke sarcastically, "Yeah. Well, that was some of that initiative you were wanting me to take. We'll get back about four times our investment."

"And if your ... investment ... doesn't work?"

Carlo was silent, an eloquent answer to Dominick's question.

"You've bet my company on a drug deal, Carlo. A deal that will kill far more people than even you and Grodin have managed so far."

For the first time, Carlo became aware of the discrepancy between *what* Dominick was saying and *how* he was saying it. It was eerie; talking about catastrophic events and killings in a conversational tone more suited to a family reunion with distant relatives. It was as if his father no longer cared about the future or had any expectations of Carlo. It was the beginning of a chilling premonition that things had changed, that he could no longer rely on past assumptions. He peered at him closely, but Dominick was deep in shadows.

Dominick said, "I met them, you know."

What the hell is he talking about now?

"Your two recent Russian imports. Over at the pier you're leasing for your cultural exchange program. Natalia and Maria. When they were still alive. They were quite beautiful. So hopeful. That was the hardest part for me. That they were so hopeful." After a long silence, he added wistfully, "And I saw them again this morning."

This morning! Not unless he's scuba diving in the middle of the Bay! He's losing it! The hell with it! He can wallow in self-pity all he wants. But it's time to stop all this self-righteous bullshit. Let's see how he deals with the whole story!

"OK, daddy! You want to talk about *initiatives?* What you call *the deal?* What's going down right now as we sit here? It includes ten more like them – your Natalia and Maria. I think one of them is also named Maria. But you can relax. You have nothing to do with any of this. So get out of my house. Go back to your own little sanctimonious life! Play golf with the mayor, go to lunch with the rest of the slobs, or do whatever it is that you do! But leave me alone!"

Dominick leaned forward in his chair, bringing his head and shoulders into the light. His expression was anguished and Carlo wondered how a person in such a state could sound so calm and composed. A vague feeling of alarm settled over him, a sense that something was being talked about that he did not quite understand.

Dominick's voice changed to match up with the tortured expression on his face. "Oh, but you're wrong Carlo. You have no idea how wrong you are. I am as guilty as you are. Maybe worse. At least you don't pretend to be something you're not. And you let Grodin do your killing."

He brought his right arm up from his side and into the light. His hand was holding a small pistol, strangely elongated by the silencer screwed onto the muzzle. He fired two shots into his son's chest. Then, for about twenty seconds, he was as still as a bronze casting, his eyes vacant.

Carlo saw the pistol come up and heard the shots. He fell face-forward onto his glossy desk, like a first-grader taking a nap in school. His vision dimmed, but he was able to see the jet black surface that his face was pressed against turn red with his blood and his father walk out of the room before it was completely dark. He was still trying to comprehend what had happened when he died.

The Players Converge

Carlo could not know it, but it was as if his death was the first and necessary step in a grand choreography staged by a master playwright, the catalyst for a series of moves and countermoves by major and minor characters, aware of one another, yet each following his own internal rhythms, destined to bring them together in time and place for a final conflict with many possible endings.

Sofia shivered as the fog streamed through the Golden Gate and shrouded the waterfront in a cold damp grayness that matched her emotional state. The hooded sweatshirt helped but was not sufficient given her position on the end of the pier. She did not know it, but she was in Harry Howden's old encampment with its view of the Bay and its exposure to the elements. However, what she did know, quite vividly, was that this was the place that she, Natalia and Maria climbed the ladder onto this pier. Somehow, the memory added to her shivering and to the anger that had been fueling her for the past two days, a simmering corrosive rage that every now and then would ebb just enough to allow the uncertainty to creep in.

Something has changed. This is not me, this woman sitting here freezing. All I have to do is walk away and I have everything I want. Absolute control over myself for the first time. I don't owe anything to Sasha. Or Natalia. Or Maria. So why am I sitting here freezing, waiting to kill someone? Or be killed!

Then she thought about McAdams and their last muddled confrontation, neither of them able to say what they wanted to say. *Like strangers in an elevator without a common language. That wasn't me either, damn it! It's dangerous to care so much about someone other than me, to be so dependent on a man's opinion ... to want to trust someone.*

Then she heard the faint sound of an engine out on the Bay, getting closer.

Three blocks away, two vehicles were parked alongside one another in an empty lot, a white box truck and a black minibus. Other than the license plates, the truck had no markings of any sort. The minibus, however, featured large neon letters advertising "Golden State Tours". Each driver sat in his vehicle, aware of the other, but knowing only his own small part in the coming events. Gomez, the driver of the tourist van, did not know that his boss, Reynaldo Vargas, was dead, but – even if he had – he would still carry out his simple instructions. *Give the man the suitcase. He will transfer five people to you. Drive them to the usual place in San Diego. Ditch the van.* He did not think about what was in the suitcase or why the five people warranted such special treatment. Gomez had survived for a long time in a hazardous trade because of his dedicated lack of curiosity.

His counterpart, the other driver, was curious but ignorant. Grodin had picked him out of the twenty or so day laborers that hung out near the exit of the truck rental yard, hoping that a contractor would hire them on for a day. He did not know enough to be afraid. He was being paid a thousand dollars in cash to drive the truck onto a pier and walk away. In his mind, the thousand dollars was already spent, committed to a full-busted woman he knew only as 'Valentina', who promised him a full weekend of sex – "whatever you want, whenever you want it, for two whole days". He thought more about what variations he would try out on Valentina than he did about the curious deal that he was part of.

The drivers stayed in their respective vehicles holding their cell phones and watching the red dot that was tracking the progress of a small boat carrying a billion dollars of cargo. They did not know the actual value of the shipment, nor did they know the exact amount of cash in the duffel-style rollerbag that sat alongside each of them in the passenger seat.

Garfield also heard the boat's engine approaching from the Bay. He was a standing on the curb across the street from where the pier was joined to the steep bank. He knew that Sofia was close by and that she had reached whatever destination she had in mind. However, from his vantage point, he could not see her pick up a rock from the shore and hammer the lock on the side door until it gave way. He thought that the only entry or exit was from the Bay itself or through the huge doors giving trucks access from the street. He wore an old army field jacket, with his hands in the pockets for warmth. The right hand gripped his revolver, surprising him by its familiarity after twelve years. His left hand was wrapped around his silenced cell phone. When he felt the pulsing, he looked at the screen, seeing the caption 'McAdams'.

Grodin was approaching the pier from the Bay. The boat was a commercial fishing boat owned by a firm with berths in Redwood City and Half Moon Bay. Its main use was as a chartered 'party boat' for individuals or corporate groups that wanted to spend the day offshore fishing or whale watching. Its passages in and out of the Bay were largely ignored by the Coast Guard, both because the boat was familiar to them, and because it rarely deviated from its routine. In any case, anybody with a badge was currently involved in tracking the four launches from the Northern Voyager. Those boats had changed course repeatedly, keeping the onshore SWAT teams frustrated and, more importantly, far away from the pier where Grodin was headed.

Unlike Sofia and Garfield, Grodin had no doubts about the unfolding sequence of events or his motivations. Two days earlier, he and Carlos had filled a canvas rollerbag with ten million dollars in one-hundred dollar bills, the final payment when the goods were handed off on the pier. The suitcase would be at the pier, along with a truck to receive the shipment. Reynaldo's man Gomez was bringing a van for the women and another bag with three million in cash to pay for the women. Grodin viewed both packages as *my money*.

Everybody gets something. Carlo could have the one-thousand kilos of drugs and its billion dollars of 'street value'. But he won't last a week without me to hold his hand. The cartels can have their forty million dollars. Grodin preferred the remembered solidity of the bag that he and Carlo had packed, the satisfying *fullness* when he towed it with its little soft polyurethane wheels that were so quiet.

I could cut out now, but then some serious people lose face and you've got all that Latin bullshit and ego to deal with. They'd come after me. And all those buyers Carlos has got lined up? The really nasty ones … they'd want a piece of me for walking away. But if the kilos and the women change hands on schedule, then it's only about money. And they get a bonus – all ten women, instead of five. They'll take the ten million out of Carlo, if they can get it. And he won't need the other three million waiting on that pier. Another thirty minutes and I'm gone with thirteen million dollars and enough passports to keep me out of reach of these amateurs!

Game Time

McAdams had stopped listening to his handheld radio tuned to the special-purpose channel. He had already decided that the four boats from the Northern Voyager were decoys, a hunch that became near certainty when they twice diverted to new destinations just before reaching shore. Whoever was directing them was playing with them.

Garfield was economical with words when he answered McAdams' ring. "Howden's pier. She's here somewhere, and waiting for someone or something." McAdams was out the door before the dial tone had stopped.

He satisfied his conscience, calling the Yerba Buena command post while accelerating through red lights on the Embarcadero. The exchange both infuriated him and left him feeling strangely satisfied. He'd finally reached Ritter, the DEA idiot that was running the operation, but only after spending three useless minutes with various gatekeepers.

"This is Ritter. Who are you again?"

"McAdams, SFPD."

"Can't you talk to your rep, what's-his-name?"

"I tried. He says you need to authorize it. And his name is Murphy."

"Authorize what? And make it quick. I'm real busy here."

"I need a team to help me cover a pier south of China Basin."

"Hell! Those boats are nowhere near that part of the Bay!"

"All four boats are decoys. The stuff is coming from somewhere else."

"Our intel says —"

"Your intel is wrong. You're being played."

"What's your name again?"

"McAdams. Yours is Ritter."

"I'll remember that, shithead. Now quit tying up the channel. Go arrest some jaywalkers or something."

The phone went dead. McAdams was surprised at the intensity of relief that he felt until he recognized his underlying fear. *Sofia's there. Face it: you don't want a swarm of cops with guns headed her way.* What he did not admit, even to himself, was that he wanted to do this alone, for Freddie and Gonzo.

He swerved around a city truck setting out traffic cones. *Howden's pier. That red spike heel caught in the planks. That's their entry point. And Sofia's there waiting. With my gun. Still three minutes away.*

The boat idled in place, floating twenty yards from the end of the pier. Grodin studied the darkened pier for two solid minutes. He saw nothing unusual, but that meant little. The cops would not advertise their presence. In any case, he had made prior arrangements to make sure that he would know if they were there. Watchers were cheap. He turned and saw that the lights on the Northern Voyager were visible briefly and then faded as the breeze altered the density of the fog. *No word from the watcher on shore. Time to go.* He signaled the captain to move to the pier and used the 'push-to-talk' feature of his phone to send a terse "Now".

Two hundred yards from the pier, the white box truck and the tourist minibus started their engines and rolled to the head of the pier, showing only parking lights. Gomez left the minibus running, but got out and used a key to open the padlock that kept the massive doors closed. He opened both doors and drove the van into the opening, leaving room for the truck to pull alongside. He closed the doors again, but left them unlocked and ajar. The parking lights from the side-by-side vehicles were absorbed by the darkness, but revealed a small forklift parked on one side of the shed. Gomez took the rollerbag filled with cash and placed in front on the van. Then he started the forklift and drove it to the end of the pier, using the lighter shades of the fog visible off the end of the pier to guide him.

The truck driver stopped the truck parallel with the minibus, took the rollerbag from the seat alongside him and centered it between the headlights. Then he turned and walked out through the doors without looking back, urged on by thoughts of Valentina.

Sofia huddled in the dark corner that Howden had once prized, only fifteen feet from the forklift when it stopped at the end of the pier. The masts of the boat swayed in front of her and she could hear hushed voices below her. She could not account for a whirring sound until the boom of a deck crane swung into view, suspending a wooden crate that reminded her of an extra large coffin. It was lowered onto the pier near the forklift. Then the operation was repeated for a second crate. At the same time, the women began appearing over the edge of the pier, swearing softly in Russian as they struggled up the ladder. Their voices reminded her of the night that she made the same ascent, and the anger surged back, driving out the fear and uncertainty. She edged closer.

Fifty yards away, Garfield slid through the main door, left ajar by the driver, keeping the two vehicles between him and the activity at the end of the pier. He could see figures moving around at the far end, but not enough detail to be useful. He almost screamed when McAdams tapped him on his shoulder.

"Where's Sofia?" A bare whisper.

"Don't know. I lost her at the last minute. Somewhere close."

McAdams whispered, "Stay here. Behind the truck. I'll go up the right side. And watch out for the driver." When Garfield moved, the light reflected from the gun that he held at his side. McAdams gripped his arm. "Put that away. If there's shooting, just run like hell!"

McAdams worked his way slowly toward the end of the pier. He was almost there when the forklift returned bearing the first crate. Its weight was apparent from the manner in which the front end bounced and swayed on the uneven planks. As it passed the point where he crouched in the deep shadows formed by some empty barrels, he could see that the driver had some kind of weapon slung over one shoulder, apparently some kind of short-barreled assault rifle.

This is not good. At one end, we've got Garfield with a handgun he's probably afraid to use, dodging a guy with a machine gun. At the other, we've got a bunch of Russian women in high heels. And one stone cold killer.

And Sofia was somewhere in the general vicinity.

The engine of the boat went from a throaty idling murmur to a steady beat that faded as it moved steadily away from the pier and back into the Bay. Looking back at the truck, McAdams could see the forklift maneuvering around the truck, preparing to drop the crate into the box. No sign of Garfield. *OK. We've got Grodin and the driver to deal with. They don't know I'm here. Grodin will have to pass me on his way out. I can take him from behind and use him as a hostage to disarm the driver.*

It's a plan. Power of positive thinking and all that. He tried not to think about the other factors, the uncontrollables. First, there were the women, what the press liked to call innocent civilians. From the muted voices he was picking up, it sounded like a significant number. If he'd decoded Torres' notes correctly, there should be ten of them. They were huddled together and sorting out the bags they had brought up the ladder, using a lone cigarette lighter for illumination. He could hear Grodin's irritated voice speaking in Russian. Then he had Garfield at one end of the pier, carrying a weapon that he was afraid to use. *But Grodin doesn't know that!*

Let's be optimistic and assume that Sofia and Garfield will wait for me to move and then back me up. Except that Sofia doesn't even know we're here. And then there's the wild card -- ten women who probably hate cops, don't speak any English, and are scared to death!

The forklift made the round trip for the second crate. The women and Grodin were backlit by the little bit of ambient lighting from the open end of the pier. *I'm seeing what Howden saw. Lots of white skin moving through darkness.* They were starting to move, with Grodin leading and the women tightly bunched behind him. McAdams heard the forklift once more and glanced back to see it emerge from behind the truck. The driver edged it against the far wall and stepped down. The parking lights of the vehicles gave enough light to see that he was carrying the rifle loosely in one hand.

Too many goddam variables! Pay attention to Grodin!

The cluster of bodies moved slowly, its progress measured more by the sound of shuffling feet than by sight. McAdams heard a distinct 'thud' from the direction of the truck and saw a figure pass in front of the truck lights. Grodin was just past him, twenty feet away, when the sound or some other impulse stopped him suddenly, causing the covey of women to pile up around him, one of them tripping on the rough flooring. He raised his cell phone close to his face, pushed a single button and spoke a few words that McAdams could not hear. The light from the phone's display created eerie shadows across his face.

Time to move!

McAdams came out of his crouching position and moved with quick silent strides toward Grodin, his gun raised.

Then the lights came on.

Standoff

Two intense beams from the truck headlights took away the darkness and all of his options. Dead silence descended simultaneously and all motion ceased, just as a flash photograph freezes all sound and movement within that single instant. McAdams and Grodin stared at one another, ten feet apart, Grodin's free hand reaching under his coat. The women were locked in place, each of them with an uplifted arm to shield their eyes from the glare.

Then a door slammed and a figure walked in front of the lights, standing precisely between the two beams with the bulk of the truck behind him and a bulky shadow at his feet. He was a silhouette without any features other than his outline. One hand held a pistol, at his side but pointing down.

Grodin said loudly, "Gomez?"

The silhouette with Garfield's voice poked with his foot at the bulkier shadow on the planks. "Is that his name? I'm afraid he'll be unresponsive for a half-an-hour or so. You're on your own."

Grodin nodded as though he had expected Garfield and turned toward McAdams. He had taken his hand out from under his coat. It was holding a pistol. From McAdams' vantage point, it looked like a forty-five caliber Colt, the 1911 model. Very casually, as though it was a gesture of affection, Grodin reached with his free hand to the woman nearest him and pulled her close. Then he did the same thing with two other women. In their heels, they were as tall as him. It was if he had created a palisade of flesh around him. The women – all of them – seemed immobilized by fright, only their heads turning from Garfield to McAdams to Grodin.

Something is not right about the women. They're wrong in some way.

Forget the women. Pay attention to Grodin. He's the one that can kill you.

287

"Give it up, Grodin. There's two of us, one of you. An army of Feds is outside. No way out of here."

Grodin was turned sideways to the high beams, so his face was bisected, one half brightly lit, the other in complete shadow. The effect was to make him mysterious and formidable, as if such a dual creature would be more than human.

He spoke conversationally, as though chatting with an old college buddy. "McAdams, isn't it? My, you are persistent! But you don't count very well. There's eleven of me – twelve with Gomez -- and only two of you. And I know about your so-called army of Feds. They're chasing their tails, and a long way off."

The muzzle of his gun came into sight, resting on the bare shoulder of one of the women he was holding and pointing up just under her chin. "I will shoot one of these ten women every thirty seconds until you both put your guns down."

Grodin's words and the sight of the gun barrel touching the soft flesh disabled whatever forces were immobilizing the women. Two or three cried out in alarm. Another cursed loudly in Russian. Confused cross-currents of motion rippled through the group as they tried to move away from the gun. Two women on the fringe, still in shadow, hugged one another tightly and were whispering frantically until the taller one of them turned and started walking away from the others, toward the street. The muzzle tracked her movement and Grodin said, "Not a good idea, Lena. I'll shoot you first." She stopped, looked back at Grodin, but then moved back to the edge of the group, cursing softly. The circle of women contracted even tighter, with Grodin more or less in the center. The woman whose shoulder his gun rested on was crying and whimpering. Again, McAdams had the impression that he was missing something about the women.

The momentary group turbulence left Grodin exposed for a second or two. McAdams fought his training and instincts. *I had a shot, and didn't take it. Shit!* But he knew why. *I need to talk to him!*

McAdams knew he had lost whatever small chance he had of shooting without hitting one or more of the women, and Garfield was much further away. *And he quit the LAPD because he killed a nine-year-old girl in a shootout. What's the chance that he'll even fire the gun?*

"Garfield," he called out. "Put your weapon down and leave. It's OK. I'll finish this."

Grodin smiled at him. He now had a clear vision of how this would end. Without taking his eyes from McAdams, he called in a loud voice, "Garfield – if that's your name – Gomez had a weapon, an Uzi. Please find it, show it to me, and then put that and your pistol down on the floor. Then come and stand over here by your friend."

Garfield's silhouette did not move for a long time. Then it seemed to slump, to collapse inward. A strangled voice came from the middle of it. "Mac, I'm sorry. I thought I –"

"Don't sweat it. Do what the man says." Then, as Garfield stooped and picked up the stubby weapon at his feet, McAdams added, "This is my story, not yours."

All eyes followed Garfield as he took three steps toward them and put the two weapons on the planking. He stood and raised his hands to show that they were empty, then walked to stand beside McAdams, his arms at his side. Just before turning to face Grodin, he winked at McAdams.

What the hell does that mean? Doesn't he know that he's about to be shot? He thinks we're Butch Cassidy and the Sundance Kid!

"Such a sensible fellow. Your turn, McAdams. Put your gun down and I'll let the two of you walk away." Grodin's speech was monotone and unaccented, as if reading for a part in a bad play that he really didn't want to be in. He didn't make the slightest effort to sound sincere.

So let's play the game for a bit.

McAdams didn't move. He kept his pistol pointing loosely in Grodin's direction. He said, "I know who you are."

"I don't think so."

"Ellerby told me. About Vladivostock and the CIA. What you do for Carlo."

"Ellerby doesn't know who I am. He didn't then and still doesn't. And Carlo's a fool who thinks he's important."

"You used him."

"Of course. That's what happens to self-important fools."

McAdams gestured at the truck. "That stuff? All those kilos? The feds will have it before it's three blocks from here. Fifty million bucks wasted."

Grodin only smiled, and it hit McAdams that Grodin didn't care about the drugs or the fifty million, that he was working an agenda that was all his own.

Grodin was growing tired of talking. "It doesn't matter whether you know who I am or not." He thought of adding, 'because you're going to be dead,' but stopped short. Instead he said, "Because that person is going to disappear. It's what I'm good at."

"You're good at lots of things, aren't you? Carlo thought it was him, but you were pulling his strings too."

Despite himself, Grodin's curiosity was growing. This person not only was not afraid of him, he really did know him. Not his name or any of the biographical history – that was buried long ago – but he knew about *him,* what he wanted, how he worked, how he made things happen from the shadows.

McAdams proved it with his next comment. "Carlo will get all the credit – for human trafficking, drug smuggling and murder. And the cartels will tear him into little bits. That's part of your plan."

Grodin smiled. "He wanted to be a big time criminal. That should make his reputation, shouldn't it? He can maybe write a best seller about it, from his cell on death row. With a good lawyer, that should give him ten years or so to finish it. Assuming he avoids those Latins you mentioned."

McAdams pointed at the suitcase that Garfield had dropped in front of the headlights. "The bag? The one filled with cash. I imagine that doesn't belong to you. Aren't you afraid of them coming after you?"

Grodin's smiled remained unchanged. "That's only ten million. They'll get it back from Carlo. Or they can repossess the merchandise if they like. I think I'll take my chances."

McAdams saw the rising impatience, first in Grodin's eyes and then in the way the angle of his gun changed, forcing the woman's head back and widening her eyes in terror. It was evident in Grodin's voice as well.

"That's enough talk. I need you to put your gun down. Now."

Garfield spoke before McAdams could respond. "I tossed the keys to your truck. You won't get very far herding ten women and carrying those crates on your back."

Grodin's smile disappeared, replaced by a calculating look. "Remember the deal? One woman every thirty seconds …"

Then, from the back of the group, a trembling voice spoke. It was the one he had called Lena. Her voice became stronger as she went on, a heavily-accented English dripping with contempt.

"You little man?" She pointed a long finger at Grodin. "You killed friends of ours -- Sasha, Anya, Natalia, Maria -- and threw them into the water like gutted fish. You would kill us all if you could. But you can't. We are too many."

She looked at Grodin in a way that reminded McAdams of Sophia's photograph. "If you fire your gun at any one of us, the rest of will kill you with our fingernails and teeth and use your bag full of dollars to bury our dead and repair our nails." She rattled off some quick Russian phrases that were incomprehensible except for the names -- Sasha, Anya, Natalia, Maria -- but the impact on the other women was apparent. All eyes turned toward Grodin and expressions changed from fearful to calculating.

Once more the tableau was frozen, as if Lena's mini-speech was going to be put to a vote and everyone had to decide 'yea' or 'nay'. The only motion was all those pairs of eyes turning toward Grodin. The four words 'Sasha, Anya, Natalia, Maria' seemed to float in the air, as though echoing from the wooden sides of the pier.

Grodin was the first to react. He did not sound surprised, flustered or angry about the sudden turn of events. If anything, he sounded faintly sad, as though a tasteless practical joke had been played on him and he was determined to be a good sport.

He shook his head, but kept his gaze firmly on McAdams. "Lena, Lena... Such a waste. I thought you might be a mistake. But you *have* changed the game. Time for new rules."

He gestured at McAdams and Garfield with his free hand. "You keep your gun; I'll keep mine. We're all going to stay in this tight little group and move down to the truck. Once there, you give me your cell phones and I and the bagfuls of cash will drive off in the truck. You can have Gomez. You two and these ten ladies will stay behind. Alive." *Unfortunately.*

McAdams thought about it, trying out alternative scenarios in his head. *He's right: it is a standoff. And probably the best outcome we can get. He won't get far in the truck. But he knows that, of course. Which means that he's already got a switch planned. That's why he was dialing two minutes ago.*

He looked at Garfield, who simply inclined his head and said, "OK with me." Something in his tone reminded McAdams of that damned wink. McAdams turned back to Grodin and simply nodded.

Grodin smiled. "All right. Let's do it. And let's hope that nobody does anything stupid."

We look like a modern dance troupe. Grodin shuffles sideways and all the rest of us match him. The unspoken rule: relative positions must stay the same. Especially the two guns and the woman with her head arched back, the gun under her chin.

He and Grodin kept their eyes locked. It would be easy to attribute that to the fact that they were the ones with the guns, but McAdams knew it was a really a non-verbal continuation of their interrupted dialogue. He knew it was time to ask the important questions, the ones that would stop the incessant pictures that kept him from sleeping, of Sasha's white skin against the black mud and the pink haze exploding from Gonzo's head.

"You *like* to kill people, don't you?

Grodin was startled by the tone. Not accusative or angry, merely curious. Perhaps that was why he thought about the question for the first time, and then answered truthfully. "No. But I am interested in *how* people deal with the reality of dying. Especially those who thought they were immune."

"Sasha? Was she one of those? Who felt immune?"

Two more shuffling steps before he answered in a lowered voice, after glancing at the women nearest to him. "No. She knew. For a long time. I was sorry … No, that's not the right word, sorry. I *regretted* that I had to kill her."

"What about Howden? Why Howden?"

Grodin looked puzzled, but quickly brightened. "Oh, the homeless guy? The bible thumper?" McAdams bumped into Garfield, who had stopped in place. He nudged him to keep moving.

"It's funny. I didn't have to kill him, but I didn't know that until after I killed him. Does that make sense?"

He didn't wait for an answer. "No one paid any attention to him or his ravings. And he bothered me. He cursed me – in the biblical sense – as I was killing him."

"Desmond? The insurance guy?"

Grodin's tone was dismissive. "Carlo pointed me at him. I think he just wanted to be able to say 'I ordered a hit today'. Desmond was no threat to anybody except himself."

They were almost at the truck. Half a dozen more sideways steps. McAdams tried very hard to keep his voice even. "What about Gonzales, the cop? That was pretty risky, wasn't it?"

Grodin picked up something in McAdams' voice that told him this question was different. More important. He responded in the same conversational tone, but made sure that McAdams saw him move the muzzle another half-inch higher into the soft flesh below the woman's chin.

"Gonzales was a mistake. Very spur of the moment. And it showed. He was supposed to be you. Desmond's phone said that he had called you. I didn't know how much he told you, so I thought you'd be worth a quick drive-by. Gonzales was just unlucky."

They were at the truck. "Was it risky?" Grodin spoke as if to himself. "I suppose. The word I would use is *ironic*. All those years and ... contracts ... all that careful planning, and the one time I do a cop, it's the wrong one."

This time, McAdams stopped dead, leaving a space between Garfield and him.

Grodin inclined his head toward the truck. "Keep moving. We're almost done with this dance. Nobody wants to be a hero at this stage."

Grodin looked at Garfield. "Now, Garfield, where are the keys to the truck?"

"In the ignition." Garfield smiled gently, as if to soften an insult.

Grodin nodded, not surprised. He said, "Garfield. That bag that Gomez brought – it's three million dollars, by the way -- Would you please pick it up and throw it in the cab for me?" He nudged the rollerbag at his feet that the other driver had left in front of the truck. "Then do the same for this one. It's ten million."

Garfield looked at McAdams, who nodded. He reached down for the bag, walked to the driver's side of the truck, staying well away from Grodin, threw the bag onto the front seat, then did the same with the roller bag, and then, finally, walked back to his place alongside McAdams.

Grodin took a half step back from the women, toward the driver's door. "Now, here's my plan for getting all of us out of here alive. I'm going to get in the truck. Garfield, I want you to walk around the truck, open the doors onto the street all the way, and then come back where you are now. Lena? When I get in the truck, I want you to move you and your friends directly in front of the truck, between me and

McAdams here. And stay together where I can see you. Can you do that?"

"Once everybody has done their thing, I will put my gun on the dash where you can see it. McAdams, you put your gun on the floor at your feet and step away. I'll drive away into the sunset and you can do your best to find me. Does that all seem doable?"

Grodin said, "I'll take your silence as agreement. Oh, and I'll take Katya here with me to the end of the street. I'll let her go if you all stay inside. If I see any one of you trying to follow me …" He didn't bother completing the threat.

He's in the truck, we're in the open. But we're mobile, he's not. Once he's on the street, we've still got Katya at risk. Still a standoff.

The tall woman in the middle of the pack – Lena -- looked around her as if seeking the approval of the others. It was not apparent what she saw, but she turned back to Grodin and nodded. However, as he tracked her eyes making the mute inquiry, McAdams finally caught on to what was bothering him about the women.

It changed the rules completely.

"One last condition," Grodin said, "I need your cell phones. It's not negotiable. Lena, please collect them for me."

The woman took the phones from McAdams and Garfield and gave them to Grodin, who dropped them into the pocket of his jacket. He lowered his gun and the woman he had used as a shield sobbed and dropped to her knees. Lena moved to raise her to her feet. Once she was standing, Grodin regripped her arm and stepped back, separating Katya and him from the group but keeping the tight cluster of women between him and McAdams. The only sound was Katya's sobbing. Grodin pushed her up into the cab and reached up to pull himself up into the cab of the truck, keeping his gun pointed at Katya.

Standing on the running board, he said, "OK. Everyone knows what to do. Let's get this over with. And remember – No heroics."

The players moved as Grodin had scripted them. Garfield made his circuit to the doors and back. Lena moved very slowly, positioning herself five feet from the center of the metal grille. The women moved to cluster around her but now all facing forward. Grodin slowly and carefully placed his gun on top of the dashboard, in sync with McAdams stooping to place his Glock on the planks at his feet. McAdams wondered if Grodin would finally see what he had just noticed – what was wrong with the women. That there were eleven -- not ten -- sets of eyes staring at him, one of them looking like she was seeing a snake crawling across her kitchen floor.

McAdams said, "Grodin", stopping him in the act of reaching for the ignition switch on the dashboard. "You're going to die. How does that make you feel?" McAdams spoke slowly and distinctly, as if pronouncing a sentence.

Grodin started to smile and say something, but then the hole appeared in the windshield with tiny spiderweb cracks around it and he looked surprised in the second before two more holes appeared and then the windshield shattered and fell into the cab and by then his throat was ripped open and his face was covered with blood. He did not feel the next six shots.

McAdams watched Sofia bring his Beretta up from her side, feet apart with both hands on the grip and fire carefully spaced rounds into the truck. He remembered her talking about Dmitri. *Every Sunday, we would go into the forest and shoot.* Much later, he tried – briefly with little real curiosity or success – to understand why he stood and watched and did nothing to stop her, even when she continued pulling the trigger long after the magazine was empty.

At that same time, he realized that he no longer cared whether Grodin would have answered his question, nor did he have any curiosity about what he might have said.

A Form of Closure

Two hours later, the pier was awash with light from floodlights, even as the eastern sky was lightening. Ritter was holding a press conference on the street at the entrance to the pier, with a carefully chosen group of DEA agents, a hundred kilos of cocaine and Gomez's cash as a carefully arranged backdrop. The crime scene unit was still swarming around the two vehicles on the pier itself, although Grodin's body was gone. The Russian women were in custody, but – from what McAdams could hear -- the several TV crews were already touting them as innocent victims of organized crime and – by implication – of an uncaring Moscow government. The word *asylum* was frequently mentioned.

Sofia was gone. She was on her way out the door before the last ejected cartridge hit the decking. McAdams figured she would win an award for "murder suspect least likely to be apprehended". Lena – whose English skills disappeared once the police showed up -- had described her to Ritter and Murphy as "a crazy Russian, an eighteen-year-old peasant girl obsessed with getting revenge for the death of her four friends". Her physical description was totally fictitious. According to Lena, the shooter was 'a blonde … a pudgy and bleary-eyed teenager, heavily tattooed and speaking with a thick Russian accent.' Neither Garfield nor McAdams challenged what she said, careful to say that they never had a decent view of the shooter, that she was careful to stay in the middle of the women and wore a large hoodie. Technically, they did not lie.

McAdams accepted Garfield's complicity in the coverup without comment. *Is he doing it for me? Or her?*

Nobody asked McAdams why a veteran homicide detective would allow the shooter to walk away untouched. Or why he had not called again for backup instead of acting out his lone wolf routine. Ritter was avoiding him and most of the cops swarming around were of the opinion that this was one of those times when the killer should be rewarded rather than punished.

Murphy brought two cups of watery and lukewarm coffee to McAdams and Garfield, who were sitting on the plank floor, leaning back against the wall.

Murphy said, "So I guess we close the three duct tape cases, along with Sasha, Desmond, Howden, Gonzo and Freddie." He spoke more tentatively than McAdams was accustomed to, leaving it unclear if it was a statement or a question. When he got no response, he prodded, "Don't you think?"

"Sure," McAdams said." *Although you've included one too many names.* "And don't forget to include the two we fished out of the Bay yesterday morning."

For some reason, that reply seemed to make Murphy even more tentative. *He isn't worried about closing cases. There's something more.*

Murphy squatted down next to McAdams and peered closely at him. "Carlo Fallon was shot to death a few hours ago. In his home. And everybody's favorite suspect – our man Grodin -- was somewhere on a fishing boat in the Bay at the time."

McAdams said nothing, wondering about his lack of surprise. *Carlo is dead. And Grodin was with me.*

"That's terrible," Garfield said in a tone that did not match the words. "He lived in Oakland, didn't he? Lots of shootings in Oakland. Was it a home invasion style robbery? They've been up recently."

Murphy didn't even bother to answer and did not take his eyes off of McAdams. He tried another tack. "The Feds want some quality time with you. They have lots of questions."

"Not Ritter. I won't have anything to do with Ritter."

"You won't be dealing with him any more." Murphy waved his arm at the crowd scene visible through the open doors. "This is his last hurrah. I've just had a long conversation with a friend of mine in Washington. I sent a transcript of your conversation with him … the one that featured jaywalking references."

McAdams smiled at the thought. "I need a couple of hours. A few things to clear up."

"Mac –"

"Personal stuff. Nothing related to the department or any of this stuff. No shooting, arresting or hassling of civilians. Purely personal."

He pushed himself up from the floor and headed for the side door. "Tell the Feds I'll be back. Talk to Garfield here. He's got interesting stories to tell."

Once outside, he stood staring at the remnants of yellow tape remaining from the investigation of the shooting of Harry Howden.

He said "The one time I do a cop …".

And then all the other pieces began to assert themselves; all those free-floating associations and disconnected little happenings that he should have paid attention to; falling into place like a time-lapse video of a jigsaw puzzle being assembled. *She was looking for somebody on the waterfront, somebody who talked like a stevedore. And Slater yesterday – she was somewhere close to Carlo's office when she got hit. And then those damned last words when he was sitting there with Ellerby -- "The killer? He's your golf part –" – with all of those alternative endings that he should have tried out, but didn't.* Then came the visual image from that barge with its pile of muck and two dead women with long white legs; the image of the man in the gray suit who couldn't lift either his head or his feet, shuffling away from the atrocity that he felt responsible for. *They got to him. And what he said: "No more. This has to stop." And then Carlo was dead. The golf partner's son…. what Freddie was trying to tell me. The spoiled kid with a father who – rumor had it – would maim anyone who threatened his out-of-control son.*

He found Dominick Fallon at home. The maid let him in. She looked worried, maybe because it was still before seven AM and the phone was ringing continuously. Dominick was sitting at the center island in his kitchen with a large coffee mug in front of him. He looked like he hadn't slept for days. A copy of the Sunday New York Times was next to the mug, open to the Business section. A small TV on the nearby counter was scrolling a banner saying 'breaking news', superimposed on a live telecast of Ritter's press conference. The volume was set to be barely audible.

When he saw McAdams in the doorway to the kitchen, Dominick nodded, not a greeting, but as if confirming an expectation. He got up and took a matching mug from the cupboard, filled it with coffee and set it on the island in front of an empty stool. McAdams sat down, still saying nothing.

McAdams sipped his coffee before breaking the silence. "Murphy just told me about Carlo. I'm sorry for your loss." He spoke as if he was reading a sympathy card before buying it, testing the phrase for its empathetic qualities.

Dominick spoke as if he hadn't heard, as if he was talking to himself. "Fathers should not have to bury their sons. It's supposed to be the other way around."

"Maybe it's for the greater good.   Remember Abraham? He was willing to sacrifice Isaac."

Dominick seemed to look at him for the first time, his expression puzzled. "But Isaac was innocent."

He continued in a wondering tone. "He mortgaged … sold … my company to finance a drug deal. He murdered young women – beautiful, hopeful young women that he promised things to. Murdered them because they became *inconvenient* to him. He had no respect. For me, for people. He -- "

"Dominick."

The word stopped the rising litany of charges against Carlo. Dominick swiveled on his stool to look directly at McAdams. *He looks like someone viewing his executioner. He knows why I'm here.*

"Dominick, I asked Grodin about the people he killed. We walked through the whole list. When I mentioned Gonzo, he said, "…the one time I do a cop…" …

Dominick looked away and slumped, as though talking required too much energy.

McAdams leaned forward, determined that Dominick see the logic that was driving him. "But you see, Dominick, there were *two* cops killed – Gonzo and Freddie. Plural. Not singular. Two times. Not one time."

Dominick's expression did not change and he did not respond, but he became extraordinarily still, like quarry hoping to escape the notice of a questing predator.

"You see, I'd been assuming that Grodin killed her too. That she got close somehow."

"And Freddie said something too. The Wednesday it rained and you went home from the course. Her last line, as it were. She said, 'The killer? It's your golf part--'. Then … there was that sound … and she died. I was sitting with Ellerby when she said it, so I assumed she meant him."

Then he said what should have been obvious at the time. "But I have two golf partners."

What she was trying to say: 'The killer? It's your golf partner's son!'

Dominick looked exhausted, like all he wanted to do was to put his head down on the counter and go to sleep. He began talking, but his voice had no energy, a reciting of events and feelings that he wanted no part of, at first soft and dreamlike, talking to himself …

"I had my head in the sand about Carlo… the kind of stuff he was into. He was my kid … and I thought I could … that if only … just this last time …. fix it for him … He'd be --"

McAdams said again, "Dominick", stopping the disjointed phrases.

Dominick sat up straighter, like someone bracing for bad news, his gaze fixed on his the palms of his hands lying open on the countertop. He kept his eyes down and resumed talking, but now hurrying, like someone telling about something unpleasant to an audience that really didn't care very much.

"That Wednesday? When it rained and I left the course early? I was in the garage at the Oakland office, taking my clubs out of the trunk so that they could dry off. She was there, talking to a couple of the stevedores. She came up to me and started asking questions. She asked me about the shipping business. She wanted to know if this was where the RO/RO's docked. Did our ships go to Russia much? Am I involved with the business? That kind of stuff... just fishing, really. Very conversational ..."

He paused, and his voice became barely audible.

"I knew she was your partner. I wanted to please her ... and you. I should have called my lawyer and stopped talking. But she was very good. She asked if I knew Desmond, the insurance guy. Very casual. 'No big deal', I thought. I didn't even know he was dead. I told her to ask Carlo, that he dealt with Desmond all the time on insurance claims. Then she showed me a picture – a very pretty young woman that I recognized – and asked me if I knew her, said that a couple of the stevedores she'd been talking to recognized her... said that her name was Sasha and that she was Carlo's most recent girl friend."

"She said, 'They're both dead. Desmond and Sasha. Murdered. And I think your son is responsible'. When she walked away to call you, I panicked."

He stopped talking, but kept his eyes fixed downward. His reluctance to continue became almost tangible between them, a silent plea to McAdams, not for forgiveness or understanding, but to absolve him of the need to finish the story. Finally, McAdams' utter indifference to his feelings made it possible for him to look directly at him and say, "I hit her with the sand wedge. It was awful."

The stark words hovered in the air around them, although neither man moved nor showed any reaction to the stark confession.

Dominick said, "He was my son", as though offering an explanation, and started to cry silently. Whether for Carlo, for Freddie, for himself, or for losses of another kind, was not clear. When McAdams did not respond, Dominick added, "And you know the really funny part? I was trying to protect Carlo … to protect him from …. I always did …"

McAdams stood up. *They talk of closure as though it ends the pain, opens up new beginnings. So why do I feel so incredibly sad? There is nothing left to know.*

But he still had one more choice to make.

Dominick reached out and slid the New York Times to the side of the counter, exposing a small handgun, still with its attached silencer. They both looked at it and considered the possibilities it represented – both past and future.

McAdams looked at the gun, then at Fallon. *I wonder why he's showing me the gun?* He turned to walk away and only as he reached the kitchen door did he realize that Dominick was giving him the choice, as if vengeance was to be governed by an ancient tribal culture rather than modern dispassionate legal codes. He also realized that it was an easy choice to make, requiring no thought on his part.

Without looking back at Fallon and in a voice as neutral as he could make it, he asked, "So. We'll see you down at the station. Later today? Right?"

When Fallon didn't respond, staring fixedly at something that McAdams couldn't see, he left, marveling at the extent of his indifference.

Still one more stop.

Loose Ends

Eileen Moresby opened the door. She was wearing a troubled expression and what looked like a satin track-suit. She did not seem at all surprised to find him on her doorstep early on a Sunday morning. She said nothing and turned away, expecting him to follow her.

Another kitchen, more matching coffee mugs. Different characters. Same old stinking lousy secrets.

Ellerby sat on one stool and Moresby took the one facing him. McAdams made it a triangle and they both turned to him, signaling with their silence that they would wait for his lead.

It's not a morning for small talk, is it? He realized that he was exhausted, that he had not slept for more than twenty-four hours. *Almost done. Then I can sleep. Maybe.*

He did not know what he was going to say until he began to speak. "You – neither of you – have to talk to me. And I have no idea what I will do about anything that you tell me. I don't even know why I'm here." *That's not quite true. What I don't know is what I want to walk away with.*

Moresby and Ellerby exchanged looks and each of them reached out for the other's hand. Ellerby spoke first. "We owe you, in ways that you don't even know about. And there's nothing that you can do or say that would surprise us, or be unfair."

Moresby continued, almost as though they had rehearsed their lines. "And we have done everything together. We have no secrets from each other."

The first lie. Everyone has secrets, especially from those we are closest to.

He asked, "Where is Sofia?"

"We don't know." They actually spoke simultaneously, as if to act out their determination to do everything together.

He looked directly at Moresby. "You *are* her mother?"

"Yes." Her response was immediate, but a look of what could have been shame, or pain, or guilt – or some combination of all three emotions – flashed across her face. In passing, it highlighted a very faint zigzag scar on her forehead. "My name is … was … Irina … never mind the last name. I left Sofia in the orphanage when I left Vladivostock with … a man … a Russian pig … who promised me much but gave me nothing. Until he died unexpectedly with all that undeclared money."

Something about the way she pronounced the word 'unexpectedly' startled McAdams and he suddenly knew without the slightest doubt: *She killed him – the man who gave her nothing that he promised.* Again, he marveled at the extent of his indifference, how little he cared about other people's felonies, large or small.

Moresby mistook his indifference for contempt and her voice rose, taking on hints of defiance. "You can't know … You … Americans have no idea … no understanding or sympathy or feeling … for what it's like to live in a world where … suddenly, without any warning … you realize that you can have all those things that were so important and so impossible … but you have to want them, really want them … and you know that you can get them … but you have to be willing to do … things … things that make you a kind of person that you despise … but you learn to bury that … to see yourself as someone strong and daring, not a ruthless selfish bitch that … that would abandon her child to get what she wanted."

McAdams was startled by the disjointed monologue, her sudden flash of temper that morphed into self-hate, and it struck him that Moresby was speaking for not just herself. *She could be channeling Sasha … or Sofia!*

Focus! Remember why you're here! So he asked in a neutral voice, "And why did you come here? To San Francisco."

She and Ellerby looked at one another. His nod was so slight that McAdams wasn't sure he had seen it. "I met Edgar a long time ago, very briefly … in another place. I knew he was here and that he might … remember me."

"You arranged for her – Sofia -- to come here?"

"No. No. To my shame, I did not see or talk to her after I left her in the orphanage until she showed up at my door, here. The woman you call Sasha told me about her and asked if I would agree to see Sofia if she came." The sentence trailed off, almost incomprehensible as the words became softer and choked off. She wrapped herself tightly within her own arms, her head down.

A full thirty seconds went by before she resumed. "I told her that I didn't want to see Sofia, that we each had our own lives now, that she could never get here anyway, so it didn't matter. God help me!"

McAdams turned to Ellerby. "But she found a way, didn't she? Thanks to you and Carlo and Grodin."

Ellerby sat up straighter and began speaking as if at a press conference.

He's rehearsed this. He knew I'd call him on it.

"Yes. The so-called 'pipeline'. I helped Carlo legitimize his cultural exchange program so that his women would come here first. To San Francisco. But I had no idea that Sofia would use that way to get here. I didn't even know of her existence until Eileen introduced her to me as 'a friend of a friend'…. Someone she'd met on a cruise."

Ellerby looked directly at Moresby and spoke so softly that McAdams had to lean forward to hear his words. "I just learned yesterday that she is Eileen's daughter."

"You knew that you were facilitating human trafficking?"

Ellerby lowered his eyes and his voice changed, all the confidence seeping out. "Yes. I could tell you that I didn't know or that I had no choice, but that would not be true. I did know. And there's always a choice."

McAdams was relentless. "You also know that at least four women have been killed because of their participation in this 'pipeline', don't you?"

"Yes." The word was whispered.

"And that Gonzo and Freddie were killed because of Carlo's obsession with protecting his precious pipeline?"

"I know that now, yes."

"And that Sofia was next on his list?"

"Yes."

McAdams watched Ellerby shrink a little bit with each question and response, his head dropping lower and his voice becoming barely audible. *I could stop now. I've made my point. Why do I have this need to humiliate him?*

But despite his self-doubts, he asked the final question, the cruelest one of all.

"And you did all this, knowing that Sofia was *your* daughter?"

Ellerby reacted as though he had touched a live power line. He seemed to expand in place, sitting bolt upright with a look of disbelief, first directed at McAdams and then at Moresby, changing to an expression that began as a pure question mark. Opposite him, Moresby seemed to contract, wrapping her arms around herself and swaying on her kitchen stool, shaking her head from side to side with closed eyes.

McAdams watched with a detached clinical interest. *She said, 'We have no secrets from one another'. I guess that was just an approximation.*

He simply stood up and left. As he walked out of the kitchen, Ellerby and Moresby were leaning toward each other across the counter that divided them, joined by their hands tightly woven together and the point where their foreheads touched.

No more of this. I've got to go home.

Home & Other Sanctuaries

He stood outside his own front door debating whether to push the doorbell or to simply walk in. The indecision bothered him, mostly because he knew it reflected his inability to resolve far more serious choices than whether to ring the bell or not. His front door seemed to require extra effort to open, as if a high wind was pushing against it.

She wasn't there. He knew it as soon as he stepped through the door. *Funny that a hundred-thousand cubic feet of space can be so obviously empty. You'd think that one would have to look around, to listen, before concluding that there's no one there, that she really is gone, taking whatever it is – an aura? – with her.* For the first time, he understood what other people felt when they first came through his front door and were confronted with so much sheer emptiness.

His Beretta was in the middle of the kitchen table, serving as a paperweight for a note.

Thanks for the loaner. It's a nice gun. I know that it has to go and I thought of throwing it in the Bay, but I don't know your police procedures well enough to feel good about that. In any case, who better than a homicide detective to get rid of evidence? I'm taking your shirt with me – you know the one. It has nice associations for me. As for all the other … intangible … stuff … the kind of baggage that I can't throw away, or leave behind or even stop thinking about … I guess I'll carry it around awhile and see if it sorts itself out. It was easier in Russia … fewer choices. Oh, and you're a lousy cop … way too much empathy. Thank you.

Somehow, those last two words – 'Thank you' – were the saddest, with all their polite civility and distance evoking a welling up of guilt, negating the stirred up memories of their common shirt. *Thank you for what?*

He slept for twelve hours and stayed in bed another four hours, getting up only to unplug the phone and disable the doorbell. He finally got out of the bed when someone began pounding on his door with what sounded like a heavy rubber hammer. It was Murphy, holding his shoe in his hand, his arm raised to resume pounding.

They stared at one another for a full twenty seconds, neither of them moving.

Murphy broke the silence. "You're not on vacation and you didn't call in sick. And I've got a departmental memo on my desk about the need to reduce chronic absenteeism. So I thought I'd take you on as a demonstration project, drag your sorry ass into the station house as an example."

McAdams just looked at him while Murphy struggled to put on his shoe while standing on one foot, still carrying on in his mild ranting style. "And since you cleared most of our outstanding homicide cases yesterday, I don't have a whole lot to do."

"So, can I come in?"

McAdams stood aside. Only as Murphy walked past him did he remember that the Beretta and Sofia's note were still sitting on the kitchen table. He walked past Murphy, who like everybody else was stopped by the impact of the physical space, scooped up the gun and note and put them in the drawer with the silverware.

"Come on in, Murphy. It's just a room."

"Yeah. Like the Taj Mahal is just a grave. Jesus, Mac! You could subdivide this and house the entire homeless population of the Tenderloin!"

"Violates the zoning ordinances." McAdams pulled on a clean shirt and said, "I'm ready. Not much point to hanging out here."

Murphy didn't move. "Couple of things you should know."

McAdams stopped and waited, incapable of surprise.

"Fallon -- Dominick – is dead. Shot himself early this morning. Same gun that was used on Carlo."

McAdams merely nodded, wondering briefly why it mattered so little to him. *A lot simpler that way.*

"And Mayor Ellerby announced that he won't be running for reelection after all. Held a sudden press conference last night. Said he was getting married and wanted some time of his own."

Murphy watched McAdams closely as he asked, "Uh, you wouldn't happen to know anything about either of these surprises, would you?"

Such a simple question! Might as well ask me whether I'm still a cop. Carlo, Dominick and Grodin – all dead. Nothing I or the courts can do to them anymore. But Ellerby! He's still out there, dirty as hell! And he suspected, maybe even knew, what was going on ... probably got some cash for not asking questions. Clearcut 'accessory'. Why am I silent about Ellerby?

An image of Moresby appeared, as if an answer to his question, saying *you have to be willing to do ... things ... things that make you a kind of person that you despise ... but you learn to bury that ...*

"Uh, Mac ..."

"Do I know anything? Nope. But I did call on Fallon early yesterday morning. Wanted to express my condolences about Carlo. He said he intended to come down to the station that afternoon. Seemed despondent. And I also saw Ellerby briefly, purely personal stuff. Didn't say anything about getting married or resigning." *How easy to lie. It isn't what you say; it's what's left unsaid.*

Murphy sighed. "Things seem to happen just after you've left the scene."

McAdams didn't respond, thinking about Dominick and the pistol on his kitchen counter.

"I think you've just run out of golf partners," Murphy said.

"That's OK, none of us were any good at it anyway. You ready to go?"

He spent four hours at the office filling out paperwork and talking on the phone with some DEA and Immigration types in Washington. They were excessively polite to him and pleased with the way his version of events fit neatly into the storyline they were building within their reports. Ritter's name was never mentioned.

When he pushed the "End Call" button in mid-afternoon, he felt as if he'd been working for days without a break. *Is this the way it's going to be from now on? Have I reached the point where I'm bored with what's around me? With what I do?* It was only when he was leaving the building that he realized that the problem was not boredom. *It's the damn emptiness. It goes with me. It has nothing to do with physical space or what I do for a living.*

Without quite being aware of what he was doing, he found himself parked outside the Fort Mason Youth Hostel. Other than Moresby's home, it was the first sanctuary she had found. *She ran here once. Maybe …* The woman at the desk was the same one as before and she remembered him. "Hello again. Are you still looking for that young woman – Anna Rubin?" He was surprised at the way her question set off a surge of emotion within him – partly fear and partly something else that he could not yet name.

"She never came back. Paid for the second night and never used it. I hope she's OK."

That's because she was with me on that second night. She found a better sanctuary. And she paid in advance for that one too. In her own special currency. And walked out before she had to. That was when the inner voice moved out of its subliminal monologue and into his consciousness: *Pay attention, stupid! You've been used!*

He headed for the Tenderloin, cruising randomly until he saw Garfield. He was in the middle of a cluster of young black males, locked in a strange static embrace with a heavily-muscled shirtless black man with orange hair and more tattoos than bare skin. The whole scene looked distinctly edgy, especially for its stillness. They looked like they were posing for a still-life with an invisible artist. McAdams double-parked and got to the perimeter of the group before Garfield noticed him.

"Hey, Mac! Just in time. I was trying to show Joachim here how to disarm someone who threatens you with a serious blade." He released Joachim and all eyes

311

turned to McAdams. They were not friendly looks. *So I still must look like a cop. That hasn't changed.*

McAdams noticed that Joachim was in fact holding a vicious looking knife. About ten inches in length and probably a switchblade. He thought, *This is the part where the Community Oriented Policing Manual says, 'Be Cool!"*

"That's nice, Garfield. But you and Joachim look more like you're learning the tango for a gay ball. Me? Somebody shows me a blade like that, I just pull out my service revolver – it's a 357 – and shoot 'em. Less embarrassing for both sides that way. And no risk of AIDS."

There was one very long second of silence and then sly grins that ballooned into general hilarity with a lot of fist bumps and hand slaps, most of which seemed to be at Joachim's expense. Garfield used the commotion to extract himself and pull McAdams away from the group.

"Nice riff there. You'd make a pretty good street cop."

"That's funny. I was just told I was a lousy cop – too much empathy."

Garfield looked at him, really looked, and McAdams remembered how he could read people, see through the perimeter defenses to what was present and real. So he said, "She's gone, Garfield. Left a 'thank-you' note – very Emily Postish – but flat-out gone."

It seemed that Garfield had no problem with conversations that started in the middle, without any apparent context or proper nouns. He nodded, somehow making that an acknowledgement of McAdams' unspoken losses.

Garfield looked off into the distance. "You know, we said about ten words to each other? I watched her drinking coffee with another woman, followed her for a couple of aimless hours, watched her shoot a man nine times and walk away like she had time to spare before her next appointment. And we have zero history."

"You shared some intense moments. Maybe that's enough to build on?" *Not a bad summary of my own present and wishful state of mind.*

"Could be. She's special, I think --".

Garfield stopped abruptly and looked intently at McAdams in a way that made him feel judged. "Special enough that I'd hate to see her sent back to what she was trying so hard to get away from."

McAdams didn't even hear what Garfield was saying. He started again, "I never told her…", but Garfield was already walking away. Then he stopped again in the middle of the sidewalk, causing the midday pedestrians to veer around him. McAdams waited, watching the new sidewalk preacher on the corner get started. He was younger, far less imposing, lacking Harry Howden's patriarchal appearance, what you might call *biblical presence,* and his voice did not carry very far, but he seemed to have Leviticus down pat.

He'll do fine, but I miss Howden.

"Sorry. I was thinking." Garfield was back in the present, again underway and apparently with a destination in mind. He looked at McAdams intently, in a way that made him fear he did not possess whatever quality Garfield was looking for, that he would fall short in some important way that he would not comprehend.

"Most of us can walk and think at the same time."

Garfield ignored him, clearly preoccupied. But, when he did speak again, McAdams was surprised at the abrupt change in the topic.

"You know that Glide Memorial Church has a Women's Center – a place where women can feel safe?"

"Sure. It's a great program."

"They use a lot of volunteers. No questions asked. Other women, mostly. Overcomers. Women that can relate to abuse of all sorts and have gotten to the other side of whatever it was."

This time it was McAdams who stopped in the middle of the sidewalk. Garfield went on a few feet ahead of him, waiting for the light to change on Mission Street. Looking back, he said, "I heard they have a new volunteer working with some of the street kids and runaways. Speaks fluent Russian and seems to have a thing about orphans, among other things."

"Garfield, what –"

But he was already halfway across the street.

It took McAdams less than ten minutes to get to Glide. During the short walk, he tried to figure out what he would say, but the words got hopelessly tangled up with his conflicting emotions and sounded exactly like what they were – prearranged edited phrases designed to hide his confusion. Scripted, therefore not to be trusted by either of them.

The Women's Center at Glide Memorial was another sanctuary, one where males were not only unwelcome but objects of scorn at best and fear at worst. McAdams found a niche in the busy hallway where he could see the entrance and leaned against the wall, waiting and watching the stream of humanity moving past him. He stood for a full hour, watching the incredible diversity of people and stories flow past, seeing what the sociologists would refer to as *the underclass*, not as a lower caste, but as a cross section of what happened to deserving individuals, both the ordinary and the extraordinary – the Garfields, Hookers, Natalias, Ellerbys, and Sofias. He did not experience an epiphany, nothing that would qualify him for the supermarket tabloids or the daytime TV shows. There was no dramatic 'aha' moment or sudden galvanizing insight. It was a simple clarity that seeped in, a certainty that life was a fragile, chance-ridden, one-shot gift and not to be wasted on waiting for some ill-defined better opportunity to come along.

So that when he saw the first glimpse of his blue flannel shirt in the cluster of women approaching, he did not hesitate or worry about what he would say.

Sofia saw him and stopped, causing the flow of men and women to divert to either side and merge again once past her, leaving a calm vortex in front of her that he could step into and say what had become so obvious and important to him.

Nine simple words, unrehearsed and factual.

"I went home. It was empty. You weren't there."

www.ingramcontent.com/pod-product-compliance
Lightning Source LLC
Chambersburg PA
CBHW071242170626
46809CB00001B/55